IF YOU

Hate

ME

NEW YORK TIMES BESTSELLING AUTHOR
HELENA HUNTING

IF YOU Hate ME

ACKNOWLEDGMENTS

Husband and kidlet, I adore you. You inspire me every day and I'm so grateful for your love.

Deb, I adore you. Thank you for always having my back.

Becca, it is such an honor to know you, as a friend, as a badass fairy plotmother, as a strong, amazing businesswoman. Thank you for coming on this journey with me. I am forever grateful for that 3 am chat that brought you into my orbit exactly when I needed you.

Kimberly, thank you for knowing what I need when I need it.

Sarah, I honestly couldn't do this without you. You've been such a huge source of support and friendship and I'm so thankful to have you on my side.

Hustlers, you're my cheerleaders and my book family and I'm so grateful for each and every one of you.

My SS team, your eagle eyes are amazing, and I appreciate your input and support.

Tijan, you're a wonderful human and I'm blessed to know you.

Catherine, Jessica F and Tricia, your kindness and wonderful energy are such a source of inspiration, thank you for your friendship.

Jessica, Erica, Amanda, Julia, thank you so much for working on this project with me, I know it was a beast, and I'm so honored to be able to work with you and helping me make it sparkle.

Sarah and Gel, thank you for being graphic gurus. Your incredible talent never ceases to amaze me.

Beavers, thank you for giving me a safe place to land, and for always being excited about what's next.

Kat, Marnie, Krystin; thank you for being such incredible women. I'm so thankful for your friendship.

Readers, bloggers, bookstagrammers and booktokers, thank you for sharing your love of romance and happily ever afters.

For the ones who do their best to show up for the people they love every day, even when it's hard.

CHAPTER 1
RIX

It smells like Cheetos, beer, possibly ball sweat, and a hint of men's deodorant in here. My stomach gurgles ominously as I lie on the futon in the loft of my older brother's condo. If I can't sleep, I might as well call my best friend and fill her in.

"I have fifteen minutes between clients. What the heck is going on?" Essie asks when she answers.

It's noisy from the big event she's working. Her makeup brushes click and clink as they're cleaned and slotted away while she waits for the next person to fill her chair.

"I imploded my life," I tell her, succinct and accurate.

"This sounds bad. What happened?"

"I rage-quit my job and moved out of my apartment."

It sounds even worse when I say it aloud. I'm so disappointed in myself. Asking my brother if I could stay at his place feels like the ultimate failure—he's a professional hockey player, and I'm now unemployed and un-homed. I'm lucky I even caught him between ice time and going out.

"Did your roommates invite you to join their sex party again?" she asks.

"They did."

"Why the hell can't they take no for an answer? That's harassment!"

I smile. I appreciate her indignation on my behalf. "Look, I respect anyone doing whatever gets their rocks off, but listen when I say no thank you. It was the worst. And then my boss dropped four boxes of receipts on my desk at the end of the day and said they needed to be sorted by nine tomorrow, so I lost my shit and quit."

And when I got home, Eugenia was tied to a pillar in the living room. Naked. That was the last straw and the reason I've ended up here. On this futon.

"Seriously?" I can practically see Essie shaking her head. "That's the fourth time that's happened! You lasted two and a half months longer than I would have."

"I really wanted it to work out, you know? It was my first real job at a firm. I had benefits and a steady paycheck, and now I have nothing." How could I be so stupid and reactive?

"You are highly employable, Rix. You graduated at the top of your class. Come to Vancouver. Where are you staying now? Please don't say a Motel Heaven."

"Almost as bad, I'm at my brother's." I love Flip. He's a great brother, and he's helped me out financially in the past, but this clearly indicates that I've failed at taking care of myself. I hate that I've messed up my life so completely after being so careful.

"Oh my God. Rix."

"It gets worse." Because not only did I lose my job and my apartment, so I get to sleep on a futon in his loft with no doors or privacy, but I also did the unthinkable.

"Worse how?" Essie asks.

"I went to the Pink Taco. And I always overdo it." Especially when I'm mid-tragedy. I love those freaking tacos.

"Tell me you didn't have the refried beans."

"I had the refried beans. And several margaritas." So stupid. And expensive.

"Rix, you know better."

"I know. My stomach sounds like a beast lives in there. A bean-fueled beast. I also might have left Rob an emotional, half-drunk voicemail."

When Rob moved across the country, from Toronto to the east coast, to pursue his master's, I wanted to try long distance. He was pragmatic and did not. We were together for more than a year, so I'm still sore about it. I'd thought we were heading toward moving in together, toward stability and next steps, so being over sucked, even if it was the right thing to do.

"Dude, you broke up months ago. Noooo." Essie groans.

"Yeah."

"What kind of message?"

"Not one I want to repeat. Maybe he won't listen to it." *He'll listen to it.*

"Babe, seriously, come to Vancouver. There are accounting jobs here."

"It's enticing." But also impractical, irresponsible, and expensive. I've capped out on all three tonight alone.

The sound of someone trying to get into the condo downstairs has me rushing to get off the phone. "I think my bro's home. I'll message later."

"'Kay. Love you more than chocolate ice cream."

"Same." I end the call and press my phone to my chest. Emotions clog my throat.

I don't want to explain this to my brother. I'm horrified by the whole thing.

The front door opens, and I take a deep breath, preparing for the inevitable embarrassing conversation. The kitchen lights flicker on.

"Ah, fuck. Shit. Too bright!" A deep voice echoes off the high ceilings.

My stomach gurgles as I tense. Stupid refried beans. It's not my brother, Phillip—Flip. That started when I was a kid and couldn't pronounce his name. Now it's an ongoing joke because

3

he's a next-level fuckboy, as in "Flip me over and do me from behind."

Unfortunately, it seems that my brother's teammate and roommate, Tristan, is home. He sounds different, though. Which makes sense since he was eighteen when I last saw him in three dimensions, and he's in his mid-twenties now. His voice is deeper, grittier.

It's hitting home exactly what I've signed up for by asking to stay here. My brother I can deal with. His best friend is a whole different story—and the condo actually belongs to Tristan. When Flip was traded to the Terror, Toronto's pro team, he was so excited about getting to play with his childhood best friend that he moved in with him, too.

"Lights off!" Tristan slurs.

The condo goes dark. There's some shuffling and then an *oof* and a grunt. "Motherhumping shitbag. Baffrum leg on!" More stumbling around in the dark. More swearing. Something hits the floor with a loud bang. "Bathroom light on." He enunciates each word slowly, with less slurring.

I stay in my coffin-style pose on the futon upstairs. He can't see me from here. I'd prefer to defer my first interaction with Tristan in nearly a decade since he's clearly shitfaced, and I've had a shit day.

I lie as still as possible and work on breathing quietly.

The fridge opens. "Fuck. I need t'order gro'ries." The door falls closed. More rustling. More swearing. "Stupid shots. Ah, shit."

I give in to curiosity and roll onto my stomach, peeking over the arm of the couch. Tristan's standing at the island, half a jug of orange juice spilled across the counter, the puddle making its way to the edge. He yanks his shirt over his head and drops it on the spreading liquid, but instead of containing the mess, it drips onto his feet. He stumbles backward into the fridge.

I'm unable to appreciate his shirtless-ness before he grumbles more profanities and disappears. Not that I want to appreciate

4

all those rippling muscles earned by countless hours on the ice. Because I don't. Mostly.

The sound of water running filters up to the loft, along with Tristan's colorful commentary about stupid orange juice, followed by something about glitter and too much perfume.

The water turns off, then turns on again a moment later. I roll off the couch to the floor, grimacing as my palms land in dirt, or crumbs, or who the hell knows what. This loft needs a serious bleaching. I stay low and crawl on my hands and knees to the railing. From here, I have an excellent view of most of the condo, including the bathroom. The door is wide open. The faucet isn't running. Tristan is peeing. He lists to the right and grabs the edge of the vanity to keep from falling over and completely misses the toilet.

I hope there's more than one bathroom in this place. Maybe my brother has his own. Crossing my fingers on that since he's not known for his exceptional cleaning skills. Tristan swears and pulls an excessively long ream of toilet paper free to mop up the mess he made.

My phone buzzes from the couch. I scamper back into hiding and check it. *Shit.* Rob is texting. A second later, the phone buzzes with a call. I send it to voicemail and quickly set my phone to airplane mode.

When the sound of water hitting water ends, I expect Tristan to stumble-weave to his bedroom. But that doesn't happen. Instead, a low groan filters up to the loft. The vaulted ceilings amplify the sound. I frown and close my eyes as I try to place the noises coming from the first floor.

"Ah fuck, yeah. So hard."

My lids flip open. He can't be... Can he?

I leave the protective cover of a gaming chair and peek through the bars of the railing again.

Oh, he totally is.

My breath catches and my heart stutters and then gallops.

Tristan is masturbating.

5

Vigorously.

Enthusiastically.

His head is bowed, eyes screwed tightly shut, brow furrowed, lip curled. I can't see what's happening below the waist, but his biceps flex and his arm moves at a furious pace. His broad back expands and contracts with each panted breath. He shifts, and suddenly I can see the goods.

And holy shit, is he packing a seriously huge cock.

Even in his massive fist, it's impressive.

I should look away.

I should not be listening.

But I can't pry my eyes away from the sight of Tristan jerking off with unparalleled zeal. Every muscle is tight and corded. A sheen of sweat covers his shoulders as his hand moves faster. God, he's rough with himself. He groans, and his head rolls back on the next aggressive tug. He grunts out a low, "Fuck yeah," and shifts so he's standing in front of one of the sinks. There are two. His hips jerk, his strokes lose their rhythm, and he blows his load all over the vanity.

I clench below the waist. My skin is dewy, and my heart is slamming around in my chest. It's not solely because of the refried beans anymore.

I just watched my brother's best friend masturbate. And based on the way my body is humming with pent-up sexual energy, I liked it. A lot. Maybe that's the vibe I was throwing out with my roommates. It might explain a few things—like why they wanted me to dress up as a pirate and join them in their sex-capades.

The water turns on, and I slink back to the futon, stretching out on the grimy cushion, feeling guilty and ashamed. Today is all about setting new personal lows, apparently. I lie there, struggling to calm my breathing while Tristan bumbles around below. It feels like a million years before a door opens and closes. My plan is to lie here until morning and pretend I was asleep the whole time. Unfortunately, the three margaritas I consumed and my anxiety over having to pretend for eternity that I didn't just watch a professional hockey player whack off without his knowledge means I have to pee. Badly.

I distract myself by reading the message from Rob.

ROB

You sound drunk. Maybe you should call Essie. Text to let me know you're safe, tho.

That was the opposite of helpful. I don't bother listening to his voicemail. I don't need to be kicked again now that I'm this far down.

I send him a thumbs-up so he doesn't worry, or call again. I can't take his brand of pity right now.

My bladder is screaming. I won't make it until morning without peeing my pants, and I'd prefer not to hit that special low. Down is the only way. I'm sure Tristan passed out instantly, considering how wasted he is.

Decision made, my need to pee becomes a physical ache. It consumes all my thoughts. I rush to the stupid fucking ladder and realize it's retracted on its own. To avoid making noise, I climb down to the last step, then hang from the rung and drop the rest of the way to the floor. It's only a few feet, but because today sucks a giant bag of assholes, I roll my ankle and land with a thud and an *oof*. I clap a hand over my mouth. And pee a little in my pants.

I hop to my feet and sprint past Tristan's bedroom, launching myself into the bathroom. I close the door harder than I mean to and turn the lock. I've barely flipped the toilet seat down before I unleash Niagara Falls. The relief is almost on par with an orgasm. Almost. I drop my head into my hands while my bladder empties.

Eleven years later, I'm finally done. I wipe and debate whether I should flush but decide against it because it could cause unnecessary noise.

The sink on the left is spotless, only a toothbrush holder and a pump soap sit on the counter. The other sink clearly belongs to my brother. The edge is rimmed in stubble, and toothpaste lumps and food particles sit at the bottom. And probably some residual jizz. The cap is off his toothpaste tube, and two razors lie on his side of the counter. Toothpaste and water spots dot the mirror on his side. I wonder if it annoys Tristan the way it annoys me.

I put myself here, though, so I don't have a right to complain.

Based on the lack of noise beyond the bathroom, I'm in the clear. I take a deep breath and channel stealth vibes so I can get back to the loft undetected. But when I unlock the door and throw it open, I realize I'm very wrong.

Tristan blocks the doorway—arms crossed, muscles bulging. He's wearing boxer briefs, and that's it.

I've seen Tristan in pictures over the years. He's a professional hockey player, and a good one at that. His stats are amazing, and he's one of the top players in the league. He's also stupidly hot. Like, my underwear wants to shimmy down my legs and throw itself at his feet.

His dark blond hair curls around his ears and at the nape of his neck. It swoops across his forehead, and the cowlick in front makes one unruly piece stick out in the wrong direction. His forest green eyes are framed with thick, enviable lashes and a day's worth of stubble decorates his chiseled jaw. And don't get me started on his chin dimple. Ugh.

He's way bigger than I remember, which makes sense since I stopped growing my freshman year of high school, and he did not. He must be six four or better, and his shoulders are ridiculous. And his abs. God, his abs. He's cut and rippling and hotter than any man has a right to be. I also think he might be sparkling, and he smells like he jumped into a bottle of cheap women's perfume.

"How the hell did you get in here? Did Flip give you a fucking key?" he demands, listing to the right.

"Um...Clarice, the super, let me in... I thought Flip checked with you."

He narrows his eyes. "You look familiar." He blinks and lists to the left this time. He's off-balance, so he uncrosses his arms and braces a hand on the wall, making all the muscles in his arm flex and pop. "You brought your friend last time, right? Suzy the screamer?" His face lights up at the memory.

I throw up in my mouth a little. "Tristan, it's me, Beatrix. Flip's *sister*."

He frowns, and his brows pull together. "Beat?"

I fight a cringe at the horrible nickname he gave me when we were kids. As in: "Beat it. No one wants you around."

His slightly unfocused gaze rakes over me, assessing. "Shit. You were a gangly, pimple-faced nerd the last time I saw you."

Ego: minus ten.

Tristan: one.

Turns out, I still really fucking hate Tristan. I cross my arms. "Still the same giant dick, huh?" I glance down for a fraction of a second, but it's enough.

He smirks. "Still interested in finding out, huh?"

"Of course that's your interpretation, you dirtbag." I roll my eyes even as my cheeks burst with heat. I may or may not have had a crush on Tristan when I was a freshman. And I may or may not have seen him completely naked once. Mostly, sort of, not even a little *not* on purpose. "Let me rephrase, still the same giant *asshole*."

His smirk grows smirkier. "Sure, that's what you meant."

This conversation is stupidly juvenile, and I'm suddenly exhausted beyond belief.

"Look, today has been a giant bag of shit," I tell him. "I get that it's been a lot of years since you've had the chance to torment me, but do you think you can put a pin in it until tomorrow? I'm wiped, and dealing with your assholery isn't high on my priority list."

When I try to slip past him, he blocks my way. "How long have you been here?"

Oh, shit. I bite my lips together and blink up at him. He narrows his eyes and steps forward, forcing me to step back unless I want my chest to brush his. Which, let's be honest, I kind of do. It's so stupidly cliché, the whole having a teen crush on my brother's best friend. But dude was hot, and sometimes, when Flip wasn't there to witness it, Tristan could be...kind. Soft. Those moments were rare, but they ignited that stupid crush flame and kept it burning throughout freshman year.

Then Tristan was drafted to a farm team out of the province, and his hockey career exploded a few years later.

"I asked you a question, Beat." He leans in closer, until his warm exhale caresses my cheek and his lips are at my ear. "I expect an answer."

A shiver runs down my spine. I inhale the scent of cheap perfume. I wonder, briefly, why he didn't bring home whoever was clearly hanging all over him tonight. Then I remember that as hot as he is, he's still seventy-five percent asshole. "Not long," I croak.

He pulls back, and his shrewd gaze locks on mine. "You're lying."

My swallow is audible. He's not wrong.

"Why didn't you announce yourself when I came home?" His voice is deceptively soft. But I'm not fooled. I remember how he used to cajole when I was a kid, and then he'd trick me into something stupid. Sometimes it was harmless, like telling me he had a chocolate bar, but really he was holding an agitated toad. When I got close enough, he would toss it in my face like an asshole and run away laughing.

Other times, though, he did things out of spite, or anger, or sheer dickish-ness. Like the time I was all dressed up for my best friend Essie's tenth birthday party and my dad was dropping Flip off at Tristan's to swim. We were early, so he went in to help Tristan's dad with some handyman project. I can't remember exactly how it all went down, but Tristan threw me in the pool fully clothed. My mom had done my hair and even made my dress. I'd been so excited, and he totally ruined it.

I feel like that's the version of Tristan I'm looking at. That version wasn't my favorite back then, and I like it even less now.

"First, I was asleep until I heard you come in." *Or I would have liked to have been...* "Second, you're wasted, and you can barely keep yourself from falling over. I wasn't super interested in dealing with my brother's drunk-ass best friend at stupid o'clock in the morning after the shitty day I've had. Third, what the hell was I supposed to say?" My voice rises with irritation and indignation. "So sorry for interrupting you, Palmela, and Fingerella? Maybe shut the bathroom door next time!"

"I thought I was alone!" he snaps. "You could've made yourself known at any point."

"'Cause that wouldn't have been awkward at all."

He leans in again and drops his voice. "Maybe you kept quiet because you liked it. Did you just listen, Beat, or did you watch, too?"

Nothing like being accurately called out by a drunk jerk. Not that I'll admit it. "Check your ego, Tristan, and back the fuck off." I shove his chest, and he stumbles back a step, maybe not expecting it. The lights in the kitchen come on.

It's tough not to admire all six-four-plus inches of cut, hot-as-fuck hockey player. It's unfair that someone as dickish as him can look as good as he does in only a pair of white boxer briefs. And I can see his dick-print. My vagina approves, but the rest of me is disgusted. Mostly. Especially when I realize there are lipstick prints on his chest and... "Are you covered in glitter?" I glance down at my hand, which sparkles in the ambient light. He's totally glittering. I shouldn't be surprised. My brother is the most notorious fuckboy in the league, and Tristan is his wingman. "You reek like cheap perfume and regrets."

For a second, his expression flashes with an emotion I don't quite understand, but a cocky smirk soon takes its place. "You sound jealous."

"Not hardly." I roll my eyes. "Get over yourself, King Douche of Assholeville."

His smile grows dark, and he takes a step backward. "Liar, liar, panties on fire. I hope you enjoyed the show." He turns and disappears into his bedroom, the door closing behind him.

I thought screwing up my life was punishment enough, but it seems dealing with Tristan is going to be my new penance.

CHAPTER 2
RIX

The first thing I learn about Flip and Tristan is that wandering around shirtless is apparently commonplace. I'm sitting at the kitchen island the next morning, nursing a coffee and eating the chocolate chip cookies I brought with me because the only food in their fridge is old pizza and a sad, squishy tomato. Grocery shopping and cleaning are at the top of my to-do list.

Right after I get my stuff from my former apartment.

Tristan saunters into the kitchen. He's fresh from the shower and wrapped in nothing but a towel. Water droplets dot his shoulders, and a rogue one tumbles gracefully over his defined pec, caressing each rolling ab on the way down. An image of Tristan fisting his massive erection pops into my head like a whack-a-mole. I shift my gaze back to my coffee cup, which is the only safe place for my eyes.

"So why are you here?"

It's not possible to make me seem like more of a burden than Tristan does with that one sentence.

To my left, Flip runs his hand through his already messy mop of hair. I have no idea what time he got in last night, but he has an absurd number of hickeys on his neck, chest, and stomach.

He's wearing a pair of gray jogging pants that hang low on his hips. I assume the hickey trail continues, but I'm thankful I can only hypothesize.

"I might have accidentally quit my job," I mumble. My first real adult job, and I blew up the opportunity after only three months. Embarrassment washes through me all over again.

"How do you accidentally quit your job?" Flip shoves his hand down the front of his joggers.

I look away, because no one needs to see that. My shoulders roll forward, and I lower my voice, as if that will make my actions yesterday less awful. "Fifteen minutes before the end of the day, my manager set four boxes filled with ten years of receipts on my desk. She told me they needed to be sorted and input by nine this morning. It's the third time that's happened in a month. I might have freaked out."

"Huh. Well, that makes sense. Your manager sounds like a dick."

"She was. Or still is." As the newbie, I expected some shitty jobs, but less than twenty-four hours with four banker's boxes is unreasonable. Especially when she did the same thing last week. And the week before that.

"We have waffles and some whole-grain bread in the freezer, if you want something other than cookies for breakfast." Tristan gives my cookie box a pointed, slightly disapproving look.

"I'm fine. But thanks." It's bad enough that I'm crashing here and drinking their coffee. I don't want to eat their food, too.

"Suit yourself."

He grabs a mug and pours himself a coffee, then turns to me and Flip. "Either of you need a top up?"

"Sure, yeah." Flip sets his cup on the counter.

Tristan gives him a look. "Dude. The fuck?"

Flip frowns. "What?"

"You're covered in hickeys, and your sister is right here." He points at me.

"So?"

14

"It's fine," I mutter. "Nothing I haven't seen before."

Tristan fills Flip's mug, still wearing his displeased-dad face, then looks to me.

"Please." I push my mug toward him.

"What does rage-quitting have to do with you staying here?" he asks as he freshens my coffee.

I really wish I didn't have to share the whys of my needing to stay in their loft. "My roommates are super into roleplay. They like to dress up in period costumes." I had a boyfriend in university, before Rob, who was big into Dungeons & Dragons. Sometimes he would dress up as a wizard. It was quirky and adorable. I loved that he was this soccer-playing guy who nerded out with his friends off the field. And as an accountant, I consider myself also a bit of a nerd. But the situation in my apartment is not at all about being nerdy.

Tristan scoffs, and Flip arches a brow.

"Anyway." I grip the edge of the island, but it's sticky with orange juice, so I go back to holding my coffee cup. "On Sunday night they were dressed up in steampunk, which is totally fine. They have great costumes." There's an entire room dedicated to their roleplay costumes and props. And Eugenia makes most of them. She's super talented. "Except they tried to get me to dress up as a pirate and...plunder them." With a pegleg.

Flip's bottom lip juts out. "Plunder them?"

"They have an open relationship, and they wanted me to join them." I said no several times in the months I lived there, but they kept asking and putting me in awkward situations. I should have known the cheap rent was too good to be true.

Tristan bursts out laughing.

"Fuck you, asshole." I flip him the bird.

"Are they hot? I mean, it'd be fun if they were hot," Flip says, oblivious to how gross that is coming from my brother.

"It doesn't matter if they're hot. They're my roommates. *Were* my roommates, because I can't live there." The roleplay isn't the issue. It's more what happened two nights ago and when I came home from work last night.

"Can't you say no and leave it at that?" Flip asks.

"I've tried. More than once. Instead of respecting my boundaries, two nights ago they had excessively loud sex until three in the morning in the living room." I was stuck in my bedroom, unable to pee until they finally went to bed. It was awful and may have contributed to my rage-quitting, although I didn't love the job to begin with.

"Sounds familiar," Tristan mutters into his coffee cup.

"Whatever, man. You've been part of the equation on plenty of occasions, so don't bitch about how hard it is to be my wingman," Flip retorts.

I gag. Those are not details I need. I hope I'm not trading a shitty situation for an even worse one. "You two are disgusting."

"I'm in my twenties, and women literally throw themselves at me. I won't be this pretty or virile forever. It's about capitalizing while I can." Flip has the nerve to sound defensive.

"What he said," Tristan agrees like the fuckboy he is.

"I can't wait for the regular season when we get to play in Vancouver." Flip's eyes are all dreamy and far away. "They have the best bunnies."

"Accurate." Tristan sips his coffee thoughtfully.

"Anyway." I'd rather talk about my ex-roommates than my brother's exceptionally prolific sex life. "They were at it again in the living room when I came home last night. I decided I'd had enough, so here I am. It'll only be for a few days. Or a week at most." *I hope.* "I just need to find a new job and an apartment." Apart from staying at a hotel, which I can't afford for long, this is my only option. My parents live three hours away in buttfuck-nowhere northern Ontario, and my best friend is on the other side of the country in Vancouver, where the best bunnies reside. God, I miss Essie so much.

"We start training camp next week and then exhibition

games, so if you need more than a week to figure shit out, that's cool. Right, Tris?"

Tristan gives me a withering look. "It's fine, I guess. Just stay out of my shit." Seems offering me a coffee refill was his one nice moment of the day.

I hate that he can make me feel like I'm thirteen again, getting in the way. "I see you're still the same insufferable asshole."

"And you're still as irritating as a mosquito. And just as crushable." His lip curls, and he has the audacity to look hot while also being a dick.

"Jesus. I forgot how awful it is when you two are in the same room. You're already giving me a headache." Flip rubs his temple.

"That's probably from the pussy shots you were doing last night," Tristan fires back.

I throw my hands in the air. "Oh my God! I don't want to know about my brother doing pussy shots!"

"I guess you should have thought about that before you threw a hissy fit at your job, lost your apartment, and decided to crash on my futon. Deal with it or beat it," Tristan snaps.

Flip snort-laughs. "Ah, man. I forgot about that nickname. Beat it, Beat." My brother raises his hand in the air, and Tristan high-fives him.

They're the literal worst. Fighting back is pointless. There's no way I'll win against them. Being thrust into the annoying-little-sister role, despite being twenty-two years old with an accounting degree, feels like a mammoth step backwards. I wish I had a pint of ice cream and a room I could mope in, but I'm here, in this crappy situation, and the only way out is to get my stuff from my old apartment, secure a job, and then find a place to live that isn't here. Once that's taken care of, I can start plotting revenge against my brother and Tristan. It's all about biding my time—and not allowing myself to be affected by their needling. I'm channeling Teflon. Nothing sticks.

While they continue laughing at my expense, I drink my

coffee, eat chocolate chip cookies, and fantasize about shaving their heads while they sleep.

"Kidding aside, what about your furniture?" Flip asks. "Does it need to go into storage?"

"The apartment came fully furnished, so I just need to grab the rest of my clothes and personal effects."

"What about your bedroom set from the old house?" he asks.

"Mom and Dad sold it."

Tristan frowns. "You don't have any furniture at all?"

I shake my head. "I always rent places that are furnished." It's easier and cheaper to move that way. "A few tote bins should cover what's left there. I didn't have a lot. I can bus over and Uber back."

"I'll drive you. You're close to that East Side's we go to, right?"

"Yeah, a couple of blocks south."

The two of us have a standing monthly dinner date at East Side's. Our parents used to take us there for a treat as kids. We'd always fill up on salad and bread because there were unlimited free refills, and then we'd take two bites of our dinner and save it for the next day.

"I'll come for the ride," Tristan announces.

Wait, what? "You don't need to. I don't have that much stuff."

His expression remains flat. "I want to meet these roommates."

Of course he does. "Why? So you can invite yourself over for a gangbang? Eugenia isn't your type."

"How do you know?"

"Because she's not a bunny." I know my brother's type, which means I also know Tristan's.

"Okay, as fun as this is, I need to shower," Flip says. "Then we'll pick up your stuff, Rix. Please try not to kill each other while I'm gone." He leaves me alone with Tristan, who is still clad in only a towel.

There's no escape.

"I should grab my keys." I'm wearing shorts, a tank top I stuffed in my bag last night, and the same bra and underwear from yesterday. Getting away from mostly naked Tristan is my current top priority.

I hustle around the island, but he's right there—a wall of hot, muscular flesh that I'd like to punch and run my nails over with equal measure, especially now that he's not covered in glitter or smelling like cheap perfume. Instead, he smells like fresh fucking rain and warm skin, and I want to hump his leg a little. Which is so, so wrong. Especially when I know what he gets up to with my brother. My emotions about Tristan should be fully channeled in the hate direction.

I consider sidestepping him, but he's a hockey player, and I only went to weekly yoga with Essie because she was allowed to bring a friend for free. And Kawartha Dairy ice cream was my reward after. Now she's in Vancouver, and I'll never yoga again without thinking of her. I give him a "come on" gesture. "Say what you're going to say, Tris. I don't have all day."

"Don't you, though?" He lifts his hand, and I twist my head away but refuse to back down or step aside. He doesn't make contact, but his fingers trail along the edge of my jaw, so close I feel his heat. He leans in until his warm, humid breath breaks against my cheek. "You're the one drinking my coffee, sleeping on my couch without anywhere to be."

His words hit home in a way I don't like. "You think I asked for this?"

He tips his head. "Is that your interpretation?"

He's playing with me. Pushing me. Needling. "Must be nice to have a throne to sit on so you can pass judgment on us peons. Of the three of us, I had to fight hardest to get where I am. I've always been the afterthought, never a big, shiny star."

His smirk slides off his face. He opens his mouth, but before he can speak, I barrel on, wanting to slice him like he has me.

"And look how quickly both of you have tarnished that shine. How lovely that you can be assholes of the highest order and no one ever calls you on it. How proud your parents must be. Mommy must love that you're a big hockey star." The words are out of my mouth before I consider their impact. His mom left when he was twelve. It was a low blow. Too low. I try to backtrack. "I didn't mean—"

"Yeah, you did." He turns around and disappears into his bedroom.

My heart is pounding, and my palms are sweaty. I may have made things infinitely worse for myself.

Twenty minutes later, we file out of the condo. The woman across the hall is letting herself into her unit.

"Hey Dred, how's it going?" Flip asks.

Tristan raises a hand in a wave.

"It'll be the best day ever as soon as I'm in comfy clothes." She's currently wearing flats, a pair of dress pants, a white blouse, and a cardigan. She looks like a librarian with her bun and her glasses.

He motions to me. "Rix, this is Mildred, Dred for short. Dred, this is my sister Rix. She's staying with us for a couple of weeks."

Dred smiles at me. "Nice to meet you, Rix."

"You, too."

"You up for a movie later this week?" Flip asks.

"For sure, just knock, I'm around most evenings."

She lets herself into her condo and I wait until we're on the elevator heading to the lobby before I say, "Is it really a good idea to bang your next-door neighbor?"

"I'm not banging her. We're just friends. We watch movies and play board games and sometimes we listen to podcasts."

"Huh." I didn't see that coming.

Two minutes later I'm crammed into my brother's car. It's a two-door, with a tiny back seat. Tristan pushes the passenger seat all the way back. There's no room for my legs, and the headrest is almost touching my face.

"Can I get a couple of inches of space?" I grumble. "Or

maybe you should stay behind, Tristan." I'm concerned my stuff won't fit in here, even without Tristan tagging along, and I'd prefer to get it all in one trip. But his enjoyment of my misery seems to be holding steady, even after all these years.

"And miss out on this quality bonding time?"

"Can it, you two." Flip pulls out of the underground lot and follows the GPS instructions to turn right.

I'm practically eating Tristan's hair, his seat is so close. And of course, they put the windows down, so my hair is blowing all over the place in a wind vortex. My hair tie is in my purse, which is at my feet, and I can't reach it.

I carefully pinch a strand of Tristan's hair between my fingers and tug it free from his head. He runs his hand through it. He loses four hairs before he clues in.

"The fuck are you doing?" His fingers wrap around my wrist before I pull out a fifth.

It sends an electric jolt up my arm and makes the hairs on the back of my neck stand on end. "Relieving you of your grays."

"I don't have grays!"

"That you can see." I try to free my arm, but his hold tightens.

He reaches between the seat and the door with his free hand and reclines further. The headrest pushes into my stomach and the backrest hits my knees, forcing me to flatten my legs.

"Stop! You're crushing me!" I yelp.

"Stop ripping out my hair!" Tristan snaps.

"Give me some space!"

"Give it a rest, you two! I missed the turn because you're distracting me."

Tristan's head is almost in my lap. He tips his chin up, his green gaze meeting mine.

I mouth, *You're an asshole.*

An amused smirk tips the corner of his deliciously full mouth. "I know. What are you going to do about it, Beat?"

He's still holding my wrist, and I'm trapped under his seat. I lean forward, my chest pressing against the top of his head, my hair forming a curtain around us. Something shifts, and a tangible, raw energy crackles between us—hate, annoyance, frustration, who knows what else. But I shock even myself when I lick the edge of his jaw.

His free hand slides into my hair and curls into a fist, holding my head. "You know what they say about playing with fire." He twists my head, his lips dragging across my cheek until they reach my ear. "Bad little Bea," he taunts, catching my earlobe between his teeth.

Warmth floods my body as he sucks the skin, then nips at it again. "Don't you dare bite me!"

"Use your manners, and maybe I'll be nice." His voice is a gritty whisper. His grip on my hair tightens, and his tongue sweeps the shell of my ear.

I can't tell if this is retaliation or foreplay. Which is…a messed-up thing to think, especially since my brother is less than a foot away, in the driver's seat. But that doesn't stop me from slipping my hand down the front of his shirt. I try not to admire how firm his pec is as I find his nipple and roll it between my thumb and finger.

His surprised sound makes my nipples peak. "Any excuse to put your hands on me, huh, Beat?"

His ego is ridiculous. I stop playing nice and pinch. Instead of releasing my ear, he sucks it, then bites harder. I twirl some chest hair between my thumb and finger and tug.

"Ah!" he grunts. "That was dirty!"

"You're biting me!" I twist my head away, but he's still fisting my hair.

The car jerks, and the tires squeal.

Tristan releases my hair, and I sit back in a rush.

"What in the actual fuck is wrong with you two?" Flip gapes at us.

We're both red-faced and panting. I have no idea why that felt equal parts aggressive and sexual.

"He started it!"

"She started it!"

"I don't care who started it. It ends right now, or you can get out and catch a rideshare home. Or call one of your fun-time friends to pick you up." Flip gives Tristan a pointed look.

"I'll stop if she stops." Tristan rubs his pec.

"Can you put your seat up so I can breathe?" I grouse.

"Ask nicely," he sneers.

"Move your seat, Tris. You're literally lying on top of her," Flip orders.

Tristan grumbles but raises the seat so the headrest is no longer digging into my ribs. I can take a full breath again.

"Don't say a word to each other for the rest of the ride," Flip snaps.

We spend the next twenty minutes in awkward silence. The closer we get to the apartment, the drier my mouth becomes. Flip parks in a visitor's spot, and I un-pretzel myself from the back seat while Tristan pulls the seat belt aside, presumably so I don't clothesline myself getting out of the car.

"This is a shitty fucking neighborhood," he announces. It sounds like an accusation. I don't know what it is about Tristan, but he always makes me feel small.

"I thought when you said you lived close to East Side's, you were in the nicer part." Flip frowns as he takes in the surrounding buildings and houses. I've met him at the restaurant all three times we've seen each other since I moved here. This is the first time he's seen where I live. *Lived*. Past tense, once I get my things. A few blocks west, the neighborhood is less run down, but also more expensive.

"How long have you been living here?" Tristan asks with a frown.

"A few months." I shrug. "It's affordable."

"But there are bars on all the windows of the corner store." Tristan flings a hand toward the Tasty Mart across the street.

"The store where Flip and I grew up wasn't any different," I point out.

"Yeah, but we knew everyone. This is totally sketch," Flip says.

"How far was your job from here?" Tristan looks annoyed.

"Half an hour on the subway, but I don't work there anymore."

"But you did, for three months. Where's the closest subway station?" Tristan's nostrils flare.

"A couple of blocks. It's a seven-minute walk."

Tristan's jaw tics. "And you walked there by yourself?"

"I have pepper spray, and I've taken self-defense classes. Besides, after today, I won't be living here, so it doesn't really matter, does it?" I don't get why he's suddenly so concerned. He was biting my ear and crushing me twenty minutes ago.

"Let's pick a better neighborhood for your new apartment," Flip says.

"As long as it fits into my budget, sure." Toronto is an expensive place to live.

Flip falls into step beside me, and Tristan follows with his phone in his hand. He's probably sexting tonight's victim.

My nerves kick into high gear as we pile into the tiny elevator with the little old lady who smells like tuna and mothballs. She makes small talk about how nice the weather finally is and how hard Canadian winters are on her old bones. It's a standard conversation. Canadians like to bitch about the six months of snow and subzero temperatures. We also like to moan when it gets too hot. There's really no pleasing us.

The little old lady gets off on the twelfth floor, and we continue to the twenty-third. The elevator clunks and groans, but the doors open, which is awesome. I got stuck in here once when it stopped between floors. I was trapped with a pizza delivery guy. He'd been worried about the forty-five-minutes-or-free situation. I was worried I'd pee my pants. Ten interminable minutes later, they pried the doors open. I'd used the stairs for two weeks after that.

Flip and Tristan follow me out of the elevator and down the hall to my soon-to-be former apartment. I stupidly dropped my fob back into my purse, so they stand there awkwardly while I rummage around searching for it.

"What's all that crinkling?" Tristan asks.

"Mini bags of goldfish crackers and a few fortune cookies," I mutter. I always carry snacks in my purse. I finally find my key fob and swipe it over the censor. I didn't warn my roommates I was coming. I figured the element of surprise would benefit me.

But as I examine the scene before me, I reconsider that strategy. On the upside, Eugenia isn't tied to the pillar in the middle of the living room. On the downside, her boyfriend, Claude, my other former roommate, is doing the helicopter, and every rotation of his wiener slaps Eugenia's cheek. She's dressed in another impressively designed period piece, her boobs hanging out.

I'd like to say this is a first, but that would be a lie.

"What the fuck?" Tristan mutters.

"Is he slapping her in the face with his flaccid dick?" Flip asks.

"Yeah," I confirm.

Eugenia is the first to notice me. My brother and Tristan are still in the hall. For now. She scrambles to her feet. "What are you doing here?" Her eyes flare as two shadows appear on either side of me. "Oh! You brought friends! Is this your way of apologizing for calling me a psycho bitch last night? I have dibs on the yummy one behind you. Claude, you can have the other one." Eugenia squeezes Claude's arm, her voice trembling with excitement.

I hold up a hand. "I'm not apologizing. I'm here to get my stuff. Then I'll try to erase this nightmarish little blip in my life, probably with copious quantities of booze." *Cheap wine, most likely.*

"You still need to pay next month's rent. It's on the lease that you have to give thirty days' notice, and you gave us no notice," Claude says. He's tucked his penis back into his pants, thank God.

"These two asked you to take part in a threesome, yeah?" Flip confirms.

"Yeah."

"And you said no, yeah?"

"That's correct. I said no."

"And they still tried to get you involved again?" Tristan asks.

"Uh, yeah."

"So they asked twice?" he presses. "And both times you said no?" For a second, I expect him to tack something shitty on the end, but after a few seconds of silence, I realize Tristan's on my team.

"They asked more than twice, and I always said no." I'm embarrassed that it's gone on as long as it has, but with the hours I'd been pulling at work, I didn't have time to look for another place. Nor the ability to comfortably afford something on my own.

"So they kept pressuring you, even though you'd made it clear you weren't interested in participating?" Tristan's nostrils flare, and I try not to notice how hot he is when he's defending me.

"I'm pretty sure that's sexual harassment." Flip looks like he wants to punch Claude.

"If someone says they're not interested, but the other person keeps pushing them, and then gets naked in the living room when their roommate could come home any minute, knowing full well it makes them uncomfortable..." Tristan and Flip exchange a look, and I'm not sure if I'm imagining it, but there seems to be a weird tension between them. "It does sound a lot like sexual harassment." Tristan turns to me. "Would you agree, Bea?"

"Um... Yes." This is the Tristan I had a crush on. The one who did nice things unexpectedly, like bring me my favorite chocolate bar for real and not throw a toad in my face.

"I could post about it on my social media, see what other people say. You know, in case we're off base," Flip says.

"How many followers do you have again, Flip? Two million, or is it three?" Tristan pulls his phone out of his pocket and starts scrolling through social media apps.

"You're lying." Eugenia crosses her arms, which thankfully cover her nipples.

"Am I?" Flip pulls up one of his social media accounts, where he has over three million followers, and shows it to Eugenia.

"Flip Madden?" Her eyes bounce from the small screen to my brother's face and then to me. "He's your brother? And he plays professional hockey?" she asks.

"Yeah." I often keep my brother's status to myself, in part because people can get weird about it. I turn to Flip. "I'm gonna get my things so we can get out of here."

"I can help," Flip says.

"It's fine. It won't take long. It's just clothes and books and stuff."

Tristan says nothing, but carries the empty plastic bins into my bedroom, then stands outside the door with his arms crossed. I frantically toss stuff in the bins, glancing over my shoulder to make sure Tristan isn't paying attention as I empty my top drawer. It contains all my most important items—bras, panties, and self-gratification toys. It takes less than twenty minutes to pack my belongings, and they fit into three bins. One for each of us.

Eugenia and Claude are sitting on the living room couch, looking terrified and slightly awestruck. Flip is standing in the doorway of their roleplay room, rubbing his bottom lip. Tristan is being his annoyingly attractive self, hair flopping over one eye as he leans against the wall outside my bedroom, wearing a pensive expression.

"All set," I squeak. I want to GTFO and forget this ever happened.

Flip turns as I set the heaviest of the bins on the floor. He makes a circle motion with his finger. "Anything out here that belongs to you?"

With my brother and Tristan standing sentinel, I scan the room for any of my personal effects. The role-playing living-room sex-capades had escalated in frequency recently, so I'd been disappearing into my bedroom most nights.

I cross over to the fridge and tuck my bottle of orange juice into my purse, as well as the half-block of sharp cheddar and two apples. My condiments will take up too much room and are mostly empty. But the freezer contains a box of ice cream sand-wiches. The good ones. They were my grocery splurge this week. I check for those. It was unopened yesterday, and now there are only three left. Jerks.

I hold up the box. "Either of you interested in an ice cream sandwich?"

"Sure. Let's take them to go. Ready to roll out?" Flip grabs one of the heavy bins and heads for the door.

I set the apartment key on the counter.

Tristan picks up the lighter bin, then he sets it down and takes the one full of books. His biceps pop under the strain. He waits at the door, keeping it propped open with his foot as I pass through with my bin.

"Thanks," I mumble.

He grunts and turns his attention to Eugenia and Claude. "You two are fucking assholes. If you cause Bea any more drama, Flip and I will make your lives a living hell." He lets the door fall shut, his expression unreadable. "Let's get the fuck out of here."

I follow Flip down the hall to the elevators.

It isn't until we're inside and on our way back to the lobby that anyone says anything. "How long has that shit been going on?" Tristan's right eye tics.

28

"It only escalated into super-weird territory over the past few weeks."

"What about your financial situation? Is it bad? Is that why you were living there?" Flip asks.

"Rent was cheap. I know why now. It meant I could save twenty-five percent of every paycheck instead of ten. I'd only planned to stay for a year, and then I'd have a cushion and could afford a nice studio or something."

I want to have at least five thousand in savings. That's enough of a buffer to cover first and last at a new place and incidentals for a couple of months. Our parents never had savings. It didn't matter that they both had full-time jobs and my dad even had a side hustle painting houses on the weekend. Every time they tried to sock away money, something would happen, and they'd need it to cover an emergency. And Flip's hockey was expensive. I don't ever want to be in the same position.

"I would've helped you out, Rix. You know that." Flip's forehead is furrowed.

"You already helped with university tuition, and that was a big enough deal. I had it mostly handled. I'll get a new job and find a decent apartment and be out of your hair."

The elevator stops on the eleventh floor, and we pick up an adorable elderly couple. We're silent for the rest of the trip. I exit after the couple, and we troop out to the car. Two of the bins fit in the trunk, which seems like a minor miracle. The third takes up seventy-five percent of the back seat.

I try to savor ice cream sandwiches because they're my favorite indulgence, but these are melting, so I'm forced to devour mine while standing beside Flip's car. Afterward, I cram myself into the back seat again.

"East Side's?" Flip asks.

I tuck my hands between my legs. "We don't have to. I know you probably have stuff to do."

"You hungry, Tris? Wanna go for lunch?" Flip asks.

"I'm always hungry," Tristan replies.

Two minutes later, we pull into East Side's parking lot.

Tristan snorts. "Dude, I haven't been here since we got drafted. Do they still do the unlimited salad and garlic bread?"

"They sure do."

"Ah, man. They're gonna hate us by the time we leave." Tristan hops out of the car.

I flip the seat forward and push it as far as I can to make it easier to get out, but he closes the door on me. Obviously the being-nice blip is over. "For fuck's sake." I grab the handle, opening it back up.

"I forgot you were back there." He holds the seat belt for me again.

I fight the sting of that comment and extricate myself from the back seat. Once I'm back on my feet, I stretch out the kinks. Despite the ice cream sandwich, I'm starving. Chocolate chip cookies aren't a filling breakfast.

The hostess takes us to a booth, and I scoot in first, Flip taking the spot beside me. Tristan sits across from us. He sets his phone on the table, screen-side up. It flashes every few seconds with a new notification.

The server comes over to take our drink order.

"Hey! I didn't expect to see you for another week!" Adelaide, our usual server, greets us with a wide smile as she approaches. "Oh! And you brought a friend."

"Hey, Addy. This is Tristan. We were in the area and figured we'd stop for lunch." Flip's smile makes her blush.

"Well, that's a nice surprise." She turns her dimpled grin to Tristan. "Hi. Welcome to East Side's."

He gives her a smirky smile and chin tip in greeting.

Such a dirtbag. He'd better not try to pick up Addy and ruin me ever coming back here.

Addy turns back to us. "Should I start you two with the usual?" She glances over her shoulder before lowering her voice. "The regular manager isn't on, so it might be harder to get two salads on the table at a time, but I'll bring two loaves of bread and put in a second salad order right away."

"Don't get in shit on our account," Flip says.

She waves a dismissive hand. "I'll tell him we've got a pro hockey player in the restaurant, and he'll probably have a mini coronary. It'll be fine."

She takes our drink orders and leaves us to look at the menu. I don't need it. I get the same thing every time.

"Have you slept with that girl or something?" Tristan asks Flip once she's gone.

"Nah, man. Rix and I come here once a month. She's usually our server." Flip looks through the menu. He typically orders one of three things.

"You could go somewhere nicer. With fewer screaming children." Tristan glances to our right, where a family with three kids, all under six, fight over crayons. The toddler is smashing goldfish crackers into dust and screaming his head off. Who is he to look down on those who appreciate unlimited salad and garlic bread?

Flip shrugs. "It's where we go."

"You're more than welcome to leave if the noise bothers you," I say with a smile.

Our server returns with drinks. Flip and I have Coke, and Tristan has a draft beer. We order our mains, and a minute later, the salad and garlic bread arrive. Addy waits while we empty the bowl onto our three side plates and tells us she'll be right back with salad round two. I spread my napkin on my lap and cross my legs. My foot connects with a shin because Tristan is manspreading.

"Sorry," I mumble around a mouthful of delicious salad.

He grunts but doesn't move his leg or comment otherwise.

Every few minutes, Addy passes by with another bowl of salad and more garlic bread.

Flip eats like someone is going to steal his food, while Tristan is methodical and mannerly. He grew up in an upper-middle-class family, so having manners and not eating like every meal might be the last one he'll get makes sense.

I'm already stuffed to bursting by the time our main courses arrive. Tristan has manspread so much that his foot keeps hitting mine. Even without trying, he manages to take up all the space—and not just on his side of the booth, but in the room. Everyone who passes the table gives him a second glance.

I kick him not-so-gently. "Can you stop?"

He arches a brow while he twirls noodles on his fork with the help of a spoon. "You're the one kicking me."

"Because you're manspreading into my space."

"I don't know if you've noticed, but I'm six-five, and these booths aren't designed to hold someone my size, let alone two people this size." He motions to Flip.

"You keep stepping on my foot!"

"And you keep kicking me in the shin. Seems like maybe we're even."

"Can you cut the bickering for two minutes? You're worse than that table over there." Flip nods toward a table of tween-girl soccer players who are shrieking and taking endless selfies.

I cross my legs and angle my body toward the edge of the booth. My heel rests against Tristan's calf. I peek under the table. He and my brother are strategically positioned so their legs don't hit each other. I stop bitching and pop a slice of spicy sausage into my mouth, even though I'm already full.

The whole point of eating at East Side's is to fill up on salad and bread and take my pasta home. I can usually make it last for an additional lunch and dinner the next day.

A minute later, a pair of twelve-year-old boys walk by and do a double take. They're wearing Terror ball caps with the raging goose mascot emblem. One elbows the other. "Holy crap. Flip Madden and Tristan Stiles?"

Flip's grin is instantaneous—he loves the fame. Tristan takes a moment to catch up, but he, too, smiles. The shift is disarming, in part because all it does is make him hotter. He and Flip entertain the boys for a minute, scooting out of their seats to take a few photos and sign the boys' hats before their parents usher them back to their table.

"You just made their day." I don't want to find how kind Tristan was to those boys attractive.

"Part of the job." Tristan's phone lights up, and he frowns as he taps on the screen. "Well, shit."

"Shit what?" Flip asks through a mouthful of noodles.

"Hendrix is coming back. I thought he was still recovering from knee surgery."

"Guess he healed up better than they expected," Flip says.

"Yeah, I guess." Tristan pokes at his noodles but doesn't spin any onto his fork.

"It'll be good to have him back on the ice," Flip offers.

"Yeah." Tristan rubs his bottom lip. He doesn't look like he feels the same way. "I wonder what line they'll start him on?"

"You're talking about Hollis Hendrix, right?" I ask.

"Yeah. He's been out since the middle of last season," Flip says.

"I thought he might retire. Isn't he in his mid-thirties?" I spear a mushroom.

"He's thirty-three."

"How many years are left on his contract?" I ask.

"Two," Flip replies.

"So maybe they want to make the most of whatever time he has left? Especially since he's pulling six million a year." Flip has three more years on his current contract with Toronto, but I don't know about Tristan. They're peaking in their careers while Hendrix is on his way out. He's played for the league since he was nineteen, which is a solid run.

Tristan's brows are pulled together, and he's staring at me with an unreadable expression.

"What?" I ask.

His phone buzzes, dragging his attention away. "I'll be back in a minute." He slides out of the booth, his phone already at his ear. "Hey, Brody, everything okay?"

Brody is Tristan's youngest brother. I think he's still in high school.

He's gone so long we have the remains of his lunch boxed up, and I offer to pay as a thank you. But Flip refuses and covers it.

Tristan is quiet on the ride home, and as soon as we arrive, he hops in his flashy sports car and says he needs to take care of something.

"Is he okay?" I ask. Not that I care about his feelings.

"Yeah. He'll be fine. Brody has hockey competitions coming up, and Tristan gets on the ice with him when he can."

"What about his dad?"

"He's not a pro hockey player, and Brody's on track to be drafted this year."

"Right. That makes sense."

I try to fit that piece somewhere into the puzzle. I don't know how to take Tristan. He's still a jerk, but he stood up for me today. And then there was whatever happened in the car.

Flip pops the trunk. "Come on, let's get you settled in the loft."

"I promise it won't be for long."

CHAPTER 3
TRISTAN

The first thing I notice the following morning is that the bathroom is clean. Totally spotless. No toothpaste dots on the mirror on Flip's side. No towels on the floor. But then I see all the bottles and jars on the counter that weren't there yesterday. And the pink fucking toothbrush. The third is the smell. It's sweet, like vanilla and citrus—lemon maybe. It pisses me off, because it smells good, and it reminds me of Beat.

Fucking Beatrix.

Everything about having her here irritates me.

Living with Flip has been a reprieve from my normal life. I don't answer to anyone. I don't have to take care of anyone other than myself. Growing up in a house without a mom, a dad who had to work long hours to support us, and two younger brothers means I've always shouldered a lot of responsibility. I made sure they got to and from school when my dad had early or late meetings, which was often. I attended practices, drove them to lessons, helped with their homework. And playing for Toronto has kept me close enough to home to take some of the pressure off my dad when I'm not on the road.

But with Flip, I've been able to indulge, let go of some of the responsibilities, and lose myself in feeling good instead of

35

always worrying. Now Beat has moved in. I don't need someone else to take care of. I don't want to be responsible for her, to worry about her, to hold her fucking hand and get her out of bad situations. And when we were younger, Beat always needed taking care of. I mean, she was a kid. But it seems like maybe that hasn't changed, even though she's definitely not a little girl anymore.

I can't tell Flip she's not welcome, though. He'll feel compelled to set her up in her own apartment, and then it'll be even more drama since those two are super paranoid about money. At least Flip is, and based on where Beat was living, she's the same. Doesn't matter that Flip's been playing for the league for the past five years, or that he makes five million a season. He's always worried it will disappear. Like one day he'll wake up and instead of being a multimillionaire, he'll be broke as fuck. That's how he grew up.

Whatever. It's temporary. And we start season training next week. I can deal with Beat in my space for a week or two.

I flip up the toilet seat and awkwardly angle my half-hard cock toward the bowl, but as my thumb grazes the sensitive spot under the crown, I harden further. There's no way I can pee like this. I turn on the shower instead. Might as well take care of all my needs at once.

The water warms quickly, and I step under the hot spray. I grab the closest bottle and squirt some body wash or shampoo into my palm and fist my erection. But instead of sandalwood and sage, I'm hit with vanilla and citrus. I stroke aggressively, frustrated that I can't escape Beat even when I'm in the goddamn shower. My nostrils flare, and I splay a hand against the tile wall as I find a steady rhythm.

I slam my eyes shut and try to conjure up an image of some generic previous one-night stand. But all I can smell is Beat, so of course her face pops into my head. Along with it comes the memory of yesterday's car ride and the feel of her tongue running along the edge of my jaw, her satiny chestnut hair between my fingers, and the salty-sweet taste of her skin when I bit her ear. Like a fucking savage. My imagination takes over. Instead of her trying to rip out my nipple hair while I'm threatening to bite off her earlobe like an unhinged MMA fighter, she's on her knees in front of me. I'm gripping her hair as her tongue drags across that plush, pouty bottom lip.

My lids fly open before I can take that disturbing fantasy any further, but it's too late. My erection kicks in my fist, and I explode all over the tile wall. I didn't even get my cock into her imaginary fucking mouth.

I wash away the aggravation with my *own* goddamn body wash.

When I leave the bathroom, Beat is in the kitchen. She's not the gangly fourteen-year-old I remember. She's definitely all woman now.

"Disappointed because I locked the door this time?"

"What'd that take you? All of five minutes?" she fires back. "If anyone's disappointed, it's your previous one-night stands. But I guess that explains why you never have a girlfriend."

"Girlfriends are a pain in the ass." Caring about someone only leads to disappointment. I learned that the hard way and never fucking forgot.

"Especially when you can't keep them satisfied."

I flip her the bird and disappear into my bedroom, closing the door harder than I mean to and jolting at the noise like an idiot. I can't stand fighting, and yet that's all Beat and I seem to do. I jab my legs into a pair of boxer briefs but don't bother dressing the rest of the way. Flip doesn't like to run the air conditioning the same way I do, which means if I put a shirt on post shower, I'll start sweating, and then I'll have to change again before we leave for this morning's team meeting. Which I'm stressed about.

I throw open my bedroom door. Beat is still standing at the island, chopping fruit. She's not wearing a bra. I know this because there's no strap on her bare shoulder. Her hair is pulled back in a ponytail, showing off the graceful slope of her neck and curve of her ear. Which I bit yesterday. My gaze drops lower, to where her nipple peaks against the pale pink fabric. I can't decide if it's an optical illusion, but I swear I can see its outline through her shirt.

I stomp across the room, angry that she's in my space, using my kitchen, and yank open the fridge. I blink a few times as I process the contents. Someone went grocery shopping. No, not someone. Beat. When Flip shops, he buys ramen, Kraft Dinner, and whatever sugary cereal is on sale. The crisper is full of fresh fruits and vegetables. There are two cartons of orange juice—the generic kind from concentrate, not the organic, fresh-pressed stuff I usually get, but still. I grab the extra pulpy one and pour myself an enormous glass. I down it and pour a second.

Beat is still chopping fruit. There's a huge fruit tray already prepared, with one empty spot left. I'm always in charge of breakfast. And most meals in general. It's been years since someone has done this for me.

I don't want to get fucking nostalgic. Or think about how much I hated going home where I had two younger brothers to help raise because my mom sucked as a human being. Flip and Beat had everything I didn't.

"I satisfy my partners every single fucking time," I blurt.

Beat continues slicing pineapple into chunks as if I don't exist.

I move into her personal space until I'm close enough to smell her shampoo, which I used to beat off. The irony is not lost on me. "Every. Time."

She stops cutting and spins around, all curves and full lips and huge brown eyes. Her tongue darts out to wet her bottom lip. It was on my skin yesterday. I can't stop thinking about that, and it makes my blood boil.

"How can you be sure?" She fingers the end of her ponytail, which hangs over her shoulder and rests on the swell of her breast. "What if they fake it for you?"

38

"They don't."

"So cocky and sure of yourself, aren't you, Tris?" Her hand goes to her chest, and she exhales a tremulous breath. "Oh." Her pink-painted fingernails skate up the side of her neck, then drift along the collar of her shirt. "Oh, God," she whimpers.

The sound goes straight to my asshole cock. "The fuck?"

She grips the edge of the counter with her free hand and meets my confused glare with a challenging one of her own. And then she moans. It's a seductive, unnerving sound coming from my best friend's little sister. "Right there. Oh, God, Tristan, you're *so big*." She throws her head back and rolls her hips.

"Seriously? What the hell are you doing?" It's like she knows what happened in the shower and she's taunting me in a pair of shorts that don't cover much.

Her bottom lip slides through her teeth and she sighs, then moans again, eyes falling closed. "Oh, oh yes! Oh, God, yeesssss! So thick. It hurts *so gooooood*."

Maybe I wasn't off base when I accused her of doing more than listening to me jerk off the other night. I'm about to call her out, but one of her hands glides down her soft, curvy body, and her thumb hooks into the waistband of her tiny cotton sleep shorts. She pushes them so low it's nearly obscene, but then they snap back into place as her hand travels lower, running along the inside of her thigh. "Fuck. Right there. That's it. Don't stop!"

Yeah, my best friend's little sister might be inconvenient to have around, but she's also hot as fuck. It's a terrible combination, apparently. Despite having taken care of myself fifteen minutes ago, my body is already reacting to this...whatever *this* is.

Her eyes snap open, and her hand curves around my nape, nails biting into the skin. Just like her tongue on my skin yesterday, the contact is unexpected and jarring. Her other hand moves to cup and squeeze her breast. I break eye contact long enough to confirm that I can see her nipple through the fabric. It's not an optical illusion. She tugs on the back of my neck, and I lean in, confused and transfixed. Her lips brush my ear, her voice softer, raspy, and a little desperate. "Please, Tristan. Oh, God. Oh, fuuu-uuuck." She drags the word out, and this time I find my earlobe caught between her teeth.

My hand moves without permission, settling on her hip, and my knee finds its way between her thighs. This is wrong. Bad. Not what I want. She's my best friend's sister, but fuck if I don't want a taste of that forbidden fruit.

She sucks in a breath, bites the edge of my jaw, and stutters, "I'm-I'm-I'm c-c-coming!"

Her fingernails retract from my neck, and she shoves my chest. I release her hip and stumble back.

"We can all fake it when we need to. Especially with an egomaniac like you." She brushes by me and disappears into the bathroom, firing the bird at me as she slams the door.

I jolt. I hate the slamming of anything.

Flip's bedroom door opens, and he stands there, shirtless, hair a mess, boxer briefs tented with morning wood. "The hell is going on out here?"

"Nothing. We have a team meeting in an hour. We should get a move on. There's a breakfast buffet." How would I have explained what was going on if he'd opened the door a minute earlier?

"Shit, that's right. They always have the best waffles. I'll be ready in fifteen."

"Sounds good."

I head for my room and close the door, then glare at my semierect cock. "Fuck you for getting excited."

"You're sure you're okay with this arrangement?" Flip asks for what's probably the seventh time in forty-eight hours.

"You should have asked me first."

"I know, man. I'm sorry. She cried on the phone, and she never does that. It'll just be for a week or two."

"I don't want another person to take care of."

"You won't have to. I can set her up with her own place if you want her out sooner." He anxiously raps on the armrest.

"It's fine." I'm not sure it's fine at all, considering what happened this morning. But I don't need him stressing about paying Beat's rent. I'll just hope she finds a job and moves out so things can go back to normal and she doesn't become my problem. In more ways than one. Besides, I have bigger things to worry about. "Is Hollis coming to the team meeting?" I tap on my knee.

"As far as I know, yeah." Flip glances at me before focusing on the road again.

"You think they'll start him off slow? Maybe second line until he gets his bearings again? He was out for almost the entire season last year." It's not that I don't value Hollis as a player. He's been with the team for the past seven years. He's seen Toronto through the playoffs twice and to a Cup win once, but his return doesn't necessarily mean good things for me.

"I guess it depends on how he performs during training camp and exhibition games. They'll want to get a feel for how quickly he fatigues. You worried about being shifted back to the second line?" Flip asks.

"I don't know. Maybe. Last season was great. I want this year to be even better, but if I end up with less ice time, it'll be hard to maintain my stats." This is my last year on contract with Toronto, so the stakes are high. "I'd like us to play together for more than two seasons, you know?"

"They'll renew. Last season was your best." Flip smiles. "And we play well on the same line. They'll take that into account."

"Yeah. I guess we'll see how it all rolls out." I had my best season by far last year, and it was the first time Flip and I had played together since high school. After Hollis was out with an injury, the team floundered. He'd been a lead scorer. But Coach

Vander Zee gave me a chance on the first line, and it proved to be a good move. Last year, we made it to the second round of the playoffs. We lost in the seventh game.

I've yet to experience the high of winning the Cup, and I'm always afraid my next season could be my last and that victory will never be mine. It's one thing to be a professional hockey player; it's another to be on a team that's won the finals. I want that so badly I can taste it. I want to establish my value so they renew my contract. The team is like an extended family. We take care of each other on the ice. It's the give and take, and I need it.

We arrive at the arena and head to the meeting room.

Ashish Palaniappa, one of our defensemen, is standing near the door. His wife, Shilpa, is the team lawyer and a total badass. "Stiles, Madden." He pops a Timbit in his mouth and offers his fist for a bump.

"Hey, Ash."

Coach Vander Zee is already at the front of the room with a young woman. "Coach get a new assistant or something?" Flip asks after his own fist bump. "She looks kinda young."

Hemi, aka Wilhelmina Reddi-Grinst, our PR person, and Shilpa appear out of nowhere. "That's his daughter, Tallulah. She's seventeen, so put your dirtbag away, Phillip."

Flip jumps. "Shit. Where the hell did you come from?"

"I'm everywhere." Hemi cackles ominously, then grows serious. "We have a meeting tomorrow morning to discuss some promotional opportunities that would be beneficial for your image." She turns to me. "And yours."

"I'm a good boy," I say defensively. At least I try to be, but Flip is out of control when we're at the bar. I always drink too much and end up doing things I shouldn't. I don't want to be a problem for the team, and that includes Hemi. "Hi, Shilpa. You look lovely as usual."

She rolls her eyes. "Sucking up with compliments doesn't make you less of a liability, Tristan."

Hemi throws her head back and laughs. Then her expression

flattens. "Did you know that your best friend posted a video of you covered in glitter, doing body shots off a woman who may or may not have been a stripper? Or possibly a go-go dancer. Either way, it's not very family-friendly behavior."

Shit. Until now I didn't even remember that happened. Flip ended up going home with her, and her friend. They were, in fact, go-go dancers at a local nightclub.

Flip frowns. "I'm his best friend. I wouldn't post that."

"Oh, but you did. So tomorrow morning, we'll meet and devise a plan so all your endorsement campaigns don't get pulled."

Flip's eyes go wide. "They won't do that, will they?"

She pats him on the shoulder and walks away, shaking her head.

Shilpa wags a finger at us. "Don't make my job harder than it needs to be." She kisses Ashish on the cheek and walks away.

"Fuck." Flip pulls out his phone and scrolls through his social media. And there it is, a video that starts with a close-up of his nostrils and ends with me sucking vodka out of a woman's navel. "I'm so sorry, man."

Clearly not my finest moment, but at least it's above the waist.

"Catching heat already and the season hasn't even started." Dallas Bright, left wing, first-line player, and one of our good friends gives us an understanding smile. "I guarantee it won't be nearly as bad as the torture she put me through this summer."

I feel myself grinning. "This I need to hear." Hemi loathes Dallas and does her best to make sure he knows it.

"She made me dress up as a clown in July. It was balls hot. I thought I was going to die. Full clown makeup, big shoes, red wig—like something straight out of a horror movie. I hate clowns. Like, *hate* them. I almost had a panic attack from looking in the mirror. It was for a charity cancer event. I guess she found out that I make balloon animals and ran with it. But I can only make dogs, flowers, and lightsabers. I can't tell you how many kids I made cry because I couldn't make them what they wanted. It was a train wreck."

"I don't understand how you can hate clowns," Ashish muses.

"Why does she hate you so much?" Flip asks.

He rubs the back of his neck. "Probably because one of my friends cut off her braid when she was in third grade."

"That's a long time to hold a grudge about some hair."

"Yeah. It's one piece of the puzzle." Dallas doesn't elaborate because Coach Vander Zee gives us the five-minute warning.

"They better still have waffles and bacon." Flip breaks rank and heads for the buffet.

Dallas already has a plate, so I follow Flip. He loads up like it's his last meal. Just as we take our seats, Hollis comes in. Everyone cheers and claps. I join in, but heaviness settles in the pit of my stomach. As happy as I am that the surgery went well and he's all healed up, I'm still worried about what that means for my career.

After the meeting, Flip goes out with a few of the guys, but my younger brother has a game north of the city. I try to attend his hockey games if I'm not traveling and they don't interfere with practice times. His birthday is in the fall, and half the time I'm out of town, which sucks. I hate not being able to celebrate with him. Thankfully, this year it falls at Thanksgiving, on one of our days off.

I get a ride home with Dallas. He has a penthouse in an exclusive building a few blocks away. I'd been looking to upgrade my place until Flip was traded to Toronto last year and suggested we be roommates.

Dallas drops me off, and I head upstairs to our place. "Hello!" I call out when I open the door, but no one answers.

The condo is empty; no Beat to deal with. It smells like

cleaning supplies and fresh lemon. The kitchen counter is free of all the random crap Flip often forgets to put away. A bowl of fresh fruit sits in the middle of the island, and there are freaking throw pillows on the couch. Two walls are all floor-to-ceiling windows, with a sweet view of the lakeshore. But it means having a TV down here is pointless because the glare makes it impossible to see the screen. Our only TV is in Beat's makeshift bedroom, the loft.

I change out of my dress clothes into jeans and a T-shirt. I grab a jacket, since the arena is always cool, and head for the door. My phone buzzes in my pocket. It's my brother, asking if I'm coming to his game, and if I am, can I please bring back his video game that he forgot here the last time he stayed overnight. I keep forgetting it.

It's in the loft, along with our gaming consoles. I toss my jacket on the counter and pull the ladder down to climb up. It smells like vanilla and citrus up here. And like the rest of the place, it's clean. Beat's bins are stacked neatly in the corner. She's folded the bedding and set it on the arm of the futon. Her off-the-shoulder shirt and shorts from this morning are folded on top of her comforter. I spot something on the floor and bend to retrieve it.

It's a pair of pale pink lace cheekies. I fight with my mind not to picture her wearing them and lose the battle. It's inconvenient that Beat has gone from annoying teen to annoyingly hot. She's got the whole girl-next-door, soft-around-the-edges angle cornered. It makes having her here even more frustrating.

I rub my bottom lip as I survey the loft. Her privacy is at zero. That situation with the roommates was pretty messed up, and as much as I don't want her here, I don't want her there, either. Whoever lived here before us hung plants from the ceiling, maybe to create a barrier?

I climb down the ladder and check the linen closet for something to hang on the hooks they left behind. I find an old duvet cover that buttons at the top end. It'll do. I climb back up to the loft and hang the duvet. It's janky and only goes halfway across, but at least it provides some separation.

I grab the game and descend again to the main floor where it smells less like Beat and more like cleaning supplies. Shoving my feet into sneakers, I leave the condo and take the elevator to the parking garage. I settle in my sports car and drive the hour and twenty minutes to my brother's game.

On the way, I call my other brother, Nate, to check in. My middle brother is away at college, in his final year of his under-graduate degree in engineering. Dude is brilliant. Played hockey through most of high school, but his brain is massive and needs to be used for other things. He and I talk several times a week. When he answers this time, he's with his girlfriend, Lisa, who he's been dating for the past year, so we cut the call short with a promise to talk in a couple of days.

Our dad is in the stands when I arrive.

"How's Brody playing?" I ask as I take my seat beside him.

"Tight. He's already managed an assist."

"Good. Good." I scan the seats for scouts, since they can show up any time, but it's just parents and a few groups of teenage girls. "We're still good to go out for dinner on Thursday?"

"Yup, his practice ends at six thirty."

"I'll try to make it to the arena. Oh, and I think I've picked out his birthday present. I just want to ensure it's the right color."

"It's pretty ostentatious," Dad comments wryly.

"Yeah, I know. But he's been trying to save up, and with his hockey schedule, fitting in a part-time job is next to impossible. I have connections, so I'll get a good deal on it. Besides, I did something similar for Nathan, so it's all about equity. I'm hoping it takes the sting away if Susan forgets to send him a fucking birthday card."

"She's proven herself highly unreliable in that regard," Dad says quietly.

Is buying my brother a car for his eighteenth birthday over the top? Maybe. But Susan, our mother who doesn't deserve that title, hasn't sent a card since he was ten. The only acknowledgement we get from her that we exist is a single Christmas card sent to my dad's house every year. There's never a phone call, a note, an email, or even a damn text message. I'm pretty sure she has her assistant write the card for her. She left when Brody was only four years old, so at least his memories of her are vague, and his expectations are low.

It doesn't seem to matter that it's been fourteen years since she walked out on us without looking back. Or that I stopped getting a call from her on my birthday only two years after she left. There's still this idiotic piece of me that wonders if one year she'll remember she has three sons and do more than nothing. But I'm not holding my breath.

So yeah, a car is definitely extra, but we make a big deal out of birthdays, so the hole of disappointment she's created doesn't swallow us up.

CHAPTER 4

RIX

The next morning, I'm sitting at the kitchen island with my laptop, sipping coffee and scouring the internet for a job. I plan to ask Flip if I can play around with his financial portfolio. It'll add dimension to my resume. Rage-quitting means I can't use my previous employer as a reference. Even putting them on my resume could lead to questions, since I was only there for three months.

Living here is not a long-term solution. Especially since it seems my brother has a habit of bringing home random women and having exceptionally enthusiastic sex until two in the morning. It was nice of him to put up the comforter curtain, but it's far from soundproof. Thank God for noise-canceling earphones. They drowned out most of the screaming and moaning last night. Except between songs. I can't do anything about that.

My phone pings with a new message, and my heart clenches. It's Rob. We haven't communicated since my whole drunken-voicemail episode. I have enough to deal with, so I figured pretending it didn't happen was in both of our best interests.

I hover over his contact and reluctantly open the message.

ROB

I miss you.

It's followed by a picture of a tub of my favorite ice cream.

I don't want to have feelings about him sending I-miss-you messages. Half the country separates us. As much as breaking up has sucked, I understand why he did it. Making a relationship work like this would have been hard, harder than he was willing to manage. That should tell me everything I need to know right there.

I still send a reply, like an idiot.

RIX

Same.

I flip my phone over, though, so I'm not tempted to continue the back and forth. Things are complicated enough without poking that wound.

At nine fifty-two, Tristan's bedroom door swings open. My eyes stay fixed on my laptop screen. The shit I pulled yesterday was stupid. Effective, but stupid. All I can think about is the look on his face. And the way his thigh magically found its way between mine. Beyond his initial confusion, there was lust—the kind that wets a girl's panties. *This* girl's panties.

He groans. Loudly.

I continue scrolling through employment ads and remind my vagina that he's an asshole, and my brother's best friend, and that I should not lube up because he made a sound that reminds me of sex.

"For a hot minute, I thought you living here was a shitty nightmare," he says as he pads across to the bathroom.

That dries up my excited vagina in a hurry. I work to shake off the sting. "Shitty nightmare is redundant. All nightmares are shitty." I shoot the middle finger in his direction.

He leaves the door open, flips the toilet seat up, and relieves himself.

I steal a quick glance. The mirror across from the toilet is visible from this vantage point. It gives me a perfect view of his sleep-messed hair, broad, thickly muscled back, and sculpted ass.

"Take a picture. It'll last longer!" he calls over his pee stream.

"Why? There's nothing worth remembering anyway," I reply.

His pee stream stops abruptly, and he appears in the bathroom doorway as he tucks himself back into his black boxer briefs. His jaw tics. There's something in his expression I can't quite figure out. Like I've hurt him somehow. But that's what we do—fire arrows and see who can hurt the other one the most. He's usually the winner, even if he doesn't know it. He pours a whole vat of salt in the wound with his next shot. "You realize you're not wanted here, right? Flip feels bad because your roommates were assholes. He'll let you stay because he doesn't want to deal with his guilty conscience. And neither do I. Especially not at the beginning of the season. But you're a problem, and I don't want you getting in the way, Beat."

I can't help it. I flinch at his words. He used to say something similar when we were teens, telling me I was annoying to have around. "I don't want to deal with you any more than you want to deal with me." *Douchebag. Fuckboy. Arrogant asshole.* I'm not the same little girl who wanted his affection. Now I wish he'd choke on his own dick half the time—the other half I wish I was choking on his dick.

"Everything you do drives me up the wall. Why is the counter covered in bottles?" He motions to the vanity.

I tried to keep all my stuff on Flip's side, but a few things have been moved since last night. "The medicine cabinet is full." Mostly of various types of condoms, plus menthol rub and a few over-the-counter painkillers.

He stalks over to the shower and pulls the curtain aside. "And how many products do you need to shower? It's like a fucking drive-thru car wash in here!"

I only have the basics: shampoo, conditioner, body wash, a

pouf, and sugar scrub. And they're all contained in a small plastic bin, unlike the leaking three-in-one wash my brother favors and Tristan's expensive shampoo and body wash.

"What crawled up your ass this morning?"

"You! Your shit is everywhere!"

Hating him is so easy sometimes. Maybe the stunt I pulled yesterday is having the same frustrating effect on him as it is on me. As soon as I think that, I brush it off as ridiculous. The knee between my thighs was reflexive. *He can't stand me.* His overt disdain makes that clear.

A knock at the door prevents me from responding. Then the condo door opens. A woman in her mid-twenties, dressed for business, pokes her head in. "Hello? Hemi incoming!"

Her long, dark hair is styled like she's been at the salon. High-waisted pants and a blue chiffon cap-sleeved blouse accentuate her curves. She's carrying a messenger bag, and she doesn't seem like one of my brother's hookups. But she looks familiar. She sets a tray of coffees on the side table.

"Hey, Hemi." Tristan pulls the bathroom door closed.

I glance between them, a weird, unpleasant feeling twisting my stomach uncomfortably. It's clear Tristan and Hemi know each other. I just don't know how. Maybe I'm wrong about the whole girlfriend thing. But he came home the other day covered in glitter and cheap perfume. I recognize the smell of Chanel No. 5 on Hemi.

She purses her lips and props her fists on her hips. "For the love of God, I said I'd be here at ten. This isn't your locker room. Put on some goddamn clothes."

She's definitely not his girlfriend. The instant relief I feel is ridiculous.

"Blame it on Flip. He was the one making a racket until two in the morning. I just got up." Tristan heads for his bedroom. Maybe that's why he's so aggravated this morning. Maybe I was an unfortunate target for his wrath.

"Where is Phillip?" Hemi asks.

"Still in bed." Tristan's bedroom door closes.

Hemi, who hasn't noticed me, huffs, and her heels click across the hardwood floor. She pounds three times on Flip's door. "You better be out here in less than ten minutes, Phillip, or I will sign you up for a herpes endorsement!" she shouts.

And then I understand why she looks familiar. She's head of the team's PR. Her job is to manage unruly hockey players and their bad behavior. Making them participate in charity events smooths out rough edges in the public eye. She also helps players secure endorsements, which earn income on top of their already amazing salaries. It's a cool job. And she seems like a badass.

She spins around, and her eyes flare. "Oh. Hi." Her gaze moves over me in an assessing sweep.

I'm wearing the same shorts and baggy shirt I slept in. I'm also braless. Mostly on purpose.

Her smile turns tight. "I'm sorry, sweetheart, but Phillip and Tristan have a meeting this morning, so you should be on your way. I can call you a car if you'd like." She pulls her phone out of her bag. "I'll just need an address."

"Oh, uh..." She thinks I'm one of their bunnies. I suppress a gag. "I don't think—"

Tristan's door swings open. He's wearing gray sweats and one of those weird workout tanks with the huge armholes, so we can see his nipples and all eleven thousand abs when he turns sideways.

"Tristan, you'll have to call your friend a car," Hemi says in that same tight, no-nonsense tone.

I kind of love her already, even though she thinks I'm a bunny.

Tristan's brows pull together. It's irksome that even that expression is hot on him. "Huh?"

She tips her head in my direction. "Your friend. You need to take care of her."

"Take care of—" His eyes go wide. "Oh! Oh, fuck."

I hold up a hand and get in a dig before he can. "Even if humanity was on the brink of extinction, I wouldn't let this fuckboy put his dirty hands on me."

His eyes narrow. "I'd rather lose my dick to frostbite."

It's early to be hitting below the belt like this, but I'm ready with the next arrow of my own. "I would rather seal my vagina shut with super glue."

Hemi, the poor thing, looks seriously confused.

Flip's bedroom door opens, and I nearly throw up my coffee. He's wearing a pair of boxer briefs with his team logo on the peen pouch, and sporting morning wood. "Are you two fighting again? I'm trying to sleep!"

"Good God! You two need to get dressed before you leave your bedrooms!" I shout. "I never, ever need to see my brother's morning wood. Never again, Flip. You will pay for my therapy bills until I'm over this. And I will one hundred percent pick the priciest therapist in the world!"

A shrill whistle has me covering my ears with my hands. Tristan and Flip have followed suit. A body rustles around in Flip's bedding.

Hemi looks less than impressed. "Phillip, get dressed and please see your guest out. Tristan, you're being a giant asshole. Get a grip." She turns to me. "I am so sorry. I was unaware you were visiting. I didn't mean to offend you."

"It's fine." I wave a hand in the air, like Tristan's nasty comments don't affect me. I truly wish they didn't. So I focus on how often I'll have to see my brother's morning wood if he continues to wander around in his underpants. It's too early for humiliation tears. I clear my throat and smile at Hemi. "I'm Rix, Flip's younger sister. I had a roommate situation, so I'm staying here until I find a new place. And a new job. It's been a week."

"Oh, God." She presses her hand to her chest. "Living with these two must be hellish."

"My previous roommates were slightly worse, which is saying something."

"You poor, poor thing." She crosses over and hugs me, whispering, "Tristan is always a dick of the first order. Just ignore him."

"I know. He and Flip have been besties since elementary school. I'm used to this. Well, I had an eight-year break from it, and I can't say I've really missed his brand of assholery, but there's comfort in familiarity, isn't there?"

She squeezes my arms. "That roommate situation must have been a real nightmare."

"They struggled with boundaries, and it got a little harass-y at the end when they kept trying to convince me to have a threesome."

"Oh wow, that's…" She glances over her shoulder at Tristan.

"Just another day in a pro hockey player's life?" I supply.

"They learn over time that their actions have consequences," Hemi says.

"Seems to be a lesson Flip isn't all that interested in."

As if on cue, a girl-woman with mascara raccoon eyes comes sashaying out of Flip's bedroom. She freezes when she sees us and tries to disappear back inside, but he blocks the way.

"Don't worry, sweetie, we're not the angry girlfriends," Hemi says. "I'm their PR manager, and this is Phillip's sister." She gives my arm an affectionate squeeze, like we're good friends, not two women who met five minutes ago. Awkwardly at that.

"Oh." The woman slaps a hand to her chest. She's wearing an altered Madden jersey that fits like a dress, and she's carrying a pair of four-inch ice blue sparkly heels. Her hair looks like it's been through a storm. "I thought this was about to get super awkward."

Hemi smiles, and I wave.

"Your brother is like, wow." She does jazz hands and makes a weird face.

"And now it's getting awkward," I say with a stiff smile.

Hemi coughs into her elbow.

"I've already ordered you an Uber. Just give them an address.

Thanks for a fun night." Flip ushers her to the door—he's now wearing shorts, thankfully—and follows her into the hall.

The door closes behind him.

"That was entertaining," Tristan says.

"Zip it, Stiles. People who live in glass houses shouldn't throw stones. You're as bad as he is. See the video that was posted a few days ago for details," Hemi snaps.

"There were shots involved."

"I know. You were consuming them out of a woman's orifice for the world to see."

I choke on my coffee.

Tristan throws his hands in the air. "It was her navel! You make it sound like I was sucking vodka out of her pussy!"

"How do we know you weren't? Being his wingman makes you as bad as he is. You don't just condone the behavior, Tristan. You engage in debauchery with him." She struts to the side table, picks up the tray of coffees, and brings them to the island, passing me one. "This was for Phillip, but since he can't respect my time, it's yours. It's one of those caramel things, so it's heavy on the sugar."

"At this point I'd drink it out of spite, but I actually like those." I pry the lid off and pour it into my half-empty coffee mug. It's like a bowl, so the entire cup fits, but I leave a few mouthfuls behind. Enough that Flip can have a taste of what he's missing for being such a player.

Flip knocks on the front door. Tristan takes a step toward it, but Hemi points a finger at him. "Don't you dare." She makes Flip knock twice more before she opens it herself.

When Hemi finally swings it wide, she makes a face. "Oh, God, you smell like used condoms and ass."

"Sounds about right," Flip says with a grin. "She was fun."

"Seriously, man, Beat is *right here*." Tristan points at me with both arms.

I don't understand why he would insult me one second and defend me the next.

"She doesn't care. Right, Rix?" Flip says.

I sip his delicious coffee, which I would not be drinking if he hadn't said yes to me crashing here. I still needle him though. "I guess as long as you don't get on my case when I bring a guy back here and have excessively loud sex, it's fine."

Tristan's head snaps in my direction. I avoid looking at him. I don't want to see his reaction.

Flip wrinkles his nose. "You can't bring guys back here."

"Why not?" I wouldn't bring a guy here for many reasons, but my brother doesn't need to know that.

He motions to the loft. "You don't have a door. Or walls."

"I'm super aware, thanks. And as nice as it was for you to put up a curtain, it's not soundproof." I motion to the hanging duvet.

"I didn't do that," Flip says.

Tristan is suddenly busy looking for a coffee mug, despite the cup Hemi brought him.

"Oh." I didn't expect that, especially not with all the shot-taking this morning. "Thanks?"

"It's as much for me as it is for you." And he's back to looking annoyed.

"Phillip, please do us all a favor and shower and change. We need to discuss how to save your endorsement campaign with milk."

"Wait, what?"

"They aren't in love with your reputation right now, and frankly, neither am I." She points at the bathroom.

He trudges past her and disappears inside, closing the door.

"Are you hungry, Hemi? I was about to make breakfast hash," I offer.

"Breakfast hash? What's that?"

"Shredded potatoes, chopped peppers and onions, sausage, ham, and bacon, and it's topped with two eggs any style, shredded cheese if you like, and fresh chopped tomatoes."

"That sounds amazing."

"I'll take that as a yes. Tristan, if you can be nice for twenty minutes, I'll even feed your surly ass." Even if the curtain was more for him than me, it was still nice, and I am staying in his place. This is my way of showing gratitude.

He nods. "I'll try my best."

"Let's hope it's good enough." I pull ingredients from the fridge. I chopped and prepared most of it yesterday so it would be easy to throw together this morning. And I already made a fruit platter because my brother's typical breakfast seems to be sugary cereal.

By the time Flip is done with his shower, the hash is nearly ready. I crack the eggs into the pan, letting them fry while I plate the hash, sprinkle it with shredded cheddar, and top it with eggs and chopped tomatoes.

"Damn, it smells good in here." Flip peers over my shoulder. "Is that what I think it is?"

"Grandma Madden's breakfast hash."

"I haven't had this in years. Thanks, Rix." He gives me a side hug.

I smile. "I enjoy cooking for other people. It's kind of my happy place." I set the fruit platter on the table, and everyone digs in.

"Shit. This is delicious," Tristan mumbles with his hand in front of his mouth. His gaze lifts to mine, and for a second I don't understand his expression. It's almost...longing? But that doesn't make sense. He says something else that sounds either like he's repeating himself or *I missed this.*

Grandma Madden's breakfast hash was one of the first things I learned how to make. It was usually mostly potatoes and left-over meat I'd squirreled away. Sometimes I'd get up extra early on the weekend if Flip and Tristan had a game and help my mom make it for them.

"It really is. And so much better than the donuts and stale pizza these two usually eat," Hemi says.

"So what's this about my milk endorsement being at risk?"

57

Flip asks. He glances at the take-out cups beside Tristan and Hemi. "Is there a coffee for me?"

"I gave it to someone who values my time more than you do."

"Here, I saved you a little." I pass him the mostly empty take-out cup.

"I deserve that." He finishes what's left in one gulp and goes back to shoveling food into his face.

"They're hosting a charity event, and it's family friendly, but your current behavior isn't in line with their mission," Hemi says.

Flip stops shoveling food into his face long enough to ask, "What does that mean?"

"It means they don't want to use someone who appears as though he has no respect for family values," she explains.

"How does my prolific sex life mean I have no respect for family values?"

"You slept with someone's wife this summer, Phillip," she reminds him.

"She said they were divorced."

Hemi purses her lips. "You dropped her off at her house, and her husband was mowing the lawn."

"I sure as hell mowed her lawn," Flip mumbles.

"She has two kids, Phillip." Hemi looks appropriately unimpressed.

"Seriously, Flip? Where the hell is your moral compass?" I'm flabbergasted.

Tristan gives him a disgusted look. "You want to sleep with every single bunny in the world, that's on you, but as someone whose mom left to shack up with one of her colleagues, maybe leave the married women alone."

Now I'm back to feeling bad for Tristan.

Flip raises his hands. "I'll stay away from the married ones and dial it back."

"And no more videos," Hemi adds. "I can't help you if you keep posting your antics for the world to see. And stop letting these women take selfies with you while you're sleeping. You'll have your own hashtag soon if you're not careful." She points her fork at Tristan. "That goes for you, too. You two are magic on the ice, but off it you're a PR nightmare. Take responsibility for your actions." She sighs. "Okay, lecture over. I need you two to get dressed. Business casual."

"What for?" Flip asks.

"You're serving lunch at a retirement home. Vander Zee's grandmother lives there, and it's her ninetieth birthday. You'll serve sandwiches and cake, and we'll take some photos and post to socials so fans see you doing something other than making out with women in bars."

They grumble but shovel in the last few bites of their breakfast hash and Tristan puts their plates in the dishwasher. Flip disappears into his bedroom, but Tristan pauses on the way to his.

He rubs the back of his neck and meets my eyes for a moment. "Thanks for breakfast, Bea."

"You're welcome."

I wait until his bedroom door closes before I turn to Hemi. "Your job is wild."

"It is. Most of the time, I love it. But these two need to get their heads out of their asses. Anyway, you said something about needing a job. Do you design meal plans for athletes? I know a few guys on the team who would love the help."

"Oh. No. I just like to cook. I'm actually an accountant." It's a stable job with options for growth, and I spent four years getting a degree to do it. Right now I'm happy that I get to cook for more than myself, and that I have a stocked fridge to work with. It's so much easier to plan meals with a full veggie crisper.

"Really? That's so cool. No offense, but you seem young to have a degree."

"I finished school in May. I had a job at a firm, but it wasn't the right fit." That is true.

She nods. "Most of our players use our recommended firm

for financial management and planning. I'd be happy to see if they have any openings."

"Really? That would be amazing."

"Great. Why don't we exchange numbers? I'll reach out to my contact and see if they're hiring, or if they know anyone who is."

We exchange numbers, and she sends me a message right away.

"Thanks, Hemi. I appreciate it."

"No problem. Let me know if I can do anything else to help."

Normally I don't like to use my brother's career to further my own, but the sooner I get a job, the sooner I can get out of here. Even if that means I'm back to cooking for one.

CHAPTER 5

RIX

After five days of living with my brother and Tristan, I've learned a few things. First, the media isn't blowing my brother's extremely prolific sex life out of proportion. He changes women as frequently as he changes his underwear. It's a little disappointing if I'm honest.

In high school, he dated the same girl for two years. They broke up when they went to different universities. By twenty, Flip was playing professional hockey, and since then, he's adopted an entirely different attitude. I get that attention comes with fame, but most players calm down after a year or two. Flip seems to keep ramping up instead.

I've also learned that it doesn't matter how often I clean the bathroom. Within twelve hours, his side looks like a bomb site. Flip has a habit of leaving his towel bunched up on the floor. Adding bleach to the wash cycle helps remove the funk.

Third, I now understand why the fridge was practically bare when I arrived. It's impossible to keep groceries in this house. I've been shopping twice already, and I need to go again tomorrow. I bought the first round, but Flip gave me a wad of cash to cover subsequent trips because he's aware they eat an excessive amount of food.

But the most frustratingly annoying thing about living with my brother and his disgustingly hot asshole of a best friend is that they constantly walk around in their underwear. Half the time they leave the door open when they pee. And apparently neither of them knows how to flush.

I'm currently hiding out in the loft, comparing grocery flyers so I can price match as many items as possible. I also use an app, but sometimes there are hidden gems in the flyers. Ice cream is on sale this week. Not my preferred brand, but I'm an ice cream addict, so I'll buy the cheaper stuff even if it isn't as satisfying. I started my price-matching mission at the kitchen island, but Tristan came out in his black boxer briefs, looking like a delicious hate-fuck. I didn't want to get caught ogling, so I moved to the loft where I can steal the occasional peek without his notice.

My phone pings with a new message. My chest tightens when I see Rob's name on the screen. His I-miss-you message has been eating at me. Mostly because it feels unfair to send it and then go back to crickets for days.

The internal battle is real. I finally give in and check the message.

ROB

Checking in to see if you're doing okay.

Responding right away puts the ball back in his court, and I'm not sure that's where I want it, so I leave it and go back to my price matching. It annoyed Rob when I did this, and he refused to go shopping with me. Which was fine because I shopped with Essie anyway.

As I finish combing through the last flyer, someone knocks on the door. Hookups usually come over in the evening, so I'm curious who it could be.

Tristan answers the door. "Hey, guys, come on in."

Two deep male voices filter up to the loft. "Where's Madden?"

I shimmy to the edge of the couch for a better view. Two guys wearing baseball caps, with broad shoulders and asses I could bounce quarters off, stand in the middle of the kitchen. One is slightly shorter, with dark hair that curls under the edges of his ball cap. The other has tan skin and short hair. They're clearly teammates. Tristan has put on shorts, but he remains shirtless.

"Still sleeping. He was out late," Tristan replies.

I can confirm this. Flip came home at three a.m. and made a racket. He ate half the contents of the fridge, left a mess on the counter, and disappeared into his bedroom. Middle-of-the-night kitchen noise is preferrable to a woman screaming her brains out, though.

"I hope he finally gets this out of his system before the season starts," the guy with the short hair says.

"We need him to channel some of that energy on the ice, instead of saving it all for the bedroom, or wherever he's getting his fuck on," his friend agrees.

"Hemi gave him shit earlier in the week, but I don't know if it's slowing him down much," Tristan replies.

I slump as his gaze lifts to the loft.

"Like you're any better, man," one guy says.

"Hey, my dudes!" Flip's sleep-raspy voice interrupts. "Give me five and we can get this party started." The bathroom door closes.

My phone pings with a message from my bestie, asking to chat.

RIX

Bro's teammates are here. Zero privacy right now.

ESSIE

Are they all dressed in underpants only?

63

RIX

Two are fully clothed. Bro is probably in underwear since he just woke up. Dickhead is wearing shorts, no shirt. It's an upgrade from the boxer briefs earlier.

ESSIE

Or a downgrade. That guy is hotter than a ghost pepper.

RIX

I know. I can't stand him.

ESSIE

You can always fight fire with fire.

RIX

???

ESSIE

Sports bra + tiny running shorts = payback

RIX

YOU GENIUS

ESSIE

Report back once mission FFWF is complete
🔥

I don't know why I didn't think of this sooner. Maybe because the only people who usually see me are Tristan and Flip. My brother won't care, and Tristan can't stand me. But with their teammates here, it might effectively make a point.

I rummage around in my clothing bin for a pair of those running shorts that barely contain my butt cheeks and a sports bra that doesn't offer much support, but it's strappy and sexy and makes the girls look fantastic. It's also white.

I duck behind the divider for changing privacy and quickly put on the outfit, removing the pads from the bra so my nipples are nipple-y. Then I put on my running shoes and pull my hair into a ponytail. My earbuds get tucked between my boobs, and my phone goes in the slot at the back so it authentically looks like I plan to work out.

Fight-fire-with-fire mode engaged.

I climb down the ladder, and when I reach the halfway mark, I hold the edges and let it carry me to the floor. It's loud, but it allows me to make an entrance.

All three heads turn my way. Tristan is in the middle of a sip of orange juice—he drinks an irrational amount of juice. He chokes and coughs into his arm.

I hop to the floor, plaster a bright smile on my face, and head for the fridge, passing Tristan. His eyes are wide, and his mouth hangs open. It's comical, really.

"What the fuck are you wearing?" he blurts.

I look down and run a hand over my bare stomach. "Gym clothes. Because I'm going to the gym. What the fuck are you wearing?" I turn my attention to his teammates. I might also flip my ponytail over my shoulder as I wave. "Hi."

"Hey, hi." The slightly shorter guy's eyes light up as his gaze roves over me, stopping at my chest for a beat too long.

I extend a hand across the island. His gaze flicks over my shoulder, to where Tristan is standing, before returning to mine. "I'm Rix, Flip's sister."

He slips his palm into mine. "I'm Dallas, and this is Roman."

Now that I see him up close, I recognize him. "Oh yeah, you're lucky number seven, aren't you? Your scoring record is impressive."

"You follow hockey?" Dallas asks.

"I try to catch most of Flip's games." I'm supportive, even if it's from the comfort of my couch. I turn to his friend and team-mate. "And you're Roman Hammerstein, the goalie."

He gives me a lopsided smile. "I am. It's nice to meet you, Rix."

Flip comes out of the bathroom, and as expected, he's dressed in underpants. He's frowning at his phone. He stops halfway between the bathroom and the kitchen and drags his gaze away from the screen. "I need to call my agent. I shouldn't be long. Oh, hey, Rix, you mind putting on a coffee for me? And get the guys whatever they want." He motions to his friends, his phone already at his ear as he disappears back into his sex den.

"I'll handle the coffee. You can grab a shirt and go to the gym," Tristan all but growls.

I head for the coffeemaker. "The gym isn't going anywhere. And you make weak coffee." I toss a glance over my shoulder. "Boys, are you interested in coffee?" Am I laying it on a little thick? Absolutely.

"Yeah, I'd love one," Dallas says.

"Me, too," Roman seconds.

Of course, the canister with the grounds is practically empty. I open the cupboard and push up on my tiptoes, reaching for the whole beans and grinder, but they're on the third shelf. While it's fine for Flip and Tristan, who are over six feet, it's too high for me. I stretch, but I'm short a few inches. I could ask for help, but that gives Tristan open season to shit-talk me. In front of their teammates. That's a hard pass.

I brace my hands on the counter and pull myself up so I'm kneeling on the cold granite.

"The fuck are you doing?" Tristan asks.

"Getting the coffee beans, genius."

"Keep your fucking eyes to yourself, Bright," Tristan snaps.

I look over my shoulder and notice I have everyone's attention. Jumping up on the counter probably put the emphasis on my ass. Perfect. I'm doing a great job of making my point.

"Here. Let me help." Suddenly Tristan is right behind me, his chest pressed against my back as he grabs the coffee beans and grinder, setting them on the counter beside me. His mouth is at my ear, nose in my hair. "Roman's daughter is your age. I don't need another problem to deal with, and you're making yourself one, Beat." His hands wrap around my waist, fingertips digging in. He steps back and pulls me off the counter. My body slides down the front of his, and I swear I feel something semi-stiff nudge the small of my back. His fingers flex, and then he releases me, stepping away. His expression is flat as he repeats himself, insistent this time, "I'll handle the coffee. You can head to the gym."

"Sure." I swallow my embarrassment and work to shrug it off. It's so easy for him to cut me down and make me feel two inches tall. I grab my water bottle from the fridge, as well as the fruit tray I prepared earlier. I set it on the counter and remove the cellophane. "In case you guys get hungry. It was nice to meet you both."

Dallas and Roman murmur their thanks, and I leave the condo without a backwards glance at Tristan. But I feel his eyes on me. I'm not sure if I successfully made my point, but Tristan sure didn't love my lack of clothing, so I'll take that as a win.

I don't go to the gym. Instead, I go to the courtyard, plunk myself on one of the super comfy chairs under a tree, and video call Essie.

"I need all the details," she says in greeting. "What the hell is going on? Why haven't I seen your face in five days?"

I smile at her familiar long dark hair, smooth tanned skin, and almond-shaped eyes. Her makeup manages to be dramatic and understated. She's a magician with a makeup brush. "I miss you, too, Essie."

"It's hard living this far away from you. They need to develop a portal between Vancouver and Toronto, like stat."

"Right? Why couldn't we live in the age of interdimensional travel?" I wish I could reach through the screen and hug her.

"You can move here. Come live with me. We'll find you a job."

"So alluring, but you know you'll find some guy and ask him to move in with you within the next three months. Then I'll be in the same position I am now, minus my brother's annoyingly hot best friend."

"He really is hot, isn't he? It's not just about camera angles," Essie gripes.

"It's so unfair. He's such an asshole. And he's stupid hot. I can't stand him." I fill her in on what it's been like living with my brother and his best friend so far.

"All the stuff in the media about Flip isn't just fodder?"

I shake my head. "I've heard it with my own ears and seen it with my own eyes. My mother must be so mortified. I wonder if that's why they moved out to buttfuck nowhere. So they wouldn't have to witness all the shit he's up to." It's not the reason. They moved north because my dad got a job offer he couldn't refuse, and it's way cheaper up there. And colder.

Essie's bottom lip juts out, and her expression is all empathy. "Babe, I'm so sorry. I know you low-key worship the ground your brother walks on."

"I'm all for sexual freedom, but his bed is almost never empty. I don't know. It all seems so hollow." If my situation were different, I might call him on it. But I don't want to create unnecessary friction, especially when he's letting me stay here rent free.

"The offer stands, Rixie. You're welcome to come here. Book a one-way ticket so you can stay as long as you want."

"Rent is three grand a month in Vancouver." I did the research when she moved.

"It would be half with you here, though."

It's enticing, but Essie is a serial monogamist. She'll have a boyfriend before long, and he'll move in soon after. Then it'll get awkward, and I'll have to figure things out again. "I love you, Essie, but moving to Vancouver probably isn't the answer. How's your job? Tell me everything."

Essie fills me in on the latest with her position as a makeup artist for one of the movie studios out there. It's clear she's happy. I miss the hell out of her, but I'm glad she's chasing her dream. It makes me wonder what mine is. I love handling the meal prep for Flip and Tristan, but that's something to do on the side. Accounting is a stable job with a good paycheck, and understanding money was paramount in a house where there was never quite enough. But the job doesn't fill me with joy. Can I do it? Yes. Is it my end goal? Probably not. Maybe it was the wrong firm. Maybe there's a better fit.

My phone buzzes with an incoming call. I check the screen and see it's Dean and Sons Financial Management. Hemi sent me a posting for a junior accountant position at the firm and said I could use her as a reference, which I did.

"I have to let you go," I tell Essie. "This might be a new job."

"Oh! Shit. Good luck. You've got this! Text me later. I love you!"

She ends the call, and I answer the one from Dean and Sons.

Five minutes later, I have a job interview and less than forty-eight hours to prepare for it. I text Hemi right away, and she calls me five seconds later.

"This is such great news! I knew you'd get an interview if you applied. You graduated at the top of your freaking class. They want you more than a hockey player wants a full set of teeth."

"I feel like I'm grossly unprepared for this."

"Come over to my place tomorrow morning. Or I can come to you. We'll do a couple of dry runs."

"It's probably better if I come to you."

"I'll text you my address. Ten o'clock work for you?"

"That's perfect. Thank you, Hemi. For everything."

"No thanks necessary. Your resume speaks for itself. I'll see you tomorrow."

I end the call feeling more settled. Flip doesn't understand interview stress. He's been highly sought after since he was sixteen. It was never *if* he would end up with a contract. It was where and for how much.

Since I'm already on a phone call roll, I call my mom on the way back into the building. I've been playing down the whole job-apartment situation so she doesn't worry.

"Hey, honey, how are you? Is everything okay? What's this about you moving in with Phillip and Tristan?"

"I just had an issue with my former roommates; it's not a big deal and Flip is being cool about the whole thing."

"What about your job? I don't understand how they could let you go with no warning?"

I also might have fibbed about how I ended up unemployed. "Sometimes these things happen. I already have an interview lined up for later in the week. So everything should work out just fine. How are you? How's Dad?" I switch the subject and we talk for a few more minutes before I let her go with a promise to update her on the job situation.

I almost head back to the condo, but I said I was going to the gym. The athletic facilities here are nice, and when I get there, the place is almost empty. I grab a magazine and hop on a treadmill.

Yesterday, I convinced Flip to give me access to his banking files and expenses so I could create a basic financial portfolio with predicted revenue streams and investment incentives. There was a lot to get through. He rarely spends more than a hundred dollars at a time, even on groceries, which may account for the frequent shopping trips.

I leaf through the magazine, frowning at the dated hairstyles. Flipping to the cover, I find it's more than twenty-five years old. I browse the contents and reach an ad that's iconic in the hockey world: the Alex Waters milk advertisement. Back then it was acceptable to be a fuckboy when milk came knocking. Although, from what I understand, Alex Waters made out with copious women, but few experienced his skill set in the bedroom.

According to some uncensored interviews with his wife, it's because most women are terrified of his junk. Those were her exact words. I stare at the ad, smiling at the old-school look that does nothing to detract from the hotness of Alex Waters in the prime of his hockey career. He's built like Adonis. He's pouring a two-liter container of milk down his body. It licks over the ridges and planes of his muscular chest and abs. The ad cuts off just below the delightful V that leads to his terrifying cock. It's a sexy ad. I wonder how this magazine ended up here.

An idea takes shape as I ogle Alex Waters. It has potential to be equally great or terrible. But I'm pretty damn sure my brother's best friend had a semi when he pulled me off that counter. I might loathe him with the fire of a thousand burning yeast infections, but if he finds me attractive, I can use that to my advantage. I can fuck with him the way he used to fuck with me as a teenager, when he viewed me solely as an annoyance. I might still be one, but it's even better if I annoy him and he finds me hot. Then we're in the same frustrating boat. I'm about to find out if that's the case.

I'm the perfect amount of lightly dewy and slightly breathless when I end my run. The magazine comes with me. I don't care if Alex Waters is old enough to be my dad now, in this ad he's total jill-off material. I take the elevator back to the condo and run into Dred in the hall. We exchange brief hellos since she's on her way out and I'm on my way in, crossing my fingers that the guys are still having a strategy meeting. Luck is on my side. They're sitting around the island.

All four heads turn in my direction.

"Hey, Rix. How was the workout?" Flip goes back to staring at his iPad.

"Good, thanks." I wave a hand in front of my face. "It's hot in here. You mind if I open a couple of windows?"

"Adjust the thermostat so the air isn't running for no reason," Flip says absently.

"Cool. Thanks." I head for the balcony. "How's the strategy meeting? You're up against Montreal first in the exhibition games, right?"

"I love that your sister knows hockey. Mine couldn't care less," Dallas says.

"Flip has always been supportive of me. I want to do the

71

same." I smile at Dallas as I open the sliding door and step onto the balcony. "Oh wow. The breeze out here is amazing."

Everyone's attention but Flip's is on me. He's focused on the two devices in front of him. Here goes nothing. I open my water bottle, take a small sip, and then tip my head back and pour the contents down my chest. Water soaks into my white sports bra, turning the opaque fabric transparent. All three sets of eyebrows rise. Roman looks away and takes a long drink of the glass he's now white knuckling. Dallas grins like he's just found his new favorite TV show, and Tristan's lip curls into something akin to a snarl. His gaze darts from me to Dallas and then to Flip, whose eyes are still on his phone.

Tristan points a finger at Dallas. "Eyes off, fucker."

Dallas holds up his hands and focuses on his coffee cup.

Tristan stalks toward me, yanking his tank top over his head. He stops when his big toe hits the end of my running shoe. He glares down at me, and I tip my head back to smile at him. I pour the last few drops right into my cleavage. His ravenous gaze dips lower, and his hands curl into fists, one holding his tank. "What the fuck are you playing at, Beat?"

"Making a point, Trissy. You and Flip are always in your underwear. Why can't I be in mine?"

His jaw clenches, and he jams his shirt aggressively over my head.

"Ow! What the hell?" I try to swat his hands away, but my arms are caught in the shirt and my hair is in my eyes.

He grabs the hem of his shirt and gathers it at my waist. "This shit is unnecessary. Everyone was already looking at you before you pulled this, Beat. It's overkill, and you have a hell of a lot more to offer than your body."

I'm so shocked by the compliment hidden in his chastisement I don't know what to say. His fingers graze the bare skin of my hip, and it feels like a direct link to my clit. And my nipples. Which he's just covered up. He ties a knot at my right side, pulling it tighter than he needs to. It takes me that long to free my arms from the tank prison, which seems impossible since it's mostly armholes.

"I already told you, I don't need another problem to manage. Stop being an antagonistic brat," he grinds out.

The whiplash is hard to handle, but that unintentional compliment gives me the courage I need to keep pushing his buttons. "Stop being an asshole. Oh, wait. You can't. It's your natural state of being."

His eyes darken, his glare menacing. "What's your plan now that you've proven your point?"

"Pretty sure Dallas wants my number. Maybe I'll give it to him."

His jaw tics. "Like hell you will."

I tip my head and drag a single finger down his chest. "It must burn your ass."

He grabs my wrist but doesn't pull my hand away. "What are you talking about?"

"Being attracted to me, even though you can't stand me. So frustrating to abhor something and want it at the same time."

His eyes flare with surprise before they narrow. "Tread carefully, or you'll wind up in over your head."

I poke him through his shorts. He's definitely sporting a semi. I bet if I looked down, I'd see the ridge pushing against the fabric. "Your body betrays you," I murmur. "What you wouldn't give right now to be able to shut me up with your cock in my mouth, eh?"

His teeth grind together, and he leans in until our noses almost touch. His body eclipses mine. I can't see Flip and his teammates, and they can't see me. I'm surrounded by Tristan. I could tip my chin up and our lips would touch. "You don't want my attention, Beat." His voice is soft and menacing, sending a shiver down my spine. "I promise you, you're playing with fire, and I will fucking incinerate you."

I smile. "That sounds like a challenge."

His expression grows sinister. "Oh, little girl, you have no idea what you're signing on for."

"Hey! What the hell's going on out there? Tristan, you can't throw Rix off the balcony, no matter how much she annoys you!" Flip calls.

I pat Tristan on the chest. "Game on, big boy."

CHAPTER 6

RIX

I've done plenty of stupid things in my life. But antagonizing Tristan might top the list. Realizing he finds me attractive even though he can't stand me gives me power. The problem is, I'm not sure how to wield it effectively.

Tristan is scarce over the next two days, which is curious. He leaves before Flip wakes, and returns in the evening, grabs food, and disappears into his room for the rest of the night. At first, I thought he was in avoidance mode. When I asked Flip if everything was okay, he said Nate was down for a visit and Brody had a hockey game, so he was spending time with family. I don't want to find that sweet, but I do. Also, my ego prefers the avoidance option.

I catch Flip between hockey practice and one of his many dates and sit him down to go over his bank statements before my interview.

"All these small withdrawals? What are they for?" I tap the yellow-highlighted expenses, most ranging from twenty to fifty dollars, but occasionally there's one for a hundred or two hundred bucks. This week he made a thousand-dollar withdrawal and gave me eight hundred to cover groceries.

He inspects the list and runs his fingers through his hair. "That's bar money."

"Are there other expenses on your credit card, too?" I ask.

He shakes his head. "Not typically. I usually pay cash at the bar."

"And you only spend between twenty and fifty dollars a night?" I confirm.

He nods. "Yeah. I only ever drink one beer and then switch to water. Sometimes it's my turn to buy a round, so those are the nights when it's more expensive, or I'll buy someone a drink. But I don't bring wasted women home, and I don't get wasted if the plan is to find a hookup, which it usually is."

"You only have one drink?" I parrot.

He gives me a look. "Bars are expensive, and getting drunk is a bad idea if I want some action."

"Right. Okay. That makes sense." In some ways, I suppose it's better that he's sober when he's bringing all these women home. But the fact that he's totally clear-headed when he makes these choices is also unexpected. I file that one away to think about later. Or not. "Okay, I'll add up your monthly bar expenses and everything else and tailor a better plan for you."

"Cool. I gotta meet with my agent this afternoon, but text if you have questions." He leaves me to my job-interview prep.

Yesterday, I spent a few hours with Hemi going over mock interview questions, so I feel more prepared. It takes most of today to come up with a new plan for Flip and turn it into a dynamic presentation, but by the time I'm done, I have projected investment-revenue streams spanning one, three, and five years based on his current annual salary.

Flip and Tristan don't come back until late, which means I don't have to deal with them before bed. Hopefully by next week I'll be gainfully employed again and I can start the apartment-hunting mission.

The following afternoon, I head to my interview at Dean and Sons. I'm nervous, but Hemi has assured me I have this in the bag. Graduating at the top of my class doesn't hurt, and neither does her recommendation. Then there's having a brother who plays pro hockey and lets me comb through his financial portfolio.

All those negligible amounts he spends at the bar add up, but it's certainly within what he can afford. And he further ensures that by living with his best friend in a much cheaper condo than he could reasonably pay for each month. My goal for Flip is to maximize his current investments, so he doesn't have to continue to live in fear of all his earnings disappearing and he'll know his lifestyle is secure even after he retires from hockey.

Dean and Sons is in a gorgeous, modern building with a great team and friendly, dynamic staff. I'm one of several candidates for two positions, and I have another interview set up for a lower-level position with a different firm early next week, in case this doesn't go the way I hope.

But they whisk me inside, and then it's all happening, and the interview goes incredibly smoothly. They love the financial-plan revisions I made for my brother—the way I consider his travel schedule and condo fees versus property management expenses for a house with a yard. I provide a budget for each option, along with the pros and cons of each. By the end, we're all laughing about creative accounting techniques for professional athletes and what expenses need the most massaging.

I text Hemi as soon as I leave the interview.

She calls me a few seconds later. "Where are you right now?"

"Just leaving Dean and Sons, heading for the subway."

"I'm a block away. Want to meet for a drink? You can tell me about it in three dimensions?"

"Are you sure you have time?" I ask.

"Yup. I just finished making Dallas's life miserable, and I need to celebrate. There's a martini bar called The Dirty Olive on the corner of Church and Yonge. Meet us there in ten?"

"Sure. Sounds great." It isn't until after she ends the call that the "us" registers.

Seven minutes later, I arrive at The Dirty Olive. It's swanky, and not a place I would typically frequent because the drinks are pricey. But I just had an interview, and it seems to have gone well. I can afford to splurge on one expensive cocktail. I'll trim my entertainment budget for the week and won't buy that tub of Moose Tracks ice cream. Totally worth the sacrifice.

With Essie in Vancouver and the end of me and Rob, I've felt untethered. I miss the comfort of Essie's friendship and the security of a long-term boyfriend. I'd hoped Eugenia and Claude would be fun roommates, but that turned into a bag of shit real fast. So it's nice to have a potential new friend, even if she's connected to my brother's job.

When I enter, Hemi is already seated at a high-top table with another woman. She has a chin-length bob, dark eyes framed with enviably thick lashes, and the physique of an athlete.

"Hey, Rix!" Hemi stands and pulls me in for a hug. "I hope you don't mind. I brought along a friend."

"The more the merrier," I reply. I'm not dying to get home and hang out with Flip and Tristan and their flavors of the night. Although so far only Flip is bringing home bedroom friends.

"Rix, this is Hammer. Hammer, this is Rix." Hemi motions between us. "Rix is Madden's sister; Hammer is Hammerstein's daughter."

"Hey!" I recall Tristan saying something about Hammerstein having a daughter my age the day of the fight-fire-with-fire mission. Hammerstein is the oldest member of the team, but he's not even forty. And Hammer looks like she might be fresh out of her teens. She's in a bar, drinking, so she must be at least nineteen. I can't see Hemi bringing her here otherwise.

"Hammer's completing her university internship with me this semester, and we're having an absolute blast, aren't we?" Hemi says with a smile.

Hammer grins. "Best internship already, and I started two days ago. And my actual name is Peggy, which is also my great-grandma's name. Rest in peace." She makes the sign of the cross. "But the team calls me Hammer."

"Got it. My actual name is Beatrix, which is also a grandma's name. My parents liked to shorten our names, so I became Rix, and my brother became Flip because I couldn't pronounce it when I was a kid. It took on a whole new meaning when he became a pro hockey player, though."

Hammer makes a face. "Oh yeah, he's got quite the reputation."

"He does," I agree.

"I'm also named after my grandmother, who thankfully is still around and full of sass," Hemi notes. "But Wilhelmina is a ridiculously long name, and I drove a Hemi in high school. The nickname stuck."

"Why did you drive a Hemi?" I ask.

"My moms wanted a safe vehicle. They thought a truck with a powerful engine that also could drive over pretty much anything qualified."

"That's legit." I still don't own a car. Living in Toronto means relying on public transit.

Hemi nods and switches gears. "So, tell me about the interview. Did you show them all your fancy charts and wow their socks off?"

"I think it went well. By the end, we were laughing and chatting. It was relaxed. I feel like they're a lot more my speed than my last job." Although I'm still not one hundred percent sure accounting is the right field for me. I do love putting together weekly meal plans for my brother and Tristan. I'm not sure how I could spin that into a money-making career, though. It would require a lot more school.

"Who interviewed you? Mike and Laura?" Hemi asks.

"Yeah, and Fergie."

"You made Fergie laugh? You're definitely getting the job. We need to celebrate your impending employment."

The server comes over, and I order a glass of water and a chocolate martini.

Hammer's phone buzzes, and she checks the screen, rolling her eyes. "Hold on a second. It's my dad." She answers the call. "Hey, I'm in the middle of a debriefing with Hemi. Can I call you back later?" She purses her lips. "You don't need to wait on me for dinner. I'll probably be another hour, maybe a bit more. We'll grab a bite… No, I don't need a ride. Dad, I've been living off-campus for the past three years. I'm super well versed in taking the subway. I'll be fine. Yes, I'll message when I'm on my way home. Oh my God, no. Do not have Hollis pick me up. That's ridiculous. I'm fine. I need to go. I love you." She ends the call.

"Is everything okay?" I ask. Maybe I pegged Roman wrong. He seemed pretty laid back when I met him.

"Yeah. Just my dad being overbearing. He already had a toddler at my age, so he gets freaked out about where I am and who I'm with. I get it, but seriously, I have no plans to get knocked up anytime soon. I'm fully committed to my vibrator these days. Which I can no longer keep on my bathroom vanity because my dad saw it the other day and nearly lost his goddamn mind."

"Why was he even in your bathroom?" I ask.

"He was washing towels and figured he'd toss mine in too. My Batdick was lying on the sink. I thought he was going to have a heart attack. He turned so red."

"Batdick?" Hemi quirks a brow.

"They have vibes inspired by comic heroes. I might have a small collection. Anyway, I'm sure he'll get over it, but having my dad as my roommate when I've been living away from home for three years is an adjustment."

"Rix's roommates invited her to join their pirate role-playing sex party, which is how she ended up living with Madden and Stiles," Hemi says, then cringes. "Sorry. That wasn't my story to share."

I shake my head. "I tell anyone who will listen. It's like free therapy. I came home to find my roommate, naked, tied to a pillar in the living room. I decided it was best that I move out."

Hammer nods slowly. "That's understandable."

"Yeah. But my brother's place only has one bathroom, and I'm sleeping on a futon in their game room-slash-loft. It has no doors, so the shower is my only private time."

Hammer puts a hand to her chest. "Please tell me the showerhead is removable."

"Unfortunately, it's not."

"You poor thing." Hammer's tone is full of empathy.

"I'm sure Stiles would be more than happy to help you out with that." Hemi smiles slyly.

I almost choke on a mouthful of martini. "We can't stand each other."

Hemi shrugs. "Doesn't mean he doesn't want you. And imagine how good the hate-fucking would be."

"Stiles is highly fuckable," Hammer says.

"I'm sure there are an extraordinarily high number of women who can attest to that," I mutter.

"I need those two to settle down. I get it during the rookie years, but Madden has sowed more oats than a farmer." Hemi stops herself. "Which I'm sure you don't want to talk about since you get to witness it firsthand."

I nod. "It's one thing to know it's happening, thanks to the media. It's another to listen to it."

"Oh, God." Hammer blanches.

"I'll be moving out as soon as I've nailed down a job," I assure her.

"Totally reasonable."

Hemi orders us another round of drinks and some appetizers. I internally cringe as I do the math and realize I've blown my entire monthly entertainment budget and cut into my grocery fund. I have savings, but without a source of income, I need to be extra careful. It's a tough line to toe, having fun with friends but not spending money I can't afford to part with.

But then we get to laughing again, and I relax. Eventually Hemi calls for the bill and waves us off when Hammer and I pull out our credit cards. "I invited you out, and this was a debrief meeting," she says to Hammer. "I got this."

"Are you sure? That was the excuse I gave my dad so he wouldn't keep texting, asking for updates on when I'm coming home."

"Still, we talked about the team, so it counts."

I thank Hemi profusely, and we part ways outside the bar with a promise that I'll message when I have job news. A new text appears as I reach the subway. Hemi has set up a group chat. I love that I've been living in this new spot less than a week, and I'm making friends. Most of my colleagues at my previous firm were older with families, so we never hung out after hours.

I'm riding the high of the interview and the buzz of two martinis as I head home. And I spend the entire train ride listening to a spicy romance audiobook, which probably isn't the best plan since I'm coming back to a doorless, wall-less room. But when I arrive, my brother's door is wide open, meaning he's out. Tristan's door is shut, so he may or may not be home.

I quietly climb to the loft. Someone was playing video games earlier, based on the empty chip bag on the coffee table. The futon and the floor are littered with crumbs.

I sweep the crumbs onto the floor and spread a blanket out over the surface of the futon, debating my options. Listening to delicious smut has me all amped up. The bathroom offers privacy, but if Tristan is home, he'll probably knock on the door to be annoying.

I can be quiet about it. I can get myself off without making a ton of noise. I rummage around in my tote bins and find my trusty purple vibrator. It's nothing fancy, but it does the trick. I grab my clit sucker while I'm at it. It's noisier, but super effective.

I lie on the futon. Mood music would be helpful, but I don't want to make unnecessary noise. I get up to shuck off my clothes and change into one of my nightshirts. Easy access is where it's at. I stretch back out on the couch, pulling a sheet over me. It's hot up here, but I can always shower when I'm done. I need some release. Maybe I can stockpile a few orgasms. That's a best-case scenario, but one will take the edge off.

I bend one leg at the knee and rest it against the back of the couch. The other one I leave outstretched. My heart rate spikes as I run my hand down my stomach and pull my nightshirt up to my waist. I'm already clenching at the possibility of getting off.

I hear movement below me. Tristan is home. A thump and other low noises follow. Whatever. It's fine. I can do this. I drag my fingers through my folds and sigh as I brush my clit. Oh yeah. It shouldn't take long. I close my eyes, sliding a finger inside, withdrawing to drag the wetness over my clit and circle a few times. I slap my hand over my mouth to muffle my moan.

I try pulling the pillow beside my head over my face, but it's too hard to breathe, so I toss it on the floor. I find my vibrator and run the smooth head between my folds, sliding it inside me to muffle the sound before I turn it on.

Tristan's bedroom door opens, and I quickly turn off the vibrator. He rummages around in the fridge. Two minutes later, he disappears back into his room. I should be good for a while. I can get this done in five minutes.

I turn the vibrator back on and angle it to hit the right spot. At the same time, I circle my clit with my fingers. I close my eyes, but I'm tense, aware Tristan is below me.

And because my brain is an asshole, it keeps going back to that first night when I watched him whack off. Now I'm picturing him on his bed, jerking it while I'm up here jilling. I try to redirect my imagination. If that magazine I borrowed from the workout room was within reach, I might look at that freaking milk ad. Anything to distract me from thoughts of Tristan fisting his goddamn enormous cock.

His bedroom door opens again. I turn off the vibrator. My

pussy is raging. I'm so on edge now. I just want to come. This time Tristan uses the microwave. I make slow circles around my clit to keep the vibe flowing—it won't be enough to tip me over. Eventually he returns to his room. Then comes out thirty seconds later. The door closes again.

I turn the vibrator to full blast and jill off in earnest. I need to come before Tristan makes another appearance. But I can't seem to get there. I'm teetering on the edge, but every time things tighten up, an image of Tristan pops into my head. And I can hear him below me. Whatever. I'll use him as fodder. I close my eyes and go back to the time I brazenly faked an orgasm in front of him. I hadn't meant to grind on him, but then he'd put his hand on my hip, and his thigh somehow ended up between my legs.

I imagine what it might have been like if we'd given in to the electric draw. If he'd pulled me closer. If his mouth had been on mine, his hands in my hair, the sting soothed by the feel of his soft lips against my neck. The rough pads of his fingers working between my thighs.

The gritty sound of his voice when he'd called me *bad little Bea.*

I give up being quiet and pull out the clit sucker. I'm so close. It won't take long now. It lights up, then promptly dies. *Shit.* It needs to be charged.

When Tristan comes out of his bedroom for a fifth time, I lose the battle to stay quiet. "Can I help you with something?" I snap.

"All your masturbating is making me hungry."

That fucker is fucking with me. I yank the still-humming vibrator from my angry, extra juicy vagina and rush to the railing, pushing the duvet-curtain aside.

He's standing in the middle of the kitchen, wearing a pair of gray boxer briefs and nothing else. My eyes rake over his ridiculously cut body, memorizing the dips and curves for later. I hate that I appreciate his hotness. My empty vagina clenches as my gaze reaches the massive erection impressively tenting the front of his boxer briefs.

"You're really going for it, eh?" He has the audacity to adjust himself.

I don't know what I'm thinking as I hurl my still-buzzing vibrator at him. Maybe that it will bean him in the head?

He catches it out of the air. His eyebrow rises as he inspects my silicone pleasure friend. "One, fuck you." He holds up his middle finger. "And two..." He maintains his grip on the vibrator as he fires a second middle finger my way. "I'm keeping this."

"Wait. What?" I scramble to the ladder and climb halfway down before I miss a step and fall to the floor, landing on my ass. "Give it back!" I jump to my feet and sprint across the condo as he disappears into his bedroom. I try the knob, but he's locked it. I pound on the door. "Give it back. Right now, Tristan!"

He opens the door enough to reveal his face, six inches of chest, and his still-straining erection. "No."

"What are you even going to do with it?" I splutter.

His smile turns downright evil. "You'll never know." And he closes the door in my face.

CHAPTER 7
TRISTAN

It's been two days since I stole Beat's vibrator. I thought I was going to lose my fucking mind listening to her moaning and writhing above me. But stealing it didn't make things better. The thing was covered in her pussy juice. It was all over my hand. I may have used my pillowcase to clean it off. And huffed it while I slept.

I have a problem. And her name is Beatrix.

I can hear her in the kitchen. It's after nine. I've been up for an hour. Flip is at some endorsement thing Hemi forced on him to help bolster his reputation. She wanted me to come too, but I told her my brother had a game. Flip's bad reputation is not my issue to solve.

I feel shitty that I used my brother in a lie, but I've been off the bunny circuit since Hemi reamed us out. Besides, I don't want Beat listening to what happens in my damn bedroom. Her being here has allowed me a slight reprieve from all the performing. So I guess it isn't all bad. Plus, she makes kickass food, and she's exceptionally organized, helpful, and generally sweet when she isn't dealing with me.

I listen to Beat move around, wondering what she's making. Probably something delicious. I'd bet my left nut she's not wearing a bra. Maybe she'll be wearing those tiny sleep shorts. Or that nightshirt from two nights ago that barely covers her ass.

I should definitely not leave my bedroom to find out. I roll over and shove my face into my pillow.

The smell is fading, but I breathe deep anyway.

I'm such a sick fuck.

And I'm pissed off.

As nice as it's been to have a clean house, amazing meals, and an incredible financial planner around, I need her to move out.

I need her out of my space and my head.

I need...to stop thinking about her in ways that will screw everything up.

I roll onto my back. She's humming a tune. She can sing. It's another item on the list of things about her that frustrates me. I roll out of bed, feet hitting the floor with a thud. I stalk across my room, already unreasonably angry. Mostly at myself. I grab the doorknob and fight not to open it. But I yank the door open with so much force it dents the drywall.

She startles but doesn't turn around, which irritates me more. If she's not ignoring me, she's taking shots at me. I don't want her here, and I'm uncomfortably aware of her at all times. There's no happy medium with us.

She's wearing my favorite sleep shorts again. And a tank top. No bra lines, as predicted. She's all curves and softness. Her hair is pulled up in a ponytail. I don't know why the graceful slope of her neck is so alluring, but I want to wrap my hands around it and feel her pulse thrum under my palms. I want to hear her make those desperate, needy sounds again, but for me this time.

Yeah. I'm so fucked.

I should have gone out last night and gotten laid.

I should have brought someone home and fucked them while she was trying to sleep above me.

I should have, but I couldn't.

Just another item to add to the piss-me-off list.

I stalk across the kitchen and yank open the drawer two inches from her right hip. I grab a spatula and a mixing bowl and slap them on the counter beside her. Then I open the drawer to her left and grab a fork. She's made a tray of bacon, there's a platter of cut fruit, blueberry muffins fresh from the oven—my fucking favorite—and she's busy making some kind of yogurt thing, probably to dip the fruit in. Everything she makes tastes amazing and is balanced and healthy.

She keeps everything in top form around here, she continually asks if we need anything. I'm always an asshole. I don't want to get used to having her around. Or worse, *like* having her here. So I say something shitty, and she dishes it right back. Like she's on to me. Because she is.

I'm in a fury trying to make some eggs. Something to take care of myself and not indulge in whatever she's made. Even I don't understand what I'm doing as I get closer and closer to her. I keep reaching around her. My erection nudges her ass when I get too close.

Everything feels out of control. Like a play gone wrong and I can't recover. I'm pissed. At Flip. At Hollis. At Beat. At those perfect little shorts.

She spins around, her ponytail slapping me in the chest. I want to wrap it around my fist and kiss a path up her throat to her mouth. *No, no, no. That can't happen.* Then she isn't just a problem, she's *my* problem. But even as I think it, my eyes drop to her pouty lips. My frayed self-control is about to snap.

"What the hell are you doing?" She tips her chin up, defiant, eyes wild and stormy. "Can you back the fuck o—"

I cup her face in my palms and slant my mouth over hers, cutting off the angry shit coming out of her. I'm right. Her lips are soft and pliant, a stark contrast to the cutting words we stab each other with all the time. She makes a shocked sound as I stroke inside. Her hands wrap around my wrists, and her nails dig into my skin. I fully expect her to shove me away and possibly slap me across my idiot face. She should. But she doesn't. Instead, she presses her hips into mine and shoves at my tongue with hers, fighting her way inside my mouth.

I'd kissed her half hoping this raging chemistry was a lie, that this attraction I feel is some strange response to how irritating I find having her around. But apparently my body is a big fan of things that piss me off. Her mouth tastes like fresh fruit—strawberries and pineapple. Her hair tickles the back of my hands. She smells so damn good.

And this kiss, this one fucking kiss is everything I didn't want it to be. It's not like any other. We're years of history colliding. Her mouth on mine is a balm, and desperation has me tipping her head so I can deepen the kiss. I shouldn't be doing this, but I can't stop. All I want is more.

I finally pull away so I can drag in some much-needed air. We stare at each other, both of us heaving like we've finished running up a mountain. I want to glue my mouth back to hers and put my hands all over her body. But she might still slap me. Maybe it's taking her a minute to get her bearings and realize this is a colossally bad idea. Because it is. It's the worst idea ever. She's my best friend's sister. The last person I should touch. Her life is a mess, and I don't have the bandwidth to help her fix it. I don't want the responsibility. But I want her.

"God, I hate you." Her voice is a soft, smoky rasp that sends a shot of lust straight to my already aching cock. She releases my wrists, and her hands twine in my hair, gripping the strands as she pushes up on her toes and tries to drag my mouth back to hers. "You drive me up the wall," she adds. It sounds like an accusation.

Before she can fire off another insult, I suck her bottom lip, letting it slide through my teeth. And then I take her mouth in another searing kiss.

I run my hands down her sides, squeezing her ass as I lift her onto the counter. She moans when my erection presses between her thighs, and she hooks her legs behind my back. When I try to push my tongue into her mouth, she bites it, then sucks on it.

She's fisting my hair, making needy noises as we frantically make out. And it's not enough.

I find the hem of her shirt with one hand and her ponytail with the other. I wrap the length around my fist as my palm skates over her ribs and cup the swell of her breast. She moans and juts her chest toward me, like she's looking for more. I thumb her nipple, and she gasps. She fits perfectly in my hand. Even that annoys me, so I pinch the tight peak, and she shrieks. I tighten my grip on her ponytail so she can't retaliate by head-butting me or using her teeth.

"Stop trying to rip my hair out." I brush over her nipple with my thumb again, a barely there caress.

"Why? Worried about premature balding, asshole?" She gives it a vicious tug.

I let her ponytail slip through my fingers and grab her wrists. After finding the pressure point that makes her release my hair, I pin her hands behind her back with one of mine and reclaim her ponytail with the other. I tug her head back, lips hovering over hers. "I told you, you didn't want my attention, but you had to keep on pushing."

"Seems like you didn't mind my pushing all that much."

I bite the edge of her jaw. "You have no idea what you're in for, Bea." My lips skim the column of her throat. The smell of her lotion and shampoo is overwhelming. Intoxicating. I should really walk away. Stop before it's too late.

"Guess I'm about to find out, eh?"

I suck the skin when I reach her collarbone and bite the swell of her breast just above her nipple. "You moan in your sleep all the goddamn time."

"I do not."

"You do. It wakes me up almost every fucking night." She makes the softest sounds. Little whimpers that have me wondering what's eating up her subconscious. "I bet you're dreaming about me. Wishing I'd come up there and give you what you think you want." It's been happening to me all week.

"Why are you still talking?"

I cover her nipple through the thin fabric of her top and bite, then suck hard. She groans and pulls against my restraining hands, pushing her chest toward my mouth.

I release her ponytail so I can pull her tank down. The stitching tears as her breast pops out. Even her nipples are perfect. A deep blushing pink. Small and delicate. Suckable. Bite-able. I do both.

She moans and rolls her hips, giving much needed friction to my aching cock. I free her other breast and lave her nipple, sucking it to a point, biting the swell hard enough to make her cry out. I palm her breast and roll the wet peak between my fingers as I kiss my way across her throat, just like I wanted to.

"You should tell me to stop." It's half challenge, half demand. This has the potential to ruin everything, but I can't find the will to walk away. I need to get her out of my system once and for all.

She scoffs. "And miss the opportunity to see you stew in your self-loathing because you couldn't help yourself?"

"And you won't feel the same way?" I work my way back down to her breasts. I can't get enough—of the sounds she makes when I use teeth, of the way she rolls her hips when I suck a nipple, or her soft sigh when I tongue her.

"Oh, for sure I will. But your suffering will make it worth it." One of her feet catches in the back of my boxer briefs.

"You're a vindictive little thing, aren't you?" I roughly suck her nipple, frustrated that I made it this way between us. Turned us into a war.

"Stop talking and show me how much I don't want your attention, Tristan."

I release her wrists and grip her ass, carrying her across the condo to my bedroom. I close the door with my foot, then lock it. Just in case. A trickle of fear slithers down my spine. If Flip finds out…

It's a risk I shouldn't take. But the only reason I'll stop now is if Beat tells me to. I unhook her legs from my waist and toss her on the unmade bed. She squeals and bounces once and then props herself on her elbows.

Her eyes rake over me. "Such a waste of a pretty face." Her expression and tone reflect her irritation.

For a moment I wish I could erase the ugliness between us. But it's better this way. If she hates me, it's just about sex. I shove my boxer briefs over my hips, freeing my erection.

Her breath leaves her in a whoosh. "Good fucking God."

I grip my cock in my fist and give it a slow stroke. "Now would be a good time to run, little Bea."

She pulls her tank over her head and tosses it aside. Then lies back and shimmies her sleep shorts over her hips, kicking them at me. I nab them out of the air and bring them to my nose, inhaling deeply. They're damp at the crotch and smell like fresh want.

Her eyes flare. "You dirty fucker."

I smile darkly. "You have no idea, but you're about to."

I grab her ankle and drag her to the edge of the mattress. Hooking her legs into the crook of my arms, I push them to her chest and spread her wide. I grip her right breast with one hand and tug at the soft patch of dark curls with the other. When I'm an inch away from her pussy, I turn my head, bite the inside of her thigh, and suck on the skin, hard.

She shrieks and her hands go to my hair, threading through and yanking roughly.

"Keep it up and I'll tie you to my bed," I warn.

"Fuck you." Her grip loosens, though.

"Mmmm..." I lick along the juncture of her thigh, close to where I want my mouth. "Soon you'll be begging me to fuck you." This is what I'm good at. This is where I can channel my frustration.

"Do you ever shut up?"

"Do you ever stop being annoying?" I suck her pussy lip and bite, not hard, just enough to make her gasp. Even her pussy is perfect. It's frustratingly pretty, with soft pink lips and a tiny clit peeking out from between the folds, begging to be licked and sucked.

I blow on it, and she whimpers.

I kiss and nibble and bite, licking up and down the juncture of her thighs, but I avoid kissing her where it counts. Once I get a taste, it'll be game over.

She keeps trying to roll her hips, but the position I have her in makes it tough.

"Tell me what you want, Bea." I can't be the only one on the edge.

"I think it's pretty damn obvious," she snaps.

"You need to ask for it." I tug at the curls again. "Nicely."

"Fuck you."

"Fuck you back." I spit on her clit.

Her eyes go wide. Maybe that was too far. But then her pussy contracts. Like she's already halfway to an orgasm. I arch a brow, waiting, needing her to be as desperate as I am.

She bites her lip, eyes narrowed with frustration and glassy with desire. "Please," she grits out between clenched teeth.

"Please what?" I nibble on her inner thigh again.

Her teeth grind together. "Please." She clamps her mouth shut and her cheeks flush. "Lick my pussy."

"Good girl. Was that so hard?" I drop my head and lick up the length of her, groaning at the taste. I fuck her with my tongue, suck her clit, and try to devour her.

Now she's chanting the word *please*, hips rolling with every flick of my tongue.

She's close to coming. Her thighs shake, and her moans grow deeper and less restrained. But she doesn't get to do that until I'm fucking her. I want to feel her clench around my aching cock.

She cries out when I stop, hips bucking against nothing as I lift my head and watch desire return to anger.

"You asshole!"

I grin. "You don't get to come yet."

I release her right leg and push two fingers into her mouth as she protests again.

She grabs my wrist, but her lips close around them, teeth pressing into my knuckles. I shudder at the thought of replacing them with my cock.

She sucks, tongue sweeping over my fingers on a low, keening sound. I pull them free and push two inside her, but I don't curl them, just pump twice, enough to keep her on the edge. When she rolls her hips, I ease them out and shove them back in her mouth, stretching out in the cradle of her hips. My cock slides over slick, hot skin, and we both groan. I drag my fingers down her chin, wrapping my pussy-soaked fingers around her throat. I don't squeeze, just rest them there, feeling her heavy swallow and her pulse thrum against my palm.

"You okay with this?"

I might talk a lot of shit, but I haven't forgotten who she is. Not for a second. As much as I hate how much I want her, and how easily this could blow everything apart, I don't want to make her feel like she can't say no.

She nods once and hooks a leg over my hip.

"I won't be gentle," I warn.

"Figured that out already. You gonna keep talking or are you going to start fucking me? Or is now when you stuff my mouth full of your cock so I can't keep annoying you?"

"Mmm...such a pretty, tempting mouth." My fingers flex, and she swallows again, maybe nervous. "But then I won't be able to hear you beg."

She snorts an indelicate laugh.

"Careful, little Bea, I sting too." I drag my nose along her cheek until I reach her ear and take the lobe between my teeth, breathing in her shampoo.

Thank God she'll be moving out soon. She'll take all her shit with her, and I won't have to deal with being surrounded by her. Won't be reminded how little control I have around her. Or how she broke me without even trying.

I release her throat and rummage around in my nightstand for a condom. "This is a one-time thing. We get it out of our system, and that's it." I can't afford to do this more than once. Though already I worry it won't be enough. That I'll want more. It's a slippery slope, and it's already too risky.

She gives me an incredulous look. "I don't even like you."

It's what I need to hear. It stings, but I've mostly been a complete asshole to her, so I can't expect any different. I push down the regret. She doesn't deserve my vitriol. It's not her fault she reminds me of all the things I want but can't have. "Good. I'll make sure it stays that way." I fold back on my knees and tear the condom open, rolling it down my length. I pinch her clit, then slap it, causing her to moan and shriek.

I push her knees to her chest again, barring them with one arm as I lean in to keep her in place.

"It's a good thing I'm bendy." She regards me with curious, lust-heavy eyes.

"For me, maybe not so much for you." I rub the head over her clit, circling twice before I drag it through her slit and nudge her entrance. But I don't push in.

She can't lift her hips. She is vulnerable and gorgeous, and for a moment I consider how fucked I'll be after this. I'll know exactly how good it feels to be inside her. I'll have that memory forever. It's exciting because it's new and forbidden and I shouldn't have her. Once it's over, that burning need will be sated, and I'll walk away. I get bored easily, anyway. These are all things meant to convince me once will be enough.

I circle her clit again, repeating the circuit once, twice, a third time.

"For fuck's sake, what are you waiting for?" Her exasperation is amusing.

"You."

"Me what?"

I smirk. "Tell me you want my cock."

"Oh my God. Are you serious right now?" Her expression is disbelieving.

"Deathly." I slide low and push in an inch.

Her eyes flutter shut, and she tries unsuccessfully to shift her hips.

I pull out again. It's not easy. But it'll be so much sweeter when she's the one who folds. I can't be the only one out of control.

"Beg for it, Bea." I bite her calf.

"Fuck you."

"I think you mean *fuck me*. Unless you've changed your mind." I back off, too close to giving in.

She bites her lips together, clearly fighting with herself. It's understandable. I'm an asshole and probably pushing her way outside her comfort zone. She'll hate herself for this after. Which is exactly what I need. For her to never want me again. To loathe me. To regret giving in so I don't have to worry about this happening again.

"You're an asshole."

"I know." I tap her clit with the head of my erection. "Are you in or are you out? Make up your mind, Bea."

She huffs. "Fuck me."

I roll my eyes. "Try again."

She glares at me. "Fuck me, *please*."

I give her an inch. "You can do better than that."

She wriggles but gets nowhere. "Fuck. Fine." She threads her fingers through my hair. It's disarmingly tender, and I like it more than I want to admit.

Her eyes soften and so does her voice, "I need you to fill me, Tristan. I'm on the edge. Please, just fuck me."

"That's my sweet girl." I push all the way in, stretching her, groaning at the feel of her tight, wet heat surrounding me. "Just remember that you begged for it." I adjust her legs so her heels rest on my back. This is as close to missionary as I'm willing to get. "You might want to hold on."

I shift my hips back, pulling out to the ridge and slamming back in.

"Oh, God." Bea grabs my wrists.

The next time she's ready for the hard thrust and doesn't move up the bed. I increase my pace, fucking her into the mattress, wringing moans and cries from her lips. Her body convulses with the first orgasm, her pussy squeezing me like a fist.

I don't give her time to recover. I fold back and rise to my knees, transferring her ankles to one shoulder. Clamping an arm around her shins, I lift and lower her, rocking her on my cock. I slip a thumb between her folds to rub her clit.

She moans and cries out, head whipping back and forth. "It's too much. Oh, God. Oh my fuuuuu—" She fists the sheets as another orgasm rolls through her. Her legs slide down my arm. I pull out and flip her onto her stomach, straddle her thighs, push back in from behind, and start pounding away again.

"Please don't stop," she whimpers.

I smack her ass and she yelps, then moans, her pussy clenching again. Every thrust makes wet shucking sounds, and her inner thighs are coated with her juices.

I stretch out over her, my chest against her back, and grab her ponytail with one hand, wrapping the other around her throat. I bite the edge of her jaw. "Listen to how wet your pussy is for me. You pretend to be so sweet, but you're a dirty girl, aren't you? And I'm going to make you filthy."

I ease my hand under her cheek and push in deep. Then I stop moving altogether. I slide three fingers into her mouth. I don't even have to say anything; she starts sucking and rolls her hips. Like she can't get enough. Like this is exactly what she wants.

Yeah. I'm definitely fucked.

I kiss her cheek and whisper, "I'm just getting started, little Bea."

That gets another low moan.

"Hands," I demand as I fold back on my knees. "Give me yours."

They're currently fisting the sheets beside her head. When she doesn't automatically comply, I grab her wrists and move her hands to her ass. "Spread for me."

She hesitates. Her trepidation is obvious in her thick swallow.

I brace my hands on either side of her head and lean in so she can see my eyes. "Am I making you feel good?"

"Yes," she whispers.

I stroke her cheek, and she chases the affection. "I won't hurt you, Bea. If you don't like it, tell me to stop, and I will, okay?"

"Okay."

I kiss the corner of her mouth, and she reaches up and wraps her hand around the back of my neck. I indulge the kiss for a few strokes of tongue, rolling my hips to the same rhythm. It's too intimate, though, and I need to remember that's not what this is about. I want to push her to the very brink of her limits, ride her hard, and tomorrow, when she's sore and moving is a monumental task, she'll think about the things I've done. Her shame will make sure she never wants me again, and my guilt will do the same for me. It's seeping in already. But it doesn't make me want to stop. Not yet.

"Change of plans." I press a knee between her closed thighs, and she parts them for me. Once her legs are bracketing mine, I fold back and slap her ass. "On all fours."

She pushes up on shaking arms. I grab her hips and pound into her, my pace as relentless as it is brutal. Bea drops to her elbows and rests her cheek against the mattress, her other hand coming between her legs to stroke her clit. But fuck if I'll let her come again, yet. I stop thrusting and drop my hands to my sides.

She whines her displeasure. "Don't stop. Why did you stop?"

"I'm doing all the work." I smack her ass. The right cheek is pink now. "It's your turn to fuck me."

She mutters something I don't catch.

"What was that?"

"I can't help out much when I'm a pretzel." She starts rocking though, slowly at first, but she finds a rhythm and picks up speed, spearing herself on my cock. Her arms shake, and she moans every time her ass hits my pelvis. Juices run down the inside of her thighs and sweat breaks out across her shoulders and the back of her neck. She's close, but she can't tip over the edge. I grip her hip and drag my thumb along the inside of her thigh, gathering wetness.

I stay deep, only pulling out a few inches before I push back in and drag my thumb along the divide. She tenses when I press against her ass.

"Relax." I rub my thumb in slow circles. "Anyone ever get in here?"

She shakes her head.

"Good. It's mine then."

"What?" Her head whips around.

"Calm down. I'm not fucking your ass, Bea. Not with my cock, anyway." But I would. If this were more than a one-time thing, I would relish being the one who gets to have her. I rock my hips so the head rubs exactly the right spot. I press against her opening and my thumb slips inside, up to the first knuckle.

She sucks in a gasping breath.

"Okay?"

"Okay," she whimper-moans.

I knead her hip, rocking to keep her focused on how good it all feels. I push in further until I reach the second knuckle.

That earns me a high-pitched, "Oh, God."

With one hand on her hip and my thumb anchored in her ass, I start fucking her again. She moans and whimpers, chanting nonsense as she comes and comes again. I yank my thumb out and grab her ponytail, pulling her up, her back to my chest.

I wrap the hand that was on her hip around her throat, holding her against me as I ram into her. My teeth sink into her shoulder, and I lick my way up the side of her neck. Biting the edge of her jaw, I slide my free hand down her stomach and cup her pussy as I drive into her. "Every time you think about the things I've done to you, and you'll think about them often—" *Probably with regret.* "—you're going to wish I'd taken your ass, too. And it's going to drive you fucking mad that I didn't, because you're too inexperienced to handle me."

That's how I'll feel about it, anyway. And I'm not above getting inside her head like she's gotten in mine. No one has shaken me the way she does, her little barbs a constant prick under my skin.

She opens her mouth to spew some shit, but I shove three fingers into it and rub circles on her swollen clit. Her teeth clamp down, and she shudders violently. I've lost count of the number of times she's come. I've never had sex with someone who can come as often and hard as she does. She must have been up in her head the other night. She'd been going at it for at least half an hour before she yeeted her vibrator at me and fucked herself out of an orgasm.

She sags against me, clearly spent. But I'm not done yet.

Then she tenses as the condo door opens and closes.

"Sweet. Breakfast!" Flip exclaims.

Panic makes my throat tight, and anger flames down my spine. He's supposed to be gone for hours. I was supposed to be able to take my time.

"Oh my God," Bea whispers around my fingers, which are still in her mouth.

"Shh..." I shut out everything but Bea, unwilling to let the guilt over what I've done—what I'm doing—sink its claws in yet. That'll hit later. But I'm still inside her. And I still haven't had enough.

I pull out and flip her onto her back, cover her mouth with my palm, and push my way back inside. Her eyes go wide, and she moans. I pinch a nipple, gently, then stretch out over her.

She asks something from behind my hand, but it's a garbled whisper. I remove it and give her my ear. "What are you doing?"

"I haven't come yet. We don't finish until I finish." Normally

I'd avoid missionary because it speaks of comfort and closeness, both things I avoid in sex partners, but I need to be able to keep a hand over her mouth. And if I only get her once, I want to see her face when I come.

I run a hand down her side, skimming her curves until I reach her knee. I pull her leg up, hooking the back of her knee in the crook of my arm. I stay deep, rolling my hips, shushing her when she whimpers.

I stroke her cheek and drop my lips to her ear. "I'm close, Bea. So fucking close. Be my good girl and stay quiet. You don't want anyone to know you let me fuck you raw, do you?"

She turns her face into my throat, teeth sinking into the skin above my collarbone. Her pussy clenches.

I pull back and take her face in my hands, giving in to the need to soak up some of her goodness. "Filthy, sweet girl." I claim her mouth and swallow her soft moan as the orgasm slams through me. My teeth hit her lip, and I taste copper, and then my vision goes white. Her nails dig into my shoulders so hard she might break the skin.

I collapse on top of her, needing the feel of her around me.

A knock on my door follows. "Hey, Tris, there's breakfast out here, if you're interested."

My gut tightens and churns. I clear my throat before I call out, "Cool. I'll be out in a few."

I don't want to move, to face what I've done, to lie to my best friend. But I need to run interference. I ease out of her, disappointed that it's over already. I'm far from sated. All I want is more.

"What do I do?" Beat whispers, her panic obvious.

I need to stay in control here. Flip can't know about this, and Beat can't see the guilt already setting in. "Stay here. I'll get food and make up some excuse to eat in here."

"You smell like condom and pussy," she whispers.

"That's not new. He'll think I brought someone home." I don't like the pit in my stomach, or the look that crosses her face.

But I've just fucked my best friend's little sister, so fucker's remorse and a heaping truckload of guilt seems pretty damn likely. "Stay here. I'll be back soon."

Against my better judgment, I press my lips softly to hers before I roll off the bed and pull on a pair of boxer briefs. Beat clambers off the mattress and grabs my arm. Her other hand covers her mouth, and her eyes are wide. She's also naked. She's a sight to behold, all softness and curves. I keep my eyes above her neck, hoping to avoid another hard-on. I give her a questioning look.

"Your back," she whispers.

"What about it?"

She points to the mirror. Besides the scratches that run shoulder to ass, there are also several bloody crescent-shaped marks from her nails. I shake off her hold, cross the room, and grab a towel from the hamper. Swiping it over my shoulders, I clear away the blood. I toss the towel in the hamper and head for the door. A wave of self-loathing hits me, not because I regret what I've done, but because I don't. And now I have to face my best friend. I steel myself, unlock the door, and open it a crack.

Flip is standing at the counter, shoving food into his face like it's going to disappear. I leave my room, stomach tightening.

"Hey, man, looks like Rix was busy this morning. Where's she at?" He turns to face me, and his eyes go wide. "Oh shit. Found yourself a wild one last night, eh?"

"Sure did." More like this morning, but that's semantics. I pause to steady myself, as the wave of guilt is crushing and deserved. Flip has been my best friend since elementary school. We've been through thick and thin together, and I just had dirty sex with his sister. She's still in my bed. The smell of her is all over my sheets and my body. I'm a selfish asshole of the first order.

I avoid eye contact and head for the fridge, grabbing the orange juice. I shake it, twist the cap off, and chug straight from the container. When I'm finished, I swipe my hand across my mouth and lie again. "I'm not sure where she is. Maybe the gym?" But Beat is naked, in my bedroom. "I thought your promo thing would take longer."

"I gotta meet Hemi again in"—he checks his phone—"shit. Less than an hour. I'm grabbing an extra suit and something casual, then I'm out. You around later? Dallas, Ashish, Roman, and Hollis are meeting at the gym, and after we'll grab a bite."

"Yeah. I should be good for that. Send me a text when you're done with your promo stuff." It's bad that I'm already considering the next three positions I'd like to fuck Beat in while I'm making workout plans for later with my best friend. Who I'm lying to. But I've already made the mistake. The guilt won't suck any less if I have her more than once.

"Cool. Your friend still here?" He tips his head toward my room.

I make a noise.

He claps me on the shoulder. "Have fun. I'll see you later."

He grabs another muffin and disappears into his bedroom.

I load up a plate with fresh fruit, muffins, and bacon, then grab a couple of bottles of water from the fridge and the maple syrup, because Beat likes her bacon to swim in a pool of it. Before I return to the bedroom, I stop in the bathroom and wet a washcloth. I want to clean Beat up before I get her dirty again. If she'll let me.

I half expect her to be standing in the same place I left her, wearing a worried expression. But she's not. At all. Apparently, she found her vibrator, because she's lying on my bed, legs spread wide, fucking herself with it. Her other hand is balled into a fist, which she's biting.

I close the door and lock it. Her eyes fly open, and she freezes.

"What are you doing?"

She stops biting her hand long enough to flail toward the door.

I set the tray of food on my dresser and cross to the bed.

"He's leaving again soon." I hold out my hand. "I didn't say you could have that back."

"It's mine," she whispers, still frozen.

I shake my head. I'm already going to hell for this. Might as well enjoy my time in the fire. "It's mine until I decide you deserve to have it back. And I'm also far from done with you, so hand it over."

CHAPTER 8

RIX

Every muscle in my body aches. Tristan wasn't kidding when he said he wasn't done with me, or that he planned to fuck me raw, because that's exactly how I feel. Raw. If there was more than one bathroom, I'd soak in Epsom salts. I've also been avoiding him since I left his bedroom this afternoon. It hasn't been all that difficult.

He went to work out with Flip and didn't come home until after dinner. And Flip left again almost immediately for one of his many "dates."

I promptly disappeared to the coffee shop down the street, and now I'm nursing a decaf tea while trying and failing to read a book. My vagina has a pulse and sitting down is a challenge.

Rob tries to call me, and I send it to voicemail. He's the last person I want to talk to—especially now that I realize our sex was meh.

At nine thirty I stop at the grocery store, pick up a few items, and splurge on a pint of my very favorite ice cream before I go home. Flip's bedroom door is open. That means I'm alone in the condo with Tristan.

I quickly put away the groceries and hide my ice cream under a bag of frozen peas. I rush to the bathroom. My plan is to continue avoiding Tristan, but he's in the kitchen when I open the door.

He's eating a fresh peach. This seems purposeful. "Regretting your decision this morning?" His voice is apathetic, like his fucks-to-give meter is at zero. But his shoulders are tight, and he can barely look at me.

I don't know what I'm supposed to say. He looks both delicious and like guilt personified.

"Of course I am," I mumble. Now I know what all the hype is about. Tristan is a filthy fucker, and I loved every goddamn minute of it. Especially when he kept shoving his fingers in my mouth and holding me by the throat. Not hard. I never felt unsafe. It was possessive, and dirty, and hot. And he spat on my pussy. Who does that?

I was today years old when I realized my previous long-term boyfriends have all been totally vanilla. But not Tristan. He leans into the filthy and wallows in it. Not that I want Tristan to be my boyfriend. Because I definitely don't. I'm a serial monogamist, but even I know where to draw the line with a fuckboy like him. We can't even have a conversation without shitting all over each other. But that was the dirtiest, hottest sex of my life. And he probably knows it.

I throw the question back at him. "How's your self-loathing meter?"

He shrugs, like he's unaffected. He still won't look at me. "Did you think you were special, Beat? That I'd buy you flowers and sneak up to the loft, looking for more?"

I don't know what I expected, but this wasn't it. I shoot an arrow before he can. "I'm not stupid enough to believe I'm more than another warm hole you got to fill. Did you actually think I'd want you again?"

His gaze is flat, expression unreadable as he leans in, lips at my ear. "You were right about one thing, though. You choking on my cock is a great way to get you to shut up."

It's the sucker punch I was waiting for, but it still hurts. "Fuck you," I spit.

"Been there. Done that. Once was enough." He disappears into his bedroom, leaving me fuming in a steaming pile of regret.

For the next two days I successfully avoid Tristan. It's too awkward. I can't look at him without thinking about the sex, or the way he cut me off at the knees after. I'm angry at myself for letting him make me feel anything at all. But my mind keeps going back to when he said he wouldn't hurt me. That if I didn't like it, all I had to do was tell him and he'd stop. Even though the sex was filthy and rough, he was tender in that moment. That's the Tristan I had glimpses of as a teen. The one who would steal a peony from his neighbor's garden and leave it on my dresser because he knew I loved them. That was the Tristan who reassured me. Then fucked the living hell out of me. It's confusing. And frustrating. I don't know how to be around him now. I still hate him, but something shifted between us the minute he kissed me. And I feel as transparent as a jellyfish. Especially when Flip is here.

So when Tristan is home, I go out. Thankfully, they're in training camp now, so they're up and out early, and they spend hours on the ice. It doesn't do much to slow Flip's sex life, but at least the three a.m. marathons seem to be over.

Four days post fuck-a-thon, I'm in the kitchen, prepping their food for the next couple of days. The amount of groceries Tristan and Flip go through is unreal. I bought fresh pasta and made marinara sauce and meatballs, because they need to carb load after long practices. Each serving goes in a microwavable container with reheating instructions. I've been out at dinnertime lately for obvious reasons. I also haven't told anyone what happened. Not even Essie—not purposely, but because every time we've talked, my brother has been around.

My phone rings as I seal the fourth container of pasta, meatballs, and sauce. My stomach flips when I see Dean and Sons flash across the screen. "Oh my God. Okay. Take a breath, Rix." I look toward the ceiling. "Please let me be employed. Sorry for always taking your name in vain. And for screaming it a lot earlier in the week." I shake my head, erasing memories before they surface, and answer on the third ring.

Three minutes later, I have a new job. And I start in two days.

"I have a job!" I dance around the kitchen, then remember the meals sitting on the counter and put them in the fridge. I call my mom right away to tell her the good news.

"That's wonderful, sweetheart. Is it a good firm? Tell me all about it."

I fill her in on the job, which isn't a whole lot different than my last one, just different clientele. "I'll start looking for my own place now that I have a steady paycheck again."

"That's good. You and Phillip are getting along okay? He must be busy with the season starting so soon."

"Oh yeah, we get along fine." His best friend is a different story, though.

We chat for a few more minutes, Mom filling me in on what her and Dad have been up to lately before we end the call.

With that task done, I decide a new work outfit is a reasonable splurge and a good reason to go shopping. I'm making a to-do list when the condo door opens. "I have some awesome n —" I turn to find Tristan toeing off his shoes. He's dressed in jeans and a T-shirt. He looks delicious and gorgeous, and for a second he actually looks happy to see me, which doesn't make sense.

"Oh. It's you." Every part of me wants to run away. But I have nowhere to go.

The right side of his mouth curls up in a mean smile. "Thinking about how I won't fuck you again?"

I give him back his own words. "Once was enough." *Lie, lie, lie.*

He chuckles, but it's a flat, humorless sound. "Is that why you've been moaning my name in your sleep?"

The ache in my chest is infuriating. He said I would regret it, and when he acts like this, I do. What we did crossed so many lines. I ignore him and pick up my phone, giving him my back as I call Hemi. "Hey! Guess who got that job?"

"Ahhh! That's such great news! We need to celebrate. Are you free for drinks? Or dinner? You can come to my place. Hammer and I are working on a project, but we'll be done in about an hour."

I need to get out of here. "That sounds great. Can I bring anything?"

"Just your sexy self. Are you so excited?"

"Super excited. Thank you so much for the recommendation."

"No problem. Does this mean you get to move out soon?"

"Not soon enough, but yeah. I'd like a place within walking distance, but at this point I'll take just about anything. The sooner, the better. Living with my brother and his asshole best friend is a nightmare I want out of."

The heavy click of Tristan's bedroom door closing startles me.

At least I'm getting under his skin the same way he gets under mine.

Over the next two days I go shopping for a few new work outfits, manage the grocery situation, meal prep for Flip and Tristan, and make sure I have food for lunches before I start my new job.

When that happens, on day one I can tell for sure that this firm is a much better fit. I have several female-identifying coworkers around my age, and everyone is so much kinder and friendlier here. But there's a lot to take in as the newest hire, and at the end of the day, I'm exhausted. I'm looking forward to vegging out to some cheesy reality TV and digging into my pint of special ice cream. Unless the TV room-slash-my-bedroom is occupied. Now that I have a job, finding an apartment is at the top of my priority list.

Flip's bedroom door is open when I get home. His wallet is on the counter, though, so I assume he's at Dred's. Tristan's shoes are on the mat, but his door is closed, and hopefully it stays that way. There's a half pint of perfection waiting for me. I practically skip to the fridge and pull open the freezer drawer. I've been eating the ice cream a few spoonfuls at a time, keeping it hidden under the frozen peas. I move the bag aside, but the container isn't there. Maybe it sank to the bottom. I empty the entire freezer, but I can't find it. Which means someone ate it and didn't leave even a little behind.

Disappointment and frustration weigh me down as I climb to the loft. My comforter is heaped on the floor, and my pillow has been used as a footrest. Sitting on the coffee table is the empty ice cream container. All that remains is a swipe of chocolate fudge at the bottom.

"That fucker." I grab the empty container and climb down the ladder. My anger isn't entirely rational and doesn't quite match the crime, but Tristan's clearly done this on purpose. Between his snide comments and making me feel like trash, this is the icing on the shit cake he's served me since we had sex. He's taking up way too much real estate in my head lately, and I'm pissed. I slam my fist against his door.

It flies open a few seconds later. His gorgeous brows are furrowed, and his nostrils flare. "What the fuck is wrong with you?"

I shove the empty container in his face. "Did you eat this?"

He bats it away, and it lands on the floor at our feet. Residual chocolate splatters my foot. "Yeah. So what?"

My voice rises. "What do you mean so what? Fuck you!" I hate how irrational I am. How out of control I feel. But all my hurt and anger is spilling out, and I'm powerless to stop it.

He flinches, but his eyes darken. "It's just ice cream, Beat."

He does this on purpose. Calls me Beat to hurt me. And it works. I try to defend myself, though I'm already overreacting. "It was on sale this week." I grew up in a house where treats were exceedingly rare. Every splurge is a big deal even now.

His jaw tics. "It was almost empty."

I clench my fists and bite back another irrational accusation. I hate that we can't stop being assholes to each other, that I crave a glimpse of the other version of Tristan. I wonder what it would be like if we didn't fight all the time.

He takes a small step backward. But he doesn't shut the door in my face or raise his voice. Instead, he lowers it to a near whisper. He appears calm, but there's a barely there tremor in his hand. "You're being unreasonable about ice cream, Beat. Just buy more."

"That's not the point!" I feel so stupid that I'm reacting this way, but my emotions are all over the place.

He throws his hands in the air, exasperated. "Then what is?"

I open my mouth, but then close it. "Nothing. Never mind." If I keep going at him, I'll make it worse. I'm already past the point of no return.

His eyes narrow. "Are you seriously getting in my face and making a big deal out of nothing just to get my attention? I've done my time handling tantrums. I don't need to baby you over something ridiculous."

"God, you're such an asshole!" I snap.

His nostrils flare again, but instead of matching my volume, his drops low, that tremor in his hand making its way to his voice. "Are you disappointed I won't spank your meltdown out of you?" He slices a hand through the air, the only aggressive action he's made during this entire heated exchange. "I don't have time for this drama. You're getting on my last damn nerve. I had a peaceful place before you moved in and took over with all your shit. How is it possible that you are more annoying now than you were at fourteen?"

My jaw drops, and my chest constricts. I feel like I've been slapped across the face, which is probably the point, I realize. "Fuck you, Tristan." To my horror, my voice cracks and my eyes prick with tears.

I spin around, wishing for the thousandth time that I could escape to a room with a door I can lock. Instead, I have to jump up to reach the bottom rung of the ladder so I can pull it down.

"Bea." Tristan grabs my shoulders and spins me around, his grip gentle but firm. His expression shifts from anger to confusion to horror. "Are you *crying*?"

I try to push his hands away, but he gathers both of mine in one of his and brings them to his chest. His expression is fierce as he cups my cheek and brushes away a traitorous tear that's escaped. "I'm sorry. I didn't mean—"

I try to turn my head away, but he's still cupping my cheek. "Don't you dare be nice to me now."

"Fuck, Bea. Don't cry. I don't want to make you cry." His voice is soft and sad.

"Then why are you so fucking mean?" I hate how desperately I want this to be different.

His eyes slide closed for a moment, and he shakes his head. "You're just here. Flip invited you into my space. And I get it, even though I don't want to. I'm glad you're not living with those fucking creeps anymore. But I never wanted anyone else to take care of, especially not here. I've done my time taking care of other people." His throat bobs, and his voice is soft as his thumb traces the contour of my bottom lip. "And the next thing I know, you're going off on me, and I don't understand why. It's one thing when we're assholes to each other, but it's another when you start yelling."

Memories surface from our childhood. Tristan always got agitated when Flip and I freaked out on each other. He'd tell us to stop, or he'd threaten to leave. Sometimes he would walk away. He used to spend a lot of time at our place when his parents were still together. And he jumped at loud noises. Flip told me once that his parents yelled and slammed a lot of doors.

This suddenly explains a lot.

"I didn't mean to yell," I whisper.

"I'm sorry for being a dick. You didn't do anything to deserve my bullshit expectations. Frankly, your brother did." He drops his head and brushes his nose against mine. "I really didn't mean to make you cry."

It's charmingly tender and unexpected.

"Hey, hey! Where my roomies at!" Flip calls.

My stomach drops. I didn't even hear the door open.

Tristan startles, steps back in a rush and rounds the corner. "Right here, my man."

"Well, get changed. We're going to the bar. Dallas is picking us up in half an hour."

Tristan runs his hand through his hair and kneads the back of his neck, all that softness disappearing. "Sounds like exactly what I need."

He leaves me standing there, wondering what would have happened if Flip hadn't shown up.

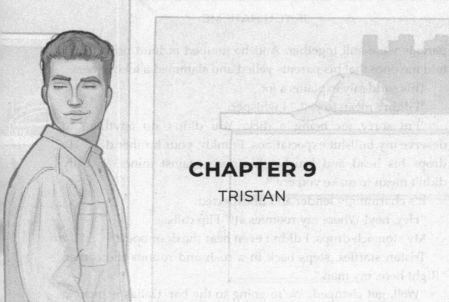

CHAPTER 9
TRISTAN

"Thanks for booking us some ice time. I know you're busy with training," Brody says as we unlace our skates. It's a Saturday morning, and I don't have to be on the ice with my team until later today.

"I wish I could do it more often. Your wrist shot has really improved since we were on the ice last." Our dad tries to make it to all of Brody's practices, but the one-on-one ice time isn't something he can give.

"Yeah. Hockey camp this summer was great." He pulls his shirt over his head and unclips his pads, revealing several hickeys on his chest.

"What's going on here?" I poke one on his collarbone. "You got a girlfriend you haven't told me about?" I frown at the marks on his stomach. He's not even eighteen yet.

He ducks his head, and his cheeks flush. "Ah, no. No girlfriend. Just uh…fooled around with a girl at a party."

I was probably doing the same thing when I was his age, or worse. "She go to your school?"

He shakes his head. "She and her friends come to a lot of our games, and they end up at our parties sometimes."

"So it was a one-time thing?" I prod. It's unsettling to think he's already into meaningless hookups.

He shrugs. "Probably. I, uh…I kinda liked one of her friends, but uh…this girl started chatting me up. Some of them have had sex with, like, half the team. It's like…" He runs a hand down his face, and his knee bounces a few times. "I don't know. Kinda fucked up, I guess. But you know what that's like. Girls are always after you."

"It can be overwhelming." And exhausting. Especially with a best friend like Flip.

Brody nods, chewing his bottom lip. "Everyone was hooking up, and she was all over me 'cause my stats are high this year. Plus, she knows you're my brother. So, yeah. She was kinda pushy and aggressive." He runs his hands over the bite marks on his abs. "But I got a BJ out of it, so I guess that's cool, right?"

I don't know if he's seeking my approval or what. We have a different relationship. I'm his brother, but I've always sort of functioned like a second parent, too, so I feel compelled to keep asking questions. "Were you into her?"

He shrugs again, removing the rest of his gear, apart from his boxer briefs. "She was all right. She just wanted to fuck around."

"Did you want to fuck around with *her*?" There's something off. Maybe it's the way he can't quite make eye contact.

"Like I said, I was kinda into her friend, but that's not gonna happen now, so it's whatever." He slaps his thighs. "Anyway, if this can stay between us, that'd be great."

"Yeah, it can stay between us. You're being safe, though, right? Using condoms, making sure you have consent?"

"I didn't have sex with her. She wanted to, but I said I didn't have a condom, so she blew me instead. I got her off first, though." He pushes off the bench. "I'm gonna hop in the shower."

"Yeah. Of course."

He disappears into a stall and pulls the curtain closed. I'm glad he feels comfortable talking to me. It's a hard balance, keeping his confidence as his brother, but wanting to make sure our dad isn't totally out of the loop.

I offer to take him out for lunch, but he has plans to meet a couple of his teammates, so we do drive-thru and I drop him off at home.

"Thanks for hanging out with me this afternoon, Tris."

I squeeze his shoulder. "No problem, Brod."

"I'll see you next week at my game?"

"Yeah. I'll be there."

He hops out of the passenger seat and grabs his gear from the trunk. He raps on the window and waves, turning toward the house.

I roll the window down as he crosses the lawn. "Hey, Brody."

He pauses. "Yeah?"

"You okay?"

He gives me a questioning look. "Yeah. Of course. Why wouldn't I be?"

"Just making sure. Have a good week."

All the way home, I think about the conversation with my brother. I remember what it was like to be his age, all hormones and testosterone. Someone always wanted to fool around. If I wanted action, I could get it. And even if I didn't, it was still available. I consider all the times Flip and I have gone to the bar. He buys me a shot and cajoles me into taking someone home. A few times I've pawned the girl off on him, if she seemed like she didn't care who she ended up under. Or if I thought my brand of sex wouldn't be her jam. Flip is always down for multiple partners.

His antics have been splashed across the internet for everyone to see, including my brother. And I've been directly involved since we've been playing on the same team, so I'm sure Brody's seen me doing body shots and who the hell knows what else. He looks up to me. Was he seeking my approval? I really fucking hope not. I've never brought anyone home to meet my dad or my brothers because they've never lasted long enough.

Three months is my cap. I get bored easily, so I always bow out before things get serious.

Later that day, I hit the gym to work out with Dallas and Roman. Flip is with one of his semi-regular hookups. He told me he was pretty sure he could get her to bring a friend along, if I was interested. But I wasn't. When we're done, I just want to go home. Huff Beat's shampoo. Maybe push her buttons if she's around. Getting a rise out of her is my favorite thing. Though seeing her cry is still shredding me.

Looks like the powers that be are on my side because she's in the shower when I get to the condo. Things have been weird since we fucked. And then there was the ice cream freak-out. She's been avoiding me since that happened. I fucking hate it.

I grab the jug of orange juice from the fridge and a box of crackers and climb the ladder to the loft. I turn on the TV, set up the gaming console, and put the headset on. I'll occupy myself until she comes up.

I'm in the middle of a level when a pillow hits me in the side of the head. It knocks off the headphones, and I drop the controller. My player dies in a hail of gunfire as Beat shrieks.

"What the hell are you doing up here?" Her body is wrapped in a towel—a regular bath one, not the sheets that act like a dress. It means most of her toned, curvy legs are on display.

"Been a while since I've heard that sound. Usually it's from me spanking your pussy, though." Oh yeah, I'm bringing my asshole A-game.

"You scared the shit out of me! Why didn't you answer when I called?"

"I didn't hear you." I motion to the headphones. "And was playing a video game. In my loft."

She clutches her towel to her chest. "Don't worry. I'll be out by the end of September."

I don't want her to move into another shitty apartment because she can't get away from me fast enough. But instead of saying something normal, I act like the dick I am. "Can't handle facing your bad decision every day, eh?" That has to be the reason she's avoiding me like the plague. Not that I blame her. I'd do the same if I were in her shoes.

"Oh, for Christ's sake, Tristan, stop throwing it in my face every time I see you."

"You're doing a good job of throwing it in mine." Running away every time I'm home. Evade. Dodge. Hide.

"What are you talking about?"

"You already said you regret it." It's a real kick in the balls. I should regret it. Hell, I want to. It'd be easier if I felt the same way. But all I want is more. I can't tell her that, though. She'll use it against me.

Her brow furrows. "We haven't even had a conversation about it since it happened."

I cross my arms. "Sure we did. The evening after."

Bea's nose scrunches up, and she rubs her temple. She's so fucking cute when she's frustrated. "You were being a dick. You said once was enough! Why would I want to be anywhere near you after you told me I'm a bad lay?"

"You said you regretted it!" I push to my feet. "I asked if you were regretting your decision already, and you said, 'Of course I am.'" I should get out of here. This conversation isn't going anywhere good. She's naked under that towel, and I'm two seconds away from admitting all I can think about is getting her under me again.

She shakes her head.

"That's exactly what you said," I snap.

She flails her hand. She's getting heated again. I can deal with that better than I can the fucking silence, surprisingly. "Yeah, but not because I regretted the actual sex," she counters. "All we do is argue. And in case you were unaware, you're kind of a giant asshole. It's pretty damn conflicting."

"So you don't regret the sex?" I don't like the wave of relief that washes over me.

She narrows her eyes and tips her head. "Why are you

pushing this so hard? Why do you even care? You think I'm annoying."

"You drive me up the fucking wall, Beat." But not because I find her annoying. After holding her in my arms the other day, I stopped hating that she's living here. It's the opposite now, actually. She's smart and funny and driven. She's helpful and thoughtful and so fucking kind. I don't deserve any part of her, but it doesn't stop me from wanting her, and that's what's making me feel like I'm losing my mind. I close the distance between us and clench my fists so I don't do something stupid like take her face in my hands and kiss her again.

She tips her chin up, defiant. "The feeling is entirely mutual." But I see hurt lurking under the surface. I wonder if that's what made her cry the other day. Maybe she's taking my admission out of context.

"I hate that you smell so fucking good all the time."

"I hate your ridiculous body and your rock-solid ass," she fires back.

"Every time you wear those tiny sleep shorts, I want to yank them off, throw you over my lap, spank that luscious ass, and finger-fuck you until you come."

"Oh, God." She grips her towel tighter and rubs her legs together. "I hate that I want that, too." Her teeth sink into her plush bottom lip.

"I hate that every time you bite your lip, all I can think about is how they felt wrapped around my cock, and I really hate that you can deep throat like a fucking champ." She got on her knees for me after Flip left. It was a fucking revelation.

"I was actually impressed with myself," she says, managing a smile. "Your dick is huge. Which I hate, by the way. Especially when you're filling me with it. *Were* filling me. Past tense. 'Cause it was a one-time thing."

"Just that one time." I nod. "You want to know what I hate the most?"

"That you still want to fuck me, even though I annoy the shit out of you?"

"Exactly." Wanting her compromises everything. It's dangerous and bad, and I'll ruin her, if she lets me.

Her nostrils flare, and her gaze drops to my mouth.

"Screw it." She grabs the back of my neck and pulls my mouth to hers.

We both make irritated sounds. I yank off the towel wrapped around her head and toss it on the floor, spearing my hands through her wet, tangled hair, angling her head so I can get inside her mouth. She tastes like mint. I spin her around and walk her backward to the futon. She grabs the hem of my shirt and pulls it over my head. I tug her towel free, then cup her breasts and dip down to roughly suck her nipples.

We're frantic hands and teeth and tongues, trying to touch every inch of each other.

"I don't think I can keep my hands off of you," I admit as I shove the coffee table out of the way and drop to my knees. "Sit down."

She spreads the towel out and drops onto it. "We should set some ground rules."

"This stops when you move out." Maybe she'll stick around longer if my dick continues to be involved. Lord knows my personality is sorely lacking. I drop my head and lick up the length of her sex, groaning as the taste of her hits my tongue.

"Fuck, that's good." She bows off the couch and shoves her hands into my hair. "No feelings. This is about fucking. I just got out of a relationship and neither of us needs the complication."

I suck her clit and smile when she shrieks. "I don't do relationships, so you don't have to worry about me getting attached."

She scoffs. "We don't even like each other. Obviously we won't get attached."

"You like my cock well enough." I circle her entrance with a finger.

"Why are you still talking?"

"Flip can't know." I palm her tit. I can't have sex with her if I'm dead. And Flip will definitely kill me if he finds out. That thought alone should give me pause, but it just makes me more desperate.

"Never. This stays between us," she agrees.

We both nod, and I ease one finger inside her. So soft, and warm, and tight.

Bea moans. "I should not be this close to coming already. It's not normal. What's wrong with us?"

"I don't know, but being ignored for the past week has been a fucking nightmare."

"Good. Serves you right for saying I'm a forgettable fuck."

"I was talking shit. It pisses me off that I can't stop thinking about the sounds you make when you're about to come."

"Stop being an asshole and use more fingers." She covers the hand currently kneading her breast and moves it to circle her throat. "I liked it when you did this last time." She pulses around my finger.

I am so, so fucked.

I rise and loom over her, my palm wrapped around her delicate throat, thumb and finger pressing into the hinge of her jaw. "Like this?"

She nods, and her fingers drift along the back of my hand, then drop to palm the breast I just released. "Yeah."

"Why do you have to be so fucking perfect?" I cover her mouth with mine as I slide three fingers into her pussy. She moans and rolls her hips.

I break the kiss and let my lips skim her cheek until I reach her ear. I nuzzle into her hair, fingers rubbing inside her. "You think I'm gonna let you come all over my fingers?"

She grabs my wrist and grinds down on my hand. "I'm so close."

"I know." I pull my fingers free and slap her clit. "But not yet."

She arches and whimpers, throat pressing against my palm as I hold her in place.

"God, I hate you." She groans.

"Yeah, but you love my cock." I stroke along the edge of her jaw and explain why I'm being an asshole. "I want to be in you when you come."

"Condom?" she asks.

I pull my wallet out and flip it open. Find the single condom and pass it to her. While she tears the wrapper open, I pop the button on my jeans, unzip the fly, and shove my boxers and pants down enough to free my cock.

My fingers flex around her throat as she rolls it down my length. I sink to my knees, run the head over her clit, line myself up, and watch as my cock disappears inside her.

"Oh my God. Oh, God," she whimpers, eyes falling closed. Her legs are already shaking, an orgasm imminent.

I sweep my thumb along her bottom lip. "Look at me, Bea."

Her eyes pop open as I pull out, all the way to the ridge, then push back in, slowly. Because I'm savoring this. At least for a few minutes. "You're so fucking beautiful."

"So are you," she whispers.

"I'm really glad you don't regret me, even though I gave you every reason to," I admit.

"I tried, but I couldn't."

"I didn't." I should. For so many reasons.

Her eyes flutter shut when I pull out again.

"Nuh-uh," I counter. "Eyes on me."

They lock on mine, lust heavy.

"Who's fucking you, Bea?" This time I thrust hard, and her body jerks.

"You are." She clenches as the first orgasm rolls through her.

"Who's making you come?" I brush my lips over hers.

"You." She arches and stiffens.

"That's right. This pussy is mine."

"Oh, God." Her eyes roll up, and she struggles to focus on me. "I hate that you make me feel so good."

"Is that why you're coming all over my cock again?" I pound into her, the orgasm still rolling through her, making goose bumps rise along her skin and a sheen of sweat breaks across her shoulders.

"Your mouth is filthy." She moans through a full-body shudder.

"You love it."

"I really do. It's so annoying." She pulls my mouth to hers, and I let her.

I want to absorb all the good parts of her. I want more of this, more of her.

And today I bought myself some time to get her out of my system. Hopefully it'll be enough.

CHAPTER 10

RIX

"Your brother is an amazing player," Hammer says.

"In every sense of the word," I reply.

She snorts and taps her plastic wineglass against mine. It's the first home exhibition game of the season, and Flip is on fire. He's already managed an assist and a goal, and we're only halfway through the first period.

"He's been keeping a lower profile," Hemi adds. She leans forward, following the puck down the ice.

We're sitting in the team box at center ice. The view from here is amazing. So are the free drinks and food.

"He's relying on his little black book of regulars." I toss a piece of popcorn into my mouth.

"Ah, that makes sense." She sips her cocktail.

Tristan is on the bench. He's tense tonight. Last night Flip stayed home, so I couldn't offer any pregame stress relief. For either of us. I don't believe that's the reason Tristan is struggling on the ice tonight, though. Access to my vagina doesn't dictate how he plays his game.

"Your brother is kind of a dirtbag," Hammer says. "It's too bad, because he's a kickass player, and he's ridiculously hot."

"He really is nice to look at." Tallulah, the coach's daughter, otherwise known as Tally, agrees.

"Yeah. And he knows it. It's irritating. Especially when he brings home his flavor of the night and she's a screamer."

Tally wrinkles her nose. "That's awkward."

"Sure is," I agree. But I never say anything because I don't want to be more of an imposition than I already am.

"Dallas is pretty yummy, and not a huge player," Hammer says.

"One hundred percent agree. He's a solid nine out of ten," I reply.

"Did you see him ballroom dancing with little old ladies? That was heart-melting." Tally presses her hand to her chest. "That makes him a ten for me."

"He only did that because I made him," Hemi grumbles.

"What's the deal with you two?" I ask.

"There is no deal. He's a dick. I can't stand him, and it's my life's mission to make him miserable as often as possible. Oh, nice save!" She whistles shrilly as the arena goes wild. "Hammerstein is definitely a hottie."

"Oh, yeah. Totally," Tally says.

I arch a brow. "Agree."

"For an older guy," she tacks on. "She's still seventeen.

"Ew. That's my dad." Hammer wrinkles her nose.

Hollis takes a shot on net but it goes wide. Flip gains control in the crease and passes it to the left wing.

"Hollis has that tall, dark, and badass vibe going on," I comment.

"I'm a little scared of him," Tally admits. "But yeah, he's hot."

"And he has two cats. Men who love animals are automatically attractive," Hemi says.

Hollis rotates off the ice, and Tristan rotates in. "Tristan is so hot it should be illegal." Hammer's gaze follows him down the ice.

"He's an asshole." Who's very adept at providing multiple

orgasms. And sometimes he's sweet at the most unexpected times. Like two days ago when he went to the store and brought back a pint of ice cream to replace the one he ate.

"A hot asshole," Tally adds.

"And he knows it." Hemi cringes when he misses a shot on net and the opposition gains control of the puck. "He's really off his game tonight."

"I think he's psyching himself out," I muse.

"How do you mean?" Hemi asks.

"He's stressed about Hollis being back this season. Obviously, he's glad he recovered from the injury, but last season he had a lot of ice time. With Hollis back, he's worried about his stats. Plus, his contract is up for renewal at the end of the season. He's up in his head about it."

He's been taking out all that stress and frustration on my vagina the past few days, since we made our sex pact. Not that I've minded. He's been less of a dick lately, and it's been nice.

"For someone who can't stand Tristan, you sure know a lot about his emotional state." Hemi side-eyes me.

"I live with him, in a loft with no walls or door. It's hard not to overhear conversations." Plus, I've become the resident meal prepper since I moved in, so I'm always around when Flip and Tristan are talking game strategy.

"Right, yeah." Hemi nods. "How's the apartment hunting?"

"Okay. I'm hoping I'll find something for October first. I got a signing bonus. It's not much, but it's enough if I find the right place."

So far every time I think I've found a place, Tristan will mention the shitty neighborhood. But it would be nice not to worry about falling in the toilet in the middle of the night. A room with a door would also be lovely.

"I might be looking for an apartment soon," Hammer says.

"Your dad's pretty cool, though, isn't he?" Hemi asks.

"He is, but I was living off-campus in an apartment before.

Interning for his team and living with him is an adjustment. I don't think it's the best long-term plan."

"I can't wait to move out," Tally says. "I love my parents, but they're totally trying to get me to live at home for university. Isn't half the point figuring out how to survive on ramen and French fries?"

"That's accurate. Where have you applied?" I ask.

"Mostly in Toronto, which I guess is kind of shooting myself in the live-away-from-home foot. I'm not sure about residence, but an apartment off-campus would be good. I'm making a pros-and-cons presentation so I can argue my case effectively."

"Let us know if you want help with that," I offer.

"Seriously?" Tally's eyes light up. She's freaking adorable. If I had a younger sister, I'd want her to be exactly like Tally.

"Yeah. For sure. Let's plan a get-together at my place later this week," Hemi offers. "We can help you go over it."

"Okay. Thanks!"

I love that I have this new group of unlikely friends. I wonder if that will change when I move into my own place. I've been eating lunch with some of my colleagues at work, but the two women closest to my age have long-term boyfriends. One takes the train in from Ajax, and the other lives with her boyfriend, so I don't know how much hanging out we'll do outside of work.

Hollis scores in the second period, and Flip scores again in the third. Tristan gets two back-to-back penalties, one for tripping and the other for interference. He freaks out on the refs and throws himself into the box, clearly unhappy.

I have to be up early for work, so I skip drinks with the girls after the game and hop on the subway home.

I have a new text from Rob.

ROB

Hey! Left a VM a few days ago but didn't hear back. Hope all is good. Would like to talk when you have a chance.

It was sent during the game. It's been days since he left the voicemail, which I forgot to listen to.

RIX

Sry. Been busy. On the way home from the game. What's up?

This is a good distraction from thinking about what bar the team will end up at tonight.

The humping dots appear and disappear a few times before a message finally comes through.

ROB

So...I started seeing someone. It's pretty new, but I figured it'd be better to tell you than you seeing it on my socials.

I want to send him a bunch of middle fingers in response. He was the one sending I-miss-you messages a couple of weeks ago. He was the one who broke up with me. My heart wasn't completely obliterated, but it sure stung. Tristan might be a dick, but at least I know what I'm getting with him.

I send a thumbs-up in reply and then silence his message alerts, because fuck that and fuck him.

By the time I get home, the pit in my stomach feels like a giant crater. My sex pact with Tristan did not include exclusivity. So it's very possible he'll hook up with someone else tonight. Nausea rolls through me at the prospect that he might bring someone back here. Yeah. I need my own place. The orgasms are great, but I can't handle the humiliation of having to listen to him fuck another woman in the bedroom under me.

I stress-chop vegetables for tomorrow so I can make omelets for breakfast and scan the want ads for apartments. I circle two potential places while I try to reassure myself that I'll be fine if Tristan brings someone home. We're just having sex. I'm a big girl. Besides, I don't even like him. He's a means to an orgasm.

Tristan walks through the door as I finish putting everything away. He's alone. Tension melts from my body so quickly I worry I'll leave a puddle on the floor. Which is bad. So, so bad. Maybe I don't not-like him as much as I thought.

"Hey." I wipe my damp hands on my jeans. I should have changed into bed wear. Or something sexy. Anything other than the jeans-and-shirt combo I'm currently sporting that now has wet spots on it.

As soon as he sees me, his jaw clenches. "I'm not in the mood."

All the relief I felt a second ago goes right out the window, along with my bruised, deflated ego. I can't handle asshole Tristan tonight.

"Neither am I."

He brushes by me, heading for the fridge. He yanks it open and pulls out the freshly squeezed orange juice. He spins around, angry. "I don't need to deal with your shit tonight, Beat."

"You're the one biting my head off, not the other way around," I snap.

"Biting your head off? What are you doing down here? Why aren't you in bed?" He tips his head. "Were you waiting for me to come home?"

I bite my lips together. The answer is sort of yes. But I won't admit it. Not when he's being like this. Instead of incriminating myself, I head for the bathroom. It's the only room I can escape to for privacy. And I could use a shower.

"Dick." I shut the door and turn on the hot water.

My frustration mounts as I strip out of my clothes. I put on some music and step under the hot spray. I've finished washing my hair when there's a knock on the door.

"If you need to pee, you have a kitchen sink and a balcony!" I say.

The door opens. Because I forgot to lock it.

"Don't you dare pee in here while I'm in the shower!" I

shout. "Or flush!"

The shower door opens a few inches. Tristan's eyeball appears.

"Fuck you!" I try to close the door on him, but he's stronger by a lot. I bar an arm across my chest to hide my nipples. "You don't get to invite yourself in here after you shit all over me."

"I'm sorry. I had a really bad game. I shouldn't have taken it out on you." He runs a hand through his hair. "Flip wanted me to come out. And it's fucking with me because I'm lying to him." He takes a deep breath.

"Then we stop doing this and tell him," I counter. "But if he knows, there's no way he'll be okay with it. So figure yourself out, Tristan."

His exhale feels like every piece of his bad mood leaving his body. "But I don't want to stop."

His conflict is real, and I get it, but it doesn't excuse his behavior. "You were a dick. I did nothing to deserve that. I'm tired of this bullshit. I'm not fourteen hoping you'll look my way again."

"I know. You're right. I'm sorry." He bites his bottom lip and has the gall to look boyishly handsome and contrite. "Can I make it up to you?"

I glare at him.

"Please, Bea? I mean it. I'm sorry."

I sigh and step back.

He strips out of his clothes and steps into the shower. He's already hard. "Will you let me make it better?" He moves to stand behind me and wraps his arms around my waist. The affection is unexpected. He drops his head and nuzzles my neck. "You know I'll make you feel good, Bea."

"What about Flip?" I tip my head back, and he bites the edge of my jaw.

"He went to the bar. He won't be home for a while." His erection presses into the small of my back. "How could I ever stay away when I know your sweet, tight pussy is right here, waiting for me to fill it with my tongue, or fingers, or my massive cock?" He kisses down the side of my neck.

I snort. "Check your ego, Tristan."

"But I make you feel good, don't I? Make you come every single time." He squeezes my breast and nips at my earlobe.

"Yeah, you make me feel good." I rest my head on his chest. "When you're not being mean."

"I'll be nice tonight, okay?" His fingers skate over the patch of curls at the apex of my thighs. He gives them a tug, then dips lower, rubbing a slow circle on my clit. I whimper and push my ass against his cock. "That's one of my favorite sounds, little Bea."

He spins me around and presses my back against the cold tiles, hands coming up to cup my face. He parts my lips with his tongue, the kiss desperate and needy. One hand stays on my cheek, and the other moves to grip my breast, his thumb brushing over my nipple. Then he pinches the peak between his fingers.

He bites his way down my neck and sucks the flesh before claiming my mouth again. His hand moves between my thighs, and he pushes two fingers inside me, pumping slowly, his thumb brushing my clit. I let my head fall back, watching him through lidded eyes.

Steam billows around us, and his biceps flex as he works another finger inside me.

"Do you like it when I finger-fuck you, Bea?"

I moan and roll my hips.

"Tell me," he murmurs against my lips, thumb sweeping back and forth along the edge of my jaw. "I want to hear you say it." There's something in his tone, a hint of vulnerability fused with desperation.

I don't understand where it's coming from or what it means, but I want to come, so I tell him what he wants to hear. It's also the truth. "It feels so good," I whimper.

"What does?" He nibbles my bottom lip.

"Your fingers inside me. I can't get enough," I tell him.

"What else can't you get enough of?" He bites the edge of my jaw. "Tell me and I'll make you come."

"Your mouth on me. The way you tongue-fuck my pussy."

He curls his fingers, hitting exactly the right spot. My eyes roll up. "Is that it?"

I shake my head.

"What else, then?" His thumb circles my clit.

"When you fuck me so hard I see stars."

"I can't get enough of that either," he admits.

"And when you call me your sweet, filthy girl. I love that."

He grins. "Yeah, you do."

He crushes his mouth to mine and starts finger-fucking me in earnest. I move the hand that's currently cupping my cheek to wrap around my throat. It's definitely my new kink, because thirty seconds later I'm clawing at his shoulder, moaning my way through an intense orgasm.

He kisses me, soft and slow. "See?" He rubs his nose against mine. "I can be nice."

I laugh and run my hands over his chest, then lace them behind his neck. My knees are weak, and my body is humming. "You were very nice."

"Will you let me take you to bed and show you how nice I can be?"

I smile and nod.

"I might be a little dirty, though," he warns. "But the nice kind of dirty."

"I can handle that."

"Good."

Tristan turns off the water. He opens the shower door, hoists me up, and wraps my legs around his waist. His cock bobs against my ass, and he drips water all over the floor as he carries me to his bedroom.

Soft Tristan is exactly what I need tonight. I wish it could stay like this. But I'll do my best to enjoy it while it lasts.

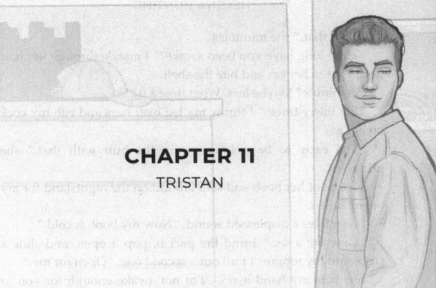

CHAPTER 11
TRISTAN

F lip messages at midnight to say he won't be home and he'll meet me at the arena tomorrow—unless I want to join the orgy at some model's house in Vaughn. I tell him I'm good, but thanks for the offer.

The next morning, I wake up wrapped around Bea. My cock is nestled in the crack of her ass, I'm cupping one of her boobs, and my nose is in her hair. I can't remember the last time I woke with a woman in my bed. I can count on one finger the number of times I've woken up with my best friend's little sister in my bed, though.

That I don't automatically want to jostle her awake and make her leave is...foreign. I check the clock on the nightstand. It's only six thirty. I told Roman he could pick me up at eight and we'd hit the pool for laps.

This means I have time to get inside Bea before either of us has to get up—her for work, me for my pre-workout swim. But I don't make a move. Not yet. I want a few more minutes like this, with Bea all warm and soft and not annoyed by my assholery.

I made up for being a giant dick last night with my giant dick, which she appreciated. Loudly. With several orgasms. My erection swells and twitches.

"I felt that," she mumbles.

"How long have you been awake?" I nuzzle through her hair until I get to her ear and bite the shell.

"A minute? Maybe less. What time's it?"

"Six thirty-three." I throw my leg over hers and rub my cock on her ass.

"Too early to be poking me in the butt with that," she grumbles.

I let go of her boob and slap around on the nightstand for my breath strips.

She makes a displeased sound. "Now my boob is cold."

"Give me a sec." I find the packet, pop it open, and slide a strip onto my tongue. I pull out a second one. "Open for me."

She bats my hand away. "I'm not awake enough for you to stuff your fingers in my mouth."

"That's not what I'm doing." I brush the strip over her lips.

She grabs my wrist. "What is that?"

"Breath strip."

"Ooh. Smart." Her lips close around the end of my finger.

When she releases it, I reach for the water bottle and take a sip before I pass it to her, along with the cap. While she takes a drink, I reclaim her boob. She puts the cap back on and moves my hand to her throat.

"Why does this one thing make my clit feel like it has its own pulse?" She shifts her hips, and my cock glides between her ass cheeks.

"It's dominating, but not in a way that makes you feel out of control, maybe." I don't tell her it isn't a go-to move for me. That, for reasons I don't understand, I'm a little obsessed with how graceful her neck is. That I want to feel her pulse pound under my palm when I fuck her. That I want to bite her and mark her as mine. Even thinking it makes me sound like a caveman.

"Maybe." Her fingers trail over mine. "Why aren't you fucking me yet?"

I roll her onto her back and fit myself between her thighs. She's wet already. My cock glides over her clit, and she wraps her legs around my waist, arching. I claim her mouth, rocking against her while our tongues tangle.

And then I kiss a quick path down her body, licking up the length of her and latching onto her clit as I loop my arms around her thighs.

"Oh, God." She fists my hair, and then it hits her. The mint on my tongue registers between her thighs. Her eyes go wide, and she gasps. "Oh my fucking God! You asshole! It burns!" She keeps trying to rip out my hair, so I unhook my arms and grab her wrists, squeezing to make her release. I keep a firm grip and settle my forearms on her inner thighs, pressing them into the mattress.

"Relax, Bea. You just need to get past the initial shock. I promise it's going to blow your mind."

"My pussy feels like it's on fire!"

"Let me make it better." I kiss her inner thigh, then lick her again, softly.

"Oh, that's better."

And then I blow on her clit.

She jerks and shrieks.

I lick her again, and she moans. I swirl my tongue, alternating between suction, hard strokes of tongue, and cool air. She comes so hard she bows off the bed. I grab a condom, roll it on, and fit myself between her thighs again. I push in on one smooth stroke and find an easy rhythm. We went hard last night, *nice* and hard, so this morning I take it easy on her. She comes twice more before I do.

When it's over, I lie on top of her, breathing in her vanilla and citrus shampoo. I consider what it would be like if this was how I woke up every day—not with some random whose last name I don't know, but with someone like Bea. No. Not someone *like* Bea...

She runs her fingers through my hair. "Let me up so I can pee and get breakfast started."

"You always make us breakfast. I'll make it for you today." I roll off her, needing space.

"Pouring a bowl of Frosted Flakes doesn't count as making breakfast."

"Ha ha. I'll make egg sandwiches. How does that sound?" I remove the spent condom and tie a knot in the end, tossing it in the trash.

"I do love a good egg sandwich." Bea stretches and log rolls to the end of the bed, where she pops to her feet.

I hold up a hand. "I'll make sure the coast is clear."

Her eyes flare. "I thought my brother wasn't coming home," she whispers.

"He said he wasn't. I'm just making sure."

"Oh." Her shoulders come down from her ears. "Okay."

I poke my head out. The condo is still empty. "You're in the clear."

"I'll get dressed."

I hook an arm around her waist and pull her against me as she passes, kissing her before I let her go. I watch her ass jiggle as she rushes across to the ladder and quickly climbs to the loft.

Our clothes from last night are still lying on the bathroom floor. Thank God Flip didn't come home. I gather them and shove them into my laundry basket to deal with later.

By the time I return to the kitchen, Bea is already there, wearing a pair of shorts and one of her tanks, making a pot of coffee. I pull items out of the fridge so I can start breakfast. Flip was always about easy food. Before Bea, I made most of the meals, unless I wanted frozen pizza or noodles. I had to learn how to cook early on, and I resent having to do it sometimes. But this is different. I want to feed Bea. Especially since she's the one usually taking care of meals these days. And grocery shopping. And almost everything, really. It's been nice not to be on the hook for everything the last little while.

"You want peameal, strip bacon, or ham on yours?" I ask.

"Whatever is fine with me. Want me to throw a fruit salad together?" she asks.

"You don't need to do that." But she makes a killer fruit salad. She puts things like fresh mango and lime rind into it.

"I don't mind." Her fingers glide across my low back as she scoots past me and picks fruit from the bowl. I grab her a cutting board, and she hops up on a stool across from me.

"How's your new job?" I ask, trying something new. Other than taking shots at each other and exchanging filthy words during sex, Bea and I don't do a lot of talking. I like this with her. The peace and comfort of doing something normal is foreign, but appealing.

"Good. Better than my last job, for sure. I don't think it's my passion, but it pays the bills, which is more important, anyway." She slices the top and bottom off an orange and carefully uses a paring knife to remove the peel.

I add slices of peameal bacon to the frying pan. "Is that why you got an accounting degree? So you'd have a stable job?" It seems like something Bea would do. Rage-quitting her job was out of character. She normally has a long fuse, except with me. I know how to push her buttons. She's the only person I can do that with.

"Pretty much, yeah. There's room for movement and growth, too."

I put four English muffins into the toaster and crack eggs into the frying pan. "But you don't love it?"

She shrugs. "I like it well enough. And I won't waste four years of university education because it isn't my dream job."

Flip and Bea grew up in a tiny house. I spent a lot of time there as a kid. Mostly, it was an escape from the fighting before my mom left. But their fridge was always half bare, and they drank powdered milk and ate a lot of Kraft Dinner and cut-up hot dogs. It must have been hard when I came for dinner. They had to make double to feed me and Flip. But they always treated me like family. After my mom left, I had to help out with my brothers a lot, so Flip came to my place more often. Always having to be responsible for other people could get tiresome. But my brothers needed someone to take care of them, and it wasn't their fault our mom bailed.

"If you could do anything, have any job, what would it be?" I ask.

"It's not as lofty as being a pro hockey player, but I'd be a dietician—plan and prep meals for people. It's a pretty linear job, though. Sports nutrition has more room for growth, but that might mean using Flip's success to further my career, and I don't want that. Also, it would definitely mean more school."

Memories pop up from over a decade ago. I remember Bea as a kid, maybe six or seven years old at the most, in the kitchen with her mom, helping pack lunches and snacks for hockey practice. They rarely had fresh vegetables. Mostly they ate frozen. Except in the summer—they had a tiny garden with cherry tomatoes and carrots. Bea would cut the carrots into circles and put the ranch dip in a Tupperware container for Flip because it was the only vegetable he would eat without complaining.

"Why wouldn't you want to use every advantage available to you?" I ask.

"Flip already helped pay for my degree. And I'm freeloading off of him and you right now. It's not his fault he's extraordinarily talented and I'm average."

"You're not average, Bea." Since she's been here, our place has been organized and spotless. We're eating better than we ever have. The fridge is always stocked, and I've seen what she's done with Flip's financial portfolio. His investments are already up thanks to her tweaks. I'm tempted to hand over mine. Plus, she has a full-time job and still stays on top of everything else. And the sex is amazing.

She drops her gaze. "You know what I mean. His career pays him assloads of money while mine is stable and respectable."

I want to brush her hair behind her ear, but I don't. "His

career will only last a decade, though, or two, if he's lucky." The toaster pops, and I arrange the English muffins on our plates.

"He'll still make more in the next five years than I will in a lifetime, no matter what job I choose. So for now, I want the one that offers me more opportunities for growth."

"I don't know that you should discount using Flip's career to your advantage. You had to give up a lot for him to get where he is," I say. *Maybe more than I realized, actually.*

"He had talent that needed to be fostered," she says, tone defensive.

Bea was always dragged along to games. She'd sit in the arena either reading a book or watching, at least until she was old enough to stay home on her own. Then she'd be in charge of things like household chores or making dinner. I remember dropping Flip off after practice and finding her home alone at age eleven, making dinner because both their parents worked shifts.

"He absolutely did," I agree. "And clearly all that time and effort panned out. But you're talented, too."

She arches a brow. "At being turned into a sex pretzel?"

"You're the complete package Bea. You're smart, savvy, resourceful, and good at more than just one thing. And you're fucking beautiful, which is a nice bonus. Me and Flip have all our eggs in this one basket, and our careers won't last forever. But you? You've got options, if you want to take them. All I'm saying is that he has some great connections because of his job, and there's nothing wrong with using them."

"It just feels wrong."

"It shouldn't." I layer the egg and peameal on top of the cheese and top it with English muffin. Then I put a second one on her plate.

"I only need one," she says as I push the plate toward her.

"I rode you hard last night. You need to fuel up." And she's always waiting on me and Flip, making sure we're fed before she serves herself.

Her cheeks flush. "And you don't?"

"I'll have breakfast round two after my workout. Besides, we're doing laps, and I'll end up with stomach cramps if I eat too much."

I scarf down my egg sandwiches in under three minutes while Bea savors hers. I demolish most of the fruit salad, but then realize she hasn't had any yet and leave the rest. Once we've finished breakfast, she goes up to the loft to change, and I tidy the kitchen. I've just finished getting dressed when Roman messages that he's here. I buzz him up since we're planning to use the pool here for laps. It's quiet during the workday, and there are fewer distractions.

I let Roman in a minute later, and Bea comes down from the loft. She's holding a pair of heels in one hand, and her giant purse is slung over her shoulder.

She gives Roman a wide, genuine smile. "Hey, how's it going?"

"Good. How about you? Flip mentioned you got a new job. Congrats."

"Thanks. I'm enjoying it so far. Now I need to find an apartment and I'm all set." She drops her purse and braces a hand on the counter, slipping on her shoes.

I immediately picture her naked except for the heels. They'd look great resting on my shoulders.

She snaps her fingers. "Earth to Tris."

"Huh?"

"Have you seen the newspaper that was sitting on the counter? I circled a bunch of ads. I want to research neighborhoods before I make more calls." She looks at me expectantly.

More calls? I don't like the sound of that. "Maybe Flip tossed it in the recycling?" I know exactly where that newspaper is. In the garbage. Where I threw it while I was cleaning up breakfast. It's under the eggshells and the extra ketchup I scraped off Bea's plate. I already know those places she circled weren't in great neighborhoods. I get that she's looking for something affordable, but it needs to be safe, too.

She checks the time. "Crap. I gotta go. If you see that paper, can you save it? Oh, and I'll be home around seven."

I frown. She gets off at five. It only takes her half an hour to get home. "Why will you be so late? Are you taking the subway or an Uber?"

She gives me a funny look. "Uh, the subway, like I always do. I have to run a couple of errands. I prepped a bunch of pasta dinners, if you can't wait, but I'm making quesadillas tonight. Roman, you're always welcome to join."

"Thanks, but Peggy and I have a dinner date tonight."

Her hand goes to her chest. "It's sweet that you have dinner dates. Tell her I said hi. Anyway, I gotta run. You boys have a good workout." She picks up her messenger bag and clicks her way to the door.

I watch her leave. I briefly wonder what a dinner date would be like with Bea, but squash that since we're just fucking and that can't ever happen.

Once she's gone, I turn to Roman. His arms are crossed.

"'Sup?"

"Dude."

"Dude, what?" I grab a dishrag and start wiping down the counter.

"How long has that been going on?"

"How long has what been going on?" *Fuck, fuck, fuck.*

He shakes his head. "I know that look, man. You got it bad."

I laugh. "You mean Beat?"

His left eyebrow climbs his forehead.

"Rix. Beatrix. Flip's sister. We can't stand each other."

He nods slowly. "Uh-huh."

"Seriously. That we managed to be in the same room and not rip each other's heads off is a miracle." Although it's been better lately. Last night was good after I stopped being a dick. And this morning was…nice. I ball the rag up and toss it on the counter,

141

then go back and smooth it out, because it drives her up the wall when Flip and I do that.

"Right. Okay. You keep living in the land of denial." Roman stands.

"I'm not in the land of denial. She annoys the hell out of me." Especially when she wears those tiny shorts when Flip's around, and I can't bend her over the nearest surface and spank her naughty ass.

"If you say so. Ready to hit the pool?"

"Yeah." I put on my slides and grab my duffle.

"One last question, though, and then I'll drop it."

I make a go-on motion.

"Does Flip know you've got a thing for his sister?"

"Fuck off. We barely tolerate each other." At least that's how I felt when she moved in. Now, though...I'm not so sure.

I push myself hard during my workout with Roman, and push myself even harder during the team skate. I need to play tighter during our next exhibition game or Hollis will take my place on first line. And rightfully so if I keep playing like it's my first year in the pros.

Then I meet my dad for a quick coffee since he's in the city and between meetings.

"How you feeling about the exhibition game this weekend?" he asks.

"All right. Hoping it goes better than last night." I shake my head.

"Hollis being back is stressing you out, eh?" He sips his coffee.

"Yeah. Got inside my own head. I'm my own worst enemy sometimes."

Dad nods.

"How's Brody doing?" I ask.

"He's okay. He had an off game the other night. He was supposed to go out with some of his teammates, but decided to stay home instead, which isn't like him."

Those hickeys and bite marks the last time he and I shot the puck around come to mind. Maybe he's avoiding that girl because he's not into her and doesn't want the awkwardness. I've done the same thing when Flip has brought home girls and I didn't feel like being part of the party. "I should call him. Make sure he knows we all have bad games."

Dad nods. "It'd be good for him to hear that from you. He has practice until eight tonight, but maybe after that."

"Okay. And once I'm back from the game this weekend, I'll come your way for dinner or something."

We talk for a bit longer, and I go over my brother's game schedule and compare it with mine. It looks like I'll be able to make a few of his games this month, but once the season starts, it'll be harder. I promise to call later in the week, and when Dad leaves for his next meeting, I head to the gym so I can run out some of my stress.

Flip and Bea are already in the kitchen when I get home a couple hours later. It smells freaking fantastic.

"Dude, we're having a quesadilla fiesta tonight!" Flip passes me a beer. "How was your dad?"

"Good. We had a quick coffee between meetings. This looks amazing. Can I do anything to help?"

"Nope. You're good." Bea keeps her eyes on the lime she's cutting into wedges.

We sit down for dinner, but everything feels off. Bea ignores my existence and gives me one-word answers. I would have expected that before, but I sort of thought we were heading for civil territory, especially after last night.

Maybe she's so quiet and standoffish because we're lying to Flip. Fresh guilt gnaws at me, along with a general unease. I can't decide why I feel bad—because I'm lying to my best friend, or because it puts Bea in a weird position. Or both. I don't want her to call off our sex pact, though. I still want more.

I get a minute with her after dinner when Flip disappears into the bathroom. "What's going on?"

She purses her lips. "I'm trying not to be obvious, and it's hard when you look like that." She flings a hand toward me.

"Like what?" I run a palm down my chest. I'm wearing a T-shirt and joggers.

She rolls her eyes. "A snack."

I smirk. "You should come to my bedroom later. I'll give you something to snack on."

She pokes my chest and grabs her purse. "Ugh. Your ego is annoying."

Flip comes out of the bathroom as she slips into her shoes.

"You heading out?" Flip asks the question I can't.

"Yeah. I'm getting a drink with Hemi and Hammer. You boys have a good night."

And then she's out the door.

"You wanna go out?" Flip asks. "I met a couple of superfans last night, and they're heading to this club tonight."

"Uh, nah. I'm not really feeling it tonight. But you have fun." If Bea wasn't so edgy, we might have had a few hours alone, and I could have gotten another fix.

"Come on, man. You've been a pretty shitty wingman lately," he presses.

I rub the back of my neck. I don't want to find creative ways to avoid sleeping with a bunny tonight. "Hemi's not wrong, man."

"Not wrong about what?"

"About this shit coming back to bite us in the ass. My youngest brother sees what's going on in my life through social media. It's not really the best role modeling."

Flip snorts. "Since when have you been worried about being a good role model?"

I can't explain it to him without adding more lies to the pile, and another side of guilt for wanting his sister. "I just… I'm not in the mood to pick up."

He holds his hands up. "Okay. It's cool. I'll call Dallas."

He grabs his phone and heads for his bedroom.

Roman's words keep rolling around in my head. I'm not staying home because of Bea. We're just fucking. That's it.

CHAPTER 12

RIX

A few days post waking up in Tristan's bed, I'm in the kitchen, prepping dinner when he walks through the door. Flip isn't with him. He has a dinner meeting with his agent.

The other night, when I got back from drinks with Hemi and Hammer, Flip had gone out, so I was alone with Tristan. I failed to resist his snack status and jumped on him like a dick-hungry puck bunny. I got three orgasms out of the deal. And again the next night. And the next. I believe that brings us to yesterday.

"Hey." Tristan drops his keys on the side table.

"Hey," I reply, but I don't look his way as he crosses the room.

He props his hip against the counter. "How's it going?"

Just the feel of his eyes on me makes everything below the waist clench. I reach for the closest vegetable, which is an English cucumber, and move to the sink. I'm making cucumber salad because I bought a three pack. "I'm good. You?"

"Spent a lot of time today thinking about last night, if I'm honest." His voice is deceptively soft. "Helped keep me occupied during the boring parts of the team meeting."

Last night Flip didn't come home, so I spent a good part of it getting railed. I slept in the loft, though, unfortunately, as we were unsure if Flip was spending the whole night elsewhere. "That's nice." I run the cucumber under cold water and, like an idiot, start stroking it.

Tristan's chest brushes my back, and he presses his hips against mine, pinning me to the counter as he sets down a pint of my favorite ice cream. "I got you a treat. Moose Tracks is your favorite, right?"

"It is. That's really sweet of you." And unexpected. I didn't realize he paid attention to the things I like.

"I felt like you deserved it after last night." His hands land on either side of me. His erection nudges my lower back as his lips ghost along the column of my throat. "What are you doing?"

"Making dinner. What does it look like?"

He nips my earlobe. "Like you're giving a hand job to a cucumber." One palm leaves the counter and slides under my shirt. His fingertips travel over my stomach, and he cups one bare breast. "You thinking about getting fucked?"

I shrug, but anticipation makes my heart gallop and my voice shake. "You're rubbing your dick on my ass. Hard not to think about it."

He steps back and tugs my shorts over my hips. "What happened to your panties, Bea?" He kneads the bare flesh and gives it a swat.

I moan as I drop the cucumber on the counter and push my ass toward him. He grabs the hem of my shirt and pulls it over my head, leaving me naked in the middle of the kitchen.

He wraps my ponytail around his fist. His other hand splays out over my stomach. "I asked you a question. Where'd your panties go?"

"I took them off when I got home." After I realized Flip would be out, I wanted to be ready for Tristan. Especially since I don't have to be quiet. The ache between my thighs is almost unbearable.

"And why was that?" His nose brushes my cheek.

"Because I couldn't stop thinking about last night either, and I soaked through them," I admit.

"Did you think about getting fucked again all day?" He peppers kisses along my shoulder.

"Yes. I couldn't stop thinking about you." It's never been like this for me. I've never felt so utterly consumed by someone.

"Even on the train ride home?" His hand glides down my stomach and cups me.

I nod.

"Did you take care of yourself when you got home?" He nibbles my neck.

I shake my head and tip it to give him better access. I love this part, when his hands are all over me, when he's kissing me, soft before he gets dirty.

"Good girl." He exhales a long, slow breath, fingers skimming my sex. "You thought about it, though."

"But I waited for you."

He pulls my head back and turns my face so he can kiss me. "I couldn't stop thinking about you either. All fucking day, Bea. I couldn't wait to get home."

Everything feels heightened. I'm aching for him. Desperate and needy. I don't want to think about how this will have to end. How, despite his mercurial moods, I want more of him. Of this. Of us.

He releases my hair and puts a hand between my shoulder blades. He pushes me forward until my chest meets the granite, making my already hard nipples tighten further. He taps the outside of my right thigh. "Bring this knee up," he orders.

I do as I'm told, and he helps get my knee on the counter. He adjusts my position, stretching my right leg along the edge of the granite. His fingers move between my thighs, and I moan when he skims over my already sensitive clit. His hands run over my ass and along the backs of my thighs, then reverse the circuit, thumbs skimming the edge of my pussy.

"Such a good girl. I want to make you feel so good tonight."

His hips press against my ass, and he leans in as he pushes his thumb between my lips. I suck as he kisses my cheek. He pulls it free and grips my chin, turning my head enough to kiss me again. When he pulls back, he asks, "Do I always make you feel good?"

"Yes," I breathe.

"But if I'm ever pushing you too far, tell me, and I'll always stop. Okay, Bea?"

"Okay," I agree. This means he has a plan, and it probably involves something new. Anticipation and anxiety spike my heart rate, and my stomach clenches.

"That's my sweet girl." He brushes his nose against mine. This is it, this is where sweet Tristan turns into dirty Tristan, and I'm here for it. One side of his mouth pulls up in a lascivious grin. "Should I get you ready for my cock?"

"Yes, please."

He shifts his position, so his hip rests against the back of my leg stretched along the counter. At the same time, he grabs the English cucumber and splays his other hand between my shoulder blades.

"Oh my God." For a hot second I consider tapping out, but he's right. He always makes me feel good. And honestly, an English cucumber isn't much different from a regular dildo. It just happens to be edible and biodegradable. And I washed it, so it's clean.

He slides the tip along my slit, rubbing over my clit, then pushes it in before pulling back again. My toes curl when he rubs it over my clit again. He keeps up with the slow teasing, only giving me an inch or two before he pulls out and rubs my juices all over the insides of my legs. I bite my knuckle to stop myself from begging for more. I have no idea if this is normal.

I seriously can't believe I'm being fucked with produce. And enjoying it.

"How much do you think you can take?" he asks.

"Why don't you find out?"

This time when he pushes in, I feel it hit my cervix and moan.

He pulls out, and I groan my irritation.

"Look at this, Bea." He holds it up for me to see. My juices are dripping down the sides onto his fist. "You haven't even come yet, and you're making a mess." He aggressively bites off the end, then slides it back inside me while chewing. I want to laugh at the absurdity of it all, but I moan when he pushes in deep, then pulls it out again.

The hand between my shoulders disappears, and he shifts again, pulling my leg off the counter. He sets the cucumber on the cutting board, pulls me to a stand, and spins me around to set me on the counter. It's momentarily disorienting. But God, the look on his face. He looks like he's ready to devour me. And I want it. Him. This version of us, where it's all about pleasure, not fighting.

"I want you to watch me fuck you with tonight's salad." He hooks my right leg under his left arm, drags me to the edge, grabs the cucumber, and starts fucking me with it again. I splay my hands out behind me so I can keep my balance.

It's obscene, watching him use the cucumber like a freaking dildo. My legs start shaking, so I know I'm getting close. "Let's make it ribbed for your pleasure." He pulls it out, then bites around the outside about an inch from the jagged top before sliding it back inside me. It absolutely does the trick. He's still chewing when I come.

When my eyes finally roll back down, he slaps his wallet on the counter. "Get a condom out so I can get in on the action." He bites off another chunk of the cucumber while I fumble to retrieve the condom. I hold it out for him.

He points to the cucumber, which is literally coated in my orgasm. It's dripping down his hand and onto the floor at our feet. "Why don't you take care of that while I have my snack?" He nibbles the end. "Best cucumber I've ever eaten. Hands fucking down." He follows that with another enormous bite.

I can't help it. I burst out laughing and slap a hand over my mouth. "Is there something wrong with us?"

"Dunno, but if there is, I don't want to fix it." He points to his crotch. "My hands are full. Do me a favor and get my cock out."

I set the condom beside me on the counter and work the buckle free on his belt, pop the button on his jeans, and drag the zipper down. I slide my hand into his boxers and wrap my fingers around his thick length, freeing him from the fabric.

He takes another bite of the cucumber and then holds it alongside his erection. He's significantly girthier, but now that he's eaten part of it—I don't know that I'll ever get over this—it's closer to his length. "I wonder if they'd both fit," he muses.

"What?" Shock makes my voice pitchy.

His gaze lifts, along with one corner of his mouth. "Nothing. Just thinking aloud." He tosses the cucumber on the counter and nabs the condom.

"About trying to get your cock and a cucumber inside me at the same freaking time?" At least I sound more incredulous than I do curious.

He tears the foil packet and rolls the condom down his length, then runs his hands up my thighs as he steps between them. He pulls me to the edge of the counter, and I reach between us to guide him to my entrance. His eyes stay on mine as he fills me.

He exhales a cucumber-and-vagina-scented breath. "All damn day, Bea."

"You thought about fucking me with a cucumber?" I lace my fingers behind his neck.

"I'll probably use that as jerk-off fodder during away games." His fingers curl around my hip. The other hand gently wraps my throat. "This is my favorite part of the day." He leans in and brushes his nose against mine. It's the tenderness I've come to relish before things get intense. "I'm going to fuck you good and hard now, okay, little Bea?"

I hook my legs behind his back. "Yes, please."

"I'm sleeping with Tristan and Flip doesn't know," I blurt.

"I knew it! I fucking knew it!" Hemi shouts.

I point to the closed door. "Shh... What about your roommate?"

She waves away my worry. "She's a gamer. Half the time she's got that whole headgear thing on so it's an immersive experience. She can't hear anything we're saying."

"Oh." I hadn't realized Hemi had a roommate until she magically appeared in the kitchen to make instant noodles, said hi, and disappeared down the hall.

"The tension between you two is delicious. I should have put money on this." Hemi sighs.

"Who would you have made the bet with?" I cross my arms. That Hemi figured this out is a bit worrisome. How transparent are we?

Hammer raises her hand. "I had a feeling when we went to the exhibition game."

"Shit. You both knew?"

"Suspected," Hemi clarifies.

"Strongly suspected," Hammer amends.

"Isn't Tristan your brother's roommate?" Tally asks, eyes wide.

She knows a lot about the team and the players.

"And his best friend," Hammer says. "This is so fantastically scandalous."

"How long has it been going on?" Hemi fills my wineglass. For the second time.

"A few weeks, maybe." I wring my hands. "This has to stay between us. Flip can't find out. And as soon as I get my own place, it stops." It has to. I can't have Tristan coming to my apartment to bang me. My sore vagina clenches at the thought. She's such a whore for his cock. But my serial-monogamist heart has ideas, and fuckboys don't make for boyfriends who love you back and dream of forever.

"Are you, like, secretly dating?" Tally looks excited.

"What? No. I don't even like him. Mostly. He's a giant asshole. It's just sex. A lot of sex." Saying that I'm sleeping with my brother's best friend, who I mostly hate, is probably inaccurate. But I'm censoring for Tally. I ran away tonight when Tristan went to the store because we've had sex at least once a day since the shower incident. Sometimes it's fast and dirty, sometimes it's hard and long. Often it's the latter. In the past week, I've had only one twenty-four-hour break, and that was when they had an exhibition game in Detroit.

Tristan fucked me into next week before he left, and then again when he came back the following evening. So yeah. My poor vagina needs a break.

Besides, Flip was home when I left tonight. So any sex would take place after he was either asleep or out. And honestly, being woken up at three a.m. for be-a-good-girl-and-stay-quiet sex is a goddamn challenge.

"Wait. What? What do you mean you don't even like him? Why are you sleeping with him if he's an asshole?" Tally chews her bottom lip, like the prospect stresses her out.

"Tristan might be an arrogant, territorial player, but the sex is out of this world. Normally I'm all about healthy, nontoxic relationships. But my ex was accepted to a master's program out of province a few months ago, and he didn't want to try long distance, so we broke up."

"I'm sorry. That must be so hard," Tally says.

"I ate a lot of refried beans, but otherwise survived." I sigh. "It was probably the right call, but my bestie had moved to Vancouver just before we broke up, so I was already in my feels. I'm not relationship ready. But I'm not above having sex with someone I dislike immensely who can provide me with multiple orgasms on the regular."

"You can have more than one?" Tally asks. I'm pretty sure her eyes are going to be permanently wide after tonight.

"Maybe we should change the subject. I feel like I'm corrupting you," I say.

"No! I'm the only virgin left in my friend group, and they all talk about sex. I'm over here still having only made it to second base! And you want to know why?"

Yeesh, she's only seventeen and all her friends have had sex? What the hell is going on in her high school? "Because your dad is the coach of a pro hockey team, and he knows what happens in their bedrooms and doesn't want it to happen to you?"

"Yes! Exactly. He's so freaking overprotective. He's a great dad, but he hovered over me all summer long. It's been a lot. And now, with this co-op placement, he gets to hover even more. I'm so grateful you're taking me under your wing, Hemi. So grateful, because if I had to deal with him being a guard dog for eight hours a day, I would lose my mind." She blows out a breath. "Sorry for the rant. It's been intense. And now I'm surrounded by all these super-hot hockey players, and I worry I'm never going to get past second base!" She throws her hands in the air.

"First, there's no rush to have sex. You have the rest of your life to worry about it. Honestly, no guy has any idea what he's doing before he gets to college. You're truly not missing out on much," Hammer says.

"Yes. This. Even the ones in their mid-twenties are fairly clueless," Hemi grumbles.

"But not Tristan?" Tally asks.

"No. Tristan knows his way around a vagina. But he's also been inside a lot of them, so that's the trade-off." I gulp my wine. I'm going to hell for this conversation.

"And you don't even like him?" Tally seems really hung up on this point.

"He's a dick who's good with his dick." Yeah. There's fire licking at my heels.

"Relationships are confusing." Tally pushes to her feet and crosses to the bathroom.

Once the door is closed, I lower my voice and admit the truth. "Tristan is fucking *filthy* in bed. *Filthy*."

Hammer's eyes light up. "Like, he makes you call him Daddy?"

I open and close my mouth twice. "Uh, no. But I feel like I've learned something about you tonight."

Hammer rolls her eyes. "This isn't about me. Sorry. I need details. Filthy how?"

"He says and does the dirtiest shit. Like the other night he spat in my mouth, and I was so shocked I just said thanks." It was dry from all the gasp-moaning. I clap a hand over my mouth and look between the two of them.

"Oh, that is high on the filth," Hemi agrees.

Hammer leans in. "What else?"

"Before the away game last week, I was making a cucumber salad—"

They both have wide eyes, and Hammer looks far too excited for her own good.

"—and he bent me over the kitchen island and fucked me with an English cucumber. And then he *ate* it."

"After he washed it?" Hemi asks.

I shake my head.

"Lord." Hammer grips the edge of the table. "Please tell me he was the only one who ate it."

"Oh yeah. He gnawed on it like it was the best thing he'd ever eaten." *And said as much.*

"Damn. That boy is dirty."

"Right?" I haven't been able to share the details with Essie because every time she calls, I have no privacy. "And last night—"

"Oh, God, there's more?" Hammer bounces a few times on her seat.

I nod. But maybe I should keep this to myself.

"Butt stuff? Did you do butt stuff?"

"Not yet." But for sure it's coming. There's no way it isn't. He's too obsessed with putting his fingers in there for that not to happen. I'm obviously nervous. His cock is huge.

"Oh my God! Not yet!" Hammer claps. "If not butt stuff, then what?"

"Have you ever watched the movie *Chasing Amy*?"

"Total classic," Hemi says.

Hammer nods. "Oh yeah. That movie is a must."

I make a circle with one hand, and put the tips of my fingers together, sliding them through the hole, until I'm gripping my wrist while making a fist.

"Oh my God!" Hammer jumps to her feet. "His whole hand?"

Hemi's jaw drops. "No!"

I hide behind my hands. "Not to the wrist, but yes." I should have known better than to think his comment about getting the cucumber and his cock inside me at the same time was offhand.

"But didn't that hurt? His hands are huge," Hammer asks.

"You would have thought so," I say from behind my hands. "But no. I did think I was going to die from coming so hard, though."

"Well, that wins the filthy trophy right there. How the hell did he convince you to let him do that?"

"I was on the edge of an orgasm for like half an hour, but he kept stopping just before I came. I would have said yes to butt stuff at that point."

"But couldn't you have finished yourself off?" Hammer asks.

"I was also maybe tied to the bed." Because I'd been yanking on his hair. It was an intense night.

The bathroom door opens. "So, um, the walls in this place are really thin." Tally thumbs over her shoulder. "Also, do you think maybe we can watch this *Chasing Amy* movie sometime?"

We all say yes.

Hemi looks toward her roommate's bedroom. "I hope she

was wearing headphones." She turns back to me. "So does this mean you're dating?"

I scoff. "Oh my God, no. He doesn't even like me. We made a deal that what's going on ends when I move out. And Flip can't ever find out." This needs to stay firmly in the sex-pact box. Liking Tristan is out of the question. I can't afford to have feelings for him.

Hemi makes a face. "You think Flip wouldn't be happy about it?"

"He'd be so pissed."

"But didn't you grow up with Tristan?" Tally asks.

"Yeah, but I was a high school freshman when they were seniors, and they both got drafted right away and called up right out of university."

"Did you have a crush on him when you were younger?" Hammer asks.

"Big time. It was ridiculous. He didn't know, though." At least I don't think he did. I tried to hide it. "He was around a lot when I was younger. Especially before his parents divorced."

"Divorce sucks," Hammer says.

"Yeah, Tristan's mom bailed. Just up and left one day. Said she needed to find herself or some bullshit."

Hemi's eyes flare. "I didn't know that."

"He doesn't really talk about it. Or her." Not that he and I have many in-depth, emotionally revealing conversations these days.

"That's so sad," Tally murmurs. "How old was he?"

"Twelve, I think. And he has two younger brothers."

"So his dad raised three boys on his own. Yeesh. That must have been hard," Hammer says.

"Yeah. One is graduating high school this year, and the other one is about my age. Tristan's tight with them." He's almost like a second parent. He's always at Brody's games, and he and Nate talk on the phone constantly.

"Well, that might explain why he's so relationship averse," Hammer says.

"Yeah. For sure." I think about how pissed off Tristan was when I moved in, about some of the comments he made. Not wanting my drama. Maybe he saw me as someone he'd have to take care of and didn't want to—other than in the bedroom.

I can't be that girl who had a crush on him back when I was a teen. Not when my current value is based solely on the availability of my vagina.

"Did you ever hang out with him and Flip?" Tally is adorably invested in my childhood crush.

"I was more of an annoyance than anything. They had to walk me home from school until they went to middle school. But we'd stop at the grocery store to pick up snacks when Tristan came over." Tristan always had cash. His dad knew how much we struggled financially and probably gave it to him. I'm sure Tristan had strict orders to spend that money on food. "We'd stop in the candy aisle, and Tristan would always let us pick something. Flip loved those candy-coated black-licorice things." Tristan had seemed so happy to be at our place back then. And he hadn't minded me tagging along as much as Flip did. Or that's how it seemed.

Tally perks up. "Good and Plenty?"

I nod. "Yes! No one else liked them, so he had the whole box to himself."

Tally shrugs. "I like them, but I'm Dutch, so it's basically a cultural prerequisite to enjoy black licorice. I think it's sweet that Tristan let you pick something."

"I'm pretty sure he had to show his dad the grocery receipt when he got home. He always pocketed it." I remember that— him fishing it out of the bag and shoving it in his pocket. "And whenever his dad would drop him off at our place, Tristan had his backpack and hockey gear, but he'd also have a cooler bag full of snacks. There was always something special for me. But again, his dad was probably responsible." If Tristan was staying overnight, his dad would send him with things like burgers and bakery buns and a fresh salad. His dad knew how much Tristan and Flip could eat.

"Maybe it wasn't his dad, though. Maybe it was Tristan. Maybe he's had a thing for you all these years." Poor Tally looks so hopeful.

I snort. "Doubtful. I was the annoying little sister. He couldn't stand me then, and not much has changed." Although he has moments of sweetness. But reading into those is dangerous and stupid.

"He must like you at least a little, all things considered," Hemi says.

"The only thing he likes about me is my readily accessible vagina. And the only things I like about him are his huge cock and his ability to make me come like a freight train." That doesn't feel one hundred percent true on my side anymore, and that makes me nervous. Liking him for anything beyond his skills in the bedroom isn't part of the deal.

"It's so romantic," Hammer deadpans.

"Totally." I clink my glass against hers.

Tally scrunches up her nose. "That's the opposite of romantic."

We all laugh. Getting my heart broken by my childhood tormentor-secret crush is way too cliché. Even for me.

On the subway ride home, I think about how things shifted after Tristan's mom left. Tristan had to be home to get his younger brothers off the bus after school, so Flip spent more time there. I was an added responsibility neither of them wanted. And Tristan's tolerance for me evaporated completely when I became a teenager. That summer before I started high school, something changed. I don't know what tripped the switch. Maybe it was my hormones, or my crush on Tristan became obvious. It was probably irritating to have me hanging around like a lovesick puppy, always vying for his attention.

There were several incidents leading up to the night he made it clear my presence was unwanted and unwelcome, but the evening he threw me in the pool wearing the dress my mom made for Essie's birthday party stands out as a turning point. I realize now that I had everything he wanted—a family that loved each other, a mom who would spend every spare minute making me a dress so I could look pretty for my best friend's party. He was angry and hurting.

Maybe he still is.

When I get home, Flip is in the loft watching a movie. Tristan's bedroom door is closed, so he's either in there or he's out. It isn't until I'm in the loft that I discover Flip is not alone.

"Oh. I didn't realize you had a friend over. I'll grab a book and hang out downstairs." I thumb over my shoulder. There are a couple of occasional chairs by the wall of windows.

"It's cool. You can watch the movie with us," Flip says. "Stacey, this is my sister, Rix. Rix, this is my friend Stacey."

"Hey." Stacey lifts a hand in an unenthusiastic wave.

"Are you sure? I can totally disappear for a while." Bed would be nice, but the café nearby is an option if it gets awkward. From what I can tell, they're about halfway through their movie, and past the first sex scene, thank God. Eventually they'll go downstairs. I hope.

"Yeah, totally. Come hang out." Flip pats the empty space beside him. "Where were you tonight?"

"I went to Hemi's with Hammer and Tally." I take the spot beside my brother.

He pauses the movie. "Oh, nice. I know it's tough with Essie in Vancouver."

"I definitely miss her."

Stacey pulls out her phone and takes a bunch of selfies that include my brother's profile.

"I bet. It'll get easier though. Especially now that you're getting settled. The new job is good?"

"Yeah. So much better. And I'm on the hunt for an apartment, so you'll have your TV room back soon." I motion to the paused movie.

"Don't rush it. I'd rather you find the right place than end up in a crappy neighborhood again," he says.

He hits play on the movie again.

Within five minutes, Stacey's hand is climbing up my brother's leg. And she's whispering in his ear. He puts a pillow over his lap.

I'd like to believe my brother wouldn't get a handy while I'm sitting next to him, but it seems high on the list of potentially awful things that could happen. The giggling comes next, followed by the sound of lips on skin. Stacey moans. I should have stayed at Hemi's longer.

I'm half a second away from calling them out, or leaving, when the front door opens. "Hey, honey! I'm home!"

I am instantly relieved that it's Tristan. And worried about why he's coming in at this hour and where he's been. Not that I have a right to care.

"We're up here watching a movie," Flip calls.

"I'll be right up. Need anything from the fridge?"

"Nope. All good here!" Flip answers for us.

A minute later, Tristan pulls himself into the loft. His brow arches when he sees me, then rises again when his gaze lands on Flip and Stacey. Tristan is fresh from the gym. He smells like sweat and deodorant. I bet his skin is extra salty right now. What I wouldn't give to lick a path from his throat to his cock. I cross my legs.

"I didn't realize you had company tonight," he says to Flip.

"Stacey, you remember Tristan, right? Tristan, we've hung out with Stacey before."

Based on Tristan's blank expression, he doesn't remember hanging out with Stacey. "Right. Hey."

The awkwardness ratchets up to unbearable levels. I do not want to know how well Tristan and Stacey know each other. My stomach twists uncomfortably, and finding an apartment climbs on my to-do list. Like, maybe I should go do that right now. End this sex pact so I don't have to deal with the hard truth: that I'm no different than Stacey. Watching a movie with someone Tristan and my brother have both slept with is more than I'm prepared for. I don't want to think about him touching her the way he touches me.

Before I can make an excuse to leave, Tristan crams himself on the futon between me and Flip. I shift over a few inches, trying to give him extra space, but he manspreads until his knee rests against mine.

He stretches his arm across the back of the couch. His fingers sift through my hair, and his thumb sweeps along my nape. I freeze, unsure how to interpret the touch. It feels illicit. Dangerous. Is he trying to tell me something? Whatever his intentions, it's incredibly ballsy. I brush his hand away, unable to handle the contact.

"How was the workout?" Flip asks.

"Good. Guess now I know why you missed it," Tristan replies.

"Planning to get a different kind of workout in." Flip snorts.

Stacey giggles.

I want to yeet her over the loft railing. Horror hits me when I finally pin down the emotion that's making my blood boil. I'm jealous. Of a puck bunny. That she's had Tristan's hands on her makes me feel sick. This is a new low. There are hundreds of women just like her—and me—who have had his unrelenting dick inside of us.

Five minutes later, Flip and Stacey decide to move to his bedroom. As they get up, Tristan's arm magically disappears from the back of the couch. Once Flip stands, he moves over a few inches.

IF YOU HATE ME

Flip sends Stacey down before him and turns to Tristan. "You want in, man?"

This time I audibly gag. Flip ignores me.

My stomach tries to turn itself inside out. That my brother is inviting his best friend to take part in a threesome in front of me is indicative of the lack of boundaries in their relationship. It's also a shot of reality I don't know how to handle. This is what I signed on for. And it was fine when Tristan and I were in this little bubble, but the season is about to start. Tristan will be on the road. Maybe fucking bunnies. Probably fucking bunnies. I'm such an idiot for thinking I could handle something like that.

Tristan coughs and rubs the back of his neck. "Uh, no, man. I'm good."

The wave of relief that follows is horrifying. He's going away tomorrow, and I'll be faced with an entire twenty-four hours of not knowing where his dick is going to be. I don't want it to be anywhere but inside me. Which is a huge fucking problem.

Flip shrugs. "Suit yourself."

"Keep in mind we have an early flight tomorrow," Tristan adds.

"I'll nap on the plane." Flip disappears down the ladder.

Neither of us says anything until my brother's bedroom door closes.

"Where'd you go tonight?" Tristan asks.

As if none of that just happened. Like I'm not over here in a panic spiral because I have feelings and don't like them one bit.

This isn't a big deal for him, I realize. And it shouldn't be for me either. But I feel ill knowing he's fucked her, had his hands on her, kissed her, probably at the same time as my brother.

And I'm about to hear her get railed all night. I should be able to shake that, but I can't.

"Hemi's." I run my hands up and down my legs. I need space. And not to have a panic attack or emotional breakdown in front of Tristan. Because this jealousy and shame aren't some-

163

thing I want him to see. This was always the deal. My stomach flops over. "I should probably get ready for bed."

He grabs my arm before I can stand. "Why don't we hang out here until Flip gets things going? Then you can come to my room."

"Wow." I blow out a breath. This is not how I envisioned tonight—or any other night—going. Although, I probably should have. This is a reminder that any feelings for Tristan that aren't lust—or hate—related is a bad freaking idea. Who knows how recently he was with Stacey. I'm just another series of holes that are conveniently available. Clearly that's what he thinks, as evidenced by his immediate invitation to fuck now that Flip will be occupied—with someone Tristan has also screwed before.

But the worst part is, for half a second I consider it. Because I don't want to listen to Stacey tonight. But if I go to his bedroom, I risk being honest about how I feel, and then I'm even more screwed. It's an impossible situation.

The whole thing feels like the absolute worst gut punch. Seriously. If I don't vomit or cry, it'll be a miracle. "It's probably not a good idea tonight."

He seems confused. "Why not?"

So many reasons. None of which I want to voice for fear of losing it, or worse, admitting I don't want to be another Stacey. "I don't know how to deal with this." It's honest without setting myself up.

"Is this because of the woman Flip brought home?" His voice drops to a whisper. "He'll be busy with her for hours."

Confirmation once again that I'm just someone Tristan fucks in secret that he doesn't even really like.

"Why are you looking at me like that?" His jaw clenches. "You can't be upset with me because Flip asked if I wanted in. I said no."

We set parameters, and he's staying inside them. But I don't think I'm capable of compartmentalizing tonight and shifting the boundaries back where they're supposed to be. I bite my lips together, taking a moment to compose myself. Calm is the only way to manage this. "As inconvenient as it might be, my emotions are mine, and you can't tell me how I'm allowed to feel."

"That's not—I'm just saying I didn't do anything wrong, so I don't get why you're stonewalling me." I can't read his expression, but he seems…anxious, maybe? I don't know. I'm confused, and the heaviness in my chest is uncomfortable.

I don't want to put myself on the line emotionally, but I need to explain this in a way he can understand. I can't listen to Stacey make the same noises I make. "I know your sexual history is extensive and prolific. You wouldn't be half as good at getting me off if it wasn't. But it's harder than I thought to come face to face with your past." What if I can't do this anymore? Maybe I'm not cut out for casual sex.

His silence is telling. And damning. "It was a long time ago," he whispers. "Why are you holding it against me?"

"I'm not trying to. I just… I didn't expect to ever run into a Stacey, which I realize is pretty stupid, but we've been in this bubble. Now it's popped, and I'm having a hard time." I don't even know that Tristan can empathize. I'm not sure that's how he operates.

He scrubs his face with his hand and presses his knuckles to his mouth. "If you stayed in my room, you wouldn't have to listen."

"But I don't want to be fucked by you tonight," I say softly. And it's the truth. I'm just another Stacey, and I don't want to be. I'm scared of what that means.

His jaw tics. "I'm leaving in the morning, though. And we're staying overnight."

Is it a threat? A statement of fact? I wish I could read him better. He has two main modes: fuck machine and asshole, occasionally tempered by the sweet side that makes my heart all melty. But I can't let him into my body tonight. Not with my head all over the place and this stupid ache in my chest. Then what will happen while he's away and I'm not accessible? I can't be that fourteen-year-old girl desperate for his attention. Not now. Not ever. If this is what ends this, so be it. It's not a risk I'm willing to take.

I swallow down the threat of tears, impressed by how steady my voice is. "I know."

His gaze moves over my face. He doesn't try to touch me. Which is good. If he did, I'd probably fold. "Okay. That's fine."

He stands and moves around me. He doesn't look at me as he climbs down the ladder. My heart is in my throat as I wait for what's next. Will he knock on Flip's door? I grab a pillow and shove it against my face. I need to get a grip. If he goes into that bedroom, I'll never let him inside me again. I will find the next available apartment and move. Doesn't matter what neighborhood it's in.

Emotions claw at my throat. Tears blur my vision. Jesus. I like him. I fucking like him, and I don't want to. I've already had my heart broken once in the last six months. I certainly don't need to hand it over to my brother's emotionally unavailable best friend.

The bathroom door closes. Five minutes later, it opens again.

I stop breathing.

Until Tristan's bedroom door closes with a thud.

I stifle a relieved sob with the pillow.

I'm terrified, but I did what was best for me. And that's more important than anything else.

"**B**ea, baby, wake up for me. Come on, Bea."

I blink into the inky gray morning light. Tristan is hovering over me. His thumbs brush along the edge of my jaw. "Time's it?" I ask.

"Early."

"Flip?"

"In the shower."

Awareness hits me. I turned him away last night. He's leaving this morning, and I won't see him until he's back in thirty-six hours.

"I get it. I get why you said no," he tells me softly. "I just wanted you next to me. I hated last night. I won't fuck anyone else while I'm gone. I haven't and I won't. There's only you, okay? You're the only one." His eyes are wild. Haunted almost. He takes my hand and presses it against his cheek. "Just don't go. Please, Bea? Don't leave yet. I'm not done with you. I need more."

I'm half awake, barely processing his words. "I won't go."

"Okay. Good. That's good." He kisses my palm. "Fuck, Bea." He drops his head and nuzzles into my hair, breathing me in. "Can I kiss you? Please? Before I go?"

There's panic in his voice. Anxiety. I've heard it before, but I can't make the connection. I'm still too out of it.

"Please?" he begs.

"Sleep breath," I mumble.

"Don't care." He cups my face gently between his palms. "Please say yes."

"You can kiss me," I whisper.

Tristan climbs onto the futon with me and straddles my hips. He slants his mouth over mine, and I feel the desperation in his kiss. The longing. The need.

Saying no last night was the right thing to do—not because this is the result, but because he came to the realization I needed him to. Actions have consequences. And last night he experienced those consequences and didn't like them.

Neither did I.

He moves my hands to his hair and stretches out on top of me. Bracing his weight on one arm, he curves his other hand around my throat.

He breaks the kiss and rubs his nose against mine. "I slept like shit. All I wanted was you." His lips brush over mine.

I run my fingers through his hair. "I'll be here when you get back."

"Promise." He pulls back, his expression fierce. "Promise you'll be here when I get back."

"I promise."

CHAPTER 13

RIX

T oronto wins the exhibition game. I don't love the gut-churning anxiety I feel knowing the team is out celebrating the win. But when they return the next day, Tristan fucks me into next week and asks for my cell number so we can sext during away games. Because he's not going to screw anyone else while he's screwing me.

Two days after they return from Winnipeg, I'm standing in front of the fridge post workout, frowning at the contents. Flip is meeting with his agent and Hemi. He brought two women back to his hotel room after the Winnipeg game, and they posted photos online. Unsurprisingly, it's causing him trouble with his endorsement campaigns.

Tristan may or may not be in his bedroom.

"Where the heck is it?" I shift the contents around, searching for my post-workout treat. There's a bakery on the way home from work that sells delicious mini cakes. I've been looking forward to the last slice all day.

Tristan's bedroom door opens. He's shirtless and wearing a pair of gray jogging pants. When the heat kicks on in the fall, it gets warm in here. Particularly in the loft. I take a moment to appreciate his rippling abs, cut chest, and popping biceps. But my appreciation fizzles the moment I spot the container in his hands. The one that used to contain my cake. It's empty.

His eyes heat as they absorb my sports-bra-and-shorts combo. I'm sweaty. It's not a deterrent for Tristan. More than once he's yanked my shorts down and bent me over the kitchen counter when I'm back from the gym. He's a big fan of licking my skin when it's salty. The guy has some strange kinks, and most of the time, I'm down for it. But right now, I'm super pissed.

He tosses the empty container on the counter and moves into my personal space. He wraps my ponytail around his fist, but before he can lick a path up my neck, I cover his mouth with my palm. "Stop."

He releases my hair immediately and steps back. "Is Flip home?"

"No." I pick up the empty container. A swipe of icing is all that remains. "What does it say on the top of this box?"

He glances at the plastic container. My name is written in bold black letters. "Rix."

"Why would you eat it when it's clearly marked as *mine*?"

"Because I was hungry, and it's been sitting in the fridge for four days."

"But my name was on it."

He frowns. "It's just a piece of cake, Bea."

"That's not the fucking point, Tris! It had my name on it. I was saving it for after my workout."

He looks perplexed. "So buy another one."

I'm heading for overreaction territory, and I can't rein it in. I fling my hand in the air. "I *can't* just get another one. The only place that sells them is by my work, which means I'd have to take a half-hour subway ride to get there. And the bakery closes in"—I check the clock on the wall—"a little more than an hour."

"The grocery store is a five-minute walk. Go there and get something else."

"That's not what I want!" I snap. I'm being exactly the kind of problem Tristan hates, but I'm already out of control. It's not just the piece of cake, but what it represents—not having enough, not being considered. I'm frustrated that he so easily plays this down while I'm heading for irrational, especially since we've done this before.

He rolls his eyes. "Why are you being so drama about this, Beat? You're harping on me about a fucking piece of cake. Are you getting your period or something?"

"One." I hold up a finger. "Fuck you, Tristan."

"Why are you so worked up about a piece of stale cake?"

I exhale through my nose, working to keep my temper in check. My anger isn't helping my cause. "Two, was I bleeding all over your face when I sat on it yesterday?"

His nose wrinkles. "The fuck, Beat?"

"It's a question. Do I need to repeat it?" I cross my arms.

"No. And no." His confusion would almost be entertaining if he wasn't such an offensive asshole.

"I realize you didn't grow up in a house with menstruating women, so let me enlighten you. My being upset with you for taking something that didn't belong to you without asking first has nothing to do with my fucking cycle. I'm a human being with emotions, and they are not tied to the goddamn blood moon."

"But it's just cake. And it was stale. Why are you so riled up about it?"

I remind myself that Tristan didn't grow up in a house where treats were rare, though I thought he understood that I did. That when we put our names on things, no one else would finish it. Sure, we might have a bite, but we always left some for the owner.

My eyes are pricking. I need to get away from him before I cry. "Just forget it." I brush by him, but his fingers circle my wrist. "Just let me go." My voice cracks, and I turn my head away.

"No." He tries to get in my face.

A stupid emotional tear leaks out. He's right about it being stale. I know how irrational I look.

"Are you *crying*?" He sounds appalled.

"Please let me go," I whisper.

Instead of releasing my wrist, he pulls me against his bare chest. One hand cups the back of my head; the other winds around my waist.

I'm shocked by the affection. Tristan isn't a hugger. He does that nose-brush thing, and sometimes he'll spoon me, but spontaneous hugs are not the norm with him.

I allow it, mostly because it's so unusual.

Eventually he pulls back, brows furrowed as he cups my cheeks. "God, I hate making you cry." His thumbs sweep under my eyes, wiping away the tears. "Can you explain why this upsets you so much?"

The only way to avoid this happening again is to be honest with him. I bite the inside of my lip. This is my thing. My hang-up.

"Bea, talk to me, please. I want to understand."

"I stick to a super-tight budget. I never want to end up in the same position as my parents."

"Okay, but Flip wouldn't let that happen."

"I won't use my brother as a bank account." I'm circling the issue. I sigh and drop my gaze to his chest. "I have food insecurities. I'm always worried there won't be enough. I plan when I'm buying a treat, and I savor it, even if it's a piece of stale cake, because I won't waste it, and what if something happens and I can't afford it again for a while?"

"We have a fridge full of food. Is what Flip and I are giving you for groceries not enough? We can give you more. I'll give you more if you need it. That's not something either of us expects you to pay for."

There's an envelope of cash in the drawer labeled *groceries* that Flip and Tristan top up regularly. I put the receipts in the envelope. When it's down to a hundred bucks, I leave it on the counter, and someone always fills it.

"That's for your food, though. I have a budget for my own, and I pay for it separately." Stupid tears keep leaking out. There's such shame attached to this for me. I hated the days when the fridge was almost bare and we were still days away from a paycheck.

His expression is tender as he puts all the pieces together. "What? Bea, baby, no. You cook all our meals, prep our food, do all the grocery shopping, and the place hasn't been this clean since Flip moved in. You don't need to pitch in more than you already are, and you don't need to buy separate groceries."

"I'm living in your space, and you didn't even want me here to begin with. And Flip's always helping me. I can't take advantage of that, because he worries about money like I worry about food. I don't want to be a freeloader." I sigh, trying to get myself together. "Anyway, that cake was a splurge for me. And last week I went out for drinks with Hemi, and that can be expensive." I wring my hands. Even talking about it freaks me out. It's not entirely rational, but some mindsets are hard to rewire. "I know I'm really weird about food. I know that. But even when we were getting by okay, there wasn't a lot extra for treats. It's hard to let go of the fear that something might happen, and I'll suddenly have nothing. I never want to resort to brown sugar sandwiches while I'm waiting for the next paycheck to clear."

"Did that happen a lot when you were a kid?" he asks.

"Often enough. I know I keep freaking out on you, but this is one of my hang-ups."

Tristan tucks a stray lock of hair behind my ear. "If your name is on it, I won't eat it. Unless it's your pussy. I'll eat that anytime."

I roll my eyes but laugh. "I'm gonna jump in the shower."

His eyes search my face. "Okay."

I'm disappointed when he doesn't join me, and I'm even more disappointed to find the condo empty after I come out. I have a new message from Essie asking about a video call, so I fire one back. A minute later, she calls me.

She makes a circle motion around her face. "What happened with the asshole now?"

I laugh. She knows we've been hate-fucking each other, but not the details. I fill her in on my freak-out, the hug, and the whole deal, including that he's now disappeared.

"But he was good about it?"

"He listened. Or seemed to, anyway."

"Maybe he had an emergency?"

"Maybe. But why didn't he tell me he was leaving? I'm probably overthinking this. I'm definitely overthinking this. I know I'm weird about food."

"You're allowed to be. It was hard for you growing up."

Essie knows what my situation was like. Her mom would pack extra snacks in her lunch for me. And Essie would trade me when I had sugar sandwiches. The next day, she always had an extra sandwich in her lunch. "It's the second time I've cried in front of him. And both times have been about food. I feel like an idiot."

"You're not an idiot. It's your childhood trauma, and you're working through it. You're used to struggling and working on a limited budget. It takes time and maybe a few years of making a stable income before you get comfortable and feel okay about loosening your purse strings. Look at Flip. He's living with his best friend like he can't afford a million-dollar house."

She has a point. Flip still has the dresser from his childhood bedroom. It's in terrible shape, and one drawer makes an awful screeching sound every time he opens it. "I feel like you tolerated a lot of nonsense when we lived together in university," I tell her. "Maybe too much."

"We all have quirks, and I love yours. It helps that we had years of friendship under our belt to work with when we moved in together. Besides, you spent four years dealing with my constant assumption that every guy I dated would be my forever."

"You're a hopeless romantic."

"I'm a serial dater, and I want every guy to be the one," she replies.

"Does that mean you've met someone?"

"Date number two is tomorrow night. I met him at a coffee shop, and we ordered the same thing. I'm trying not to turn him into my new husband right away. You'd be proud. I haven't even merged our faces on that app that shows me what our children would look like."

"You're saving that until date six?" I ask.

"Maybe even number seven."

I smile. "Have you kissed him yet?"

"Oh yeah. We sucked face for a good ten minutes at the end of our first date. My next goal is to hold off on sex until after date five, but my libido gets in the way." Essie cringes. "I'm trying to stay mysterious, at least with what's going on in my pants."

"Seems reasonable. What are you doing on date two?"

"Having lunch and then grocery shopping."

"A grocery-shopping date? That's new."

"But also smart. His food choices will tell me so much. Does he price match? Does he buy things on sale? Does he binge or impulse buy? Does he only buy brand names, or will he get the no-name kind to save a little since it's the same product in a less flashy container?"

"That is smart. Who suggested it?"

"Me, of course. I really need groceries, and it seemed like an unconventional way to get to know him better."

"So smart. I miss grocery shopping with you. And going through the flyers," I admit. We did it every Thursday when the new ones arrived in the weekly paper.

"We were the price-matching queens. We should have had T-shirts made." Essie smiles.

I return it, but talking about this makes me miss having her close. If she wasn't halfway across the country, I'd probably be on my way to her house right now. "Our system was unparalleled."

"What else is going on? You and Dickhead still hate-fucking each other?"

"Yeah. I think I might not hate him as much as I should."

"He's softening you up with the D, huh?"

"Maybe. I don't know. Sometimes he can be almost…sweet." Like earlier when he wouldn't let me walk away. Or when he's not busy saying filthy things and turning me into a sex pretzel. "I need to find an apartment, but I can't secure anything before October first." And maybe that's okay because moving out means the sex with Tristan ends.

"The offer stands. You can always move in with me. I have a king bed. We could make it work."

"Unless this new guy turns into your boyfriend. Then it would just be awkward."

"True. And despite my best efforts, I'll probably have us married by date four. It's sort of my thing."

"It kind of is."

"What if I come visit you? We'll time it when the guys are away. We'll go to a bar, get drunk, and dance on tables. Flirt with dirtbags. It'll be like old times."

"You mean like last year's old times?" I ask.

"Exactly."

"That would be awesome." A visit from Essie is exactly what I need.

"I'll look at their schedule and check flights. I'm between events, and I need a reason to get out of Vancouver for a few days, so I don't fall for this guy too fast."

"This is perfect. I need some bestie time."

The condo door swings open, and Tristan appears, laden with grocery bags.

"My roommate just got home," I whisper.

"The one you're fucking?"

"Yeah."

"Love you. Play safe. Bye!"

She hangs up before I can tell her I love her back.

"I'm coming up whether you're decent or not, Bea!" Tristan pulls the ladder down, and his head appears a few seconds later, followed by the rest of his body. He sets several bags on the floor, then pulls himself the rest of the way up.

"What's this?"

"Stuff." He grabs the grocery bags and one brown paper bag with handles and sets it all on the coffee table. He crosses his arms. Then uncrosses them and runs a hand through his hair. "For you."

"For me?" I echo.

"Yeah. I went to that bakery. I hope I got the right one. I think it is. I ate three different kinds of cake to make sure." He pulls out a full-sized version of the mini cake he ate.

"That's four times the size." And a fifty-dollar cake.

"Seemed like a small price to pay if I can make up for being an asshole." He pulls out three more boxes. "These are the slices I bought. I ate half of each of them. They can be yours too, if you want them."

"You didn't need to do this." My heart is at risk of pooling at my feet.

"Yeah, I did. I made you cry. Twice. So I'm making up for it. Plus, I got you this other stuff." He motions to the grocery bags, then shoves his hand in his jeans pocket.

I peek in the first bag. "How did you find Thrills gum?"

"There's a vintage-candy section in a grocery store about twenty minutes from here. It's on the way back from the bakery. I'll take you sometime, and we can get whatever you want."

I riffle through the contents. It's literally all my favorite treats. "How did you know I like all this stuff?" I'm at risk of getting emotional again. Part of me wants to squirrel it all away and eat it one piece at a time.

"I remembered from when we were kids, I guess. It's all the

crap your parents got you for your birthday one year. Or am I not remembering that right?" He rubs the back of his neck. "One year you had a mountain of freaking candy."

I stare at him. "You remember that?"

He lifts one shoulder. "It was a lot of candy."

My bottom lip trembles. Yeah. My feels are extra big tonight.

Tristan frowns. "Are you going to cry again?"

I cover my eyes with my hands, press my lips together, and shake my head.

His fingers circle my wrists and, despite my best efforts to keep my hands in front of my eyes, he's way stronger than I am. But he's gentle as he moves them away.

"Hey, hey." He kisses my cheek. "This was supposed to make you feel better, not make you cry again."

"My parents didn't buy all that candy. I did," I whisper.

"Oh." He's still holding my wrists. "Flip and I almost made ourselves sick on it."

"I know." My feelings are on fire.

"I'm missing something important here."

I sigh and drop down on the couch. My arms are still raised because Tristan is holding them. He lets them go and takes a seat beside me.

I pick up a package of Fuzzy Peaches. "I'd mentioned to Flip earlier in the week that I wanted to have a movie night on my birthday. Looking back on it, he probably wasn't paying attention. I was an annoying barely-teenager, and you were seventeen and probably already getting blow jobs in the back seat of your car from the bunnies."

"That's about right. The part about the blow jobs, I mean." He makes a face. "Which you probably didn't need me to confirm. Anyway, you weren't really annoying. I know I said that a lot, but mostly coming to your place was an escape from having to take care of my brothers. Hanging around with Flip was a reprieve, because at your house, all the responsibilities didn't fall on my shoulders."

I shake my head. "I drove Flip nuts. He hated it when I had to tag along."

"But it wasn't your fault you were a kid with parents who worked long hours, just like it wasn't my brothers' fault our mom bailed."

"You had to take on a lot of responsibility, didn't you?"

He shrugs. "I didn't want them to think they weren't important."

I wonder if that's how he felt when his mom left. Unimportant. Maybe even unloved. He had no mom to hug him, give him affection. His only female role model abandoned him. I open the package of Fuzzy Peaches and offer some to Tristan.

He shakes his head. "They're for you."

"I'm not going to eat all of this on my own." I pop a pink one in my mouth.

"I can't stand those; they make my mouth peel so they're all yours." He stretches his arm across the back of the couch, fingers sliding under my hair. "Tell me more about the candy birthday."

"I asked my parents for money for my birthday that year, instead of a gift. I bought candy and all the ingredients to make cupcakes and buttercream icing." With real butter. Not lard or margarine, which were cheaper. "I was so excited. Essie was coming over, and Flip said he'd watch a movie with me. I said you could come, too."

The smile slides off his face. "We didn't stay for the movie."

"It was stupid anyway. No seventeen-year-old wants to hang out and watch action movies with his younger sister." I'd gone to change. Essie was coming over after her dance lessons to sleep over.

"Fuck, Bea. I was such a dick to you that night." He rubs his bottom lip.

I can't believe he remembers this at all. "I was being a pest."

He shakes his head. "You were being a normal girl who wanted to celebrate her birthday." He runs his hands through his hair. "Fuck. *Fuck*." His expression makes my heart clench. "I thought your parents had done all this stuff for your birthday, decorated and made it all fun and special, and I was so pissed off that my mom couldn't even be bothered to send me a fucking card, let alone remember to call. I was so mean to you. I'm sorry."

When I'd come back out in my pajamas—my cute ones, for obvious reasons—Flip and Tristan had polished off half the candy and were on their way out the door. I'd asked if they were staying to watch a movie, and Flip had looked at me like I had two heads. Tristan said they were going out, and no one wanted their little sister tagging along. It felt like my heart had been stomped on.

"I was a kid with a dumb crush."

"Wait. What?" His jaw drops. "You had a crush on me? When you were a teenager?"

"No. I don't know why I said that." My face is on fire. I can't look at him. That was a stupid thing to admit.

His hands wrap around my waist, and he moves me to straddle his legs. He takes my face in his palms. "Look at me, Bea."

I side-eye him.

"I was really fucking mean when you started high school."

"I was annoying."

"You weren't. You were sweet, and kind, and thoughtful. You're still all of those things and more. But I was a fucking nightmare of a human being. I was angry, and hockey gave me a place to channel that energy. I spent a lot of time in the penalty box. If I'd known you had a crush on me back then..." His jaw clenches. This is the most open Tristan has been with me, and I see that angry boy inside him. His wounds are still raw.

He wraps his hand around my throat, thumb stroking along the edge of my jaw and down the side of my neck. "I'm sorry for the way I treated you, and the way I sometimes treat you now. I just..." He looks to the side. "You deserve so much better." His gaze shifts back to mine. "I used to hurt you, sometimes on purpose. Maybe I wanted what you had. And now I just want...you." His other hand sneaks under my shirt, skimming my ribs. "You were so fucking sweet, and now I've corrupted you."

"You don't get to claim the corruption card. Thanks to you, I've discovered that vanilla soft serve isn't my jam. I don't feel bad about the things we've done. You shouldn't either."

"I should, though. You're my best friend's little sister." He tips my chin down and covers my mouth with his. This kiss isn't possessive. It's soft and sweet. Something shifts between us, elating and terrifying.

Before we can take it any further, my brother walks through the door. I'm out of Tristan's lap and across the couch between one heartbeat and the next. What if we'd been in the kitchen instead of up here?

"Hey, party people! Who wants to hit the bar?" Flip calls.

"We're up here watching a movie," Tristan calls back, quickly cuing up one of my favorite old-school action movies.

My heart is in my throat and my stomach flip-flops.

A minute later, Flip's head and shoulders appear. "Come on, man. Let's go out."

"We have early practice tomorrow. Maybe take a night off. Plus, we have snacks." Tristan motions to the ridiculous mountain of sugary treats.

Flip surveys the coffee table. "I could skip the bar tonight, I guess."

He joins us on the couch, eats an obscene amount of sugar, and crashes within half an hour. Tristan puts his arm around my shoulders and presses his lips against my temple. "I'm going to fast forward to the end, and Flip can put himself to bed," he whispers.

"Okay. I'll use the bathroom while you deal with him."

I'm in the kitchen filling my travel mug with water when my bleary-eyed brother disappears into his bedroom with a mumbled good night. Tristan puts the full-sized cake in the fridge and sets the three half-eaten ones on the counter. He grabs a fork and takes a seat at the island, patting the stool beside him.

I climb up and prop my cheek on my fist. He slides the fork through the cake and touches the tines to my bottom lip. I part my lips and take the bite. It's lemon cake with a berry buttercream in the center. Tart and sweet and delicious.

"I like this." He eats a forkful of cake.

"They make the best cakes in the world."

He flips open the second container and forks a chunk of carrot cake. "Not the cake. I mean, you're right, it's awesome. But I like this." He motions between us with the fork before offering the bite to me.

"You like feeding me cake?"

"Yeah. I like the way you savor things. How you don't rush to get to the end too fast." He takes another bite. "Which one?"

I tap the first box, and he cuts me another bite. I finish chewing before I say, "I like this, too."

He sets the fork down and tucks a finger under my chin. "I really hate it when I make you cry. I'll try not to do it again." He presses a soft kiss to my lips. "Come to bed with me?"

I nod.

Tristan closes the lids on the mostly eaten cake slices and laces our fingers, tugging me toward his room. If Flip came out right now it would blow this whole thing apart. My heart is racing, and my palms are damp as Tristan pulls me into his room and locks the door. He takes my face in his hands and kisses me.

Just like in the loft, it's soft and sweet. And it continues as we undress, his fingers skimming my curves, touching all the places that make me sigh and bite my lip to contain my moans. He kisses a path down my stomach and makes me come with his mouth and fingers, then rolls a condom on and fits himself between my thighs.

"Aren't you going to turn me into a pretzel?" I ask as the head nudges my entrance.

"Not tonight." He pushes in on one smooth stroke, and his

eyes flutter shut for a second. When they open, he caresses my cheek.

"Why are you being so nice?"

"I'm making up for all the times I've been needlessly mean. Don't worry, I'll go back to being my asshole self after the orgasms." He smiles, but there's an emotion lurking behind it that I can't pin down.

He drops his head and kisses me, rolling his hips. The sex is slow, intimate. The orgasm builds, and I fight back a moan as it threatens to pull me under.

"Look at me," he demands as his hand circles my throat. "I want your eyes on mine when you come on my cock."

I force them open and struggle to keep the low keening sound from bubbling up.

"So fucking good, Bea. It gets better every time," he whispers.

He crushes his mouth to mine and swallows my desperate sounds.

Everything is changing.

Reframing.

Shifting.

And I worry how my heart will manage when this ends.

Because it has to.

Just not tonight.

CHAPTER 14
TRISTAN

"**Y**ou're on fucking fire tonight, man!" Flip crashes into me.

We're in the last ten minutes of play in the third period, and I've scored as many goals this game. It's only an exhibition, but it's against the team who took us out of the play-offs last year. I needed this.

"Beautiful goal, Stiles." Dallas slaps me on the shoulder as we trade places. He glides out onto the ice, and I take a spot on the bench next to Ashish, who gives me a fist bump.

"You're owning the ice tonight," Coach tells me.

More of my teammates pat me on the back as I take a drink and catch my breath. I can't stop smiling. I scan the arena and spot my brother and dad. Bea is in the box with Hemi and the girls.

Flip pats me on the back. "I said you'd kill it tonight, didn't I?"

"Yeah, you did. That was a great setup." Flip isn't playing his best tonight. He's usually cleaner on the ice, but he was out late last night. Regardless, he recovered a fumbled pass, and I scored the goal.

"We're a kickass team, but you really pulled it out." He taps his temple. "You gotta stay out of your head."

"I know. I'm my own worst enemy sometimes."

He pats me on the back like he understands, but Flip usually lets things roll right off him. If he has a bad game, he says he'll do better next time. If he has a great game, he'll give his teammates credit. If I have a bad game, I worry the next one will be worse, that I don't deserve my spot on this team. It's a shit mindset to get into, so I need to roll with this high.

After a few minutes, we rotate back onto the ice. The opposition scrambles for a goal to close our lead, but they can't get the puck to stay past the center line, so we win the game, four-two.

I stop to chat with my dad and brother before I hit the locker room.

"Beautiful game tonight, son." Dad claps me on the shoulder.

"Thanks. We played tight, and I had good setups."

"You kicked ass!" Brody gives me a fist bump. "My friends are blowing up my phone. Can we snap a pic?"

"For sure." I throw my arm over my brother's shoulders and smile as he snaps a bunch of selfies. "Things are good? We can get on the ice together next week?"

"I don't want to ruin your flow," Brody says.

"You never ruin my flow." I squeeze his shoulder. "We'll make it happen. I'll check your schedule and mine and toss out a couple of dates."

"Okay. Sounds good." Brody's all smiles.

"Everything going okay? Is Beatrix still staying with you?" Dad asks.

"Uh, yeah. She is for a while longer." I rub the back of my neck. "Her last apartment wasn't great, so we want to make sure she's in a safer neighborhood this time."

"It's good you're letting her stay with you. Her family didn't have it easy growing up."

"No, they didn't. But she's got a good job now."

"And Flip helps her out, I'm sure."

"When she lets him, yeah. She's pretty independent and does most of the caretaking, actually."

"You two have that in common, then." He fishes around in his pocket for his keys. "All right, Brody. You've got school in the morning. Let's get you home." Dad smiles at me. "Nice game tonight. I'm real proud of you."

"Thanks, Dad. I'll call you later in the week."

"Sounds good." He ushers Brody down the hall.

The locker room is buzzing with the high of handing our biggest rivals their ass. When Flip sees me, he whistles and claps.

"Fuck off, man." I flip him the bird, but I'm smiling. I needed this win and these points. I needed my team to see that I can play my ass off, even when it's just an exhibition game, that I can score goals against the team who slapped our balls at the end of last season. I like Hollis, but I don't want to give up my spot on first line for him. I want to be on the same line as Flip during the first game of the season, and I hope my game play tonight will help secure that.

"You're coming out tonight." Flip points an accusing finger at me. "We are celebrating the fuck out of this win."

"Yeah, I'm coming out," I agree.

"That wasn't a question. You have zero excuses for getting out of shots tonight." His smile is wide and infectious. "You play this hard during the season and teams will fight over you come contract time."

"That's the hope." I want Toronto to renew. I want to keep playing for my home team and with my best friend. I want things to stay the same.

"And when we've slept off the hangover, you and I will run some drills with the guys tomorrow afternoon. We need some bro time. Get your gear off and get in the shower. You're buying the first round."

I ride the high all the way to the bar. I have a text from Nate congratulating me on the win. I promise I'll call him tomorrow so we can catch up.

The second we step through the doors, we're swarmed. Fucking Flip posting shit on social media. I fight my way through a throng of excited bunnies, a few of whom I recognize. There are always locals who show up when they find out where we're going. I do my best to avoid them and head for the bar. We don't have practice until later tomorrow, so I plan to have a good time tonight.

I glance over my shoulder, making sure none of my teammates are around, and that Flip is occupied before I check my messages. Bea is saved in my contacts as #1. With us traveling soon, I needed to be able to contact her in ways that don't include me throwing shit into the loft at two in the morning.

According to her most recent message, she's waiting to order a drink. I scan the bodies and spot her ten feet down the bar. At the game, she was wearing jeans and a team hoodie. Her hair was down and wavy. Now it's pulled up in a ponytail, and she's wearing a cropped tank. Some dude is trying to chat her up, but she ignores him. I want to knock his teeth out for even looking at her. But I can't do that unless I want Flip to figure out what's going on. Her chin is propped on her fist, and her gaze is fixed on the bartender, who happens to be female. And someone I know. Not because I've slept with her, though. I know better than to screw the people who serve us drinks. I can't say the same for Flip.

I'm stopped for a couple of selfies as I try to edge my way closer to Bea. The guy beside her leans in, trying to strike up conversation, but Bea gives him a tight-lipped smile and a one-word answer. I need this jerkoff to get a clue and leave my girl the fuck alone.

I put myself between them and address the guy. "She's not interested in you, so back the fuck off." I don't know what my expression must be, but he abandons the bar and disappears into the crowd without a word.

I turn to Bea. Her delicious mouth is tipped up in a knowing half grin. I barely resist the urge to lean in and drag my lips up her throat. She looks amazing, and I'm not the only one who's noticed. I want to put my hands on her, pull her onto the dance floor, and let everyone know she's mine. But I can't, because if Flip finds out, he'll murder me. Not for the first time I wonder, briefly, how bad it would be if he knew. Then I think about that Stacey woman. Yeah. Probably really bad.

Bea pokes at her lip with her tongue, eyes roving over me. "Fuck, you look good in a suit."

"You always look good, but my favorite is you under me, about to come all over my fingers or my tongue."

She throws her head back and laughs, giving me a saucy look. "Nice work on the ice tonight. Watching you dominate made my panties unreasonably damp."

I lean in again. "You should take them off and bring them to me so I can verify that."

"Or you could stick your hand down my pants and find out." She grins deviously.

"That sounds like a dare."

Her eyes dart over my shoulder, and she steps back. "Flip and teammates incoming."

Flip edges his way between us and throws an arm over both of our shoulders. "Try not to rip each other's heads off tonight, eh?"

It's not her head I want to rip off. It's her clothes. That guy who was flirting with her, though? I wouldn't mind separating his head from his body.

Flip waves to the bartender, and Dallas edges in beside me. "Pretty sure Hemi brought her entourage to babysit Flip's ass tonight. Shilpa and Ashish even came out."

"Where is she?" I glance over my shoulder. Hemi sometimes comes out with the team under the guise of celebrating. She rarely has more than one drink, if any. Her primary goal is to ensure we don't make the team look bad.

"Seven o'clock. She's wearing a team shirt tied at the waist, black jeans, and fuck-me heels," Dallas grumbles.

The fuck-me heels comment has me doing a double take when I spot her. She's wearing ice blue stilettos with the team logo. "She still making your life miserable?" I ask as Bea makes her way back to Hemi and Hammer.

"Every damn chance she gets."

The bartender approaches and gives Flip a tight smile before she turns her attention to me and Dallas. "Nice game tonight. What can I get you boys?"

"A round of shots on this guy!" Flip slaps me on the back.

I roll my eyes. "Dude. When have shots ever been a good idea?"

"They're always a good idea."

The bartender quirks her brow.

"Go on. Line 'em up," I tell her.

We down the shots, and of course, because it's on my dime, Flip orders a dozen more and calls the rest of the guys over. We toast the win, and Flip orders one more round, but he pays for these, which is rare for him. Hemi, Shilpa, Hammer, and Bea get called over to join us. Hemi and Shilpa give us judgy looks as we pass them out. I bite my tongue when Hemi passes her shot to Bea. Two beers and Bea's tipsy, so adding shots probably isn't the best idea.

She and Hammer have their heads together. I don't like Bea's smile. It's the one she wears when she's planning something devious, like pouring a water bottle down her chest while she's wearing a white sports bra. I considered gouging Dallas's eyes out for a second that day.

Flip makes another toast to the team, and I shoot my tequila and chase it with beer. Ashish sniffs his before knocking it back.

"The only time I like tequila is when it's in a margarita," he notes. He chases the shot with water.

Shilpa gives him an arched brow as she dumps her shot into a lowball glass with juice.

"I don't know why I didn't do that," Ashish mutters.

Hammer and Bea rub their lemons on their collarbones, then sprinkle each other with salt.

"That would have been an even better idea." Ashish glances

at Shilpa, who's watching the girls with a knowing smile from behind the rim of her glass.

"Those two are a problem waiting to happen," Dallas notes.

I grunt and take another swig of beer.

They lick each other's collarbones, shoot their tequila, and finish with the lemon. That's *my* neck Hammer is licking, my girl she's getting up close and personal with. Pretty sure the entire bar, except for Flip, just watched that happen. He's busy flirting with a bunny. I'm busy fighting with my body to stay where I am and not stake my claim. Especially when I spot a couple of guys eye-fucking her from across the bar.

"I need a drink," Hollis mutters and walks away.

Roman sighs and drains the rest of his beer. "Pretty sure this is payback for last week."

"What happened last week?" My gaze returns to Bea, who's now doing Hemi's shot. This time she salts the webbing between her thumb and pointer finger and her eyes swing my way as she drags her tongue over her skin.

Roman snaps his fingers.

"Huh?"

"You two are about as obvious as a flashing neon sign."

I yank my gaze away from Bea. "I'm nowhere near her."

"You're looking at her like you want to eat her."

Or spank her ass while taking her from behind. She's pushing my buttons on purpose. "Flip's busy flirting with the bunnies."

"Just because he hasn't noticed doesn't mean other people won't. Clearly, whatever was going on still is."

"It's not a thing." I drain the rest of my beer. I need him to drop it, and I need to be less fucking conspicuous. But having to stay away from her? I don't like it. At all.

"Saying it doesn't make it true."

"What's Hammer getting you back for?"

"She saw my business end by accident. It's the second time it's happened, and she wants to move into her own apartment. I can't say I blame her. And changing the subject won't make this shit go away, Tristan. The longer you go behind his back, the harder it'll be to come clean."

"It's supposed to end when she moves out." I don't like the tightness in my chest that comes with that admission.

"Which is when?" Roman asks.

I rub my bottom lip. "When she finds a place, I guess. We're closing in on the end of September, so there's a good chance she'll be living with us through October."

Roman gives me a look. "Do you hear yourself, man?"

I realize I'm back to staring at Bea, who's now dancing with Hammer and Hemi. I force my gaze away again. "She probably won't find a place next week."

"Look, man, I get that you can't help the way you feel—"

"I don't feel anything. We're just fucking." That sounds and feels like a big, shitty lie. Sure, I like being inside Bea. But I also like being *around* Bea. I hate when she's upset, but I like buying her treats, even if I have to drive an hour to get them. I love watching her eat cake. And feeding it to her. She takes tiny bites and saves the icing for last. She makes little happy noises.

"So you'd be fine if it ended next week?" Roman presses.

"She doesn't have an apartment yet." My shoulders are tight.

"She's been talking about apartments with Hemi and Peggy."

My head snaps toward him. "What? How do you know that?"

"Because my daughter lives with me and hangs out with Hemi and Rix. And she talks to me."

I run a hand through my hair. "Just because she's talking about it doesn't mean she's found a place. I'd know if she had." She would tell me. She wouldn't just leave.

"Right, because aside from the *just* fucking, you talk about your living situation."

I try to sip my beer, but it's still empty.

He nods toward Hammer and Bea. "And in the same vein of

just fucking, you're totally okay that some dude bros are planning to make a move on Rix and my daughter?"

The two guys who were eyeing Hammer and Bea when they were doing body shots have moved in. Bea has her back to them, but Hammer keeps looking their way. I take a step toward them, but Roman grabs my arm. "You're just fucking, huh?"

My throat tightens, and my chest does this weird thing that makes me want to rub it. "Flip will kill me if he finds out." And he has every right to bury me in a shallow grave. I'm doing very dirty things to his baby sister. And she fucking loves it.

"The longer you hide it, the harder it'll get," Roman repeats. "You're inviting all kinds of drama if you keep doing this behind Flip's back. If he finds out, will you fight for what you want?"

I stare at him. "I'm not supposed to like her."

But I do. And if I'm totally honest with myself, I probably always have. Sure, she was kind of annoying as a kid, but when she started high school, things changed. Though I wasn't lying when I said I was too angry and destructive.

"But you do. You should tell him before he figures it out. It'll still be hard, but at least you can tell him on your terms." He claps me on the shoulder. "I'm going to cockblock those dude bros so your head doesn't explode and I don't punch out a kid ten years younger than me."

He heads for the girls, and I go back to the bar.

I need to figure a way out of this pact. Maybe we can make an amendment. Maybe the sex doesn't have to end. We could still see each other after she moves out. It might even be easier because she'll have her own place and I could go there. If that happened, we could keep it from Flip a little longer—until we got each other out of our systems. Or she got tired of my shit. The latter seems more likely.

I end up beside Hollis at the bar. He downs a scotch, and the bartender pours him another. He motions to me. "I'll get his too, unless it's more shots. Then he can get mine."

"Just a beer." I specify the brand, and the bartender grabs me a bottle. I thank her and wait until Hollis has his scotch before I clink my bottle against his glass. "Thanks for the drink."

"You kicked ass tonight on the ice," he says.

"So did you." He managed an assist.

He makes a sound. "Thanks. I spent a lot of time in physical therapy so I could be an asset to the team this year and not a liability."

"It's healed up good, though, yeah?" He's playing tight so far.

"Yeah. But with injuries like this, it'll never be quite the same. It's one day at a time. I'm good for now, though." He sips his scotch. "I know my being back screws with the starting lineup. Just remember you're younger, in better condition, and you're not contending with any long-term injuries." He tosses back his scotch. "I'm gonna head out. Have a good night."

"You too, man."

He glances over at the girls, maybe making sure they're safe before he disappears into the crowd. Bea's not hard to find. Because she's dancing on a table with Hammer. For someone who usually follows orders and routine, and mostly has her shit together, Bea sure is a wildcard when she's had a few drinks.

I search for Flip and spot him dancing with two women. All three of them are making out. It's one of those nights. I push through the crowd to the table where the girls are dancing. Bea and Hammer have quite the audience. It doesn't hurt that they're both hot and rubbing their boobs on each other.

Hemi is watching them with a mixture of amusement and longing. Roman stands beside her with his arms crossed. Shilpa and Ashish are off to the side, completely absorbed in each other. Which isn't unusual. I approach the table. Bea rolls her eyes, gives me her back, and shakes her ass at me. Hemi glances my way and mirrors my facial expression.

"FYI, Flip's on the dance floor making out with two women, and there's a high probability someone is recording it for the world to see."

"Why didn't you stop him?"

"That's not my job." Flip is a grown-up responsible for his own actions. And I don't want to get dragged into a situation that will be tough to get out of.

"Fuck you. You're an asshole."

I give her a tight-lipped smile. "I know."

Hemi heads in Flip's direction and I tap Bea on the shin and hold out a hand. "You should think about coming down before you fall and break your leg."

"Or you could come up."

"I'll break the table." I glance around the bar. Roman is holding out a hand to Hammer. Flip is busy dealing with Hemi. I wrap my hands around Bea's thighs, just below her ass, and tug her forward. She stumbles a step, and I pull her down from the table. Her chest ends up mashed against my face for a second, and then she slides down the front of my body.

"What're you doing? I was having fun!"

I set her on her feet, aware that I need to let her go before the wrong person—namely Flip—sees us all up close and personal, but she grips my tie and wraps it around her fist. Her eyes are hazy and unfocused. "Isn't this the tie you used when I was ripping out your hair?" She tips her head back, and her eyes light up. "The night you got your entire hand in my cock holder. It totally is. Did you wear it on purpose?" Her tongue glides across her bottom lip.

"It's my favorite tie." Also, yes. It's my new lucky tie. And that night will forever go down as a spank-bank favorite.

Her smile widens. "Buy me another drink, and I'll let you do it again. You can tie me to your bed and fist fuck my pussy."

I'm about to tell her she doesn't need another drink, and that I'll fuck her any way she wants, when someone cough-chokes beside us.

"Come on, Peggy. We should go home."

Fuck. Roman definitely heard that.

"Can you not call me Peggy in public, please? We've been

over this before. I'm not eighty-five. Either call me Hammer like everyone else or use my middle name."

I glance to my right as Hammer shoulders her way between us and hugs Bea. "Might want to use your inside voice when you're asking to get fist fucked. We'll talk tomorrow." As she releases her, Bea weaves slightly and gives me a cringey face, like she didn't realize we were in a bar full of people. I can't be mad because I forgot we were in public for a minute there, too.

"Okay. Well." Hammer glances at my hands. "Yeah. No. Maybe use a lot of lube."

I say nothing.

Roman's face is a shocking shade of red.

Bea looks drunker by the second. Those shots are finally hitting her, I guess.

"This never happened." Hammer makes a lips-zipped-and-throw-away-the-key motion. "Okay, Dad, let's go before your blood pressure hits lethal levels."

He shoots me a glare and allows Hammer to guide him toward the exit. I glance around to make sure no one else is paying attention. Dallas and Spencer, a second-line right-wing rookie, are talking to a couple of women. His gaze meets mine for a second, but he turns back to the woman with her hand on his arm.

"Sorry. I wasn't thinking," Bea whispers.

"Don't worry. Roman won't say anything. We should probably get you home, though." I can't keep my hands to myself any better than she can. I don't know if it's the shots or the beers, but I don't want to, either. Which is reckless—and stupid.

"I'll call an Uber." She pulls her phone out from between her breasts.

"I'll go back with you." I'm not sending her home alone.

"Is that a good idea?" she asks.

Hemi appears at my side. "Where's Hammer?"

"Roman took her home," I say.

"I'm calling an Uber," Bea announces.

"I can drive you," Hemi says.

Bea pushes her lips out into a pout. "But we've been drinking."

"You've been drinking," Hemi says. "I've had a glass of soda water."

"Shouldn't you stay so you can monitor Flip?" I motion to the dance floor. I want to take Bea home and find out if she meant what she said about tying her to my bed.

Hemi gives me a tight smile. "That gets to be your job for the rest of the night."

"But I'm taking Bea home. I want to make sure she gets in okay."

Hemi looks between us. "Maybe be a good influence for your best friend tonight. I'll make sure Rix gets into the condo."

Arguing will make things worse, so I let Bea and Hemi leave. Bea glances over her shoulder once on the way to the exit. She looks worried. I abandon my beer, because I don't want to make decisions that will fuck shit up for me. More than it already is.

Turns out Flip is a hot mess. Usually he has one beer and switches to water, so all those shots have hit him hard. I'm used to dealing with sober Flip and his entourage of women, but now he's so drunk he's barely making sense, and the women he's been buying drinks for aren't in much better shape. I remind him that he's been buying them drinks all night, and he can't take them home. They're too out of it to be able to consent to anything but a glass of water and some painkillers for the inevitable headache.

I haven't missed my wingman role the past few weeks—entertaining women in my house, performing, doing what's expected of me instead of what I want. And she's already on her way home with Hemi. I call the women an Uber, and Flip and I get into one of our own. He doesn't seem to realize they're not coming to our place.

I get texts from both Hemi and Bea to let me know she made it home to her bed. And that's good because Flip insists we stop for pizza. If I feed him, maybe I won't have to carry him down the hall. We sit on the bench outside our building while we demolish most of the pizza, but I convince him to leave two slices for Bea.

"Shit. I left my sister at the bar," he slurs as we pass the doorman.

"Hemi took her home." I take his elbow to keep him from walking into a window.

"Oh. That's good. Hemi's good people even though she rides my ass a lot." He stumbles into the elevator. "I can't believe I left my sister at the bar."

"She can take care of herself."

"I fed her a lot of shots. I'm not the best brother." He leans against the wall. "What happened to those girls I was dancing with?"

"They went home."

"You could've taken care of them for me."

"Then who would make sure your drunk ass got fed?"

"You're a good friend, Tris. The best. Thanks for making sure I didn't do something to totally fuck up my career tonight."

I don't feel like a good friend, especially since my plan had been to leave *him* at the bar so I could take his sister home and get her into *my* bed. And I would have if Hemi hadn't intervened. I swallow the guilt and pat him on the shoulder. "No problem."

I don't know what it means that I'd rather continue lying to him than stop this thing with Bea—other than Roman is probably more right than I want him to be.

The elevator doors open, and Flip weaves down the hall.

He's still too hammered to function, so I let us into the condo. He almost face plants into the floor. "Rix, we brought you pizza!" he shouts.

"I'll eat it for breakfast," she mumbles. "Do I need to wear headphones tonight?"

"No," I call back.

"Why would she need to wear headphones?" Flip asks as he weaves toward the bathroom.

"To drown out the sound of your one-night stands."

"Ha. Good one." He disappears into the bathroom.

I pull out my phone and message Bea.

> **TRISTAN**
> The bathroom will probably be a mess tomorrow. Sry in advance.

> #1
> Me too.

> **TRISTAN**
> I'll clean it up and make sure you don't sit/step in pee. Did you eat something before you went to bed?

> #1
> A cucumber

And I'm instantly hard.

> **TRISTAN**
> (⊙.⊙(Ō_Ō)⊙.⊙)

> #1
> JK. We stopped for ramen. Carbs for the win.

> **TRISTAN**
> Good.

Flip stumbles out of the bathroom and into his bedroom. I clean off the toilet seat, then follow to make sure he sleeps on his side, and I put a puke bowl beside his bed, just in case. He passes out cold when his head hits the pillow. Bea is sitting at the kitchen island with her cheek resting on her crossed arms when I come out of the bathroom. I incline my head to my bedroom, and she slips off the stool and pads quickly after me, checking over her shoulder twice on the way.

"I'm so sorry about tonight. I wasn't thinking. Hammer won't say anything, though. I trust her."

"Neither will Roman."

"How can you be sure?" She bites her fingernail.

"He's known for a while. I mean, not the part about me tying you to my bed or the—" I make a fist and shake my head. "I still can't believe I did that." Not up to the wrist or anything, but Bea is small compared to me, and my hands are definitely not.

"I meant it when I said you could do it again," she whispers. Then her eyes widen. "What do you mean he's known for a while?"

"He, uh... He figured it out somehow. Said he could tell by the way I was looking at you or whatever." My gaze roves over her. She's wearing the tiny sleep shorts and a tank. I can see her nipples through it. "But he's kept his mouth shut so far, so we're safe." I take her face in my hands and cover her mouth with mine. "And tonight I just want to make you feel good, if that's okay with you."

"Totally okay. Better to save the other stuff for when Flip's not home since it's hard to stay quiet when your fingers aren't in my mouth."

I peel her out of her clothes, and she struggles to get me out of mine. She clambers up onto my bed and kneels in the middle. Her fingers go to her lips, and she bites one, her eyes guileless. "How do you want me tonight?"

"So many fucking ways, Bea." I climb up after her, tucking a finger under her chin and tipping it up. "Are you gonna be my good girl and stay nice and quiet?"

She whimpers and nods.

"Lie on your stomach, legs together." I release her, and she scrambles into position, stretching out on the bed.

I run my hands down her back and squeeze her ass. Then I slip my hand between her thighs and push two fingers inside her. She buries her face in a pillow to muffle her soft moan. I lean in to bite her ear. "Shh, little Bea. I can't make you come if you don't stay quiet."

She nods once, and I curl my fingers. She fists the sheets and turns her face into the mattress. I'm jittery, like I'm not sure what to do with myself. I'm too amped up from this night, frustrated that I had to wait this long to touch her. And terrified that Flip will find out and it will have to end.

I roll a condom on and lie on top of her, bracketing her legs with mine. I push in, all that tight warmth surrounding me. Her eyes roll up, and she bites her lip.

I kiss her cheek. "The next time we're alone, I want to make you scream until you lose your voice."

She shudders under me and whimpers.

"Shh, you want to come, don't you?"

She nods and whispers, "So badly."

I thrust my hips, and she pushes her ass up, her breath leaving her on a whoosh.

She grabs my wrist on the next hip thrust and brings my fingers to her lips, sucking three into her mouth. She bites down on the next deep push. She makes another small sound, a quiet whimper, and strokes along her throat.

"You want my other hand?"

Another affirmative whimper.

I curl my palm around the back of her neck. She sucks my fingers, and her whole body convulses as she comes, pussy squeezing like a fist. "Look at you, coming already, my sweet, filthy girl. I'm not even close to done yet, though, so you'll have to be quiet a little longer, okay?"

She nods.

She comes twice more before I do, each time harder than the last. I don't want to send her back up to the loft after. I want to tuck her body against mine and hold her, wake up with her next to me. But she's exhausted, and we can't take that kind of risk.

So she steals out of my room at two in the morning and goes to the loft.

Despite being tired, I can't fall asleep right away.

TRISTAN

I've been thinking

#1

About cucumber salad?

TRISTAN

Among other things

#1

Such as…

TRISTAN

We should rent a hotel room so you don't have to disappear up to the loft.

#1

You want to spoon with me?

TRISTAN

No. I want to spork you.

#1

Ur romantic side is really shining through

TRISTAN

And you wouldn't have to be quiet either

You could moan my name as loud as you want

#1

I'm turning off my alerts

TRISTAN

It's a good idea. U can't deny it

#1

Night, Trissy

TRISTAN

I can smell your shampoo on my pillow

#1

You're four texts too late for being
sweet/stalkery

TRISTAN

And your pussy on my fingers

#1

Ah, there you are. Seriously, g'night. Some of
us have to be up early

TRISTAN

Night. I'd be sorry that tomorrow is going to
suck for you, but you were the only person I
wanted to celebrate with tonight.

#1

*Notifications have been silenced, notify
anyway?*

She has to get up in four hours. She needs sleep.
Hopefully Bea can read between the lines.

CHAPTER 15

RIX

"Oh my God, did you steal your brother's car?" Essie's jaw nearly hits the sidewalk as she rolls her suitcase to the trunk.

"He left me the keys. Driving it freaks me out." It's practical, considering he makes millions a year, but I've never driven a car worth more than fifteen-thousand dollars, so getting behind the wheel of his Tesla makes me nervous. But making Essie Uber or take the train was silly when Flip said I could use it.

We hug briefly, and I help her heft the bag into the trunk. We hustle into the car and out of the chilly September rain. I fight a cringe as I take my place behind the wheel. Pre-away-game sex with Tristan is turning into a full-body event. Muscles I didn't even know existed hurt. I'm not sure what it indicates that he feels the need to have extra-intense sex anytime we won't have it for more than twenty-four hours.

"Trixie Rixie, are you having trouble sitting down?" Essie inquires as she moves my purse from the passenger seat to the floor. She tucks the fortune cookie that fell out back inside.

I focus on leaving the Toronto airport without getting into a fender bender. It's the worst. "How was your flight?"

"It was decent. The guy next to me was hot, which is much

better than my last flight, where I ended up beside a grandfather who farted every fifteen minutes and seemed shocked by the smell."

"Was the hot guy also nice?" I'm not above distracting her.

"He was self-absorbed. Talked about all the money he makes in finance. I did a lot of nodding and smiling. I also drank three glasses of wine, so that helped quell the boredom. His pretty face was a bonus." She adjusts her position. "Nice try changing the subject, but you sat down rather gingerly. I've been dying for details, so spill them."

"Some details are rather filthy," I warn.

"I would expect nothing less from Tristan, considering he's best friends with your brother and the stories floating around on the bunny sites are unreal. There has to be some truth to them."

I avoid the bunny sites like the plague. I already know enough about my brother and his sex life. And I have no desire for any insider scoop on Tristan. But I finally have privacy to speak to Essie, so I fill in the gaps—there are many—in the dirty story since Tristan and I started sleeping together.

"Holy shit. He really is filthy. I can't believe he ate the cucumber."

"Yeah. He really commits."

"I also can't believe Flip hasn't suspected anything," she muses.

"He's pretty busy with his own social life."

"Does that bother you? Especially since Tristan is the same way."

I consider telling Essie about the woman Flip brought home who Tristan had previously slept with but decide that's one situation I don't need to relive. "It's awkward witnessing it firsthand," I tell her. "There's almost always someone in his bed. He had a long-term girlfriend in high school, and our parents have been married for over thirty years. It's not like he's had bad modeling." I wave that away. "Anyway, I don't need to psychoanalyze my brother, and you'll probably see him in action when they get back tomorrow night."

I pull into the underground lot and park my brother's car, help Essie unload her suitcase, and take her up to the condo.

She lets out a low whistle and crosses to the wall of windows. "Wow, now that's a view. The waterfront is amazing from here."

"Right? It's a great location."

Essie surveys the rest of the condo. "It's a sweet pad."

"It is. Minus the single bathroom and the ladder to get to the loft."

"Yeah, that's a weird design flaw."

Once we get Essie's suitcase into the loft—no easy feat—we catch up while we make dinner together. I work in the morning, so Essie will visit friends from university while I'm gone.

The following evening, we're snuggled together on the couch in the loft, eating buttered popcorn and watching a movie, when Flip and Tristan return from Ottawa. They won the game, and Flip and Tristan scored a goal apiece.

"Hey, sis! Hey, Ess!" Flip shouts.

"Hey!" we call back.

"Gotta shower off the sin," he says, probably to Tristan. Two seconds later, the bathroom door closes.

Tristan grumbles something, and his suitcase rolls across the floor.

Essie side-eyes me and whispers, "Now we're getting to the good part."

I roll my eyes. "Nothing will happen while you're here."

"We'll see how true that is, won't we?"

Less than a minute later, Tristan pops into the loft.

"Hey." I give him a questioning smile. This should be interesting.

"Hey." His gaze shifts to Essie as he pulls himself up. "Essie, it's been a while, eh?"

"It's been a few years." She pops a piece of popcorn into her mouth. She hasn't seen him in the flesh since freshman year of high school.

He tucks his thumbs into his pockets. He's wearing distressed black jeans and a long-sleeve shirt pushed up to reveal his delicious forearms. The look does a fantastic job of highlighting all his exceptionally defined muscles. His gaze shifts from us to the TV and back again. "What are you two up to?"

"Uh, watching a movie." I motion to the TV. It seems obvious.

He kneads the back of his neck. "You look pretty cozy."

We're currently sharing a blanket. "Do you want to join us? We're only about twenty minutes in."

His brow furrows, and he bites his bottom lip.

Essie glances between us and holds up her insulated wine-glass. "I need a refill." She tosses off the blanket and untwines our legs. We're both wearing shorts, those terrible-but-comfy reading socks, and hoodies. "I'll be back up in a few. Holler if you need anything."

Tristan's eyes go to my mostly bare legs.

"Maybe bring the bottle up," I say.

"Will do." Essie skirts around him and disappears down the ladder.

Tristan glances over his shoulder before he moves closer. He leans down, bracing a hand on the back of the couch. Aside from looking confusingly upset, he smells fantastic. Two days of stubble decorates his cheeks. I bet that would feel great rubbing all over my lonely, neglected pussy. "Are you spooning with Essie?"

"She's my best friend. Why do you look upset?"

"I thought I'd get some time with you. Alone." He fingers the end of my ponytail, and his lips brush my cheek. "Come to my room when everyone else goes to sleep so we can spoon naked."

"I haven't seen Essie in months. I live here, Tristan, at least for the next little while. You can wait until Essie goes home before you get me naked again."

He backs up. "How long is she here?"

"Until Sunday."

He buries his face against my neck. "I haven't been able to touch you for almost two days, and you'll be up here, all cuddly."

"Are you jealous?" I ask.

"No." His brow furrows. "Wait. All you're doing is cuddling, right? With your clothes on."

"Oh my God." I laugh. "You *are* jealous."

"I'm not. I just had an away game. Back to this cuddling business—you and Essie just snuggle? That's it?"

He seems so skeptical, like he can't believe it's possible to touch someone and not want to take their clothes off.

"We're affectionate people. We like to cuddle. So that's what we do when we watch a movie." It's affection without intention. I wonder how many people touch Tristan without wanting something from him. "Maybe a weird concept for you, but not for us."

"Oh." His palm rests against the side of my neck, his gaze slow to lift. "I don't know why I asked that."

My heart clenches. Sometimes he's such a broken little boy. "Maybe because you and my brother have slept with the same woman at the same time."

Something like shame flashes behind his eyes before they drop. "Maybe. I didn't want to cuddle with them, though. Or Flip."

"Good." I was nervous last night. My brother and Tristan routinely share a room during away games, and Flip can't seem to keep his dick out of a vagina for more than twenty-four hours these days. Not that I'm any different, but at least it's the same dick, as opposed to his vagina variety.

"Did Flip bring someone back to your room?" It's hard not to look away.

"I said I wouldn't fuck anyone else, and I didn't." His thumb sweeps across my jaw, and his palm shifts to rest against my throat.

"What'd you do then? Just watch?" I hate that he can feel my nervous swallow.

"No. Of course not." His expression softens. "I went to Roman's room and fell asleep on his couch."

The wash of relief scares me. "Oh."

"Were you worried?" he asks.

"I didn't want to be."

"It's just you I want, Bea. I meant it when I said it." He brushes his nose against mine. "Now that we've cleared that up, can I kiss you?"

"Yes, please."

"Fuck, I love that coming from your sweet mouth." He slants his over mine and groans as our tongues tangle.

"Hey! Can someone help me? Climbing a ladder with full arms is impossible!" Essie yells.

Tristan breaks the kiss. "I missed the way you taste. I need to be in you."

My vagina really loves that idea, but the logistics are not the best. "Same, but you'll have to wait." I push on his chest. "Coming!"

He straightens and adjusts himself while Essie passes the stuff up before climbing into the loft. She flops back on the couch. "You joining us, Tristan?"

He glares at the screen and runs a rough hand through his hair. "Pass. I'm gonna hop in the shower when Flip's done. You girls enjoy yourself."

He climbs back down, and after a moment his bedroom door closes.

Essie gives me a look.

"He's jealous," I whisper.

"Because we're watching a movie together?"

"Because we were making physical contact."

She arches a brow. "Boy has it bad."

"For my pussy."

She makes a noise as she tops up my glass, but her smile is sinister.

"What is that look?" I gulp my wine.

She daintily sips hers while grinning. "Nothing."

"It's not nothing. You're scheming."

"Since tomorrow is Friday, we need to plan a girls' night. I want to meet Hemi, Hammer, and Tally. We should go to a club."

"Tally is only seventeen."

"Fake ID?"

"Her dad's the team coach, Hammer is the goalie's daughter, and Hemi is their PR person. Fake ID or not, it wouldn't go over well."

"Hmm... Okay. Girls' night in tomorrow with Tally, and then Saturday club night?"

"That would work."

"I bet you a visit to Vancouver that once the boys get wind of our plans, they'll stalk us to the bar." Her eyebrows bounce on her forehead.

"Oh, I see where this is going."

"You and me on the dance floor."

"He'll lose his mind." I grin. "The sex will be out of this world when it finally happens."

"Intergalactic, baby."

F lip goes out after his shower. He returns with two giggly women as Essie and I are getting ready for bed. He disappears into his room with them. And then the real fun begins.

Essie looks beyond disturbed as the moaning-giggling continues from behind his bedroom door. "How often does this happen?"

"Fairly regularly. And it'll continue for some hours, so use these to minimize the emotional scarring." I pass her a set of plug-in earphones. It's easy to lose wireless headphones in bed. It took me two nights to learn that unfortunate lesson. Especially when my left earbud cut out halfway through an epic fuckfest.

Essie crams the earphones in and pulls a pillow over her head.

I'm about to do the same, but my phone buzzes with a message. I'm unsurprised it's Tristan, but the content is unexpected.

TRISTAN

Wish it was me cuddling you tonight. I hope you sleep okay.

My stupid heart clenches. I need to get a handle on these feelings.

RIX

Sporking doesn't count as cuddling. The headphones are in. Enjoy your door.

TRISTAN

I would settle for spooning with no sporking just to have you next to me. Night, Bea.

210

In the morning, I wake to the smell of freshly cooked bacon. I climb down the ladder and find a woman I've never seen before making breakfast. "Hey. I'm so sorry. I hope I wasn't too loud," she says with a slightly chagrined smile.

"I had to get up for work anyway. I'm Rix, Flip's sister," I explain.

Flip's bedroom door opens, and two more women come out, both dressed in Flip's T-shirts and sporting epic cases of bedhead. My brother is behind them, wearing boxer briefs and a sleepy half smile.

"You were busy last night," I observe. I swore there were two women with him when he came in, so the breakfast-making third one is a mystery.

"Sure was." He kisses the breakfast-maker on the cheek. "This smells great."

"I figured we could all use a nutritious breakfast after last night," she says brightly.

Yeah. This is super weird, but she's cooking, which is better than most of Flip's bedroom friends. Essie comes down from the loft, and Tristan eventually joins us too. He seems as surprised by Flip's entourage of women as Essie and me.

After breakfast, Essie and I both head out. I have to work a half day, so Essie is once again visiting some friends who live in the city—they're lucky enough to work from home. But she meets me at the office mid-day, and we stop at the grocery store to pick up stuff for our girls' night. It's the first time since she's moved that I have a grocery-shopping partner. I've missed the little things.

Stocked with essentials, Essie and I head to Hammer's place and make dinner with the girls. They absorb Essie into the group like she's been part of it the entire time. Roman stays long enough to eat—he goes back for seconds and thirds and keeps complimenting us—then leaves to meet Hollis and Ashish to talk strategy about the upcoming season.

We don't get home until late. There's a rare note on the counter from Flip saying he's next door watching a movie with Dred. My phone buzzes with new messages from Tristan after I've crawled into bed.

> **You need to come to my room**

Essie snuggles up beside me and snickers. "Are you going?"

"No. You're here. He can wait another forty-eight hours for pussy." I compose a response:

RIX
> **For what?**

TRISTAN
> **...**

RIX
> ***shifty eyed gif***

TRISTAN
> **My balls ache. I'd feel a lot better if I could bury my face in your pussy—or other parts.**

RIX
> **Palmela and Fingerella can take care of you**

TRISTAN
> **Your hands are softer than mine**

RIX
> **Essie is here. We're cuddling**

I send him a selfie of Essie and me snuggled in bed together. It's a grainy, terrible photo.

TRISTAN
> **Fuck that. She's had you for three damn days. When do we get to cuddle?**

RIX

Not until Essie goes home

TRISTAN

I'll book her a flight and drive her to the airport. First class. And I'll fly you out for an away game in Vancouver so you can see her. On a weekend.

"Oh my God, he's desperate for you," Essie whispers.

"Desperate for my vagina, you mean."

TRISTAN

I want you to come on my face

You can pick the position

I need to be inside you

I'm dying

Of blue balls

I'm about to compose a reply, but Flip comes home. Alone for once.

O n Saturday, Flip and Tristan have an early practice and a promo thing in the afternoon. Essie and I make breakfast together and lounge around, soaking up the comfort of being together. In the afternoon we take over the guys' bathroom, and Essie does my makeup since she's a wizard with contouring. I'm not big on the nightclub scene, but Hemi has connections thanks to the team, so we're going to some exclusive place and dressing up like thirst traps.

Tristan and Flip return from their day of volunteering at a food bank as we're leaving. I'm fastening my strappy heels while Essie checks her clutch for her ID.

"Essie, looking good," Flip says.

She gives him the bird. "Don't say things like that to me unless you want me to projectile vomit all over your expensive shoes, Flip."

He frowns. "I just said you look good."

"Yeah, but your tone was all bow-chica-wow-wow, and that's a *no* all the way around." Essie turns to me. "You ready to roll?"

"Where are you going anyway?" Flip asks.

"Out with Hemi and the girls," I reply.

"Weren't you together last night?" Tristan asks.

"Last night we had dinner because Tally is underage," I explain as I slide off the stool.

Tristan's eyes pop when he catches the full effect of my outfit. "You're going to a bar dressed like that? What bar?"

I pretend I can't remember the name. "Some place downtown." I check my phone. "The Uber arrives in three minutes. We should head down." I smile brightly. "You guys have a good night. Don't wait up."

Essie says nothing until we're in the elevator. "Based on the way Tristan couldn't take his eyes off you, there's an eleven million percent chance that they'll end up at the bar with us."

"Probably, yeah."

Three hours and many text messages later, Flip, Tristan, Dallas, and a bunch of other guys from the team are sitting at a table reserved for people with deep pockets. Hollis and Roman opted out because the club scene is not their jam, and Hammer didn't want her dad to hover like a bodyguard.

Essie, Hemi, Hammer, and I are shaking it on the dance floor.

"Tristan has zero chill," Essie says as we move to the beat. One of her hands is on my hip and my forearms are resting on her shoulders, like we're slow dancing. I glance at the table. He's frowning in our direction. Flip gets up to dance with some woman. Dallas keeps trying to engage Tristan in conversation, but eventually, he gives up and turns to one of his other teammates.

We spend most of the night dancing, and Tristan spends most of it watching us. He doesn't look particularly impressed. At some point, Flip goes home with a woman, and when my feet feel like they're about to fall off, we hit an all-night diner. Tristan goes back to the condo. I fully expect him to be asleep when we get there, so I'm surprised when I open the bathroom door after Essie and I finish brushing our teeth and he's standing on the other side. His button-down is open at the collar, and the sleeves are rolled up. The forearm porn is delightful.

"Essie, I need fifteen minutes alone with Bea, please," Tristan grinds out.

"Cool, yup." Essie moves around him and rushes for the loft.

Tristan steps into the bathroom and closes the door, flipping the lock. "This fucking dress." His gaze rakes over me, and his nostrils flare.

I cross my arms. "I look good."

Tristan pokes at his cheek with his tongue and shakes his head. "No, you don't."

"Well, fuck y—"

"Good doesn't begin to describe how you look tonight. You are fucking sinful." He takes a step forward, and I take one back, bumping into the vanity. "I couldn't leave the table all goddamn night because of the constant hard-on."

"That must have been frustrating." I grip the edge of the vanity.

"I thought my head was going to explode with the way you and Essie were all over each other. I assume that was intentional." He plants a fist on either side of me and his knee presses against mine.

"Maybe a little."

"I wanted it to be me out there with you." He drags his tongue across his bottom lip. "Please don't make me wait until Essie goes home."

I part my legs. Between one blink and the next, Tristan seals his mouth over mine and lifts me onto the vanity. I expect him to tear my clothes off, but instead he cups my face in his palms and slows the kiss. Our tongues tangle and his hands roam, easing down the side of my neck. His lips follow, and he nuzzles in. He wraps his arms around me as he fits himself between my thighs and lets out a plaintive sigh.

"I hate not being able to touch you," he mumbles.

"I'm here now." I run my fingers through his hair, surprised by the affection.

"I don't want to need you." His lips move along the edge of my jaw. "But I do."

This time when he kisses me, it's not soft; it's desperate, frantic even.

He starts rocking his hips. His hands are everywhere—in my hair, palming my breast, squeezing my ass. He shoves my dress up to my waist and yanks my panties down, then drops to his knees. He pulls me to the edge of the vanity and rubs his face all over my pussy, like a cat marking its territory. He groans as he licks up my center and latches onto my clit. I grab a fistful of hair and clap my other hand over my mouth to stifle my moan. In less than a minute, I'm on the verge of an orgasm.

He rises, his cock already in his fist. He crushes his mouth to mine and rubs the head over my sensitive clit. I pull his wallet free from his back pocket and search for the condom.

"Fuck. I stopped carrying them around when the away games started," he admits. I don't have time to unpack that because he adds, "I know you take the pill. I got tested after our first time. I'm clean. We could go bare this once. But only if you want to." He swallows hard, like he's waiting for me to deny him.

"Okay. We can go bare."

He lines us up and both our gazes drop as he pushes in, one slow inch at a time.

"Oh, fuck." His head drops to my shoulder, and his breath leaves him in ragged pants. "You feel so fucking good, Bea. Why do you have to feel so good? It's never enough. I always want

216

more." He turns his face into my neck and his lips part, teeth sinking into the flesh as he makes a tortured sound. "My control is really frayed right now."

I run my fingers through his hair. "It's okay if you need to lose it."

One hand curves around the back of my neck. "You should hold on to something," he grinds out.

I grip his forearm and wrap the other hand around the nape of his neck.

As soon as I do, he starts fucking me. Hard and fast. Pulling out to the ridge and slamming back in. I can't stop the moans that bubble past my lips. He releases my hip and covers my mouth with his palm. He leans in close, lips brushing my cheek. "Shh, little Bea, Essie's in your bed right now, listening to you get fucked."

I whimper and clench, the orgasm a few dirty words away from dragging me under.

He bites my earlobe. "You gonna come all over my cock, like a good girl?"

I bite his palm to keep the moan from slipping out. My legs are shaking, nails digging into his skin.

"The next time I get you alone, I'm going to fuck you for hours."

I come so hard the world goes dark for a second and comes back into focus in a burst of white and stars. Tristan crushes his mouth to mine, swallowing my cries as he pounds into me. I can't stop coming. It goes on and on, endless pleasure that's so intense it's almost pain.

"Fuck. Shit. No condom. I'm sorry." He pulls out, angling his erection toward the sink. For a second I contract around nothing. And then his calloused fingers slide inside me and find a rhythm, dragging the orgasm out.

"Fuck." He warms a washcloth for me and gently cleans me up, then tosses the cloth in the towel hamper. He tucks himself back into his pants and I push my dress down. We're still both fully clothed, apart from my panties being on the floor.

He takes my face in his palms and kisses me. He's back to being gentle.

When he finally breaks away, I say, "You know Essie is leaving tomorrow, right?"

"Yeah. But I needed you now." He wraps his arms around me and rests his cheek on top of my head for a moment. "Tell her I'm sorry...-ish."

I push on his chest. "No you're not."

"You're right. I'm not. She's the one who gets to hold you tonight."

I roll my eyes. "You have to go. I need to pee."

He kisses me on the cheek and leaves the bathroom.

Essie is lying in bed when I return to the loft.

"Sorry about that." I'm mortified.

"Never apologize for getting laid."

I disappear behind the screen and change into my pajamas, then climb into bed beside her on the futon.

She rolls onto her side. "How much longer can you do this before Flip finds out?"

"He can't. And it ends when I move out." I should already have a place secured, but Tristan and Flip keep shooting down every apartment I find.

"You really think you two can quit each other like that?"

"It's just sex." It sounds like the lie it is.

She makes a noise but doesn't call me out. "Well, Vancouver is always an option. And it'll be a lot easier to stay off his dick if there are thousands of miles between you."

CHAPTER 16
TRISTAN

I make sure Flip is in the bathroom before I pin Bea against the counter with my hips. She's cutting fruit for her lunch. Her hair is down, so I sweep it over one shoulder and lean in to press my lips against the sensitive spot behind her ear. "Did you leave a bag upstairs for me?"

"Behind the privacy screen." She tips her head, as if she's waiting for my lips to keep moving along her neck.

It's tempting, but once I start, it's hard to stop. "Good. I'll pick you up after work." These stolen moments when I get to touch her like she's mine are my favorite part of the morning.

I step away a few seconds before the bathroom door swings open and Flip comes out. I need to watch myself. There have been a few close calls recently. Hence the reason for tonight.

"Can you make me a coffee, Rix? I'll be ready in ten," Flip calls as he heads for his bedroom.

I bite my tongue so I don't call him out for his lack of fucking manners. "You'll have to take breakfast to go."

"You're driving then." His bedroom door closes behind him.

This morning Flip and I are volunteer coaching a special-needs hockey team with my brother. Brody and I have done it a bunch of times. These kids get so excited about playing, and

219

Hemi loves the positive promotion. She gave me a bunch of team swag, including water bottles, pucks, and baseball caps. They're already in my car.

I notice the newspaper on the counter is open to the ads section. I'm quick to squash apartment options by sending her articles about crime in the neighborhood. Truthfully, all I want is more time with her. Also, I don't intend to stick to the plan of this thing ending when she moves out. Maybe I'll broach that subject later tonight, when it's just the two of us.

She finishes separating the fruit into plastic containers and heads for the coffeemaker.

"Flip can get his own coffee," I say behind the rim of my mug. Lately it irks me how much he takes advantage of Bea. She's not his personal fucking assistant. And she never complains.

"I'm already pouring one for myself." She fills two travel mugs. "Can I pour you one, too?"

"Fill yours first. I've already had two cups." In the weeks since she's been living here, I've noticed that Bea always makes sure everyone else has what they need first. She'll take the smaller portion and wait until we're finished eating before she goes back for seconds.

She fills hers three quarters of the way and pulls out a travel mug for me. I cover the top with my hand. "Yours first."

"I need room for cream and sugar. There's enough left for you."

We stare each other down.

She gives me a look. "Really? You want to argue about who gets the most coffee this morning?"

"Do the two of you ever stop fighting?" Flip asks.

"Occasionally." A grin tips the corner of Bea's mouth.

I move my hand and avert my gaze, because that expression makes me want to do dirty things. Well, I always want to do dirty things to her, but I'm getting a hard-on, which isn't conve- nient with Flip in the room.

"Flip, you'll have to doctor your java. I've gotta run, and I'm out tonight, so you'll be on your own for dinner. There's lasagna in the fridge and directions to reheat it here." She taps the Post-it stuck to the fridge.

Flip's eyebrow rises. "You got a date or something?"

"I'm out with work friends for dinner, and Hemi and Hammer invited me over later. Depends on how late dinner goes, though." She tucks her phone in her purse and slides her feet into her shoes. Her cheeks flush pink and the tips of her ears turn red with the lie.

"Right. Okay. That's great that you're making friends at work." Flip lifts his head. "You're liking the job, then?"

"Yeah. It's good. You guys have a good day." She heads for the door.

"Your coffee." I hold it out to her.

"Right. Thanks." Our fingers brush, and our eyes meet for a second. If Flip wasn't here, I would kiss her. Instead, I watch her walk out the door.

Tonight, she's all mine. No interruptions, no being quiet, no her sneaking back up to the loft, no feeling guilty that we're lying to Flip. Or less feeling guilty. It's getting harder to remember not to touch her when he's around.

"We should go, too." I put the lid on my travel mug and grab my car keys.

"Sounds good."

"Thanks for agreeing to come with me today," I say once we're on the way to the arena.

"No problem. It'll win me points with Hemi." He digs into the fruit and yogurt parfait Bea made this morning. It's got all his favorite fruits, high-protein yogurt, and a separate container of granola and nuts to preserve the crunch. "How are you feeling about our next exhibition game?"

I tap the wheel. "Okay. I get why Coach wants to start Hollis on the first line."

"You know it has nothing to do with you not being the better player, right? They want to be careful with Hollis this season and playing him on first line when he's fresh is better for him," Flip says.

"I know. It's a rough transition from last year. I'm still hoping I'll be on the starting line for the opening game of the season."

"You will," Flip assures me.

I want to believe he's right, but I don't know where I stand. Hollis has been visiting Coach regularly. Lots of private meetings. He's upped his PT to make sure he's in good condition for the start of the season. It's tough not to worry about where my value to the team will fall. If Hollis makes a comeback, will I slide down the ranks again? Was last year the highlight of my career?

I sigh. "Maybe. We'll see."

"It'll be fine," he says through a mouthful of yogurt. "Man, this is good. I should have taken two." He scrapes the bottom of the container with his spoon.

"I've got those almond muffins in my bag, if you're still hungry." I thumb over my shoulder.

"Really? I didn't even know Rix made those."

That's because I asked her to, and because I hid them so Flip wouldn't eat them all before I could. "Save me at least one."

He pulls the plastic container out of my bag. "Damn, you've been holding out!" He pops the lid. "You want one?"

"Sure. Yeah." He passes me a muffin.

He eats the first one in two bites, crumbs falling into the container in his lap. "You and Rix seem to get along better these days."

He doesn't know the half of it. I accidentally inhale a crumb and start coughing. Thankfully, we hit a red light, so I set the muffin on the dash and cough into my elbow. When I've got myself under control, I wash it down with coffee. "She's helpful around the condo," I offer.

"Yeah, it's been nice having meals prepped, and not having to do the groceries and stuff. I know it's been a lot having her in the loft, and she's looking for an apartment, but I don't want her to end up in the same position again. She was looking at some place a few blocks from her work, but the neighborhood wasn't the best, so I told her to skip it."

"It's fine if she stays a while longer. We're traveling soon anyway, so we won't be there half the time." My stomach tightens. I don't want her to move, but the guilt is eating at me.

"I appreciate you being cool about it. I know you two rub each other the wrong way."

I grip the wheel tighter and fight with myself not to confess. If I do, this thing with Bea ends, and I want that less than I want to unload my conscience. "I don't mind her."

He snorts a laugh. "You don't mind having someone picking up after us."

"Nah, man. I mean, that part is nice, but she's cool to hang out with. She's got good taste in movies, and she's smart as hell. I just didn't want someone else to look after."

"She's too proud sometimes. I wish she'd let me help her with rent. Then she could get a decent place."

"She doesn't want to mooch off you."

His expression reflects surprise. "She say something to you about it?"

I scramble for something plausible. "I overheard her talking to Essie. You paid for her university, right? Maybe she thinks that's enough. Plus, she's living with us rent free."

"Yeah, but she's taken over as our personal chef and housekeeper. And she's managing my finances, and the change has made me like twelve grand in interest since she's been living with us, so it's not like she's loafing around, playing video games. And I only paid for what her scholarship didn't cover. She worked a part-time job throughout university to cover her rent and stuff. I think I gave her twenty grand," he says.

"Twenty thousand is a big deal to her, no?" I reply. "This new job she has. What does it pay? Like sixty grand a year or something?" I don't even know the answer to that. And I feel like I should. We spend most of our time together naked, but sometimes we talk after, before she falls asleep.

He frowns. "I don't know. I never asked."

"Renting an apartment in Toronto is expensive." I tap the steering wheel. "A nice studio is around two thousand a month. If she's making between sixty and eighty thousand a year, twenty-five to thirty of that goes to rent. She's pretty careful with her money. She price matches groceries every week."

He glances at me. "How do you know that?"

"The flyers are always covered in Sharpie, and she makes a spreadsheet. She leaves them on the counter." I've also tried to entice her into sex when she's been in the middle of price matching more than once. She gets really fucking annoyed.

"Huh. I didn't realize that."

I bite my tongue. If he hung out with her more he might have a goddamn clue about his sister. Then again, he might also realize what's going on. It's getting harder to keep this secret for a lot of reasons. I pull into the arena parking lot, which thankfully ends the conversation.

My brother is already dressed in his gear, so we get changed and meet him on the ice.

"Damn, Brody." Flip claps him on the shoulder. "You're filling out, eh?"

He grins. "Been spending a lot of time at the gym lately."

"Yeah, you are. Bet the girls are all over you," Flip says.

"Sorta, yeah." He rubs the back of his neck. "Can we take a couple of pics for my socials?"

"For sure."

We flank Brody while he takes selfies.

"You're gonna be eighteen soon, right?" Flip asks while Brody posts a photo.

He sets his phone on the bench. "Yeah. Thanksgiving weekend."

"Next year we'll take you to the bar to celebrate, show you a real good time." Flip winks.

Brody looks to me like he's unsure.

"Your version of a real good time won't win any points with our dad," I say. "But we can definitely take Brody out for dinner and feed him too many beers."

"There's always booze at hockey parties. It's not like I've never been drunk before," Brody gripes.

I'm not surprised. I was drinking at parties at his age, but I worry about what he's getting himself into.

The kids show up. I brought my Polaroid so we can autograph pictures and add them to the swag bags.

We spend the next two hours on the ice. It's great to see Brody with these kids. He's a natural, and they adore him. And he's a skilled teacher. Flip is good at encouraging the kids and giving Brody pointers on how to help them.

Halfway through, a few girls show up to watch.

"Looks like you got some fans." Flip tips his head to the group sitting on the bench.

They look like they're ready for the club, not watching hockey. And they're a bit of a distraction for the kids on the ice.

Brody mutters an expletive under his breath but spins it into *fudge*. He gives them a tight-lipped smile and waves but refocuses his attention on the kids. It's good to see he's got his priorities straight. For now.

At the end of our practice, we pass out the swag bags and take a team photo before we hit the locker room. Brody is hickey free this time, but when pass through the lobby, the girls are waiting around for him. A dark-haired girl breaks rank and rushes over to throw her arms around his neck. He gives her his cheek when she tries to kiss him.

A girl with strawberry-blonde hair stares uncomfortably at her feet. She's wearing a hoodie with the name of Brody's high school on it.

Brody introduces us, and it isn't until after we sign a few napkins and give them leftover swag that Lana, the girl who's all over my brother, asks if he's going to the party this weekend.

He's noncommittal about it, saying he has games and home-work, but maybe if he can swing it.

"Got yourself some real fangirls, eh?" Flip says once the girls leave.

Brody stuffs his hands in his pockets. "The one who was all over me is that girl I told you about."

"The pushy one?" I ask.

He nods. "And Enid, the redhead, is the one I like. Liked. It's just awkward, and there's nothing I can do to fix it."

I clap him on the shoulder. I wish I had some advice, but my relationship history isn't great. Realistically, if he's drafted, he'll end up playing for a university team before he gets called up. The attention he gets now will only compound. But I don't tell him that. "I'm sorry, Brody. It's a shitty position to be in for sure." I invite him out for a bite to eat, hoping I can get him to open up more about the situation. But he has a school project, so I drive him to his friend's house instead.

"He's a good kid, eh?" Flip observes as Brody waves goodbye.

"Yeah, he is." I'm worried about that girl who won't back off. He doesn't seem comfortable with her, and she seems clueless about it. "I don't think he's ready for what it'll be like if he makes the pros."

"He's solid on the ice," Flip observes. "A few years playing university level and he'll be ready for the pros."

I'm about to tell him that's not what I meant, but I decide to leave it alone. Flip doesn't mind the attention. And for a while, I was right there with him. But now I see what Hemi meant about consequences, and not just with my brother, but with Bea, too. That Stacey situation was shitty. I hated everything about it. And then there was Essie's visit. I know Bea needs time with her, but it made me hyperaware of how much I wish I could touch her just to touch. It's too risky with Flip around, though.

After practice, Flip and some of the guys suggest going out for dinner, but I tell them I have plans to meet my dad.

What I actually do is drive across town and get everything ready for my night with Bea before I pick her up from work. When she comes out of her office building, she's wearing sunglasses even though it's overcast, and she rushes to the car, throwing herself inside and sliding down.

"What are you doing?"

"Being incognito. You drive an expensive, flashy car."

"It's not that flashy or expensive." Not compared to the cars my teammates drive. Although next to Flip's ride, my Mercedes is pretty sweet.

"You should go." She motions to the windshield.

I slide a hand under her hair and curve my palm around the back of her neck. "Come here."

"What?"

I lean in and tug her toward me, but she resists. "I want your lips."

"What if people see us?"

"The windows are tinted. Come here, Bea." I caress her cheek with my thumb.

She relents, and I claim her lips. I curve my other hand around the front of her throat, and she moans.

"I would finger-fuck you right here if there wasn't a police car parked across the street," I say against her lips.

She wrenches her mouth free. "What? Where?"

"Maybe I should anyway." I drop my hand to her thigh and bite the edge of her jaw.

"Fuck that. I don't want an indecent-exposure charge."

"I'm kidding, Bea. There's no police. But I wouldn't mind fucking you in my car sometime." Then it would smell like her, and I'd have that memory until I traded in my car. Or maybe I'd keep it forever.

"That would probably be tragically awkward." She fastens her seat belt.

"You're bendy. We'd make it work." I adjust my hard-on and signal into traffic.

"What's the plan? Are we going to a hotel so we can order room service and fuck like bunnies?"

"That's later. I have something else planned first." Do I want to be inside her? Absolutely. But I want this time with her more.

"I'm still in my work clothes, though. And we can't go out in public. You're way too recognizable, and people would take pictures. Then Flip would find out. We can't have sex if he kills you, or me, or both of us. Besides, I haven't found an apartment yet—not that I would need it if Flip killed me."

I push down the guilt over the lies we're telling, and the uncomfortable feeling that comes with having to hide what's going on. "Don't worry. We're not going out in public, and the place we're staying is private, so you don't have to worry about Flip." A few times over the past week I've considered what would happen if I told Flip. He'd be pissed off at first, but eventually he'd get over it. Wouldn't he?

But I don't want to put that on Bea, or strain their relationship. Not with her parents hours away and her best friend in Vancouver. Besides, I don't have a great track record with actual relationships, and I can't imagine she'd want more from me than fun between the sheets and maybe the occasional secret date night. Hopefully she wants that.

She seems to relax a little. "So where exactly are we going before we get our fuck on?"

"It's a surprise."

"A surprise?" She shifts in her seat, angling her body toward me, eyes lit up with excitement. "Can I guess?"

"If you want." I like this. Making her happy feels good.

She taps her lips as we drive across town. That I pulled this off is a damn miracle.

"Are you taking me to an escape room?"

"No. Not an escape room."

"Drive-in movie?"

I snort.

She bites the end of her finger. "So, it's not in public, and it's not an escape room or a movie. What about a virtual experience? Like a virtual sex show or something."

"I don't know if those things exist, and even if they do, we could just get those VR headsets and watch it in the privacy of a hotel room," I point out.

She keeps lobbing ridiculous ideas at me, and I keep knocking them down until we arrive at the restaurant. It's cozy, with only twelve tables, but they have the most amazing dining experience and a chef who's also a certified dietician. She's worked for some of the best hockey players out there. She retired a few years ago and opened this place. It's by reservation only. I park in the back and get out of the car, rounding the hood in time to open Bea's door.

"Are we playing underground poker or something?"

"Nope. You're out of guesses. Come on." I extend my hand.

She stares at it for a few seconds before she finally takes it. I lead her down the stairs.

"Please tell me you're not taking me to some secret underground sex club," she says when I knock on the door.

I snort. "No one touches you but me."

"And Essie. She's my cuddle friend."

I make a noise in the back of my throat. Can't say I was sorry to see Essie go.

The door opens, and Eliza Van Horn smiles widely. "Right on time, Tristan. Come on in." She ushers us inside and turns her bright smile on Bea. "And this must be Beatrix. I've heard such lovely things about you."

Bea's gaze shifts to me and back to Eliza. "Really?" She extends her hand. "That's, uh… It's nice to meet you. I go by Rix mostly." She side-eyes me. "Or sometimes Bea."

Eliza introduces herself, and I see the moment it clicks for Bea. Her head whips my way. "Is this for real?"

I nod and tuck my hands in my pockets as she turns back to Eliza. "You were the lead nutritional consultant for professional

229

hockey players in Ontario. I've read two of your books. I love your recipes."

"I hear you're quite talented in the kitchen." She motions for us to follow her through the restaurant.

"Oh, I don't know about that. This guy was living on stale pizza and sugary cereal, so anything is a step up from that." Bea gives me wide eyes and mouths, *Oh my God*.

"She's being modest," I say.

"I'm not—oh!" Bea comes to an abrupt halt when we reach the entrance to the kitchen. It's set up with ingredients laid out on the metal work surfaces. "Are we cooking? With you?" she asks Eliza.

"She's teaching us how to make her famous stuffed ravioli."

Bea's mouth drops open, and she brings her hand up to cover it. "You set this up for us?"

"I thought you might like it."

She waves her hands in front of her face. "I get to cook with Eliza Van Horn! Like, what?"

"And me. Don't forget that part."

She shoves my shoulder and wraps her arms around my waist. I give her a squeeze and kiss the top of her head. Yeah, it's totally worth the guilt and sneaking around to see her this happy.

"You two are so cute." Eliza hands us aprons and shows us around the kitchen.

Bea keeps squeezing my hand and grinning. She's giddy, and it's fucking adorable.

Bea is naturally gifted when it comes to cooking pretty much anything. It turns out, I'm not. Which I already knew since the only thing I'm proficient at are boxed frozen food from the grocery store, grilled cheese, and egg sandwiches. I kind of like the way we work as a team, though, and how patient she is when I don't get something right the first time. When I was a kid, my mom would freak out if I made mistakes. But you can't get it wrong if you don't try at all.

Bea slides between me and the prep table so she can show me how to knead pasta dough properly. "Gently, but firmly, Tristan. You don't have to pound everything into submission."

Eliza's in the back getting more fresh Parmesan. I wrap my arm around her waist and whisper, "Should I take notes for later?"

"Even I appreciate a gentle touch on occasion. Especially when I'm getting railed every night of the week."

The fridge door closes. I release her and step to the side before Eliza appears.

Bea gives me a sidelong glance.

"Duly noted on the gentle touch," I murmur.

We make three types of ravioli, marinara and vodka sauce, a salad, and chocolate lava cake for dessert. Bea and Eliza chat like old friends, and I love how animated they are. This is her passion, like hockey is mine. They talk about the science of feeding athletes. When our diets need more protein, when simple fuels and complex carbohydrates are best. Why loading up on cereal meant to entice small children is terrible before a game. This explains why, even when I was being a giant asshole, she still made meals for me and Flip. She loves doing it more than she hated me.

When we sit down to eat, Eliza brings us a bottle of wine and disappears into the kitchen, saying she'll keep an eye on dessert and bring it out once it's ready.

Bea's smile fills her entire face. I can't get enough of it.

"I can't believe you set this up," she says. "No one has ever done anything this thoughtful for me before."

"No one?" Hasn't anyone else ever paid attention to what makes Bea tick?

"Not really. I mean, I've gone out for nice dinners, but this is...it's really sweet."

"I had some help," I admit.

"From who?" Bea cuts into her ravioli and drags it through the sauce. She pops the bite in her mouth, and her eyes flutter closed on a soft moan. "Oh, this is fantastic. I'll never eat store-bought stuff again." Her eyes open, and she looks at me expectantly. "Well?"

"Well, what?"

"Why are you looking at me like that?"

"Keep moaning and we'll be visiting the bathroom together," I warn.

She rolls her eyes. "You have me all night."

"I know. My plans for you later are extensive."

"No doubt. So, who helped you plan this?"

"Roman has worked with Eliza in the past, and Hemi has connections, so I called in a favor."

She pauses with her fork halfway to her mouth.

"Do you think Roman would say something to Flip?" She worries her bottom lip.

"It's not his business to tell. And I trust him."

She nods slowly. "Okay."

It's on the tip of my tongue to ask her if we can amend the pact, but Eliza comes out with sparkling water. When she leaves us alone again, the moment and my nerve have passed.

"You should really rethink the whole dietician thing. I think you'd be great at it," I say.

"I'd have to go back to school for four more years, though. And come up with the money for that. Besides, I have a perfectly good degree that makes me a solid salary. It would be a waste of money to walk away from that."

"What if you didn't have to walk away entirely? You can still manage Flip's portfolio. You could use your accounting degree and work in nutrition with sports teams. There has to be a way to pair those two things."

"I can't afford another four years in school." She cuts her last ravioli into four small bites and spears one. It must be cold by now. "It's too hard financially."

"Money shouldn't be the thing that prevents you from achieving your dreams," I argue. Flip could put her through school, and so could I, but explaining that would be hard. And she wouldn't accept it from me. "Eliza teaches some courses. What if you started with just one? Or a night course? Not too expensive and then at least you could see if it's something you wanted to pursue?"

"Maybe something to consider in the future. Some people spend their lives chasing dreams. I've spent mine chasing financial stability," she says softly.

"It's okay to change your mind and decide you want to chase something else," I counter.

"What else do you want, aside from an illustrious career as a professional hockey player?" She pops the last bite of her ravioli into her mouth.

You, I want to say. *For this not to end. For the things I'm afraid of not to ruin this. To give you the things you want. To make you smile like this every day.*

But I don't say any of that. "To win the Cup before my career is over." I don't want to talk about hockey right now, though, not when things feel unsteady there. I glance toward the kitchen to make sure Eliza isn't around and drop my voice, changing gears. "And to hear you scream my name when we're alone later."

"Well, I can definitely guarantee you the second if I don't end up in a food coma."

"Should we take dessert with us? Save it for later?" I want to be alone with her. If there's one thing I'm skilled at, it's making her feel good in bed.

She bites her lip. "Might be a nice midnight snack."

We thank Eliza, and she invites Bea to come back any time for a free cooking class. She sends us off with leftover ravioli, sauces, and our desserts. I don't know that the whipped cream with the cakes will make it, but that's a risk I'm willing to take.

I drive us to the house I rented for the night—another favor I called in. Hotels are great, but we'd have neighbors, and I don't want Bea to hold back. I want those moans, and sighs, and shrieks, and giggles.

"Whose house is this?" Bea asks when I pull into the garage.

"A friend."

"What kind of friend?" She side-eyes me.

"A guy I used to play hockey with in New York."

"You went to a lot of trouble to set this up, didn't you?"

"It wasn't trouble, and it was totally worth it." I grab our leftovers from the back seat and extend my hand.

She slips her palm into mine. I like this kind of easy contact. I wish I could do it more often.

I lead her through the house, put the food in the fridge, and grab the bottle of champagne I had in there. "Let me show you the rest of the place."

"You mean the bedroom, right?"

"If that's what you want to see first."

I stop at the second door and flip on the light.

"This is like something out of a freaking fairy tale." She bites her lip and hugs my arm. "You better be careful, or I'll start thinking maybe you actually like me."

I skim her cheek with my fingers. "I do like you, Bea."

"You like my vagina." She nudges my arm with her shoulder. "The rest of me annoys the shit out of you."

"I am a big fan of your pussy, but"—I curve a hand around the back of her neck, brushing my lips across her cheek—"the rest of you is pretty great too."

Before I can claim her lips, she spins out of my grip and grabs her bag from the end of the bed. "Hold that thought for like two minutes."

"What?" I move toward her.

She holds up a finger as she races across the room. "Two minutes. I need two minutes." She disappears into the bathroom and slams the door. The lock flips as my fingers wrap around the knob.

I knock a few times. Gently. "Don't make me break this door down, Bea."

"Two minutes. I promise it'll be worth the wait!" she calls.

234

I brace a hand on either side of the door. I want to spend all night worshiping every inch of her. No worrying about Flip. No going back to her own bed. I want to wake up beside her. I need to amend this pact we've made. Two minutes later, the door swings open.

"Sweet fuck." She looks like my favorite sin. She's dressed in black, strappy, lacy lingerie.

"Worth it?" She bites her lip and ducks her head, looking up at me from under her lashes.

"More than worth it." I take her hand and lead her to the bed. I tap the edge, then wrap my hands around her waist. "Up you go."

She folds her legs under her and kneels at the edge of the bed in front of me. I drink her in as she raises a hand, trailing her fingers down my arm. When she reaches my hand, she moves it to skim her waist, lifting it so my fingers graze the swell of her breast. She drags it higher, over her collarbones until my palm rests against her throat. Her eyes flutter shut for a moment as she adjusts the position, and then her fingers rest over mine, pressing them into her delicate flesh.

"Fuck, Bea." I curve the other hand around the back of her neck and brush my lips over hers. "I'm sorry if this lingerie doesn't make it through the night, but I will definitely replace it if I ruin it."

I move my mouth over hers but remember what she said about being gentle. I should probably start off easy if I don't want to wear her out in the first hour.

So I'm soft with her. I kiss her like I'm not in a rush, like she's my favorite ice cream and I'm savoring her. When I stretch out between her thighs, I'm all soft strokes of tongue and teasing nips, and when I push inside her, I fuck her with long, lazy strokes. She comes on whimpers and sighs, and I find I want her soft pleas for more. I want her wrapped around me when she unravels. I like how gentle feels with her. I want to stay here, in this bubble where the guilt doesn't eat at me and there doesn't have to be an end.

When we're both spent, I gather her up and arrange her so I can breathe in her shampoo. I kiss the back of her neck. "Stop looking for an apartment for a while."

Her fingers drift over the backs of mine. I lace them together. "We start traveling soon. Just stay until the end of October at least."

"Okay," she whispers.

"Yeah?"

"Yeah."

I kiss the back of her neck. "I promise I'll make it worth it."

Her breath evens out a few minutes later.

"I wish I could keep you happy like this forever," I murmur. "I wish I deserved to." But I don't know if I'm capable of making anyone happy long term. So I'll keep her as long as she'll let me.

I wake up at six in the morning and pat the mattress, but all I find are cold, tangled sheets. "Bea? Come back to bed!" I call.

But I get no response. I sit up and scrub a hand over my face. My phone is on the nightstand. I have a text from Bea. A long one.

She said she would stay, and she's gone. She fucking left me. Memories surface, the kind that make me want to punch things. To rip the whole house apart.

My stomach twists, and panic makes my throat tight. My hands shake. I hate this weakness. Hate that I'm suddenly sweaty and nauseated. I grit my teeth as I scan the first few lines.

#1

> I'm sorry you're waking up alone. I didn't want to leave, but I worried if neither of us was home in the morning, Flip might realize something is up. And if I'm sticking around until the end of October, I don't want to give him a reason to be suspicious.

Last night was amazing. It was fun and thoughtful and completely unexpected. Thank you for doing that for me. I wish I could have stayed. I wanted to, but I didn't want to take that kind of risk. There's a thank you blow job with your name on it the next time you get me alone. (ɔ◦◦_◦)ɔ ♥

I read the message over three times. For a few seconds, it felt like someone had put my heart in a vise. I rub my chest, trying to relieve the ache. I get her reason for leaving, but the secrecy is harder to deal with. I'd rather have more last nights and waking up with her beside me than the promise of a BJ.

Maybe Roman is right. Maybe these feelings for Bea are real. I guess I bought myself some more time to figure shit out.

CHAPTER 17

RIX

There's a shift with Tristan after our date night. He's the first person to text me in the morning and the last person to text me at night. And he's more affectionate. Or as affectionate as he'll allow himself to be. He'll come up behind me and wrap an arm around my waist. His other hand ends up around my throat. He'll nuzzle into my hair and press his lips to my skin. At first, I expected him to whisper something dirty in my ear, but he just stands there, breathing me in for a minute. Then he kisses my cheek and walks away.

As the first game of the season approaches, I hold off on looking for an apartment, like Tristan asked. Eventually this has to end, but I'm in no rush to get there. And it seems he isn't either. We're definitely not hate-fucking anymore. But qualifying it as anything else seems like a bad idea.

It's a Saturday afternoon, and Tristan is working out with Dallas and Roman. I'm prepping meals. I want them eating the right food for peak performance.

Flip walks into the condo looking like he needs a nap and a shower. "Hey, sis." He gives me a side hug, and points to a freshly made yogurt parfait. "Can I eat this?"

"Of course." I pass him a spoon and the box of granola.

238

"Thanks." He takes a seat across from me, and dumps granola on top. "I haven't seen much of you lately," he says before he digs in.

"That's because you've been keeping the bunnies happy." I squeeze lemon juice on the apple chunks and add those to another parfait. The apple cinnamon ones are Tristan's favorite, whereas Flip prefers melon.

"Fair. You got plans this afternoon? You want to hang out?" he asks.

I stop cutting fruit. "You and me?"

"Yeah. We haven't done much of that since you moved in. Hell, we haven't done much of that since we were kids." He frowns, like this bothers him.

"To be fair, when we were kids, you were forced to bring me along until I could stay home on my own," I point out.

"You got dragged to a lot of street-hockey games and arcades," he muses.

"The street-hockey games I didn't mind. The arcades were boring as hell."

"Wanna play a round of mini putt and eat some East Side's?"

"I could be convinced. I just need to finish up here."

"You want help?"

"I'm good, but thanks."

"Cool. I'll hop in the shower. Then we can roll out."

I put away the prepared food while Flip showers, and when we're both ready, we take the elevator to the parking garage. I bring a cooler bag with an ice pack for my leftovers. I'm always prepared.

"The job is still a good fit? You liking it okay?" Flip asks once we're on the road.

"Yeah. It's so much better than my old job, and more interesting. Thanks for letting me tweak your financial portfolio. It helped during the interview."

"My investments are up more than fifteen grand since you did that."

"That's great!" I can't imagine making fifteen grand in a span of weeks from investments, but it's all relative.

"I had no idea how much I was spending on takeout and bars. Well, I could've guessed about bars, but the takeout was a lot. I'm gonna miss all the good food when you get your own place. And having someone do all the shopping and food prep..." He runs a hand through his hair and frowns. "How are you getting all that shit done and working full time?"

I shrug. "It's no big deal. I like grocery shopping and making meals. It's my happy place, and I'm not paying rent, so this is one way I can contribute."

"We're giving you enough for the groceries? I don't want you spending your money on food when you're doing all the prep and shopping. I know you're used to taking care of that stuff on your own, but I can help," he says.

"Between you and Tristan, there's always more than enough." I don't say anything about my own food budget.

"I noticed the OJ from concentrate, Rix, and the fakle syrup. You don't need to buy separate stuff." That's what we always called fake maple syrup.

"I like it better."

"No you don't." He stops at a light. "You can and should be using what's already there. I get where you're coming from. Logically, unless I develop a serious drug problem, I have enough money to last a couple of lifetimes. Sometimes I worry, but I don't need to. So let me and Tristan take care of the groceries while you're staying with us."

"I never want to go back to the way we were," I admit.

"Me neither. It's why I have all the investments and endorsement campaigns. You're making okay money now, though? They're paying you well?" he asks.

"Yeah. Eighty thousand a year to start, with end-of-quarter bonus opportunities. I should be able to afford a nice studio." I just have to get over paying two thousand a month for four hundred square feet of space.

"How's the hunt for an apartment going?" he asks.

"Okay. I'm probably looking at a November first move date, though." Because Tristan has asked me not to get a place before then.

"Don't worry about it. The season's starting. I want you in a nice place, and I want to help you with that," Flip says.

"You helped with university. I can cover my own rent." He already helps our parents. I can make my own way.

"I know you can, but I can make it easier on you, Rix. So let me, okay?"

"We'll see." I hate taking money from Flip, but he has a point. A little help would open options for a better apartment. "I'm sure you guys would like your game room back."

"Eh, it's been nice having you around—and not just because you're a master at meal prep. We haven't lived in the same house since I was called up. It's been cool seeing you rocking it at life." He taps the steering wheel. "You and Tris seem to be getting along okay. Or at least being civil?"

"Oh yeah. Mostly, we stay out of each other's way." When he's not busy turning me into a human pretzel, anyway.

Or taking me on the most thoughtful date I've ever had.

"He's not a bad guy." Flip sounds defensive.

"I didn't say he was." I honestly think he's a great guy. He's thoughtful, and the way he is with his brothers makes my heart melty. He's a caretaker. Maybe not on purpose, but I see it.

"His mom leaving really fucked him up." Flip stops for a red light. "Like, more than I think he's willing to admit."

"I vaguely remember when that happened, but I was only eight, I think?" I try not to sound too eager for information. Tristan is pretty closed off when it comes to talking about any emotion apart from lust. And sometimes anger or jealousy.

"Her leaving was probably the best thing that happened to that family. She was...not a good mom." He taps on the steering wheel. "Not like ours. I know we struggled a lot, but we were loved. Are loved."

"Yeah, we really are." I message my mom daily, and we talk on the phone twice a week. Though I haven't said anything about Tristan for obvious reasons. My parents couldn't give us financial stability, but they gave us love, and a lot of it.

As if she knows we're talking about her, Mom messages. I set the phone in Flip's holder and take the opportunity to call her.

"Well isn't this lovely! My two babies spending time together." Mom says. "Are you in the car? What are you two up to?"

"Heading to East Side's for lunch."

"You're still doing that once a month?" Mom asks.

"We try."

We chat for a few minutes, Mom asking Flip about the upcoming season and me about my job. My dad has taken a cash job over Thanksgiving weekend, so we'll have to figure out another time to see them. They only have two days off, anyway, so the drive would have been hard to manage.

After we end the call, I ask, "What was Tristan's mom like?" I only met her a few times. His dad would come by and have beers with my dad sometimes, but his mom never came.

"She had a short fuse, and she was hard on everyone. She was always yelling. Always. I don't remember ever being at Tris's house when there *wasn't* a fight. Not until after she left. She went off about anything and everything. Once she even screamed at me. I think I left an empty pop can on the coffee table or something. I remember being confused by how upset she was over something that wouldn't have been a big deal in our house," he says.

"I didn't know it was that bad," I muse.

"Yeah. It was messy. And Tristan took the brunt of it because he was the oldest. He hates yelling. Like, *hates* it. Last year he was seeing this woman for a while, not long, maybe a couple of months, and she threw this absolute fit about something. A picture someone took, maybe? It was out of context, as stuff often is. But she lit right into him. I've never seen anybody shut down the way he does." He runs his hand through his hair, shaking his head at the memory. "She was screaming her head off, and he went into his room, got all her shit, tossed it into the hallway, and told her to get the fuck out. And that was it. He blocked her contact and never spoke to her again."

"Yeesh. Sounds like she needed some anger management."

"Yeah, she was on fire for sure. But he doesn't deal with conflict well."

"Maybe he has his reasons." And it explains so much—like his reaction to me getting upset over the ice cream and cake. Tristan and I push each other's buttons, often on purpose, but he never yells. He gets agitated, and cruel, but he doesn't raise his voice.

"Yeah. And his brother's eighteenth birthday is coming up. He's stressing because he doesn't think their mom will call Brody," Flip confides.

"Why wouldn't his mom call on his birthday? Is she off the grid or something?" Tristan never talks about her. Ever.

"She only ever sends Tris a Christmas card. He hasn't heard from her in years. I guess she was better with his younger brothers, but the past couple of years she's missed Brody's birthday, and she stopped sending cards and calling Nathan a few years back."

"Geez. That's awful." I knew Tristan's relationship with his mom wasn't good, but I didn't know it was this terrible. If my mom didn't remember my birthday, I'd be heartbroken. No wonder he has so many walls.

"Yeah. She's a real gem. Tristan tends to go all out for his brothers on their birthdays. He's getting Brody a car." Flip pulls into East Side's parking lot.

"A car? A real one? Like *vroom-vroom*?" I pat the dashboard.

"Yup. He consulted with his dad and made sure it wasn't something that would get Brody a million speeding tickets or anything. But he did it for Nate, so he's doing it for Brody, too."

"That's sweet, even if it is a bit extra," I say.

Flip and I exit the car and head for the restaurant. The smell of fresh bread and garlic butter instantly makes my mouth water.

"His mom is a waste of air. He's trying to make up for it," he says.

"I can see that. He's doing his best to be a good brother." He's at one of Brody's hockey games right now. This conversation sheds so much light on so many things. Those backwards hugs mean even more now. That's Tristan letting his guard down.

Adelaide is our server again today. We plow through several bowls of salad and loaves of bread. Flip eats his entire meal, and I do what I always do, eat a few bites and save the rest for later. We still get dessert, though.

Afterwards, we head to the indoor glow-in-the-dark mini putt.

By the third hole, I'm kicking his butt. "For a professional hockey player, you sure suck at mini putt."

Flip keeps overshooting. By a lot. He's almost hit three people, and he can't get the ball in the hole in fewer than seven tries. Even the five-year-olds are better than he is.

"Shh... You're killing my concentration with all your smack talk." He takes a few practice swings.

My phone buzzes in my pocket. I pull it out. Tristan wants to know where I am and whether I feel like bouncing on his cock. Obviously, I'd love to, but seeing as I'm with my brother, who is still unaware that we're fucking on the regular, sex will have to wait.

RIX

I already have my hands full with balls and sticks.

I snap a quick pic of my golf club and neon yellow ball and send that along.

TRISTAN

Is that glow-in-the-dark mini putt?

244

RIX

Yup

TRISTAN

Who are you with?

RIX

Flip

TRISTAN

Oh. Cool. I was two seconds away from plotting a murder FYI

RIX

Why I sent the photo.

jellyfish gif

He ignores the dig.

TRISTAN

Which location are you at?

RIX

The one close to Vaughn.

TRISTAN

I'm coming to play with balls too while I wait for you to play with mine

RIX

Uh. Maybe text Flip in five first, otherwise the jig is up????

TRISTAN

Right.

RIX

Got excited about having your balls slapping my chin later, eh?

TRISTAN

Maybe. *shifty eyes*

"Hey, Rix, you're up." Flip snaps his fingers.

"Right. Sorry."

"Who are you texting?"

"Just the girls. We're getting together sometime next week for dinner at Hemi's." This is not untrue, and they did text a couple of hours ago, but I told them I was with Flip and I'd catch up with them later.

"You're spending a lot of time with those girls lately, eh?" Flip stands off to the side while I take my first putt and get it within a foot of the hole.

"Yeah. They're great. And it was super nice of Hemi to help me get that interview." I approach the ball and try to decide what angle to hit it from.

"I would've put in a word for you." He almost sounds hurt.

"I know, but this feels less like direct nepotism. I've gotten more than enough legs up from you." I miss the hole the first time, but now I'm only six inches away.

"But Mom and Dad funneled most of their savings into my hockey, so me helping you out is balancing the scales," he argues.

"They saw your talent and were smart about making sure it was realized." This time I get the ball in the hole. This is the hard part of growing up in a family where money was tight. Now that Flip is making a lot, he feels like he owes everyone something. We all knew he was going to be a shining star. Investing in his future was a sure thing.

"You have lots of talents, too. Like outside of financial planning, which you're amazing at, you know exactly how to feed us for games. That's a huge skill. Players pay a lot to have someone do what you're doing for me and Tris. I had no idea you were good at that stuff. Well, that's not entirely true. You could always cook. It's like you were born to dominate the kitchen." He makes a face. "Sorry, that probably sounds sexist."

"It would be sexist if you said I was born to be a kept housewife. And I love that I get to do that for you." I pick up my ball, and we move to the next hole.

"My energy levels have been way up, and I know you're the reason." He sets up his ball for the putt.

"They'd be even better if you spent more nights actually sleeping," I mutter.

"I'll slow down during the season." His phone pings, and he checks the message. "Uh, you okay if Tristan joins us?"

"Sure. That's fine." I roll the ball around between my fingers.

"It's okay if you'd rather he didn't," Flip says.

"Do *you* not want him to come?"

"Sometimes you two get under each other's skin."

He doesn't know the half of it. How upset would he be? How betrayed would he feel? I don't want to risk telling him to find out. "It's seriously fine."

"If you're sure…" He sounds unsure.

"Really. I promise not to bludgeon him to death with a putter." I give Flip two thumbs-up.

"That's not super reassuring."

I roll my eyes. "Just tell him to come. We can be civil."

"Okay." He still looks skeptical as he fires off another message. "Looks like he'll be here in ten minutes. Should we step aside and wait for him?"

"We could go back to the beginning and start over? Or he could skip the first few holes?"

"Tristan won't want to skip holes."

I cover a snicker by coughing into my arm. "So we wait here or we go back to the beginning. Up to you." We step aside for a birthday party of seven-year-olds and supervising parents who are trying to keep the boys from using their putters as swords. Someone ends up getting hit in the shin and starts crying. That makes our decision to go back to the beginning easy.

Tristan arrives a minute later.

"It smells like the inside of a sneaker in here," he complains.

"That should not be a surprise." I inspect my nails so I don't eye-fuck him. He's wearing a pair of dark wash distressed jeans and a black T-shirt with his brother's hockey team logo. He's also wearing black running shoes and a black belt. He looks delicious and entirely too fuckable for his own good. "If I remember correctly, your running shoes used to smell like something died in them."

"If you two could not bicker for the next hour, that would be awesome," Flip grouses.

"She's not wrong. My running shoes had a funk when I was a teenager. I learned later it was because my asshole cat took a dump in them."

"Oh, shit! I remember that!" Flip laughs.

A mom gives him the stink-eye.

"Sorry. My bad." He motions for them to pass. "You go ahead of us."

We step off to the side so the mom and her two kids can putt putt their way to happiness. "How did you figure that out?" I ask.

"We watched the cat go into the closet and cop a squat over his shoe." Flip chuckles.

"I guess my brother accidentally locked the cat in the closet once, and he did his business in my shoe while he was in there. My brother dumped out the mess, but the damage was done. And he kept doing it every time the closet was left open."

"Why didn't your brother just fess up in the first place?" I ask.

"They were Tristan's lucky shoes. He wore them to every game," Flip replies.

"Ah." I nod knowingly. "Superstition shoes."

Tristan rubs his bottom lip. "I tried everything to get the smell out, but eventually I had to get a new pair. I swear it was the reason we lost our chance in the playoffs that year. And to the second worst team in the freaking league."

"Or it was because our team captain broke his ankle on the ski hill the week before and our number one goalie got mono and couldn't stay awake for more than fifteen minutes at a time,"

Flip counters. "But yeah, it totally could've been because your cat took dumps in your shoes and you had to replace them."

I tip my head. "I didn't know you were superstitious."

"Just about certain things." He swings his club. "Who's ready to get their as—paragus handed to them?" He amends his swear on account of the family behind us.

The tween girl giggles.

We start again. With Tristan added to the mix, Flip's competitive side comes out. He still keeps overshooting. And I keep hitting the balls within inches of the hole.

Tristan steps up and gives Flip a chin tip. "Watch and learn, Madden." He takes a golfer's stance, and I try not to ogle his butt. "You're not trying to slam the balls into submission. Caress the balls. Be firm but gentle." He smirks as he taps the ball. It rolls along the turf and circles the hole, dropping in on one shot. "That's how it's done."

It's my turn, so I step up and take aim. I fully expect I'll need a second shot, but to my surprise, I sink it in one.

"For fuck's sake," Flip mutters.

"Nice shot. Looks like you know how to handle your balls." Tristan turns to Flip. "You're up. Any words of wisdom, Bea?"

"Firm and gentle. Tap, don't slap."

He overshoots again, and we heckle him.

Every time Flip is up, Tristan stands beside me, and we talk shit. He also keeps touching me. A soft brush of fingers down the back of my arm, skimming my hand, sliding under my hair to squeeze my neck. They're all innocent touches, and it's dark so the balls, sticks, and courses can glow, but they ramp me up all the same, because Flip is right here. Of all the naughty things we've done, this feels particularly scandalous. I don't want to ruin what we have by slipping up and making a mistake, but it's hard to keep my hands to myself.

By the time we reach the end of the course, Flip is seriously annoyed because he's had his ass handed to him by both of us. Tristan suggests we drop the cars off at the condo and walk over to the pub. Philly is playing against New York in an exhibition game. Kodiak Bowman, one of the most sought-after rookies in the league, started his career with Philly but got traded to New York along with another member of his team. His dad played professional hockey for years, and Kodiak is on track to blow all his records out of the water. It doesn't hurt that he's nice to look at, either.

We grab a table with a great view of the game and order drinks and appetizers. I'm tucked into the corner with Flip beside me and Tristan across from me. These booths are bigger than the ones at East Side's, but despite that, Tristan manspreads into my leg room. When he feels my foot against his shin, he lifts it and tucks it beside his leg.

"New York is playing tight." The score is already two-zip and Bowman has a goal and an assist.

Flip glances at the screen as Connor Grace, another recent trade, takes a shot on net. "I can't stand that guy," he mutters, then turns his attention back to Tristan. "How was Brody's tournament, anyway?"

"Good. They won the first two games, lost the third, but pulled it together in the fourth and won the final. Brody really needed the wins. He played well and scored a bunch of goals, which is good because he's had a few off games recently, and he's a lot like me and gets up in his head." Tristan kneads my calf under the table as the server drops off our drinks.

"I'm glad they won. That's good for him. Any scouts at the game?" Flip asks.

Tristan nods. "A couple recognized me. There was one from Ottawa and one from Montreal. The ones from the States usually come up later in the year. But they're looking at him, so that's good news."

"Is he excited about his birthday?" Flip takes another swig of his beer.

"Yeah. And it falls between games this year, so I'll be able to celebrate with him. Are you two visiting the 'rents for Thanksgiving?" Tristan motions between us.

I shake my head. "My dad took a job on Sand Lake. He's working the whole weekend for cash, so we said we'd find another weekend to do the turkey thing."

"Do you want to come to my dad's? Nate is coming back from uni for the weekend. Brody has games on Saturday, but he's off Sunday and Monday, so we're deep-frying a turkey in the backyard. There's always way too much food and leftovers for days." Tristan's gaze shifts to me. "You're both welcome to join us." He squeezes my leg, then runs his hand through his hair.

"I'm down for deep-fried turkey," Flip says and looks to me.

"Sure, that'd be great. I can bring pumpkin pie, or whatever kind of pie you want. Tell your dad I'm happy to help with whatever."

"Pecan pie. I want pecan pie. And your candied sweet potatoes," Flip says.

"I can do both. All three even."

"Cool." Tristan's smile is genuine. "I'll let my dad know you're in."

CHAPTER 18
TRISTAN

"Hey, Stiles, come to my office when you're showered, yeah?" Coach says as the team heads for the locker room.

"Yeah, sure. Is everything okay?" I had a good practice, and last game I scored a goal and an assist.

"Yup, just want to have a word." His smile is tight, though, which worries me.

Flip claps me on the shoulder. "Stay out of your head, man. You've been killing it on the ice lately. I'm sure it's good news."

"Yeah." But I can't shake the heavy feeling in my stomach as I change out of my gear and shower.

Flip offers to wait for me, but there's a free lunch buffet, so I tell him I'll meet him up there. I knock on the door to Coach's office and wait until he tells me to come in.

He and Jamie Fielding, the GM, are sitting at his small conference table, papers strewn across it. He shuffles them into a pile and slides them into a manila folder. "Have a seat, Tristan."

I drop into a chair and try not to fidget. "What's up?" I don't love their expressions. It's like they're trying to keep them neutral.

"We wanted to talk to you about the starting lineup for the opening game." Coach taps his pen on his knee.

I glance between them. Yeah, this isn't reassuring. All my gains from last season are slipping through my fingers. My value to the team isn't where I want it to be. "You're starting Hollis, aren't you?"

Coach raises his hand. "It has nothing to do with your performance on the ice. Your preseason play has been top tier, and you're on track to have a great season if you keep it up."

"So why aren't I starting the game?" I cross one leg over the other, then uncross them. I'm restless and frustrated.

"Hollis is strong at the beginning of the game," Coach says.

"He's been out for almost an entire season, and he's been playing for Toronto for nearly half of his career," Fielding adds.

I can read between the lines. It's good for team morale to start Hollis on the first line for the opening game. He's a fan favorite, and he's part of the fabric of this team. He's taken the Cup home twice. I nod slowly. "So I'm second line opening game?"

"We'll put you on first line for the second game of the season," Coach says.

"Okay. You know what's best for the team." My mouth feels full of cotton. "Is that all?"

"That's all." Coach and the GM exchange a look. "This isn't a reflection of your on-ice performance, Tristan."

"Yeah. I get it. I can go?" I do get it, but it rattles my confidence. What's coming at the end of the season if this is how we're starting?

"You can go. Get some rest. Tomorrow's a big day," Coach says.

I leave the office feeling worse than I did when I went in. I want Bea. I want to lose myself in the feel of her under me. I want her to look at me like I'm a fucking god. It's Friday. She should be home in an hour. I can get inside her and release some of this tension.

I'm on the way out of the arena when I run into the last person I want to see.

"Tristan! Hey, man, can I have a word?"

I turn to face Hollis. "Now really isn't a good time, man."

He raises his hands. "I know you're upset about tomorrow. You have every right to be." The empathy on his face makes me want to punch him. "I know it's shitty for you, and you deserve to start this game, but you've got a lot of great years of play left, man. Lots more opening games of the season to start. This will be a rock-star year for you. Just know this isn't about you."

"I get it. See you tomorrow." I walk away. I know I'm being an asshole, but it's the best I can do right now. I understand their reasoning, but it doesn't make it suck any less.

Flip messages to let me know he's meeting a "friend" for some pre-game stress relief. That means he'll probably be occupied for at least a few hours.

I slide into the driver's seat and message Bea.

TRISTAN
I'm on my way home and I'm in a shit mood.

Might be a good idea to vacate the premises if you're not interested in being ridden hard

#1
Thanks for the warning. What about Flip?

TRISTAN
He's occupied with a friend

#1
I'll be ready

TRISTAN
You should probably visit Hemi

#1
Is that what you want me to do?

I compose and erase the message three times.

#1

I'll take that as a no. See you soon

When I get home, Bea is in the kitchen. She's wearing a pink lace bra and a matching lace thong. And that's it. Her hair hangs over her shoulder in a long braid. She leans against the island, gripping the edge, her head tipped to the side as I stalk across the room. I stop before my body collides with hers.

"I'm not going to be nice," I grind out.

"I gathered that from the text messages," she says softly.

I clench my hands into fists. I should walk away. She doesn't deserve this side of me. "You're not going to like this version of me."

"Maybe it'll be my favorite." Her eyes flash.

I hate how much I want her, how much I don't want her to see me like this, how I don't want to be this person with her anymore. I could fuck everything up. If she sees me at my worst, she'll probably end this, and maybe she should. It would be better for her. I'm barely tolerable on a good day, let alone boyfriend material. I'm so pissed off that I need her, and she's still standing here. "Last chance, Beat. You should really fucking run."

"But I don't want to." Her voice wavers.

I reach out and trace the contour of her bottom lip, murmuring *I'm sorry*. But I'm out of control. My career is hanging in the balance because of someone else's legacy. I'm lying to my best friend, betraying him every fucking day. And I'm putting Bea at risk every time we do this. She has nowhere else to go, no apartment to move into because I keep asking her to stay longer. And worst of all, I'm lying to myself. Because it's not just about the sex. It's about her. About the way she makes me feel. But I don't want to stop. I can't.

I spin her and curve my hand around the back of her neck, pushing her down until her cheek meets the counter. I slap her ass with my free hand, and she gasps and moans. "God, I love

255

that fucking sound." I unbuckle my belt and pop the button on my jeans, yanking the zipper down to free my erection. "You sure this is what you want?" I kick her legs apart. "To get fucked?"

"Yes."

She sucks in a shaky breath as I slip my finger under the thin strip of fabric. "Tell me to stop."

"I don't want you to," she whispers.

"You will." I follow the strip of satin down between her thighs. I skim her clit and she moans. This shouldn't be happening. I shouldn't be doing this. She should be tapping out. I push two fingers inside her and pump twice, then withdraw to slap her ass again. "How about now?"

"I want more," she rasps.

I lean in, sliding my cock between her ass cheeks. "So fucking filthy. Feel how wet you are for me." I wipe her juices on her cheek, then lick over the spot as I push my fingers between her lips.

They close around them on a greedy moan.

"Such a dirty girl." I pull my fingers free, grip my cock, and bite her earlobe as I line myself up and push inside her on one hard thrust. "So ready to be fucked."

"Oh, God," she whimpers.

"Tap out, Bea." I'm almost begging. This could be the last time she lets me inside her. I could ruin it all right now. "Tap the fuck out."

"No. I want you."

I pull my hips back and slam in. She moans, and her legs tremble. She tries to snake a hand between her thighs, but I release the back of her neck, spear her with my cock, grab both of her wrists and fold her arms behind her back, holding them with one hand to keep her in position.

"Still want me now?" My breath is ragged, heart hammering, waiting for her to tell me she's done. For good. To quit me. She should. I'd quit my demented ass if I were her.

"Don't stop. I'm so close," she pleads.

"You think I'm going to let you come?" I pull out to the ridge and spit on my cock before I thrust. "You haven't even asked nicely yet."

"Please," she moans.

"Not good enough. Try again."

"Please, Tristan." She whimpers and tries to roll her hips.

She grunts her displeasure when I pull all the way out. "Please what? Please stop?"

She shakes her head. "No. Please don't stop."

I keep her on the edge, close to coming, never going over. Her legs shake and juices coat my cock and drip down the inside of her thighs. I come all over her ass and keep fucking her. Keep pushing. Keep pleading for her to tell me to stop. But she doesn't. She just keeps taking it, keeps asking for more, keeps begging me to let her come.

But I don't.

It's fucking cruel. I know it is. I hate this version of myself, when I feel too fucking much and don't have control the way I should. I hate that I need her. Want her. Can't get enough of her. But she doesn't tell me to stop.

It isn't until I'm close to a second orgasm that I pull out. I slide a hand under her and pull her to standing, quickly wrapping my arm around her waist because her legs are too weak to hold her up. She's a rag doll as I spin her around and set her on the counter. The cheek that was pressed against it is red. I wrap my hand around the back of her neck as her head lolls.

Her eyes are glazed and unfocused. Her hands glide down my chest and rest limply on the counter. "Hey, hey." I cup her face in my palms. "Bea, baby? Tell me to fucking stop. Tell me you've had enough."

"No." She shakes her head. "You need this, and I need to come."

I step between her parted thighs, line myself up and push back in. Her eyes roll up when I brush her clit with my thumb.

"Please, please, please," she whimpers.

I rub circles on her clit, and she jerks and shudders, eyes flaring before they roll up again.

"Oh, God, oh my God..." She makes a low keening sound, and her body quakes with the orgasm. Her pussy clenches around my cock, and she sobs as sensation rockets through her. I hold her hips, pounding into her as she cries out, the orgasm relentless as it drags her under. I don't pull out when I come this time.

She sags against me. We're both covered in sweat. Her body convulses every few seconds, and she makes these little hiccupping whimpers when it happens.

I cup her cheek again, my hands shaking. My stomach feels like it's bottoming out. I pull back so I can see her face. She looks beyond exhausted. Tears leak out of the corners of her eyes.

"Fuck, Bea." I brush them away, panic taking hold. "Why didn't you tell me to stop? I didn't want to hurt you."

Her tongue drags along her bottom lip. "You didn't hurt me."

"I made you cry again." Every time it makes me want to stab myself in the eye.

Her hand brushes over her cheek and drops to her lap. "Not hurt tears. Orgasm-relief tears."

"Oh." I smooth them away, still not liking their presence. "Fuck. I thought I pushed you too far."

She shakes her head. "I knew you wouldn't." Her fingers drift along the edge of my jaw. "I would like you to kiss me now, please."

I slant my mouth over hers and wrap my arms around her. This kiss is penance, languid strokes of tongue. A soft apology. Eventually I pull back. "Are you sure you're okay?"

"Absolutely okay. But walking might be a challenge for the next couple of days, so I guess it's good your first game is an away one."

I laugh, relieved, and cover her mouth with mine again.

She hums and runs her fingers through my hair.

That she's gentle with me after I was so rough makes me feel like an even bigger asshole. "I'm sorry."

"I'm not. I would have told you to stop if it had been too much, but it wasn't. I'm glad I could be what you need."

"I don't deserve you." I drape her arms over my shoulders and pick her up.

"Says who?"

"Says me."

"Where are we going?" she asks against my lips.

"Shower. I want to clean you up."

Half an hour later, we're up in the loft. After the shower, I got Bea settled in with water and a huge glass of fresh-squeezed OJ. Then I ran across the street to the convenience store to buy treats. Now we're cuddling on the couch. As someone who hasn't experienced a whole lot of cuddling, I find I kind of like all this closeness. Especially when it's Bea, and she's all warm and smells like my favorite things.

"So what prompted the rage-fuck?" she asks, taking a bite of an Oreo Drumstick. I recently learned she loves them.

"Hollis is starting the game tomorrow. I'm second line."

Her brow furrows. "But you've been kicking ass in preseason. You've scored the most goals and have the most assists on the team. Hardly anyone in the league has better stats than you."

"Yeah."

"So why…" Her eyes close and her lips purse. "Because it's good for team morale."

"How do you know that?" I ask.

"Hammer overheard her dad and Hollis talking the other day." She props her cheek on her fist. I'm grateful the red spot has disappeared. "That's so shitty, Tris. First line belongs to you."

"I get why they're giving it to Hollis." And I do. But it makes me question where I stand and what's coming at the end of the season.

"Doesn't make it suck any less."

"Not really, no."

"Well, you'll just have to play your fucking ass off and show the hockey-watching nation why you should always be in the starting lineup. And of course, my pussy is always available for a rage-pounding when shit's unfair."

I kiss her on the cheek. "I can't believe you didn't tap out."

"I trust you. You might keep me on the edge, but you'd never hurt me. I honestly thought I was going to die if I didn't have an orgasm soon, though. When I finally did, holy fuck." She makes the mind-blown gesture at her crotch. "Best orgasm ever."

"Don't tell me that. I don't want the green light to be an asshole like that again."

Every time I think I've pushed her past her limit, she steps right up and takes what I give. It makes me want to keep her, take care of her, even though I know I can't. But how long can we reasonably keep doing this?

She shrugs. "You were rightfully upset, and you came to me for what you needed. If it had been more than I could handle, if *you* had been, I would have told you. I've seen all your sides, Tristan. None of them scare me."

"Come here." I pull her into my lap, wrap my arms around her waist, and shove my face into her hair. I'm so glad to have her, but everyone leaves eventually. It's the story of my life.

I do exactly what Bea says. I play my fucking ass off. And Hollis is rotated out in the third period, so he doesn't tax his knee, and I take his place. It puts things in perspective. I may not have started the game, but I finished it with a goal.

For once, Flip doesn't bring bunnies back to the room. Not by choice. Hemi is on him, and milk is one bad press statement away from pulling his endorsement campaign. Dallas is also trying to stay under the radar. His campaigns aren't at risk, but he doesn't want to give Hemi a reason to dress him up like a clown again. That's why we're all here in our hotel room, like it's some kind of slumber party.

"You kicked some serious ass tonight." Dallas clinks his beer bottle against mine.

"We all did," I say. "It's a great start to the season."

Flip nods. "It really is. I wish I was celebrating balls deep in a bunny, but losing a million-dollar endorsement over sex seems stupid, even for me." He tips his bottle back and drains half of it.

We stopped at the liquor store to grab a case. We also stopped at Walmart to grab snacks. It's a Flip thing to do. Room service is pricey.

"You should probably slow your roll now that the season has started," I suggest.

"Seems like I'll have to, no matter what, at least until the milk campaign settles. Or I'll have to rely on a few regulars to get by. Although too many repeats gives them ideas." Flip taps his temple.

"You could try dating someone for a change," Ashish offers.

"I'm not interested in commitment." Flip polishes off his beer and grabs another from the fridge.

I shake my head. "You have this great stable family, parents who have been together for more than three decades, and you're more relationship averse than even I am." I trade my empty for a full one, too.

"They're part of the reason I'm relationship averse," Flip admits.

"They love the shit out of each other, don't they?" At least they seem to. As a kid, I couldn't believe how nice they were to each other. They didn't have a lot of money, but every Friday, Flip's dad brought his mom a bunch of wildflowers in the summer. In the winter, he'd bring her a single rose. I could do something like that for Bea. Bring her flowers. She loves peonies. I used to steal one from my neighbor's garden every once in a while for her when she was a kid.

"Yeah. Exactly. I can't get in that deep with anyone. Not now.

It's too much pressure."

"Too much pressure how?" Dallas asks.

"It's someone else to worry about. You know what that's like," he directs the comment at me. "I already have my parents and Rix. I can't add another person to that when I'm focused on my career."

"Why are you worried about Bea?" She's got it together; she has a good job and nice friends. Not much to worry about apart from the one thing we're hiding from him.

"You saw where she was living. She's used to shitty neighborhoods because of how we grew up. But small town and big city are different. I want her somewhere safe, but she refuses to take money from me, and she's super paranoid about not having enough of a cushion. That roommate situation must have been way worse than she's admitting for her to end up at our place."

"Why would you think that?" Once we got her out, I didn't think much about it.

"Rix doesn't do anything without a plan. She organized her university pathway starting in grade school. She figured out how much she'd have to save every year, how much she'd need in loans, and how long it would take to pay it all off once she had a full-time job. She even calculated things like inflation, trajectory, and how quickly she could reasonably climb the ladder with the right company. It takes a lot for her to go off, and she'll put up with a lot of shit before her fuse gets lit," Flip says.

"Huh." I sip my beer, considering. Maybe that's why she won't say anything to Flip about his fuck-a-thons. She's already had to get herself out of one shitty situation. Maybe this is the lesser of the two evils. Or maybe if we weren't going behind his back she would say something, but she feels like she can't.

"Huh, what?" Ashish asks.

"Eh?" I give Ashish my attention.

"You said *huh*. Huh, what?"

"I seem to be able to light Bea's fuse." In more than one.

"And she lights yours. Although you've been fighting less

lately," Flip says.

"I wonder why that is." Dallas eyes me from the side.

"What was that?" Flip asks.

"We should check out the New York game," Dallas says. "See how they're playing so we know what we're in for later in the season." He flips through the channels until he finds replays of tonight's other game.

My heart is pounding, though the guys have moved on. It seems Roman isn't the only one who's noticed.

The hall leading to our condo smells like pumpkin spice. My mouth is watering by the time I open the door, and not just because the house smells like freshly baked pies. Bea is standing in the kitchen wearing a pair of ridiculous socks, shorts, an oversized T-shirt, and an apron. Her hair is fixed on top of her head in a knot, and she has smudges of flour on her neck.

"Damn, it smells good in here." Flip drops his bag and heads for her.

She turns around, a wide smile on her face, and accepts a brief hug. I look away, jealous that he can do that and I can't. Not being able to touch her when other people are around is wearing on me. I crave those stolen moments when Flip disappears into the bathroom or his bedroom and I can hug her from behind and bury my face in her hair. It makes me wish we hadn't started this with a pact I don't know how to get out of.

"Your timing is perfect!" she says. "I made an extra pie. I figured waiting until dinner tomorrow night would be torture. Come sit down, and I'll cut you both a slice. I also made too much filling for the pecan pie, so there are tarts. You can try those, too!"

There's a bottle of red wine on the counter and a mostly empty glass beside it.

She grabs plates from the cupboard and rushes back to cut slices of pie. She tops them with fresh whipped cream and pushes them toward us.

Flip drops into the chair opposite her, and I take the one next to him. He digs in, shoveling a huge bite into his mouth. "This is so good," he mumbles. After he swallows, he asks, "Grandma Madden's recipe?"

I slide my fork through the pumpkin and pastry, gathering whipped cream before I take a bite. It's incredible. But then everything Bea makes is.

We eat the entire pie, and Flip passes out. Thanks to his food coma, I take Bea to my room. I'm soft with her. Gentle, because last time I was hard. I don't want to be too much for her. I want to give her a reason to stay, not leave.

The next day, we wake up and get ready to drive over to my dad's for Thanksgiving dinner.

"I have an idea," I say once we've loaded Flip's car with pies, sweet potato casserole, and the gift Bea picked up for my brother, since we're also celebrating his birthday. She offered to make a cake, but Brody only likes ice cream cake, and my dad has taken care of that.

"What's that?" Flip asks as he closes the trunk.

"Bea should drive my brother's car over. That way, he'll think it's hers, and it'll be more of a surprise."

"Uh..." Bea pushes her lips out. "I haven't driven to your dad's place like...ever. And this is a brand-new car. I don't want that kind of responsibility."

"How about I drive most of the way, and we switch spots when we're around the corner?" I suggest.

"Yeah, okay. That would work," Bea agrees.

She rounds the passenger side of my brother's soon-to-be-birthday present, and Flip frowns. "Why doesn't Rix drive with me until we get close to your dad's? Don't want you two killing each other before we even get there."

Because I want half an hour to huff Bea's shampoo before we have to spend the rest of the day behaving. "Sure. That works."

When we're two streets away from my dad's place, Flip pulls over, and Bea hops out of his car and into my brother's birthday present.

"I saw what you tried to do there," she says as I tell her where to turn. My dad lives in the same house my brothers and I grew up in.

"I thought we'd get half an hour without an audience."

"So you could get a car handy?" Bea glances at my crotch before she turns right.

"Mostly so I could tell you all the dirty shit I want to do to you later. But I wouldn't have been opposed to a car handy."

She rolls her eyes and smiles. "Brody will be so excited when he realizes this car is his."

"Yeah. He's been drooling over this one for a while. He only works one shift a week because of hockey, so saving has been hard," I say.

"You're a great brother."

"Eh, I do what I can. Our mom sucks. She hasn't called him or sent him a card on his birthday in a few years," I admit.

Bea reaches over and squeezes my hand. "I'm so sorry. That's beyond shitty."

"It is what it is. That's why we make such a big deal about birthdays. Try to take the sting out, you know? He was only four when she left, so he doesn't remember her much. Mostly she's been an occasional voice on the phone and someone who sends him a card once a year." This isn't something I talk about, mostly because it makes me feel like garbage.

"It still sucks for all of you." Bea pulls into my dad's driveway. "Oh wow. It's the same, but different." She puts the car in park.

I spot my brother in the window, and a second later, the front door opens. His smile falters as Bea gets out of the driver's seat.

He schools his expression and comes down to greet us. "Sweet ride."

"Right?" Bea tosses me the keys and bites back a smile.

Flip parks on the street.

I wait a moment before I toss the keys to Brody. "Happy birthday, buddy."

He catches them, eyes bouncing between me and Bea. "Are you fucking serious?"

Nathan and my dad appear in the doorway.

"Yup. It's all yours."

"It's a smooth ride. You should check it out." Bea pats the hood and steps aside.

"Rix, right? My dad said you were coming. I haven't seen you in like...a long time. You're like..." His gaze moves over her, and his cheeks flush pink. He's all over the place. Trying to be polite while freaking out. "Yeah. Holy shit. It's nice to see you. This fucking car, man! Sorry about the swears, Dad."

"Why don't we take it for a spin?" I suggest.

"Can we?" Brody looks over his shoulder. "Is that okay, Dad?"

"Yeah, of course it's okay." Dad turns to Bea and Flip. "Beatrix, it's wonderful to see you again. You remember Nathan." He squeezes my brother's shoulder.

"Hey! Hi!" Nathan wipes his hand on his leg and holds it out. "It's been a long time." His eyes are wide, and he looks shocked.

"Hey. It's good to see you." She grins and shakes his hand, then nods to us. "You should probably go for a ride, too."

"Come on." I beckon him over. "We'll be back in a few."

Nathan climbs into the back, and I take my place in the passenger seat while Brody gets behind the wheel.

"This is so sweet. I can't believe this is my birthday present. Like, dude..." Brody is vibrating with excitement.

He drives it around the block and hops on the highway for one interchange, but it's slow going thanks to the holiday weekend, so he exits and drives back to my dad's.

Nathan checks his reflection in the rearview mirror before he gets out.

"What are you doing?" I ask.

He gives me a look. "Making sure my hair isn't a mess."

"Why? Who you looking to impress?"

"Dude, did you see Flip's sister? She's hot."

"You have a girlfriend." Unless something has changed in the past few days. Lisa was supposed to come for Thanksgiving, but she has a midterm paper to finish, so she had to bow out.

"I can still make a good impression." He sniffs his armpit.

I roll my eyes. "She's involved."

"Oh yeah? With who? Is one of your teammates brave enough to date her?"

"It's none of your fucking business. Don't flirt with her. She's Flip's sister, and she's off-limits. Got it?"

He raises his hands. "Geez. Don't get your panties in a knot, Tris. I wasn't gonna flirt. I just want to make sure I don't have shit in my teeth."

Bea's in the kitchen with my dad when we get inside. I'm unsurprised to find that she's taken over food prep. I'm also unsurprised when both of my brothers suddenly want to help. Nathan's right. She is fucking gorgeous. She's smart, and fun, and funny. She has an infectious smile and a laugh I can't get enough of. And watching her with my family makes me wish for things I shouldn't. Like permanence. Which is impossible.

She'll stick around for the sex, because I'm good at giving orgasms. But I'm not the kind of guy anyone wants long term. Ask my mom about that.

Flip hands me a beer. "Thanks for inviting us, man. Rix needed this. She's missing Essie and our parents, even if she doesn't want to admit it."

"Yeah, of course." Essie is another piece of the Bea puzzle I can't ignore. There's always a chance she'll end up where her best friend is. Those two are tight. And Essie is the stability Bea needs, emotionally and otherwise. I can't give her that.

And anyway, we're just supposed to be fucking.

CHAPTER 19

RIX

I t's Saturday morning, almost a week post-Thanksgiving with Tristan's family. He and I have found a rhythm. Most nights I sneak into his bedroom for quiet sex while Flip is either out or in the middle of making a bunny happy. Afterward, I disappear back to the loft.

But Flip has a promo thing with Hemi this morning, so we have the condo all to ourselves. And we're making damn good use of it.

Tristan licks up the side of my neck and bites my earlobe. "Next time I fuck you from behind, I'll be taking this sweet virgin ass of yours."

"Oh my God, you'll split me in two." I groan.

His hand curves around my throat, as usual. My ponytail is wrapped around his other fist, my back is arched, and my breasts bounce with every thrust. His balls slap my inner thighs, which are wet with my excessive coming. I'm watching our reflection in the mirror across the room. And I'm on the verge of coming again. Especially with the promise of what's coming when he gets back from his next away game.

Sure, I'm nervous. But currently there's a plug in my ass, and

I can't deny that the orgasms are out of this damn world. So that gives me courage for what lies ahead.

"We'll go nice and slow—at least until you get used to my size," Tristan assures me, his voice a low rumble. "Even if it takes all fucking night, your ass will be mine."

I shudder, on the edge, but I can't let go of his forearms to rub my aching, desperate clit. I moan as my thighs quake.

There's a knock on the bedroom door, and to my horror, it flies open.

"Is there room for one more?" My brother's voice singsongs as light floods the room.

Flip is standing there. In the doorway. With his hand still poised in the air. He quickly reaches for the knob. "Oh crap, so sorry."

"Shit." Tristan releases my hair and throat, which means I fall forward, but not before I watch my brother's expression turn to shock.

I don't have time to put my hands out, and we're close to the end of the bed. I go tumbling over the edge. My ankle slips through Tristan's fingers, and I break my fall with my face. "Ow! Fuck!" The rest of my body lands gracelessly on the floor.

"Rix? What the fuck? You're fucking my goddamn sister?" The door slams into the wall, the knob lodges in the drywall.

"Flip, man. It's not—" Tristan clambers off the bed, and his feet appear in my line of view. I'm still lying on the floor.

"Do not say it's not what it looks like!" Flip shouts. "Your dick is fucking *glistening* right now, so you were absolutely balls deep in my sister!"

"Can you give us a fucking minute!" Tristan snaps as he drops to his knees beside me and yanks the covers off the bed, draping them over me. He pulls me up to sitting, his eyes moving over my face. "Are you okay?" He cups my cheek, and I flinch. "Shit. I'm sorry. I panicked."

"You're a couple of fucking traitors!" Flip shouts.

I already have a headache. Tristan makes sure I'm covered

with the sheet before he grabs his shirt from the floor and pulls it over his head, which does nothing to cover his now-softening wiener hanging out the bottom.

What a mess.

Not to mention, there's a butt plug still lodged in my ass.

"Dude! Of all the fucking women in the world, why my sister? You don't even like her. She annoys the hell out of you." Flip is pacing. He shoves his hands through his hair and laces them behind his head. "I can't believe you're fucking my sister."

Tristan steps around me and follows Flip into the kitchen, glancing back with apologetic eyes. I find a T-shirt on the top of Tristan's dresser and check my face in the mirror. With my luck, I'll end up with a bruise.

"I'm sorry, man. I'm sorry. It just happened. We shouldn't have kept it from you." Tristan is cupping his junk.

"It just happened? It sure didn't look like your dick accidentally slipped into her!" Flip hauls off and punches Tristan in the face.

He stumbles back a few steps, and now cups his junk with one hand while cupping his nose with the other. "I deserved that. I know I deserved that."

"I'm gonna kick your fucking ass!" Flip shoves Tristan.

"Can you two stop?!" I shout.

Flip's angry gaze lands on me. "How could you let him touch you? How? We've fucked the same woman at the same time! And not just once, but many, many times." He motions between himself and Tristan. "We've been in the same pussy at *exactly* the same time. My dick and his dick." He slaps his palms together. "Like this."

"Flip, man, I know you're angry, but she doesn't need to know that shit. She's your sister, for fuck's sake," Tristan snaps.

I grab a pair of boxer shorts from the dresser and throw them at the back of Tristan's head. I can't even with these two. I hold up a hand. "I can do without the visual. You two have no boundaries. Flip, since the moment I started living here, you've paraded an entourage of fuck friends through this condo with no consideration of me or how I might feel. At all. I have listened to you do gross, unholy things to countless bunnies. Who, in case you weren't aware, aren't just a series of holes to fill. They also might be someone's sister! Women are human beings with value outside of your goddamn bedroom."

I pause a moment, trying to breathe. "I'm an adult woman capable of making my own adult decisions. And that includes who I decide to fuck, whether you approve or not. Grow the fuck up!"

"How long has this been going on?" Flip's furious gaze whips back and forth between me and Tristan, who has now jammed his legs into his boxer shorts and positioned himself between me and my stupid brother.

"A while." I should've known this would happen eventually. I just didn't envision it as a total dumpster-fire situation.

"What's a while?" Flip crosses his arms. "A week? Two weeks? A month? Longer?" His expression turns incredulous. "Someone answer me!"

"Stop yelling at Bea," Tristan says, his voice low and threatening. "The first time was about a week after she moved in, and I'm the reason it happened. And the reason it kept happening."

"A week after she moved in?" Flip echoes. "You've been fucking my sister behind my back for almost two months? You asshole!" He points an accusing finger at me. "And you! I let you move in here because you needed a place to stay, and you let my best fucking friend put his dick in you! Repeatedly! What the fuck, Rix?"

I cross my arms. "You put your dick in pretty much anything with two X chromosomes and a pulse. At least I'm not fucking the entire team." I'm going for sarcasm, but Tristan whirls to stare at me, and he makes a sound sort of like a growl.

I give Tristan a look. "Seriously? Put your double standard away." This is the least ideal scenario I could imagine. Especially considering my cheek hurts and my ass is still full of fucking plug. I was ninety-five percent of the way to an orgasm, so my clit is all achy, too.

"What the hell is even going on with the two of you? Are you…dating?" Flip spits the word like it's poison.

"No. We're just fucking. That's it," Tristan says before I can even open my mouth.

That stings. We're not dating. That much is true. But while Tristan and I are doing a lot of fucking—like *a lot* of fucking—I wouldn't say that's *all* we're doing. We went on a date. We sometimes hang out. He brings me thoughtful treats. Texts me all the time. I spent Thanksgiving with his family, for shit's sake. I give him a look.

"It's true." His eyes dart all over the place, and he runs a rough hand through his hair. "We fuck all the time. That's what we do. We fuck."

I huff and shake my head. One second he's defending me, and the next he's acting like we're nothing to each other. I can handle a lot of Tristan's shit, but this is next level. "Screw this." I head for the bathroom.

"You're gonna walk away? Is that it?" Flip calls after me.

"The bathroom is the only room with a door that doesn't belong to either of you!"

"Fuck both of you." Flip grabs his shirt from the counter and storms out of the condo.

I slam the bathroom door. Four seconds later, Tristan knocks. "Bea, come on. I was trying to smooth things over with Flip."

I turn the lock and open the door. He's wearing a forlorn, panicked expression. But he's turned me into the one thing I don't want to be: just another person to trade orgasms with. And it's my damn fault for wanting more than that. I yank the plug out of my ass and throw it at his chest. "I need some alone time, so if you can fuck off, that'd be great." I close the door in his face and turn on the shower.

Now I really need to find an apartment.

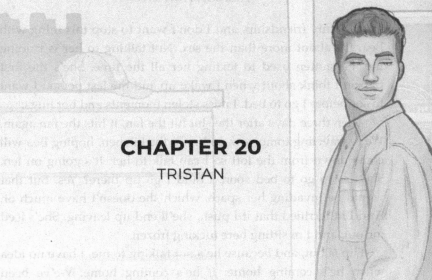

CHAPTER 20
TRISTAN

Shit has officially gone sideways. It's been two days, and Flip isn't talking to me. I get it. I went behind his back and fucked his sister. Repeatedly. Excessively. If the roles were reversed, I'd feel the same. But because we live together and play on the same team, it's doubly difficult to manage.

And to make things worse, Bea has turned to ice. Sure, she still makes food and leaves it in the fridge for us. And she still cleans the house and smells amazing and looks like my personal wet dream, even when she's scowling. But she's freezing me out. She leaves extra early for work and comes home late. She's also not responding to my text messages.

Not seeing her smile, hearing her laugh, or being able to wrap my arms around her is killing me. I thought Flip finding out would be the worst thing that could happen, but it turns out Bea avoiding me is even more fucking terrible.

I don't know how to fix this. I don't know if I can fix this, and it's freaking me out. My best friend won't acknowledge me, and Bea won't let me near her. I'm screwing up my life. Losing everything good. The only things left are my family and hockey. Before it was enough, but now… I don't know. I don't want to implode my friendship, and I don't want to stop this thing with Bea. It's about more than the sex. Not talking to her is ruining me. I'd gotten used to texting her all the time. She's the first person I think about when I wake up and the last person I want to see before I go to bed. I miss stolen moments and her hugs.

Then three days after the shit hit the fan, it hits the fan again. We're traveling tomorrow, so I'm in the kitchen, hoping Bea will come down from the loft so I can talk to her. It's going on ten. She has to go to bed soon. Could I go up there? Yes. But that would be invading her space, which she doesn't have much of. And I'm terrified that if I push, she'll end up leaving. She's iced me out, and I'm sitting here fucking frozen.

Flip is out, and because he's not talking to me, I have no idea when he's coming home. *If* he's coming home. We've been driving separately to practice.

This week is hitting high on the shitty barometer.

At ten fifteen, Flip walks through the door. He's not alone, which is unsurprising. Nor are the two giggling women trailing after him. What is a surprise, and a kick in the balls, is that they're familiar. Their eyes light up when they see me.

"Tristan! Hey! We didn't know you were here." One of them shoves at Flip's chest. "We had so much fun the last time we hung out, didn't we, Trinity?" She runs her nails down her friend's arm.

"So much fun." Her heels click on the floor as she shuffle-runs over and throws her arms around me, then tries to climb into my lap.

I untangle myself from her arms. The only person's hands I want on me are Bea's. "Sorry, I'm not part of the package tonight."

"You sure you don't want in?" Flip gives me a tight smile and throws his arm around not-Trinity's shoulder. "We had a lot of fun last time, didn't we?"

"So much fun," not-Trinity says.

Of course now Bea comes down from the loft.

"Oh! Hey, girl! You joining the party?" Trinity asks.

"That's my sister," Flip says flatly.

"Fuck you, Flip." Bea fires the bird at him.

"I think it's my best friend you're fucking," he calls back. "Nice to know where everyone's loyalty lies around here."

"Eat a dick." The bathroom door slams shut, and the shower turns on.

"She's probably got her period," Flip tells his friends.

"She doesn't have her fucking period, you idiot. She's mad at you for being a hypocritical asshole, and she's mad at me for..." I don't actually know why she's mad at me, but I can guess. "... being me." I run a hand through my hair and give the girls a tight-lipped smile. "Can you give Flip and me a minute?"

He pats not-Trinity on the butt. "Go get comfy. I'll be right there."

They hustle off to his bedroom.

"Look, Flip, I get that you're pissed, and you have every right to be. I lied to you. Bea lied to you. But how does this make anything better?" I motion to his closed bedroom door. "Why are you throwing this shit in our faces?"

"Before Rix moved in, you would have been all over those two with me. In fact, you *were* all over those two *with* me." He says it loud enough that I'm sure Bea can hear.

"You didn't leave a lot of room to turn you down," I snap.

"I never heard you complain." He crosses his arms.

I rub the back of my neck, frustrated. I expected his anger, but this is blatant, in-your-face sabotage. "What could I say when you brought two or three women home and told them we'd all party together? If I ever wanted to tap out, you'd tell me you needed me as your wingman, that I had to take the pressure off. Before you moved in, you want to know how many times I tag-teamed a woman?" I make an O with my fingers. "Zero times. And now you're bringing home these women for what reason? To remind me of all the shit I've done in the past? You're disrespecting Bea. Like she needs to see this."

"She doesn't need to be here. She can get her own damn apartment. And it's never bothered her before, so why would it bother her now?"

"How do you know it doesn't bother her? Have you asked her? Or do you assume because she only jokes about it that she's cool with it? Because that's what you did with me. Just assumed I'd want to get in on your fuck parade." I'm so angry that I've gotten myself into this shitty situation, that I sat by and allowed this to happen. I hate that I was so hung up on keeping Flip happy that I went along with his plan.

"I didn't hear you complaining."

"It was something we did, and I fully participated, but it was really your thing, Flip, not mine. Think about how things have been since Bea moved in. How many women have I brought home since the day she started sleeping in the loft?"

"You had that one who left all the scratches. Right at the beginning of training camp."

I cross my arms, waiting for him to figure it out.

"You started sleeping with my sister back *then*?"

That was literally the first time. Not that Flip needs the specifics.

"What's your plan with Rix, huh? You don't do relationships. The last girl you dated lasted all of what, two months before you tossed her out? What's your record? Three and a half months? Rix has had three long-term boyfriends, all of them for at least a year. She does monogamy and stability, and you can't give her either. Or is this your attempt at settling down?"

I rub my bottom lip, the sting of his words hard to take. He knows me better than anyone. Knows my history, what I'm like. I want Bea to talk to me. I want her to stay. I want this to not just be about sex, but maybe he's right. Maybe I can't be what she needs. "She doesn't want anything serious."

"Is that what she said? Was that your agreement? You were

going to bone each other until what? I found out?" I open my mouth to speak, but he holds up a hand. "You know what? It doesn't matter. I know you, man. You don't commit. I can't see you starting now."

"That's not fair." Just because I haven't doesn't mean I don't think about it. Or want it. I just don't trust that I can have it, or that it can last, and Flip's lack of faith underscores those worries.

"Dude, don't talk to me about fair," Flip counters. "I have been there for you. My whole family has been there for you—including my sister, even though you treated her like shit half the time, even when we were kids. Hell, my parents half raised you before your mom bailed. We've always treated you like family. Always. And you turn around and sleep with my sister?" His lip curls. "I know what you're like. *What* you like. I know exactly how you are. I've seen it. So you can say I pressured you or whatever, but you can't tell me you didn't get down and dirty right along with me." He shoves two fingers into my chest. "You better not fuck her up, or I'll fuck you up right back." He turns around and disappears into his bedroom.

"Shit." I run my hands through my hair. Guilt rolls my stomach. Over the lies. Over the betrayal. Because I'm too chickenshit to admit what I really want.

Giggles filter through Flip's door.

I wait for Bea to come out of the bathroom. When she finally does, she's freshly showered and smells like everything I want. She looks exhausted, though. I know the feeling. I've slept like shit the past couple of nights.

She tips her head back to look at the ceiling but doesn't say anything. When I raise my hand to touch the bruise on her cheek, she twists her head away and puts both hands up.

"I'm sorry I panicked. I should've stopped you from falling." I should have done a lot of things.

She shakes her head. "A bruised cheek isn't the issue, Tristan."

I swallow past the lump in my throat. Memories I've worked

to keep in a box surface. *"There's nothing you can do. I'm leaving."* I should have handled things differently. But I didn't, and I don't know how to fix it. "You don't have to stay in the loft, Bea. You can stay in my room."

"Why?" Her gaze shifts to the side. "So you can drown out the sound of their orgasms with mine? So you don't have to deal with feeling like shit for the choices you wish you didn't make? Thanks, but no thanks." She brushes by me and heads for the loft.

The rejection is acid burning through my veins. I could give her my room. I could sleep in the loft so she can have some peace tonight. "I could—"

She cuts me off with a wave of her hand. "I don't want anything from you." She disappears up the ladder.

I don't stop her. I don't know what to do anymore. I want her. I want to wrap my arms around her and make her stay with me. But I can't be what she needs. And she was always going to leave.

An hour later, I stealthily open my bedroom door, partly to see if Flip is still going strong, and also because I can hear Bea talking, and I want to eavesdrop on the conversation.

"I fell face-first into the freaking floor. There's a stupid bruise… Yeah, it wasn't the best. I thought Flip was out all morning, but apparently not. Yeah…yeah. I wouldn't be in this situation if I'd moved out last month."

Silence follows. "Flip is being an asshole, and Tristan is…it's a mess all the way around." She sighs. "I wish I could come for a visit, too. Maybe soon. Then I won't have to miss you so much or deal with my idiot brother losing his shit over my sex life. The double standard is unreal." Another pause. "Yeah, my boss did mention a position out your way." She laughs. "It wouldn't be the worst idea."

My stomach sinks. Of course she's thinking about going to Vancouver. Why wouldn't she? It's only a matter of time before she's out of the condo. Who knows how long it'll be before she's on the other side of the country.

CHAPTER 21

RIX

"**W**hat are you doing?" Tristan's hands are on his hips. He's blocking the ladder and thwarting my ability to toss shit into the bin at the bottom.

"Packing." I load stuff into another empty bin, since he seems disinclined to move.

"But...why?"

"Because I'm moving out."

"But...but..." He runs his hands through his hair. "We're done if you move out."

I stop packing to look at him. He's anxious; that much is clear. His eyes are wild, there are circles under them, and his jaw keeps ticking.

"That was part of the deal," I remind him.

His hands are on his hips again. He doesn't seem to know what to do with them. They drop to his sides, and then he crosses them.

"Flip also wasn't supposed to find out, and he did, so our sex pact is effectively dissolved. Also, we haven't had sex in the past week, so me sticking around for more awkwardness seems pointless, don't you think?"

I'm hurt that we still haven't had an actual conversation since

Flip found out. Tristan keeps coming up with elaborate ways for me to sneak into his bedroom, though. Which I've refused to do.

"I was away for three of those days." He's back to running his hands through his hair. "How can I make it better when you won't let me do what I'm good at? Who's going to fuck you like I do?"

I would laugh if every sentence out of his mouth wasn't a punch to the heart. If Tristan replaced the word *fuck* with *love* or *take care of* or any combination of words with feelings attached to them, this would feel like an actual relationship. Which is a problem. Because he's made it clear this is not a relationship. I might like having sex with him, and I might like him as a human being when he's not being an emotionally stunted idiot, but if there's one thing I've learned this week, it's that Tristan and talking things through do not go hand in hand.

They had two back-to-back away games, and when they returned, Flip and I continued to ignore each other, and Tristan tried to get me back into bed via late-night texting. Sneaking into Tristan's room before my brother found out was one thing. But I can't do it when he's here and he knows. And for whatever reason, Tristan doesn't get that. Or doesn't want to. Either way, it's been horrifyingly awkward. I need space. So I'm getting out.

"Right now I'm packing, and honestly, I'm not in the mood to fuck."

That's not one hundred percent true.

Tristan looks damn well edible with his frustrated, furrowed brow and his low-slung gray jogging pants and team T-shirt. I could happily peel him out of his clothes and ride his face or his cock to multiple-orgasm bliss. But I don't want to be *just* fucked by him. I want connection. I want him to rub his nose against mine and be all sweet and soft before he fucks me like a savage. And there's also the whole matter of not dealing with the fallout of Flip finding out still hanging over our heads. Not to mention that Tristan refuses to acknowledge that what's going on between us has escalated from hate-fucking, to fucking, to actually sort of maybe liking each other while also fucking. Throwing more sex on top of that slice of avoidance cake is a bad idea.

"When are you moving?"

"This afternoon."

"This afternoon?" His eyes flare and the color drains from his face. "But that's...how did you find a place so fast? Where are you moving? Is it even safe? Do you have roommates again? What if it's the same situation you just got out of?"

My heart aches. I wish he could admit that he cares. But Tristan is a broken boy living inside an angry man, and I can't fix that. "I'm moving in with Hammer. There's a sublet in her dad's building, and it's a two bedroom." Fates aligned yesterday when we were in the elevator on the way up to Hammer's dad's place. A woman a few floors down is moving to France for a year, and her tenant fell through at the last minute. We were in exactly the right place at exactly the right time. The apartment is fully furnished, and she left for France this morning, which means we can move in this afternoon.

"So you're staying in Toronto?" Tristan asks.

"Yeah." I glance at him, and my stupid heart clenches at his relieved expression. "I'm staying in Toronto."

"And Hammer will be your roommate?"

"Yes."

"Okay." He nods once. "I can drive you over."

"Hammer and the girls are coming to pick me up." Hammer has a truck. How she drives it in downtown Toronto amazes me, but it's big, and all my stuff will easily fit in the back, and no one has to eat their knees, so it's a win.

"Tell them you don't need a ride."

I cross my arms. "Why do you want to drive me?"

His jaw clenches. "Because I just do."

"So we can fuck guilt free?" I press. I need him to meet me halfway here. I can't be the only one admitting this turned into something else. "When this started, we agreed that Flip couldn't

282

know, and it would stop when I found an apartment. I'm moving, and Flip has found out." Not to mention the whole part about no feelings, which I definitely have a lot of, some positive, some negative, but there are feelings, and they are real. "Based on those two factors alone, that means this has to stop."

"Fine. It stops when you move. But you're still here, and Flip is at some promo thing for the rest of the day, and you can't just fucking leave with no warning." He steps into my personal space.

His chest is heaving, he looks like he wants to break something, and he's tenting his gray sweats. He has a point. My departure is sudden, and while it shouldn't be entirely unexpected, I didn't give him much in the way of a warning. But he hasn't given me a reason to stay and fix this.

"When will the girls be here?" he grinds out.

"An hour."

"A fucking hour? That's all you're giving me? One goddamn hour?" One hand wraps around my throat and the other snakes around my waist, dragging me against him. He crushes his mouth to mine in a punishing kiss.

I spear my hands in his hair, suddenly frantic. This is it. This is the last time. My chest aches in a way that's become unpleasantly common this week, and my pussy throbs in a way that's familiar and comforting. My heart, head, and vagina are all on separate pages, but my vagina is clearly winning this fight.

"You're a fucking liar." Tristan bites my lip, then sucks it before releasing it so he can bite his way across the edge of my jaw.

"What are you talking about?"

"You said you weren't in the mood to fuck and you're humping my goddamn leg."

I realize I have one leg hooked around his and I'm grinding for all I'm worth. "My pussy wants to fuck, and apparently she's in the driver's seat."

Besides, I'm not the only liar in the room. It annoys the hell out of me that Tristan maintains all we're doing is fucking when it feels like more than that. But maybe that's all this is for him. Maybe I'm the only one who feels anything other than lust. And if that's the case, it's good this is the last time.

He releases my throat, grabs the hem of my shirt, and yanks it over my head. I'm wearing a boring black bra. He pops the clasp and tosses it on the floor, groaning as he cups my breasts in his palms and pinches my nipples. And then we're back to kissing, aggressively, desperately.

Like reality is finally setting in.

We tear at each other's clothes, shove each other's pants down. My thong doesn't survive removal. And then he grips my ass and hoists me up. I wind my arms and legs around him, and his shaft glides over my clit. I wiggle around until the head nudges at my entrance.

"You don't get my cock yet." He shoves all my crap off the futon—I honestly won't miss sleeping on it because it's not particularly comfortable—lays me out on it, and grinds his hips, cock sliding through my folds. I'm wet and needy and there's no barrier between me and the futon. We'll probably make a mess, but I can't find it in me to care.

He squeezes my ass. "This was supposed to be mine."

"So take it now." The words are out before I fully consider what I'm saying.

"I'm too pissed off to be nice about it," he snaps.

"So take your anger out on my pussy, then."

"Oh, I plan to." His hand circles my throat, kneading gently as his nostrils flare. His gaze moves over my face like he's trying to memorize this moment.

I know I am.

He shoves the coffee table out of the way with his foot, so aggressively that it bangs into the entertainment console and several things topple over and land on the floor. He grabs a pillow and drops it on the floor. Then he grips my ass and shifts, so he's sitting on the couch with me in his lap.

I'm dizzy and disoriented as I grip his shoulders. But he doesn't give me time to get my bearings. Instead, he tips me backwards, hand splayed between my shoulders to guide me until they hit the pillow on the floor, along with my head. I'm halfway to somersaulting backward off the couch, but he grips my thighs and pushes my knees over my head to the floor, so my ass is in the air. This is a position I've seen plenty of times in porn, but never experienced in real life. I'm completely at his mercy, exposed and on display. Unless I tell him I don't want or like this. Then he'll stop, adjust, and make sure I'm good before he keeps going.

His jaw tics, and his chest heaves. His hands glide up and down the backs of my thighs. "Okay?" he grinds out.

"Okay." I nod as much as I can in this position, which is basically a modified plow in yoga, seeing as my knees are beside my freaking ears.

He slaps my ass, then bends and licks up the length of my pussy on a growl and latches onto my clit, sucking hard.

"Ah!" I shriek and grab his hair, but his fingers encircle my wrists and he plants my palms on my ass and covers them with his hands, keeping them in place.

"It's my fucking pussy, and you're taking it away from me." It's an accusation.

"I have to go." My heart can't handle staying.

He makes desperate sounds as he licks at me and fucks me with his tongue. His hot, angry gaze stays fixed on mine as he slides two fingers inside me, pumps several times, slaps my clit, then stuffs his fingers into my mouth.

He gets me close to an orgasm but doesn't let me tip over the edge. I squirm and moan and beg, but I know better. I'm not getting what I want until he's inside me.

"Please," I rasp.

"Please, what?"

"Please fuck me. I want you in me. I need you in me." And I do. I need the feel of him stretching me. I need to wake up

285

tomorrow and remember what it felt like to be wanted so fiercely. To want just as desperately. "Please, Tristan. I need you."

"Then why are you leaving me?" There's real anguish in his expression.

But he doesn't give me time to form a reply. Of course not. Tristan doesn't want to talk, to figure things out, because that would mean admitting this is about more than sex.

One second I'm a pretzel on the floor, the next my legs are wrapped around his waist and my chest is pressed against his. I grip his shoulders, light-headed and disoriented all over again. And then he's pushing inside, filling me up.

He wraps his arms tight around me, buries his face in my hair, stays deep, and rocks his hips. I come so hard the world turns black. And then I'm on my back on the futon again and he's pumping into me, hips slapping, wet sounds accompanied by my high-pitched moans.

I search for his hand and try to move it to circle my throat, but he shakes his head. His lip is curled, almost in a snarl. His hands are splayed out on either side of me.

"Tristan, please." My fingers brush over his.

"You gave me an hour fucking notice, Bea. A fucking hour." He's still pounding away.

I'm seconds away from another orgasm. "I can't." I can't keep doing this without it becoming glaringly obvious that I have feelings for him. Big ones. Scary ones. I can't let him convince me to stay when every conversation we have devolves into orgasms. I can't watch him and Flip give each other nasty looks and refuse to talk. I can't be the reason their friendship falls apart. I can't let him see that he'll break my heart if I don't go.

I reach up and wrap my hand around his throat. My hand is comically small compared to the thickness of his neck. But I feel him swallow, feel his pulse hammering under my fingers. "Please," I beg. "Please, please, *please.*"

His jaw clenches and tics. But he adjusts his position, dropping to his elbow. The fingers of his other hand drift down my cheek and then his palm rests against my throat and his thumb and finger press firmly into the hinge of my jaw. His lips hover above mine. "Is this what you wanted?"

"Yes. Thank you. Oh, God." The orgasm slams into me with the force of a tidal wave. I cry out, back arching, body convulsing, contracting. I wrap my fingers around his wrist to keep him from taking his hand away. Not that I'm strong enough to stop him if he really wants to move it.

"Open your eyes and look at me, Bea." His fingers flex against the side of my throat. "At least give me that."

I pry them open and find his angry, fiery, forlorn gaze locked on my face. He's hurting as much as me. But he can't or won't admit it. And I can't force him to.

I shudder as the orgasm continues, wave after wave of intense pleasure. It keeps building, expanding. And as I'm about to hit the peak, he releases my throat, sits back on his heels, and pulls out. He fists his erection, stroking aggressively, and comes all over the inside of my thighs as I clench around nothing.

I scramble to grab his arm, but we're both slick and sweaty. He's still choking his cock and I'm still trying to figure out what the hell just happened. In one smooth motion, he stands up and puts distance between us. It's not just physical, though.

"You don't have to go." His voice is a gritty whisper.

"I do, though." Because staying will only make this harder in the end.

His expression flattens. "It's been fun. See you when I see you." He gives me his back and disappears down the ladder, still completely naked. He doesn't even take his clothes with him.

I lie on the futon, trying to catch my breath, covered in sweat and an unreasonable amount of bodily fluids, and wonder how someone who can make me feel so damn good one second can also make me feel so damn bad the next. Until now, I always knew what I was getting with Tristan. Sure, he could be an asshole, but at least he was honest about what he wanted. Dealing with an honest dick was a hell of a lot better than a guy who broke it off with me, moved across the country, sent I-miss-you messages, and a few weeks later started dating someone else. But all that honesty is out the window now. And I can't keep doing this to myself.

I don't have time to wallow in self-loathing, or Tristan-loathing, because five minutes later, the girls show up. At least I'm dressed again.

Hemi and Hammer both wrinkle their noses when they see me. Tally just smiles because she's still sweet and innocent.

"Oh, girl. The freshly fucked vibe is strong." Hemi pats me on the shoulder.

"So is the freshly fucked scent," Hammer mutters.

"One day, hopefully in the not-too-distant future, I'll be able to personally identify the freshly fucked vibe and scent," Tally announces.

"We're all going to hell," I say.

"At least we're going together," Hemi replies brightly.

"Where are your roommates?" Hammer asks.

"Tristan is in his bedroom, and Flip is at some promo thing?" I end on a question because I don't really know where Flip is. He and I aren't exchanging more than grunts and side-eyes.

"He's with Dallas. They're selling pierogis at a church bazaar. Dallas hates the smell of sauerkraut, so it's perfect for him." Hemi's smile is downright evil.

"You're a mean one, Miss Grinst." I motion to my half-full bin at the bottom of the ladder. "I got distracted, but it shouldn't take long to pack the rest of my stuff."

"You and I can pass stuff down to Hemi and Tally," Hammer offers.

"That'd be great."

Hammer follows me up the ladder. She takes in the huge wet spot on the futon. "Needed one last round, eh?"

I nod. It sucks that we've ended on such a low note. That he pulled out in the middle of an orgasm and came on my thighs basically sums up the entirety of our messed-up non-relationship.

"Need a hug?" she asks quietly.

"Later. I'll probably cry, and I don't want to give him the satisfaction of seeing or hearing me lose it," I whisper.

"Fair. Let's get your stuff and get out of here."

I throw clothes into the bin at the bottom of the ladder, including Tristan's shirt, boxers, and jogging pants. *Finders keepers.* When that bin is full, I toss my remaining clothes into another one, make sure I have all my things, and lower the other bins down.

I grab my stuff from the bathroom, fill a cooler bag with fridge items, and do one last check to make sure I have everything. Tally and Hemi both take a bin full of clothes, and Hammer and I each take one end of the heavier bin.

Tristan's door remains closed as we file out into the hall. It's not a surprise. But it hurts. A lot. We're quiet as we trek down the hall to the elevator. Dred, the woman who lives across the hall, holds the elevator door for us and eyes the tote bins. "You find your own place?"

"Yeah."

"Hopefully I'll still see you around when you come visit," she says with a smile.

"Yeah, for sure." I lie, because I plan to be angry at Flip for a long time.

"Who was that?" Hammer asks once the doors close.

"Our next-door neighbor," I explain. "Flip is friends with her."

"Like friends with benefits, friends?" Hemi asks.

"Surprisingly no. They're totally platonic."

"I sort of expected Tristan to come running out and ask you to stay," Tally says as we head for the lobby.

"Tristan doesn't do vulnerable. He doesn't even really do feelings." I tip my chin up even as it trembles. Feelings are

annoying and inconvenient. Especially when they're not reciprocated.

"Are you okay?" Hemi asks softly.

"I'm fine. I'll be fine. It was just sex. That's all we were doing.
Just fucking each other." Which is why it feels like my heart has
been ripped out of my chest, stomped on, and kicked into a meat
grinder. "It's better that it's over."

Two stupid tears leak out of the corners of my eyes.

Tally's arms come around my waist first. Then Hammer's
and Hemi's.

"Men are idiots," Hemi says.

"Tristan's a dick," Hammer says.

"Maybe he'll realize he's in love with you, too," Tally says.
Bless her sweet, innocent, observant heart.

"Shit. How did that even happen? How did I fall in love with
an emotionally unavailable asshole?" Because I did. I'm such an
idiot. The elevator dings, and the group hug comes to an
abrupt end.

We file out as my brother strides through the lobby. His brow
furrows when he sees us. "Rix? What's going on?"

I fire the bird at him. "I'm moving out, genius. You can go
back to tag-teaming the bunnies like the good old days. Sorry for
cramping your style."

His gaze shifts to Tally for a second and he flinches, like my
words have physically hurt him. Or maybe he realizes she's the
coach's daughter and I'm over here calling him out about
screwing bunnies with his best friend, who just robbed me of
orgasm satisfaction because he's mad that I'm taking my vagina
away from him. It's admittedly on brand for Tristan. At least he's
consistent.

"Rix, come on."

"You suck, dude," Hammer says.

"Come on, let's get you out of this nightmare." Hemi throws
a glare my brother's way.

Tally just looks at him like he's a huge disappointment as we trudge through the lobby and out the door.

We lift my bins into the bed of Hammer's truck and climb into the cab. Tally takes the passenger seat, and Hemi and I sit in the back. There's enough room for three full-sized hockey players, even with the front seat slid all the way back. No one will recline their seat and make it impossible for me to breathe.

Even that thought makes my eyes prick with tears.

"How did this happen?" I throw my hands in the air and let them land in my lap. "How did I manage to fall for my brother's asshole of a best friend?" I lean my head against the seat and bang it twice. "Ugh. What a cliché, stupid thing to do."

"Eh, don't beat yourself up over it. He's hot. And we've all seen the way he looks at you. Yeah, there's a lot of lust, but that guy has it bad. It's not your fault he can't tell you how he feels," Hemi says.

"If Tristan doesn't usually talk about feelings, or show them outside of safe ones, like lust and happiness and anger, then there's a chance he's not even aware of the depth of his feelings for you," Hammer says.

Tally twists so she can give me an empathetic smile. "And Flip is his best friend. So that makes it even harder, because now two important people in his life are at risk."

"These are all valid points," I agree. But they don't make me feel better about how things went down. As we drive toward my new apartment, I consider how blindsiding Tristan might not have been the best plan. Maybe him inviting me to his bed was his way of trying to smooth things over. Maybe sex is the only way he knows how to express himself. That's its own problem and not something I can fix for him.

"We're making a pit stop," Hammer announces.

We stop at the LCBO and pick up all manner of tequila-based drinks and an unreasonable amount of wine while Tally waits in the truck. Then we make another stop at Hammer's favorite Mexican restaurant, where we pick up an absurd number of tacos. She skips the refried beans, though, because she knows I already feel bad enough.

Twenty minutes later, we troop up to the new apartment with my bins and our Mexican fiesta. It's a great apartment, and I have a bedroom with a door. And my own bathroom.

I try not to give in and eat too many tacos, but I'm weak, and they're delicious. Besides, I don't need to worry about any gastro distress coming my way later since I have a private bathroom.

It's bittersweet. My heart hurts, but it's better to get out now and let it heal than stay and have it smashed into smithereens.

CHAPTER 22
TRISTAN

Everything sucks. Especially me. On the ice, I'm a mess. I keep missing easy shots, fucking things up during practice. Three times Coach Vander Zee has pulled me aside to ask if I'm okay. The answer is no. I'm not okay. I'm miserable.

I miss Bea. There's a physical ache in my chest that won't go away, and it makes me edgy. It reminds me of how I felt when my family fell apart.

And everything is worse because Flip still isn't talking to me. Bea has been gone for five days, and it's been nearly two weeks since he found out. I've been sleeping on the couch in Roman's room during away games because I can't deal with the tension. When we're home, I hide in my room.

We're scrimmaging today. Tomorrow, we play Philly for the first time this season. I'm not on starting line. That's not a surprise, considering the way I'm playing. And the tension between me and Flip is bleeding onto the ice.

I'm only half paying attention as the puck comes my way during practice, and I'm not taking stock of my teammates, which is admittedly terrible form. I snag the puck before it passes and spin around, heading down the ice. But Flip is right there, so I slam into him, knocking him down. I should offer him a hand, but I'm pissed that he walked into my bedroom and fucked everything up. If he hadn't found out, Bea would still be in the loft, and the empty, gaping hole in my chest wouldn't feel so fucking huge.

He scrambles to his feet and shoves me. "The fuck is wrong with you?"

Coach Vander Zee blows the whistle, but I'm already in Flip's face. "You got in my way." I'm not really talking about on the ice, though. The hit was completely my fault.

"I got in your way? Are you even paying attention to what's going on around you? Or are you so fucking self-absorbed that you do whatever you want without considering the goddamn consequences?" He tosses his stick aside.

"Everything was fucking fine until you got in the way!" I shout, sending my stick flying as well.

Yeah. We're not talking about the game at all.

Coach blows the whistle again.

Dallas tries to get between us, but we grab each other's jerseys, elbowing him out of the way.

"I got in the way? I got in the fucking way? You're the one getting in your own goddamn way!" Flip yells.

"That's rich coming from you!" I shout back.

Roman skates over and pulls us apart. "This argument doesn't belong on the ice."

"What the hell is wrong with you two?" Coach looks to Roman. "You know what this is about?"

"I have an idea."

Flip's eyes flare. "You have an idea? You knew what was going on?"

Roman gives him a withering look.

Coach blows his whistle again. Shrilly. Two feet from my ear. "You two shower and change. I want you in my office in twenty. Roman, you go with them and make sure they don't kill each other."

I don't argue. I head for the gate and Roman follows, Flip muttering behind him.

"I can't believe you fucking knew, and you didn't tell me," Flip snaps once we're in the locker room. He removes his pads, flinging them aside.

"That you didn't know says more about your priorities than anything, Flip," Roman fires back.

Flip frowns. "What the hell does that mean?"

"It means if you were actually paying attention to something other than yourself, you might have clued in that there was something going on! I haven't looked at anyone else since Bea moved in with us, dipshit." I toss my pads on the bench.

"You've been lying to me this whole fucking time!"

"No, I haven't." Not once has Flip asked me who I'm fucking.

"You were sleeping with my sister behind my back the entire time she lived with us!"

"That's not the same as lying," I argue. Which is idiotic. I knew it was wrong, but I did it anyway. And kept doing it.

"You betrayed me!" He points a finger at Roman. "And you kept his dirty little secret."

"Well, considering your reaction, it seems like I made the right choice." Roman crosses his arms. "I get that you're upset, Flip, but you need to step back and get some goddamn perspective. I don't know if you've noticed, but Tristan is a fucking mess. He's playing like shit, he looks like shit, he's not eating, and he's been walking around for the past week with a black cloud of doom hanging over his head, doing a solid impression of Eeyore."

"Thanks, man," I grumble.

"I'm trying to help you out, asshole," Roman snaps, then turns back to Flip. "Do you really think, if Tristan didn't give some sort of a shit about your sister, that he would be this upset about whatever the hell is going on?"

"He's upset that Rix moved out and he can't get into her pants." Flip storms off to the showers.

Roman shakes his head. "You two are idiots." He scrubs a hand over his face. "Get your shit together, Tristan."

He's right. I'm in this predicament because I can't be honest with myself about my feelings for Bea, let alone anyone else. But that doesn't give me a way out of it.

I shower and change, and Flip and I get chewed out by the coach. Flip throws me under the bus and tells him I've been sleeping with Bea behind his back. Coach tells us to keep our personal lives off the ice and deal with our shit. If I can't, I'll end up on second line for more than just tomorrow's game.

Flip and I ignore each other in the locker room and leave the arena separately. I can't deal with being home. Everything about the condo reminds me of Bea. She left half a bottle of her lotion in the bathroom—it fell behind the garbage can—and I routinely sit around sniffing it, wishing she hadn't moved out. So I end up going for dinner with some of the guys at our local watering hole, including Dallas, Roman, Ashish, and Hollis. It's the one place we can go and no one makes a big deal about our presence. My appetite is for shit these days, but I order food anyway, hoping I'll feel like eating it when it arrives. I miss Bea-made meals. I miss Bea period. Hollis gets a salad with cucumbers, and I barely resist the urge to yeet it across the room.

"So you and Rix, eh?" Dallas chugs a glass of water. "Can't really say I'm all that surprised with the way you two look at each other."

"Which is how?" I ask.

Ashish offers his perspective, "Like no one in the world exists but her."

"I honestly can't believe Flip didn't see it," Roman muses.

"He's too busy getting laid to pay attention to anyone or anything else," Hollis says. He checks his phone and composes a message before setting it facedown on the table. "It'll be easier for him to get over it if you give him a reason to."

"I don't know what that means," I tell him.

He doesn't have a chance to answer because Flip appears.

The smile slides off his face. He points at Dallas. "Fuck you." He aims the double bird in my direction and spins around.

Hollis grabs the back of his shirt before he can go anywhere. "You two need to sort your shit out, and we're here to moderate." He slides out of the booth and forces Flip in before he takes his spot again. Flip is stuck between Hollis and Roman. And I'm sandwiched between Dallas and Ashish, so I can't go anywhere either.

"You assholes orchestrated this." I glare at Roman.

"You two got into a fight on the ice during practice. Your personal drama directly impacts this team. We have a home game tomorrow night against Philly, and last season they handed us our asses. If they get wind that there's dissension in the ranks, they'll use it to their advantage. So yeah, we orchestrated this little chitchat," Roman snaps.

"And as much as I appreciate being on the starting line, I don't need the added stress that you two are going to fuck our game if you end up on the same line later in the game," Hollis adds.

"I like the nachos here," Ashish says.

"I'm mostly here because I wanted the dirt on this little development," Dallas admits. "But Hollis and Roman are right. You two need to solve your problems, and we're here to make sure you don't kill each other in the process. We can't have two of our best players suspended this early in the season."

"Flip, I understand you're upset, but you and Tristan have a lot of years of friendship under your belt," Roman says. "Before you go throwing it all away, maybe you need to talk this shit out." He motions between us.

Flip glares at me, and I stare at my half-empty beer. Guilt is heavy on my shoulders. I shouldn't have gone behind his back, but he wouldn't have understood. And now I've lost Bea, and I stand to lose my best friend. It's the worst possible outcome.

Roman huffs. "Tristan, maybe you can start by apologizing for keeping your involvement with his sister from Flip."

"We're not involved anymore, thanks to him," I spit. Being angry is better than being hurt.

"Thanks to me? You were sleeping with her behind my back for two months!"

"I don't understand how you didn't notice, Flip," Ashish muses.

Roman sighs.

Dallas shakes his head.

"Why is it Flip's fault that you're not involved with Rix anymore?" Hollis asks.

"Because we said it would end when she moved out. And when Flip found out, he was a real fucking asshole about it. Bea shut down, and I didn't know how to make it better, so now she's living with Hammer." I mean, the last part is pretty damn obvious.

"I think I have a right to be pissed off. She's my little sister, and you hid it from me." Flip tries to cross his arms, but he doesn't have enough room.

"What could we say? Hey, Flip, hope you're cool with us sleeping together? We didn't even like each other to start with. We drive each other up the wall! Drove each other up the wall. Past tense."

"If you irritate each other so much, why did you end up sleeping together? Repeatedly?"

"I don't know. We pushed each other's buttons until we broke, I guess." I poke at my cheek with my tongue. "It was only supposed to be one time. It just happened. And we never planned to let it happen again." I give him an imploring look. "I tried, Flip. I really tried not to want her. But she just...smells so good all the time, and she's sassy and smart, and she was there every day, being beautiful and kind, even when I was a giant dick."

"So you kept giving her yours," he mutters.

"I thought maybe it would last a week or two." I was sure her tolerance would give out. "We said it would stop when she moved, but then I convinced her to stay until after the season started," I admit.

"Why would you do that?" Flip taps agitatedly on the table.

"I didn't want her to leave." I focus on my beer.

I wanted her to be there when I got back from away games, and practice, and on weekends, and every fucking day. I wanted to see her smiling face, to push her buttons, to touch her, be close to her, absorb some of her goodness since I have so fucking little of my own.

"So it was just about sex, then?" Flip grinds out.

"It wasn't supposed to be about feelings." That was the agreement. I don't know when it changed, but it did. And now I'm screwed because she moved with no warning. Just up and left me.

"For the love of fucking God." Hollis slaps the table. "What this idiot is trying and failing to say is that at some point, it *stopped* being just about sex. If it was just about sex, Tristan wouldn't be a mopey, depressed, lovesick fool. And we're learning that he's apparently more emotionally repressed than most serial killers, since owning up to his feelings seems to be impossible, despite his team's welfare and his relationship with you being on the line—not to mention his relationship with Rix."

"I don't know if I'm lovesick." Apparently in addition to being emotionally repressed, I'm also a complete idiot.

"Does all food taste like garbage?" Hollis asks.

"Yeah."

"Do you intentionally listen to her favorite songs or watch her favorite shows because it reminds you of her, even if it makes it feel like your heart is being shredded? Or, conversely, are you avoiding all those things for the same reason?"

"Uh, yeah."

"Does it feel like there's a giant, empty hole in your chest and the only thing that will make it go away is Rix?"

"Yeah."

"You're lovesick." Hollis turns to Flip. "And maybe I'm going out on a limb, but I'm guessing the reason they tried to keep it under wraps was to avoid upsetting you. Especially if they both thought they would be able to keep feelings out of it. That might have worked if it had lasted a couple of weeks, but no one sleeps with someone they claim to hate for weeks if they don't actually like them."

"So you have feelings for Rix that extend beyond getting into her pants?" Flip asks.

It doesn't make sense to lie anymore, even if my feelings aren't reciprocated. Can't say I'd blame her after the way I acted the day she moved. I hadn't expected to only have an hour. I frittered away my last days with her because I couldn't tell her how I felt. Feel. "Yeah."

"So why haven't you tried to contact her since she moved?" Roman asks.

"How do you know I haven't?" I challenge.

"Because Peggy lives with her, and I see my daughter every day. There've been an unreasonable number of ice cream bars consumed over the past week. And not even the good kind."

"The no-name brand vanilla and chocolate sandwiches?" I ask.

"Yeah."

"Bea only splurges on the good ones once a month. The rest of the time, she buys the cheaper stuff." Her favorite are the Oreo ones, and second are the Oreo Drumsticks. But nothing hits the mark quite like a pint of Kawartha Dairy Moose Tracks.

"Wasn't she doing all the shopping? And weren't you giving her money for that?" Dallas asks.

"Yeah, and we kept telling her to buy for herself, too, but she refused," Flip explains.

"And neither of you could manage a ten-minute trip to the store to pick her up a fucking treat for cleaning your house, making all your meals, and whatever else she did for you?" Dallas looks appalled.

"I bought her a cake and all her favorite candies." After I ate her treat with her name on it for the second time, but he doesn't need to know that part. "And I got her ice cream a few times."

"You two have been sleeping together for two months and you bought her ice cream *a few times*?" Ashish is looking at me like I'm the biggest idiot in the world.

"I took her out on a date, too. But it had to be low-key, 'cause no one was supposed to know," I admit.

"When did that happen?" Flip asks.

"Before Thanksgiving. I would have done more of that, but for obvious reasons, I couldn't." This whole conversation is making me antsy and uncomfortable.

"Maybe you should check on her," Roman says.

"What if she doesn't want to hear from me?" She wasn't responding to my texts when she was still living with us. I don't know why she'd respond to them now.

"You won't know unless you make a move, will you?" Hollis asks.

"And it wouldn't hurt to send her something nice," Ashish adds.

"Noted." I can't believe I'm getting relationship lessons from these guys.

Roman turns his judgy eyes on Flip. "Rix isn't very impressed with you."

"I'm not the one sleeping with her best friend behind her back."

"You freaked out and didn't let either of us explain, and then you gave her the silent treatment for a week," I say.

"You're the one who said all you were doing was fucking," Flip points out.

"Because that's what we were supposed to be doing! I didn't expect the feelings part." I still don't know how to manage that. But the guys are right. If I don't make a move, I'll never know if I'm alone on feelings island. "And you sure didn't help things by bringing home women we'd been with before *after* you found out."

301

"You did what?" Roman looks like he wants to flip the table.

Dallas shakes his head. "Are you telling me that after you found out Rix and Tristan were sleeping together, you brought home women you and Tristan had previously tag-teamed? While your sister was sleeping in her doorless, wall-less loft above you?"

Flip looks at the table.

"Yes. That's exactly what happened," I say, since he won't confirm or deny it.

"That was a real asshole move." Ashish sounds disgusted.

Dallas shakes his head in disapproval.

"I thought they both needed a reminder of what Tristan is really like," Flip says, then grimaces as he takes in the horrified expressions around the table. "Which was a really shitty thing to do."

"Ya think?" Hollis scoffs. "Like the stakes weren't already high enough with Rix being your sister, then you gotta throw his past, which you're complicit in, back in their faces?"

"I didn't think about it that way until now." Flip looks embarrassed.

"Going behind your back was a shitty thing to do, though," I say. "And I didn't mean for it to happen. Or keep happening. Or to catch feelings for Bea. But I did. Catch feelings." I rub the back of my neck. I feel like I'm about to have an allergic reaction.

"I mean, you passed up a repeat with Tiff and Trinity, and those two were up for anything," Flip says.

"I don't want to talk about other women's pussies. Especially not other ones I'm familiar with, because it makes me feel like a steaming pile of garbage, and I already feel shitty enough."

"At least I'm upfront about who I'm sleeping with instead of hiding it," Flip counters. For a moment it seems like he's going to say more, but then he takes a swig of his beer and sighs. "I guess if you want to try to date my sister, I won't punch you out again."

"For real? You'd be okay with it?"

"Yeah. For real. Just don't break her heart," Flip warns. "If you do, I get to punch you in the face again."

"That's fair."

Dallas claps me on the shoulder. "Look at you two. That's some real personal growth."

Now I need to grow a pair of balls and apologize to Bea for being a giant asshole. If I'm lucky, maybe she'll let me do more than make up for that orgasm I shortchanged her. Maybe she'll let me try to date her, too.

CHAPTER 23

RIX

"These reports are flawless, Rix. You're such a fantastic addition to this team. I almost regret telling you about that position in Vancouver." Agatha Boycott, my boss, gives me a rueful smile. She prefers to be called Aggie. She's a super funky woman in her early fifties with two grown children, a Great Dane, and a hairless cat. There are pictures of her entire family, pets included, all over her office.

"I just moved into an apartment with a friend, so I'm not looking to transfer." Although, if ever there was a time I should consider getting out of Dodge, it would be now, while my heart is bruised and my vagina is devastated. But it would be uncool to move in with Hammer and promptly bail for Vancouver.

It's nice to have a fun roommate. And as enticing as Vancouver sounds, I can't handle more change. I need time to get over what happened with Tristan. The whole *"I'll see you when I see you"* parting still stings. And the lack of communication makes me question whether I was wrong about him having feelings.

"We'll happily hold on to you as long as you'd like to stay," Aggie assures me. "There will be plenty of opportunity for movement inside the firm."

"Thanks, Aggie. I really like it here." And I do. I like my colleagues, I like my boss, and the job is dynamic enough to keep me on my toes in a good way. I enjoy financial planning and helping people establish good spending habits and work within a budget or helping someone maximize their investment potential. Is it my passion? No. But for now it's enough. I need one stable, consistent thing in my life.

I return to my office to finish end-of-the-day paperwork. Beryl, who I share an office with, in addition to Mavis and Burt, hops up from her desk when I walk through the door.

"There was a delivery for you."

"Really? I didn't order office supplies."

"It's not office supplies." She clasps and unclasps her hands while pursing and un-pursing her lips.

I frown. "Is it an NSFW delivery or something?" I wouldn't put it past Hemi and Hammer to send me dick-shaped donuts or cookies to cheer me up. They're good friends, but sometimes they forget that I don't work with a team of alpha males who handle sticks and pucks for a living.

"No. It's on your desk." Beryl follows me to my cubicle.

I suck in a breath when I see it. Only one person I know would send this kind of gift basket—and to my work, of all places. It's enormous and ostentatious. And there's no way I want to open it in front of Beryl. That will only make the contents more visible, and then I'll have to explain. That's a big, huge *nope*. I peel the card free from the cellophane and open the envelope.

> *Bea,*
> *I'm sorry I was a dick.*
> *I fucking miss you.*
> *Tristan*

"Who's it from?" She stares at me expectantly.

"This guy I was...involved with." For obvious reasons, I have not told my colleagues I was banging my brother's best friend who also happens to be a professional hockey player.

She peeks at the basket. "Sort of seems like he still wants to be involved."

"It does." Without the note, I might have questioned his motives. As weird as the contents are, the message is clear.

"Do you think he wants to have dinner with you?" She's obviously fishing.

I can't blame her. It's an unusual basket. "That's a definite possibility." I turn the basket and scan the contents. "Oh man, I have to take this on the subway."

"Or you could Uber. Or maybe he'll pick you up!" That possibility seems to excite her. She reminds me a little of Tally right now.

"He's working tonight, so probably not." They have a game this evening. It would be impossible to drive me home and make it to the arena on time.

"He must be a real health nut, eh?" Beryl says.

"Totally."

I take my basket on the subway. It's ridiculous and cumbersome, and I get a lot of looks. It's understandable. Hammer is in the kitchen when I arrive home, which puts a smile on my face. After less than a week of living together, we've found a groove. She loves price matching and going through the flyers with me. There's a grocery store across the street and another one around the block. It's still about a thirty-minute commute on the subway to my job, but the location and my roommate make it worth it.

"What the hell is that?" Hammer asks as I set the basket on the kitchen table.

My arms ache from holding it. "A gift from Tristan."

She abandons the carrots she's slicing into coins.

Her lips pucker. "Was this at the front desk?"

"No. He sent it to my work."

"How did you get this home? Can we open it?"

"I took it on the subway. And yes, we can open it."

"Dude. Why didn't you text me? I would've picked you up."

"The drive is twice as long as the subway ride." I tear the cellophane wrapping.

"Fucking Tristan." Hammer shakes her head. "Only he would send you a basket of dick-shaped vegetables as an apology. That's what this is, right? An apology basket?"

"Yup." I pass the note card to her.

"He *fucking* misses you, Rix." She presses the card to her chest.

"Or he misses fucking me," I reply. I'm still hurt about the way he left things. There's being upset and then there's shitting all over what we had, and that's exactly what he did. "Damn him and his stupid sense of humor. There are three English cucumbers and a field one."

Hammer holds up a white, carrot-ish looking vegetable. "What the hell is this?"

"It's a daikon. It's part of the radish family and would go well in a fresh salad, thinly sliced," I explain.

"Huh. And this? It looks extra ribbed for no one's pleasure." She holds up a green, tubular, warty vegetable.

"It's a bitter melon from the cucumber family and is used primarily in Chinese cooking. We could add it to a stir fry."

"Cool." Hammer is way too excited about this basket. "But I think tonight you have to make cucumber salad with a creamy dill dressing and take a photo to send to him."

"Oh yeah. That's a must. We should take videos and send them in stages."

"Have you thanked him for it yet?" Hammer asks.

"Not yet."

"But you will, right?"

I sigh.

"Seriously, Rix, just text him. Send him a picture of the basket with an eye roll but send something. You two are miserable without each other. I mean, you're doing a good job of being fake chipper, but you're looking at that cucumber with actual longing. And he and Flip got into a fight during practice yesterday, and my dad staged an intervention with Hollis, Dallas, and Ashish."

"Wait. What? Why didn't you tell me this until now?"

"Because I found out an hour ago." She nudges me with her elbow. "Text him. They're probably still in the locker room."

I blow out a breath. But she's right. I should text him. He's reaching out, and that's a big deal for Tristan. I find my phone and see I have a message from my mom asking if we can chat after dinner tonight. I reply with a thumbs-up and give her a time, then scroll down until I reach Tristan's contact. Rob's is a few down from his, with unread messages since I muted him weeks ago. I continue to ignore him and snap a pic of the basket.

RIX

You know I have more than one vibrator, right?

I want to unsend it as soon as I press Send, but it's already done. There are so many other opening lines I should have gone with. I never did get the vibrator I threw at Tristan back. I didn't need it. When he was away, I took Epsom salt baths to expedite the healing process, so I'd be ready to go to Pound Town when he came home.

My phone rings. I'm so nervous I almost drop it. I also accidentally put it on speakerphone. Hammer slaps her hands over her ears and rushes out of the room as soon as Tristan speaks.

"I didn't know that, but thanks for arming me with knowledge for the future."

My chest and my vagina clench at the sound of his voice. I'm still so angry at him, but I miss him, too. "Don't make me regret my honesty."

"I will try my best, but we both know I'm the kind of asshole who would use that to my advantage."

"That's true. I'll temper my expectations."

"It's really good to hear your voice, Bea," he says softly.

"I won't moan for old times' sake." I make a noise that isn't a moan, but it isn't not a moan. "I'm using humor to deflect a lot of feelings," I admit.

"I get it. I turn into an asshole when I have feelings." He clears his throat. "I'm sorry. I didn't know how to deal with you moving out. I miss you. I want to see you."

"You want to see me or my vagina?" This time I'm not deflecting. I swallow down the fear that comes with such a bold question.

"*You.* I miss you. I mean, yes, I miss all the parts of you, too, but I hate how shitty things are without you. Can I take you out? On a date? Tomorrow night maybe? We could go for dinner. Please say yes, Bea. I want to apologize in person. Please give me a chance."

Hammer gazelle leaps across the room and mouths, *Say yes*. So much for not eavesdropping.

"Okay. Yes. We can go for dinner." I need to clear the air and confront him for being such a horrible dick.

"Can I pick you up at seven thirty? At your place?" Tristan asks.

"Yes. My place. Seven thirty. You can pick me up."

"Great. That's great. I promise you won't regret it, Bea. I gotta go. We're taking the ice. I'll see you tomorrow."

"Good luck tonight."

"Thanks." He ends the call without saying goodbye.

"I'm so nervous. Why am I so nervous?" My palms are damp, and I hold my arms out so I don't sweat in my dress. "Is this outfit too much? It's too much. I should change."

Hemi steps in front of me to prevent me from making a beeline for my bedroom. "Take a breath, Rix."

"And a drink." Hammer hands me a glass of bubbly rosé.

When I try to chug it, she gently pries it out of my hand. I've changed my dress three times. I finally settled on an emerald-green satin number with a plunging neckline and ruching. My heels are gold and so is my purse. Hemi helped me with my hair. It's in an intricate ponytail. On purpose. Tristan is a little obsessed with my neck.

"Little sips, sweetie. We don't want you on your back before the date even begins." Hemi squeezes my shoulders. "You're smokin' hot. You don't need to change."

"You look great," Tally agrees. "I wish I had a butt like yours."

"You're gorgeous," all three of us say in unison.

Tally opens and closes her mouth a couple of times before she ducks her head and says, "Thanks. A guy I went out with last year told me I have a flat butt."

"That guy is an idiot. I'm glad you're not dating him anymore," I say.

"If you need me to vacate the premises for the night, I can stay at my dad's," Hammer offers.

"I'm not sleeping with him tonight." It comes out sounding like a question.

"You need to do what feels right for you, but considering what he did the last time you had sex, leaving him hanging tonight might be the better move," Hemi suggests.

"You're right. I know you're right." Sex is what got us into this mess; having it tonight won't solve our problems. Even if it will feel good.

"What happened last time?" Tally asks.

"He came, and she didn't, which happens sometimes. But she was literally in the middle of an orgasm, and he pulled out and finished on her thighs and left her hanging on purpose," Hammer explains helpfully.

Tally's mouth drops open. "Oh my God."

"Seriously. We are all going to hell for corrupting Tally," I say.

"At least we'll be there together," Hemi reminds us.

"Why are you going out with Tristan again when he did that to you?" Tally looks baffled.

Her confusion is understandable.

"I gave him an hour's notice that I was moving."

"You only gave him an hour's notice?" Hemi seems shocked.

Maybe I failed to share that part. "Yeah, but to be fair, things were pretty tense the week after Flip found out, and he didn't do much to help smooth things over." Apart from invite me to sleep in his room when Flip brought home a couple of ladies they'd tag-teamed before. "None of us were talking, and I didn't want to be responsible for imploding two decades of friendship. Besides, they're teammates. They needed to be able to sort things out, and it wouldn't happen with me living there." I take a deep breath. "I feel like this dinner will be more of a therapy session than anything else. So yeah, jumping back into bed when that's the reason things went so sideways seems unwise."

A knock on the door has me panicking all over again. Hammer rushes to open it.

"Oh, hey, Daddy." She twirls her ponytail around her finger. "Hi, Hollis. What's up?"

"We thought we'd check in. Tristan mentioned a big date tonight, so I wasn't sure if you'd be on your own for dinner." Roman lifts a hand and waves. "I see your girl gang is all here and accounted for."

"You look nice, Rix." Hollis gives me the thumbs-up.

"Thanks, Hollis."

"So do you Peggy, I mean Hammer." Hollis's gaze darts to

Hammer and then around the room. "You all look nice." He doesn't seem to know what to do with his hands. He crosses his arms, then uncrosses them and tucks his thumbs into his pockets.

There's a collective murmured thanks from the girls.

"You could have texted," Hammer says.

"We were on our way to the diner and thought we'd extend the invite. You're all more than welcome to join us. Except you, Rix. I doubt Tristan will be all that inclined to share you."

"That's kind of a relief, actually." The words are out before I think them through.

Hollis coughs into his elbow.

"That's...yeah." Roman nods.

Hemi snickers.

Tally looks confused, God bless her.

"Uh, we're going to hang out and watch Chris Hemsworth movies, but thanks." Hammer gives her dad an expectant look.

"Okay. Well, you girls have fun tonight." They can't seem to leave fast enough.

A minute later there's another knock on the door. Hammer opens it enough that she can see through the crack. "Geez, Daddy, what now? Oh, hey, Tristan."

"Daddy?"

"It annoys him," Hammer explains as she opens the door.

Tristan stands on the threshold dressed in a blue suit. Not navy, but a deep royal blue. His shoes are black and polished. His shirt is pale pink, and his tie matches his shoes. He looks delicious, and I approve.

As soon as his eyes land on me, he strides across the room. He's holding a bouquet of peonies in one hand. He stops about a foot away. "Hey."

"Hey."

His free hand rises, and his fingertips skim the edge of my jaw until his pointer reaches the hollow behind my ear. His thumb follows the line of his fingers in reverse, traveling all the way to my other ear. His palm settles against my throat. He steps in closer until our faces are inches apart and his knee touches my thigh. His eyes are on my lips. "You look fucking gorgeous," he murmurs.

"Wow. That's some unreal chemistry," Hammer says.

"Seriously," Hemi agrees.

"Is he choking her?" Tally whispers.

Tristan drops his hand and steps back. "Sorry. Hi. You look amazing. I brought you flowers." He thrusts them at me and glances toward the girls, who wear a mix of expressions. Tally looks scandalized, Hemi knowing, and Hammer seems envious.

"They're beautiful. Thank you." I bring them to my nose and inhale. "How did you get up here, anyway?"

"Hollis and Roman were going out as I was coming in. I probably should have texted. I didn't think everyone would be here." He gives the girls a constipated smile.

"They're my support team."

He bites the inside of his lip. "I don't know that you needing a support team to get ready for a date with me is a good thing."

"I'm nervous," I admit. "It's been a while since I've been on a date. And I've never been on a not-secret date with my brother's best friend who was railing me on the downlow for two months until Flip found out. Just a lot of never-before-experienced variables."

"That's legit." His tongue drags across his bottom lip. "I'm nervous, too. I'm probably better at railing you than I am dating you."

"You've had a lot more practice railing me, so it makes sense you'd be better at it." I pat his chest. "Should we give this whole date thing a fair shot? You can't get better at it if you don't try, right?"

"That's some good logic." He glances at the girls, who have taken front-row seats to all this awkwardness. He opens his mouth a couple of times, but nothing comes out.

"We see you, Tristan." Hemi's smile is downright evil.

He frowns. "I don't know what that means."

"Have a good time! But not too good a time!" Hammer winks.

Tally looks shellshocked. Poor thing. "We'll put your flowers in water."

"Thank you." The girls come in for a hug and whisper words of encouragement.

I grab my purse and usher Tristan out the door.

Being alone with him in an elevator is a test of my restraint. We're both used to deflecting feelings with sex. Thankfully, another couple joins us, so I don't have to worry about humping his leg on the ride down. We do the polite, Canadian thing and talk about the weather.

Tristan is parked out front in the ten-minute spot. He opens the passenger door and holds out his hand. I slip mine into his and lift my dress, so it doesn't get stuck in the door. Once I'm settled, he rounds the hood and drops into the driver's seat.

His nostrils flare as he inhales. "Fuck, I missed the way you smell." He runs his hands down his thighs. "Sorry about what I did in front of the girls. I just saw you, and I wasn't thinking, and I haven't touched you in a week, and you look amazing, and yeah."

"You can join me, Hemi, and Hammer in hell for corrupting poor little Tally."

His eyes flare. "Why? What did you do to Tally? She's not even eighteen."

"We didn't do anything. She's been around for some NSFW conversations. Anyway..." I wave my hand. "Enough about that. Where are you taking me tonight?" I'm not ready to deal with the heavy stuff, yet.

"It's called Scaramouche. I've never been there, but Dallas and Ashish said it's a great place to take a date." He pulls out of the spot and heads for the exit.

He stretches one arm across the back of my seat. "Is this okay?"

"Yeah, it's okay."

"I missed touching you," he says.

"I missed you touching me," I admit.

"How's the new apartment? How have you been?"

"The new apartment is nice. Having a bedroom with a door obviously has perks, and I have my own bathroom, so I don't have to worry about falling into the toilet in the middle of the night if I forget to make sure the seat is down." Yup, we're avoiding the hard stuff for now.

"Did that happen a lot when you were living with me and Flip?"

"A couple times. Falling into post-drinking pee-water has a way of sticking with you, though." I tap my temple.

"That's fucking gross."

"Yes, it is."

"Sounds like the move has been good for you. Better than living with me." His thumb sweeps back and forth along the nape of my neck.

"Living with you had some perks." I adjust my position so I can look at his profile.

He's gorgeous. Just so pretty. And so filthy between the sheets. I remind my vagina that we are not letting him near her tonight, not after what happened last time. We need to deal with feelings first.

"And some pretty serious downsides," he says softly.

I let that go for now. "How are you and Flip? Hammer said you two got into it during practice?"

Tristan frowns. "Haven't you talked to him?"

"Not really. I'm pretty pissed at him, so I'm waiting on an official apology that isn't him inviting me out for East Side's in a text message. If we're here, I guess you two have resolved your issues?" I motion between us.

"Roman, Hollis, Ashish, and Dallas mediated a conversation after we got into a fight on the ice, so yeah, Flip and I are okay.

We did go behind his back for a lot of weeks. And he knows what I'm like." His grip on the wheel tightens.

"So it's fine for him to rail everyone else and post about it all over social media, but it's not okay for his younger sister to get railed by one guy she's hot for in private? It doesn't matter if it's vanilla sex or filthy sex, or anything in between, that's my prerogative. I understand that he's upset we went behind his back, but he can't live in a land of double standards where what he does is okay and what I do isn't."

"I think it's more that he knows I can be aggressive in bed."

I can't read his tone or his facial expression. "And if I wasn't on board, we would not have continued to have sex," I assure him. "And again, why is it fine for you to be aggressive with other women, but not with me, if it's what I want? I refuse to be ashamed for liking what I like, even if it's being fucked with a cucumber and then watching you eat it like a savage." My thighs clench at the memory. We're still circling the bigger issues, but one thing at a time.

He squeezes the back of my neck. "We should shift conversation gears if I want to get out of this car without ending up on the front page of the tabloids for rocking a public hard-on."

"Good point." Besides, jumping him in a public parking lot would garner a lot of attention neither of us needs. "How do you feel about the upcoming away series?"

He exhales a long, slow breath. "I'll be starting on second line for the next few games, so not fantastic, to be honest."

"Because you and Flip duked it out on the ice like man-babies, or because they still want to pull Hollis in the last period to make sure he's still in peak condition?" I ask.

"More the latter than the former, but I sure didn't help myself out by fighting with my teammate during practice."

"Better practice than an actual game."

"Yeah. Hollis is having a kickass season so far. I know it's good for the team, but it messes with my head."

"That's fair. Hollis was strong in the first two periods last game."

"You watched?" His eyes flare. "I didn't know you were at the arena."

"I wasn't. We watched from home. Hammer's worried someone will get wise to their game strategy."

"One knee injury is bad enough. No one wants to be forced into retirement because of a reinjury." He pulls into the parking lot adjacent to the restaurant, which ends our conversation.

Tristan hustles around to help me out. I accept his offered hand, but he lets go as soon as I've found my footing. I fall into step beside him. He's used to wearing suits when he travels and before and after games. Most of the time he carries himself with an air of arrogant confidence. But he keeps looking over at me like he's not sure what to do.

I lift the hem of my dress when we reach the stairs up to the door and use the railing for balance. Halfway up he realizes I'm a few stairs behind and comes back down. "Do you... Can I?" He offers his arm.

"Thank you." I slip my arm through his.

"Anything for you, Bea." His fingers find the small of my back as the doorman holds the entrance open for us.

The host clearly knows who he is and addresses him as Mr. Stiles. We're led to a private table. This is probably the nicest restaurant I've been to. Rob's family was upper middle-class, so sometimes we'd go for nice dinners, but this beats that by a long shot.

We're given the option of still or sparkling water, and the server comes by to take our drink order. I choose a glass of white wine and Tristan opts for a beer. That's his go-to drink of choice when we've been at the bar.

He crosses and uncrosses his legs—sets his elbows on the table, then removes them and leans back in his chair.

"Are you okay?"

"Yeah. Good. Why?" He rubs his bottom lip.

"Don't take this the wrong way, but you look...uncom-fortable."

He taps on the arm of his chair. "It's been a long time since I've been on a date."

"How long is a long time?"

He pokes at his cheek with his tongue. "Junior year of high school."

"What about that cooking lesson? Didn't that count as a date?"

"I mean...I guess, yeah. But before that, not since junior year."

The server returns with our drinks, and we order the burrata salad and crab cakes to start.

Once the server leaves, I dig back into this interesting and probably uncomfortable conversation. "But you've dated women?"

"Sure. Yeah. I guess." Tristan takes a huge gulp of his beer and then another.

"By *dated* I mean you've spent time with a woman that extended beyond a one-night stand, and you did things together apart from have sex," I clarify.

"I guess. Does watching movies count?" he asks.

"In a theater or at home?"

"At home."

I raise an eyebrow. "What about events—did you ever take anyone to one? Like a charity gala or a team thing?"

"Maybe once or twice, but mostly that was for promo ops and mutually beneficial." His knee bounces under the table.

Clearly this isn't his favorite topic, which means I want to explore it more. "What about the girl in high school? How long did you date her?"

"Most of junior year."

"What was her name?"

"Darla Fitzgibbons."

"Did you go to the same high school?"

He rubs his lip. "Why are you so interested in my dating history?"

"Because you haven't been on a date since high school, apart from a couple of charity galas. And if they were promo ops, they don't count. But the high school girlfriend counts, so I'm interested in her and why you went out with her for so long."

"Mostly because her parents worked long hours so we could go to her place after school or practice and have sex."

"That's the only reason you dated for a year? It must have been some great sex." I'm needling him on purpose.

"She was nice. And smart. And fun to be around for the most part," he offers somewhat grudgingly.

"Why did you break up?" I sip my wine.

"Because I couldn't give her more and hockey took up too much of my time," he replies. "I don't know that much has changed."

"Well, we're here, doing this thing you don't normally do, so I think that counts as personal growth. And you play hockey for a living, so it makes sense that it takes up a lot of your time," I say.

"I had a hard time getting close to people after my mom left. I still do," he says softly.

Now we're getting somewhere. "That must have been really difficult for you and your brothers and your dad." I want to reach out and touch his hand, but I don't know how receptive he'll be to contact meant to comfort. I don't think it's something he's used to, and I don't want to give him a reason to shut this conversation down yet.

"I came home when she was leaving." He focuses on his beer glass. "It was super random that day. I was supposed to go to your house after school, but Flip hadn't been feeling well. He'd caught the flu, so I went home instead and found her throwing her suitcases into the car. She was just gonna disappear. I mean, she did just disappear on Brody and Nathan. They came home

319

an hour later, and she was gone. I had to tell them. And my dad."

This time I do reach across the table and cover his hand with mine. No wonder he never talks about his mom. No wonder relationships are hard for him. "I'm so sorry, Tristan. That must have been awful for you."

"I thought maybe she would come back, but she never did." He shakes his head. "Why the hell am I talking about this? You don't want to hear this shit. I gotta use the bathroom." He pulls his hand away and pushes his chair back. He strides across the room and disappears down the hall.

I want to chase after him. To hug him. To tell him she never should have made him shoulder that responsibility. That his mother is a horrible coward and he deserved so much better. But if there's one thing I've learned about Tristan over the past few months, it's that when he feels anything uncomfortable, making him confront it causes him to shut down.

And this explains his anger when I told him I was moving, and I only gave him an hour. I left him. Without warning. Just like his mom. Of course his reaction was to lash out and shut down.

Our appetizers arrive while he's gone, and I half expect him not to come back. But two minutes later he returns, sliding into his seat like nothing happened.

This little glimpse into the fall of his family makes me see him differently. I wasn't wrong about him still being that hurt little boy hiding inside a closed-off man.

"Are you okay?" I ask.

"Yeah, sorry I left you on your own like that. I don't really talk about that stuff. It's too hard." He sets his napkin in his lap. "Which one do you want to start with? You eat half and I'll eat half and then we can trade?"

I let it be for now. "I'll start with the crab cakes, if that's okay with you."

"Yeah, for sure." He sets the plate in front of me, then moves the burrata salad in front of him.

We're both quiet for the first couple of bites. The crab cakes are decadent and delicious. The flavors burst on my tongue.

"You need to try this." I slide my fork through the tender meat and lean in so I can offer it to Tristan. "It's literally the best thing I've ever put in my mouth."

"Really? The best?" He gives me a cocky grin as his fingers wrap around my wrist. His plush lips close around the tines, pulling the bite free. He chews thoughtfully. "It's good. But you taste infinitely better."

"You're not getting in my panties tonight," I warn him.

"I know." He peeks up at me. "Doesn't mean I can't think about it. Or fantasize aloud."

"Is that your attempt to wear me down?"

He lifts a shoulder and lets it fall. "Mostly I'm grateful you said yes to seeing me." He cuts a small piece of tomato, fresh basil, and burrata, and drags his fork through the oil-balsamic reduction. He lifts it to my mouth.

His eyes spark as he watches the fork disappear into my mouth.

I let my eyes flutter closed and moan as I chew. On purpose, of course.

"It's gonna be a while before I get to hear that sound for the right reasons, isn't it?" Tristan asks softly.

"You weren't very nice last time, so yeah." No point in pretending I'm over how that ended.

"I'm sorry I was such a dick." He cuts another bite but doesn't make a move to eat it.

"Do you want to explain why you were?"

"I knew you would move out eventually. I just didn't expect it to happen like it did. I thought maybe you needed space after Flip found out. I didn't want to make things worse, and then you were packing and I couldn't stop you from leaving me," he admits.

His phrasing is everything, I realize. "To be fair, you had an entire week to talk to me about Flip finding out and how you wanted to deal with it." If we're ever going to move past this, he has to own how awful he was, and I need him to understand that I can't allow that to happen, not ever again.

He sips his beer, then takes a hefty gulp. "I did try."

"To get me into bed. Not to talk," I point out.

"That night Flip brought those two women home, I said you could sleep in my room, though." His knee is bouncing again.

"You didn't correct me when I asked if you planned to drown out their moans with mine." My stomach twists uncomfortably. I desperately want him to open up, to give me something to work with. To show me he cares enough to try, even if it makes him uncomfortable.

He looks like he wants to bolt. His gaze darts to the side, and his fingers go to his lips. He looks like a scared boy, not a badass hockey player. "If that was what you wanted, I would have done that. But that wasn't how I meant it. I didn't want you to have to listen and think about how I'd been involved the last time. I didn't want that shoved in your face."

"Why didn't you say that, then?"

"I started to, but you were so upset with me." He pushes a piece of tomato around his plate. "You were always going to leave. I didn't want you to. But if I asked you to stay and you said no... I couldn't handle that. And I would fuck things up again eventually. I always do."

It's heartbreaking the way he holds on to blame, like everything was his fault. Like he's the problem, when really the whole thing was doomed from the start.

"You didn't even give it a chance, Tristan. You told Flip all we were doing was fucking."

"Because that's what we agreed on." His jaw works. He looks so uncomfortable.

"But was it the truth?" I ask.

He shakes his head. His gaze lifts, and his voice is barely a whisper. "I have feelings for you. And not just I-want-to-fuck-you feelings. I have a lot of those, but I have other feelings, too."

"You were awful to me when I moved out."

He drops his head and pulls his bottom lip between his teeth. "I know. I'm sorry."

"You treated me like I meant nothing to you."

His swallow is audible. "You were leaving me, and I couldn't get you to stay. It hurt, and I couldn't handle it."

"So you hurt me back?"

His head snaps up, and his eyes go wide.

I hold up a hand. "Not physically. With your actions and your words. You were cruel."

He drops his head again. "I shouldn't have left you hanging like that."

"It's about more than that, Tristan. You discarded me. You treated me like I meant nothing to you, and it gutted me. It wasn't just about the sex. It was how easily you turned off your feelings. You made me feel used. Do you understand how awful that was? You can't do that to me again. Not ever. I won't stand for it. I deserve better."

"I'm sorry. I wish I could go back and do that differently." He wrings his hands, then hides them under the table. "I hated myself for what I did and how I acted. Everything was changing, and there was nothing I could do to stop it. But I care about you, Bea. A lot. More than I know what to do with sometimes. It scares the shit out of me."

And there he is, that broken boy I've come to know well. "I care about you, too."

"Yeah?" The way his face brightens with hope makes my chest ache.

I nod. "Yeah."

"Good. That's good." He fidgets with his fork. "I, uh, I was hoping you'd want to do more of this after tonight." He motions between us and almost knocks his glass over.

"More talking and dinners?" I won't make this easy for him.

"Yeah. Exactly. We don't always have to go out for dinner, though. We can hang out and not just naked hanging out. But we could do that, too. Whenever you're ready."

"So you want to go on dates?"

"If you do, yeah."

The table is jiggling like there's a low-level earthquake happening under it. For as cocky as he is in the bedroom and on the ice, he's definitely unsure of himself off of it.

"We can go on more dates."

"Yeah?" His eyes light up, and my heart clenches.

"Yeah."

We spend the rest of dinner talking about the upcoming games, and my job, and how he misses hanging out with me in the kitchen while I prep food and all the other little things he'd gotten used to with me living there.

At the end of the night, Tristan offers me his arm as we go down the stairs. He opens the car door and helps me with my dress. Instead of dropping me off at the front door, he parks and walks me to the elevators.

"I'm not inviting you in tonight," I inform him as we get in the elevator.

He nods. "I know. I want to make sure you get in okay. And I want every minute I can get with you." He leans against the mirrored-glass railing as we ascend, and I fidget with my purse strap. The doors open, and he laces our hands as we walk down the hall.

"I had a nice time tonight. Thank you for dinner, and the flowers, and for opening up."

"I...I know I'm bad at it, but I'm trying to be better. For you." His bottom lip slides through his teeth. "Thank you for agreeing to a date."

"You're welcome."

"Would it be okay if I hug you? Please?"

I nod, and he wraps his arms around me. He presses his face

against my neck and shamelessly sniffs me. "I missed you so much, Bea. So fucking much."

"I missed you, too." I rest my cheek against his chest. "Especially this version of you."

He holds me for a long time. Eventually he pulls back, swallowing thickly. "I know I'm probably pushing it, and maybe you're not ready yet, but can I kiss you good night?"

My heart clenches—hell, everything clenches. "I would like that."

"Cheek or..." He trails off.

I tap my lips.

His fingertips drift from my temple to my chin, and he tenderly cups my cheek. He tips my head back and lowers his mouth to mine, just a soft brush of lips at first. His arm winds around my waist, pulling me against him as he angles his head and I do the same. I part my lips, and his tongue strokes inside on a quiet groan. I grip the lapels of his suit jacket, whimpering as my body warms and I feel his erection against my stomach. He adjusts his grip, and his palm settles against my throat. But still, the kiss is soft. An apology. A promise of what could be. I'm afraid to hope for more than this. But I want to try. I want to see what this can be outside of the secret bubble we were living in.

He ends the kiss before it grows heated and brushes his nose against mine. "Thank you. I'll do everything I can to deserve you." He pulls me in for another long hug.

I melt into him. Into possibility. Into what this might become.

Eventually he pulls back. "Can I see you again soon?"

"I'd like that." His smile is so boyishly charming, I almost invite him in so I can sit on his face.

"Can I call you tomorrow?"

"That'd be great."

"Night, Beatrix." He kisses my hand and steps back.

"Night, Tristan." I manage to get inside the apartment without pulling him along with me. My vagina is confused, but my heart is happy.

CHAPTER 24
TRISTAN

Away games have never been my favorite. I prefer home-ice advantage to sleeping in hotel rooms. Especially lately, since Flip is still being Flip. It's stupidly awkward now that I'm dating his sister. I often end up on Roman and Hollis's couch. Or Dallas and Ashish's. It's better than trying to pretend shit isn't going down in the bathroom or the bed next to mine.

Instead of hitting the bar after the game, I go directly to the room. Flip will be at the bar for at least a couple of hours while he trolls for tonight's bedmate, or bedmates, so I can get in some phone time with Bea.

I fire off a text message on the way to the room to tell her I'm calling in two minutes, and when I get there, I put the DO NOT DISTURB sign on the door.

I strip down to my boxers and a T-shirt on the way to the bed and hit the video button as I flop down on yet another hotel mattress.

"Hey, nice game tonight. Those two goals were magic." Bea's gorgeous two-dimensional image appears on the small screen in my hand.

My earbuds are close by, but I leave them out for now so I

can hear what's going on beyond our conversation. "We're playing tight."

"How was your day?" She's fresh from the shower. Her hair is wet and pulled over one shoulder, the damp ends soaking into her white tank. I bet she smells fantastic. What I wouldn't give to bury my face in her hair and smell her skin.

"Good. Better now. Yours? Did you have cake for dessert? Have you run out? Do you need me to send you another one?"

She smiles. "I did have cake for dessert. There's still a slice left, though, so I'm good for now."

"Are you doing that thing where you savor it so slowly it's basically sawdust and requires half a pint of ice cream to be palatable at the end?"

She gives me the shifty eyes.

"I'm sending you another one tomorrow so you better eat up," I warn.

"Okay. I'll finish it." She grins. "Tell me about the game—the highlights and the lowlights."

I love that she talks hockey with me every night, like she gives a fuck about the actual game. Because she does. She knows it. She's spent an inordinate amount of time sitting in arenas because of Flip.

"Highlights were the two goals," I tell her. "Lowlights... Flip is off his game, and it cost us our lead in the second period, which I expected with us playing New York."

"Bowman's been a good addition to the team," Bea says.

"Yeah. We were lucky tonight. Especially since Flip can't keep his shit together when he's on the ice against Grace."

She makes a noise as she braids her hair. "Flip can't stand him."

"Have you even talked to him? Flip, I mean."

She side-eyes me.

"He asks about you every day, Bea. And he's been calling your parents more than usual, and he sought Hemi out before we left. He never does that."

Flip is off—even when he's not in the same arena as Grace. He's worried about Bea. And I don't like that I'm the reason they're not speaking.

"I'll talk to him when you get back from away games," she concedes. "How's Brody? Did they win their game tonight?"

"They did, which is great. Their team is in second place now. I think he'll be drafted this year."

"How do you feel about that?" Bea asks.

"Okay."

"Just okay?"

"Good, I guess. It's what he wants. He's professional material in the player sense."

"But?" she presses.

"But I worry about all the other stuff. He'll be fine with the pressure of the game. He's got a good head on his shoulders, but he's a lot like me."

"That's not a bad thing. You're an incredible player."

"The game play isn't my worry." I glance to the side and rub my lip. All the shit Flip and I got up to last year has been eating at me. I don't want Brody to think he has to fall into that pit, and I don't love that Bea has had to meet more than one of my previous one-night stands. Sitting on the other side of those choices, I wish I'd realized there were consequences sooner.

"The lifestyle is the issue?" she asks softly.

"I don't know if he's built for it. He's a good kid."

"Flip's path isn't the only one out there. Look at Roman. Hammer has been surrounded by the team her entire life. She's been part of the family, had a tutor, been immersed in this world since she was a kid, and she's well rounded. Roman is a great guy, and I know Hollis is a sore spot because you're fighting for position, but he's levelheaded and not a player."

"He wasn't like that in his early years," I argue.

"For all of two years. He had a string of short-term girl-friends until he started dating that one actress. After that he settled down and focused on the game and stopped letting fame

328

dictate his actions. Dallas has one scandalous night a season and reins it in. Flip is an anomaly, and you've gotten used to it. But it's not the norm, Tristan."

"I guess I've been so immersed in it the past year, it's hard to see anything else," I muse.

"Makes sense. But you're on the outside looking in now, so you view it differently. He at the bar now?"

"Yeah."

"Do you think he'll be there for a while?"

"Oh yeah. He's licking his wounds from those flubbed shots on net tonight, so he'll be looking to score off the ice. Especially with it being our last away game." Flip typically brings home multiple partners after a bad game, like he needs to prove that he can score all the goals in some capacity. I'm not sure he realizes how transparent he is.

Bea rubs her bottom lip. "Does that mean you'll be sleeping in Hollis and Roman's room tonight?"

"Yeah. But he won't be up here for a while. Is Hammer home?"

Bea shakes her head. "She's at an event tonight with Hemi. She probably won't be home for another hour." She fingers the wet end of her ponytail and tips her head. "What are you thinking about over there?"

We went on another date before the away series. I have a feeling Bea would have invited me in, but Hammer was home, so I got a good-night make-out session in the hallway and a hard-to-hide boner.

"How much I'm looking forward to getting past first base with you when you're ready." Might as well be honest with her.

"We could get past first base right now, if you're interested." She circles her nipple through her damp tank.

"You mean, I watch you fuck your hand, and you watch me fuck mine?" My cock kicks in my boxer shorts.

"More fun than doing it alone, don't you think?" Her smile turns sly, and she pulls her top over her head, discarding it on the bed. My gaze rakes over her as she shimmies out of her shorts and panties. I haven't seen her naked in weeks. Haven't done more than hug or kiss her. I need to earn my way back into her bed and her body after what I did the last time.

"You're so fucking beautiful." I set my phone on the holder beside the bed, angling it so she can see what I'm doing while she does the same.

"So are you." Her fingers glide over her bare breasts, skimming her nipples on the way down. I follow the path, fisting my erection as she dips between her thighs. She takes her time, fingers pushing inside, then circling her clit. I have to stop halfway through, or I risk losing it too soon. Just before she comes, her free hand glides up her body, pausing to squeeze a breast before she wraps her fingers around her throat. Her legs tremble, and her hips roll and jerk as the orgasm sweeps over her. And I let go, too.

We're both panting and sweaty, but at least we're semi-sated.

"When you get home tomorrow, you can come over," Bea says.

"Over as in…" I let that hang.

"As in, I'll show you my bedroom."

I wake up at three in the morning because I have to pee, and I see that Flip messaged an hour ago to let me know his friends were gone. I could go back to our room and sleep in a bed, or I can catch an early flight back to Toronto and take Bea out for breakfast. Maybe I can even convince her to take the day off. I've been away for almost a week. I'm not used to missing someone, and I don't like how antsy I am about having to wait until the end of the day to see her.

Decision already made, I book a flight, get dressed, and leave a message for Flip and one for Coach to let him know I went home early. The team flight doesn't leave for several hours.

I text Bea once I've boarded to let her know I'll be home in less than two hours, and I want to take her to breakfast. She video-calls me right away. We're still fifteen minutes from takeoff.

"I thought the team wasn't flying back until later this morning?" Her voice is sleep raspy. It's barely six a.m.

"They aren't. I'm coming home early so we can have breakfast. I haven't seen you in six days, and last night made me hungry for more of you."

The businesswoman next to me gives me the side-eye.

"Is this because I said I'd show you my bedroom?"

"I want to see you regardless of whether I get to see your bedroom," I say. "I'll be back by eight. Can you go in late? Or take the day? I promise I'll make it worth it. And not just orgasm worth it, if you decide you want me to give you some of those."

The woman beside me makes a disapproving sound.

"I want the day with you. Just us," I add.

Bea is quiet for a few seconds. "Jane, in marketing, went home yesterday with the flu after our morning meeting. I can always say I think I've come down with the same thing."

"Yeah?" I haven't had a whole day with Bea before. I definitely need to make it worth her while.

"Yeah."

"I'll be at your place by eight thirty."

"I'll be ready."

Two and a half hours later, I knock on Bea's door. She's wearing a robe.

"Hi." I don't make a move to touch her.

"Hi." She steps back, and I cross the threshold.

"Is Hammer home?"

"She left for work half an hour ago."

"Can I hug you?" I ask.

A small, surprised smile tips her mouth. "Yeah. Of course."

I wrap my arms around her and pull her body against mine. Dropping my head, I bury my face in her hair and breathe in the scent of her shampoo. "Fuck, I missed you," I mutter. I've never really been much of a hugger, but with Bea, it feels good. I want to hold her all the time.

She gives me a gentle squeeze and runs her hand up and down my back. "I missed you, too."

We stand there for a minute, and I absorb all her warmth and goodness. The only people I'm used to caring about are my dad, my brothers, and my teammates. I've never allowed myself to get close to anyone else. Not like this. But I want it. I want her.

Eventually I pull back. "Can I kiss you now?"

"Yes, please."

I take her face in my hands and put my mouth on hers. She parts her lips, and our tongues tangle. She tastes like mint and home and everything I need.

Her hands go to my belt and she tugs, pulling it free from the clasp.

"I don't have expectations, Bea."

"I know." She pops the button, drags the zipper down. "But I'm done holding out."

I groan as her hand slips into my pants, her fingers wrapping around my erection. "Fuck, that feels good. I missed you touching me."

"Same." She pulls my mouth back to hers for a few strokes of tongue. "I just need you in me, so can we save the part where you torment me and hold out on giving me an orgasm for later? Like, after you take me out for breakfast?"

"Any other time, you saying that would make me inclined to do the opposite." I grab her ass and hoist her up. Self-control will be tough to find, but I don't want to rush this. Not when it's been weeks since I last put my hands on her.

She wraps her arms around my shoulders and her legs around my waist. "But not today?"

I carry her to the kitchen island, biting the edge of her jaw. "Not today."

"Why not?"

She reaches for my cock again, but I grab her wrists and quickly pin them behind her back with one hand, then wrap my free hand around her throat. If she gets her hands on me again, I'll lose it. And I want this to be about her. "I need to make up for last time."

Her eyes go soft. "So touch me."

I ghost my lips along her cheek. "Tell me where you want my hands."

Her eyes flip open, and she licks her lips. "Anywhere. Everywhere. I just want to feel you again."

I brush my lips over hers, release her hands and tug the tie at her waist. She's naked under the robe. I soak in the sight of her as the fabric drops to the counter.

"I missed this," she whispers.

"I missed this, too." I circle her nipple with a fingertip. "Why don't you unbutton my shirt while I show you how sorry I am for being such a dick?"

"That sounds like a great idea."

She pulls my tie loose—even though I wasn't flying with the rest of the team, I still wore a suit home—and pulls it over my head, then gets to work on the buttons. Her hands are shaking, so she struggles with the first two.

And I'm no help because I ease a single finger inside her and pump twice as a distraction. She whimpers when I remove it and bites her lip when I suck it clean. I add a second finger and pump twice more, repeating the same action, sucking my fingers clean before I fuck her with them. I purposely evade the spot inside that makes her eyes roll up—not to be a dick, but because it makes her orgasms more intense. It takes an eternity for her to unbutton my shirt.

When she does, I release her throat and drop to my knees so I can kiss a path up the inside of her right thigh. She runs her fingers through my hair and grips the strands. But she doesn't try to shove my face into her pussy.

"Not gonna try to rip my hair out this morning?"

I blow on her clit, then start kissing the same path from her left knee up the inside of her thigh.

"It doesn't usually work to my advantage." Her toes curl against my side.

I hum in agreement. "I'm trying to hold back, but I'm too hungry for the taste of you." I push her thighs wider and lick up the length of her.

"Oh, fuck." Her fingers tighten in my hair and her hips roll.

"So fucking good, Bea." I bite the inside of her thigh. I want to keep her balanced on the edge, to savor her slowly, but my need for her is overwhelming.

All it takes is a few strokes of tongue and one clit suck and she's moaning my name as her body quakes. I stand, drag the head of my erection along her slit, and push inside. Her eyes roll up as she clenches around me. I take a moment to savor the way it feels to be with her again. How fucking lucky I am that she's so damn forgiving.

But I don't start moving. "Look at me, Bea. I want your eyes on me when I'm fucking you."

They flip open, hazy and hot with need.

"That's better." I stroke her cheek. "Wrap your legs around me and hold on."

She laces her fingers behind my neck and hooks her feet at the small of my back. I hold her hips and start thrusting—lazy strokes that make her moan and clench around me. But I can't get enough of her, can't get deep enough, close enough.

"Can I see your bedroom now?" I slide my hands under her ass.

"First door on the right." She wraps her arms around my neck and kisses my jaw.

I carry her across the apartment to her bedroom. I don't turn her into a pretzel. Instead I stretch out on top of her and keep her wrapped around me. I go slow, taking my time, because I don't want this to end. I want to stay here with her, in this place where we can't get enough of each other. Where I can make her feel good. Where I can't do something else to fuck this up.

Two hours later, Bea and I are tucked into a booth at a diner across the street from her place. She's suggestively eating a sausage link. "Nothing beats the real thing." She dips the end into the pool of maple syrup on her plate and nibbles it before dragging it through the syrup again. "I remember that time your dad sent you over with a huge bottle when we were kids. That was the first time I had the real stuff, and nothing else compared after that."

I smile. "I remember that. Your pancakes were swimming in it."

"I didn't expect it to be so runny. I was so sad when the bottle ran out and my mom replaced it with the fake stuff. I always secretly hoped you'd bring more over some time."

Real maple syrup costs four times as much as the fake stuff, and that was an indulgence her parents couldn't afford. "I have a friend who has a maple farm. We could go there this afternoon if you want?" I suggest.

"It's not harvest season, though," Bea points out.

"They have riding trails and a bakery. We could go for a hike and buy maple candies."

"Do you have time for that?"

"Yeah. Totally. It'll be fun." I want to spend time with her, hold her hand and make her smile.

We finish breakfast and drive out to my friend's farm. On the way, my brother Nate calls.

"Hey, bro, what's up?"

"Just checking in. You back from your away series?" he asks.

"Yeah, flew in this morning. I'm in the car. Bea's with me, and you're on speakerphone," I warn.

"Bea? As in Beatrix, your best friend's sister? The one you

didn't want me flirting with at Thanksgiving?" I can hear the smile in his voice.

"Oh, this is news. Do tell, Nate." Bea's eyes light up.

"He said you were already involved with someone. He just failed to mention it was him."

"Yeah, well, now you know. Besides, you have a girlfriend," I remind him. "So you shouldn't be flirting with other girls. Especially not mine."

"Oh, I'm your girl now?" Bea smiles mischievously.

I stretch my arm across the back of the seat and sift through her hair. "You all right with that?"

She turns her head and kisses my wrist.

"How you doing, Rix?" Nate asks.

"I'm good. How about you?"

"Yeah. Doing all right. This semester is kicking my ass a bit," he says.

"You okay? You need help with anything?" I can't help him with his courses since he's in engineering, but I can make things easier by sending him premade meals or grocery deliveries.

"Nah. I've got it under control. Lisa's buried in work, though. I haven't seen much of her the past few weeks."

"She still planning to come this way during the holidays?" I ask.

"Hopefully, yeah. I know Dad's really looking forward to seeing her. Anyway, I'll let you go. Call me later, okay? We can catch up."

"Okay, sounds good."

I end the call.

"How long have he and Lisa been dating?" Bea asks.

"Over a year. She visited last year at the holidays."

"Your dad said as much at Thanksgiving. He really likes her."

"He does. And she seems good for Nate." She was shy around me, but she seemed sweet. And into my brother.

We arrive at the farm, and I introduce Bea to my friend Carter, whose family has owned the farm for more than fifty years. Bea has never been horseback riding before, so we take her out on the trails, and afterwards Carter takes us to the maple syrup house. It's cold today, below freezing, so they set up the maple toffee trough.

Bea jumps up and down and hugs my arm. "Oh my gosh, I haven't had this since I was a kid."

I kiss her temple. "We couldn't come here and not have the full experience."

She tips her head up, her smile wide and infectious and so fucking beautiful it makes my chest tight. "Thank you for this. The last time I did this, your dad took us."

I remember, vaguely, Bea as a preteen tagging along with me, Flip, and my brothers on a few family outings. She and Nate were close to the same age, so they were likely tasked with managing Brody. I probably hadn't paid much attention to her, but her excitement triggers a memory of her standing in the store at the end of our trip, counting out change to see if she could afford the smallest bottle of maple syrup.

She eats four maple syrup toffee sticks before we visit the store.

I put everything she gets excited about into a cart. I love seeing her like this. And she's never self-indulgent, so I want to do it for her. I spend close to five hundred dollars on maple-infused condiments, frozen foods, and three pies.

When we get back to her place, I head for the trunk.

"What are you doing?" She frowns as I hand her a couple of bags.

"This stuff is for you—except for one apple custard pie. I plan to eat the entire thing later tonight and have serious regrets when it makes me feel like puking."

"That sounds like my relationship with refried beans." She grabs the front of my shirt and suctions her face to mine. It goes on long enough that my body starts to react in inconvenient ways. She breaks the kiss before it becomes an embarrassing problem.

I smile down at her. "What was that for?"

"For being sweet."

"You might change your mind about my sweetness factor when I fuck your mouth later."

She grins. "Want me to make gagging sounds and get really sloppy about it?"

"Why are you so damn perfect?" I feel like I've been missing out all these years. I've never spent a day hanging out with someone I'm seeing. But this is Bea. I've known her most of my life. It feels...normal. Right. Like something I want to do more of, with or without the sex. And that's a serious first.

"We should get this stuff upstairs." She closes the trunk for me. "I don't think Hammer will be home from work for another hour or so. Lots of time to gargle your balls."

It's a good thing we're not alone in the elevator on the way up to her apartment or she'd probably make it hard for me not to embarrass myself in the hallway.

Five seconds after we walk in the door, Bea gets a call from Essie. "Let me tell her I'll call her back, okay?"

"Sure thing." I start to unpack all the maple nonsense.

She puts her on speakerphone. "Hey, bestie!"

"Hey, babe, I've missed your gorgeous face," Essie says by way of greeting.

"So much same. When will they develop teleportation so I can see you whenever I want?"

"Just move out here and you won't need teleportation skills. The winters are so much less frigid in Vancouver."

"So tempting. I could really live without the minus-thirty temps and four months of snow. Listen, can I call you back in a bit? Tristan's here."

I don't love that I'm standing right here and she's talking about moving across the country. Especially not after the day we've had. Here I am, feeling like for the first time in my life I want more out of this with her, but I can't compete with her friendship with Essie. They're tight, and it's really cool that they have each other. But there's a sinking feeling in my gut. I'll do something stupid and mess up this good thing I've got going. That's usually how it goes. And she's already left once. She could do it again.

Suddenly I feel a little panicky. "You know what? I didn't realize what time it was. I need to get in a workout, and I have a game strategy meeting with Flip and Dallas. You catch up with Essie."

"Hold on a sec, Es." She lowers her phone. "I thought I was supposed to gargle your balls and choke on your cock?"

"You forgot to mute yourself," Essie says.

"Sorry." Bea wrinkles her nose and hits the mute button. "Seriously, you don't have to go."

"Save it for next time. I'll talk to you later." I move toward the door, but Bea grabs my wrist.

"Thanks for today. I had a great time." She pushes up on her toes and kisses my cheek.

"Me too." I manage a smile, but I don't make a move to kiss her back.

Even though I want to.

Fear propels me out the door. *What the fuck am I thinking?*

I don't want to go, but this is more than I can handle right now.

CHAPTER 25

RIX

"Delivery for Beatrix Madden," says Harold, the guy who works the front desk, when I answer the phone. "I can bring it up for you, unless you'd like us to hold it in the lobby."

"I can come down." I ordered new running gear—on sale seventy-five percent off—but I figured it would take a few days to arrive.

"I have three other deliveries. It's really no problem," Harold says.

"If you're sure."

"I'll be up shortly, Miss Madden."

"Thanks, Harold."

A minute later, there's a knock on the door. Except it's not Harold, it's Roman and Hollis. "Hey, Rix. You and Hammer ready to roll out?"

"Hammer's changing for the seventeenth time. And Harold is coming up with a delivery. Otherwise we're good to go." Tonight, it's a home game against Florida. Last time we lost, but their goalie is out with an injury, which gives Toronto a distinct advantage. "Ready for tonight's game?"

"Looking forward to putting another win under our belt," Roman says.

"Same here," Hollis agrees.

"Any special requests for meals next week? I'm shopping tomorrow." I've been prepping a few meals a week for Hollis and Roman since I moved in with Hammer. I missed doing it for Tristan and Flip, so I was excited when they asked me. It's a nice side hustle, and they pay me cash, which goes into my entertainment fund.

"That breakfast hash. I could eat it three meals a day," Hollis replies.

"And your Bolognese sauce. I only have one container left," Roman adds.

"Got it." I pull out my phone and make a note in my grocery list. "If you think of anything else, just let me know."

Hammer comes out of her room. She's wearing her ice blue and black Hammerstein jersey, a pair of black jeans, and knee-high boots. Her hair is curled.

I give her two thumbs-up. "You look hot."

"So do you." She high-fives me, then gives gun fingers to Hollis and Roman. "And so do you and you. This calls for a selfie."

"I hate selfies," Roman grumbles.

"Same," Hollis says.

"Don't be a curmudgeon, Daddy. You either, Hollis. It's good for your social media." Roman rolls his eyes as she pulls out her phone. She pokes Hollis in the cheek until he reluctantly smiles. She gives kissy lips to the camera and snaps a pic.

There's another knock on the door. "That's Harold. I think my new workout gear arrived."

Hollis opens the door. The box Harold is holding most definitely doesn't contain workout gear. Hollis gives him a twenty-dollar tip and takes the box. I try to give him the money back, but he waves it away.

"Your workout gear looks more like it might be a cake," Hammer says.

"It's from my favorite bakery." The other day I said I would

341

give my left boob for a slice of white chocolate mousse cake after Tristan and I had three-hour marathon sex. But it was late, and the only thing open was the convenience store down the street. Tristan brought back a cake from the frozen section. It curbed the craving but doesn't hold a candle to anything from Just Desserts.

"Is it your birthday?" Hollis asks.

"No. It's in the summer."

"Did Tristan buy you cake because he loves your vagina?" Hammer asks.

Roman coughs.

"Chill out, Daddy. Everyone knows they're boning. It's borderline NSFW when they look at each other." She waves her dad off. "Is there a card? Let's see what he got you."

"I don't know for sure that it's from Tristan." Although the odds are in his favor. There's no card though. I peel the sticker free and flip open the lid.

Hammer barks out a laugh. "Only Tristan would do this."

"I'd like to say I can't believe this, but I can totally believe this."

Roman looks over my shoulder and chuckles while rubbing his chin. "Boy's in deep."

"What do you mean?" I ask as my face heats.

Hollis moves in for a closer look. "For fuck's sake."

"Any man who has a cake like this made has to be head over ass in love. He literally can't get enough of you. And it's good to know he's taking care of all your needs. He's not worth your time if he's not going downtown. Isn't that right, Hollis?"

"Oh my God, Dad." Hammer looks scandalized.

"Yup, one hundred percent." Hollis thumbs over his shoulder. "I'm going to pull the car around. I'll meet you downstairs."

"Seriously. If he's obsessed enough to send you this cake, the guy is in love." Roman pats me on the shoulder.

I snap a pic of the pretty icing flowers and the loopy cursive that reads *Please sit on my face.* In a few clicks, I send it on to Tristan with a message.

"Looks like I'm spending the night at your place, Dad," Hammer says.

"**O**h my God, that's it. Don't stop, don't stop! So goddamn close." I'm gripping the headboard, straddling Tristan's face while he hoovers my clit like he's performing an exorcism. They won the game tonight. We went to the bar, I humped his leg and ground my ass on his cock on the dance floor, and now here we are. Me doing exactly what his cake requested.

"You gonna come on my face?" Tristan slaps my right ass cheek.

I moan, grab a fistful of hair, and grind down on his mouth. How he can breathe with his nose jammed against my pubic bone is a wonder, but he's not tapping out. He grabs my ass and helps move me over his mouth. My legs are shaking as the orgasm builds. He knows exactly how to keep me on the edge and make me want more. Suddenly a finger presses against door number two.

My grinding falters. "What are you doing?"

He takes a brief break from fucking my pussy with his tongue to reply, "Priming you." He eases a finger into my ass and latches onto my clit, sucking hard.

The orgasm slams into me like a bulldozer. I make a bunch of excessively loud noises that are half moan/half scream, interspersed with garbled words that don't make any sense. The world turns into a starburst for several seconds as sensation drags me into the blissful abyss. I'm so out of it that I don't even realize he's flipped me onto my back until the world comes back into focus and I'm staring at the ceiling.

Tristan is stretched out between my thighs, massive shoulders forcing my legs wide. His chin glistens with girl-gasm. His hot gaze meets mine as he gently laps my clit and that insidious finger slides in deeper.

"Oh my God." My hips buck involuntarily. I'm on sensation overload. And I'm still coming.

He prowls up my body. When we're face to face, a second finger presses against my opening and joins the first, stretching me. "I'm getting in here tonight, little Bea."

"What if I can't handle it?" I whimper.

"You can and you will." His lips brush mine. "First, I'll get you ready with my fingers." He curls them as they slide out to the first knuckle, then pushes back in deep.

My eyes roll up when his thumb circles my clit.

"My sweet, filthy girl." He sucks my bottom lip and drags it between his teeth. "You're gonna come from having your ass finger-fucked, aren't you?"

I nod and bear down as they ease back in. His free hand comes up to circle my throat. "How close are you?"

"So close." My legs are already shaking.

He circles my clit again and adds a third finger.

I groan at the hot sting as he stretches me further. His thumb doesn't stop circling my clit, though, and his fingers flex against the edge of my jaw. And then I'm coming, my entire body rigid as I moan, and my hips roll and jerk.

The hand around my throat disappears as Tristan rummages in my nightstand, where all my sex toys are. Two items land beside me on the bed: anal lube and the butt plug. We've used it several times since we started seeing each other for real.

"I'm going to plug your ass and fuck your pussy, but you don't come again until my cock is in your ass, understand?"

"Okay?" I'm delirious from the endless orgasm, so I don't fully consider what I'm agreeing to. One second I'm full of his fingers, the next I'm empty.

"I'll be right back." Tristan kisses me, then rolls off the bed, his erection straining.

"What? Where are you going?"

He disappears into the bathroom and the water comes on. *Right.* He's washing his hands so he can touch me again. Nerves make my hands shake as I grab the plug and the lube. I squirt some onto the tapered tip, coating the black silicone. He returns as I set the lube on the nightstand.

"Look at you, all eager to get your ass filled." He strokes himself and holds out his other hand. "Let's get you ready for my cock."

I pass him the plug, but before I flip over onto my stomach, he cups my cheek in his palm and leans in to kiss me tenderly. "We'll take it nice and slow, okay?"

I nod. "Okay."

"We only do what makes you feel good." He straightens. "On your stomach for me."

I flip over. Tristan sets the plug on the nightstand and runs his hands from my shoulders all the way down to my calves. I'm nervous, obviously, but everything about the way he touches me is gentle, reverent. I feel worshipped. Cared for.

"So fucking beautiful." He kisses the dip in my spine and taps my ass. "On your hands and knees."

I push back, like a cat stretching, so my ass is in the air. The bed dips behind me, and Tristan's hand glides over my ass. He kisses a path up my spine, then brushes his lips against my cheek as he grabs a pillow and tucks it under my head.

"I promise you'll love this, little Bea."

I bite my lip and nod. He tucks his hand under my cheek and twists my head enough that he can slant his mouth over mine. His erection presses against me, and I moan.

"Soon, baby." He folds back on his knees and sits on his heels. The smooth plug glides between my cheeks, and he presses the tapered tip against my opening. He pushes in, his other hand sliding under me so he can tease my clit and pussy as he fills my ass with the plug, inch by slow inch. He keeps checking in, making sure it feels good before he gives me more. Eventually, I rock back, pushing the plug deeper on my own. And when it's finally seated fully, Tristan exhales heavily and runs his hands over my ass. "You're doing so good, baby, so fucking good."

He flips me on my back and hooks my knees into the crooks of his elbows as he stretches out on top of me. His hips settle into the cradle of mine. His gaze moves over my face on a gentle caress that's echoed by his fingers skimming from my temple to my jaw. "You're so damn beautiful." He brushes his lips over mine. "I promise I'll be careful with you. Make you feel good the way you always do for me. Okay?"

I nod once and his mouth meets mine. The kiss is soft, unhurried. His thumb sweeps along the edge of my jaw as he rocks his hips until his blunt head nudges my entrance.

He pulls back so he can see my face. "You want more?"

"Yes, please," I whisper.

"This is about making you feel good. You tell me if it's too much, okay?"

I run my hands through his hair, nerves and anticipation warring. "I trust you." Everything about this experience is heightened. It's not just about sensation, the feel of his body surrounding me, protecting me. It's more than that. I feel safe in his arms. Revered. Precious.

We both groan as he pushes inside, his thick cock stretching me, the head putting pressure on the plug.

He cups my face in his palms and rests his forehead against mine. "Fuck, Bea, nothing compares to this feeling."

It's so much tighter like this. And the intimacy is heady and overwhelming. I'm already so close. It won't take much to make me come. But Tristan doesn't move, doesn't pull out and push back in, doesn't rock his hips and give us what we both need.

"Do you remember what I said?" His fingers tremble against my cheek.

"Huh?"

"When do you get to come?" He kisses the corner of my mouth.

"Tristan."

"I promise it'll make it even better."

"But I'm so close already," I admit.

"I know. I need you on the edge, Bea. That's where I always am when I'm with you." He shifts his hips back, and I fully expect him to push in, but he doesn't. Instead, he pulls all the way out. I clench around nothing and whine my displeasure.

His smile is salacious as his cock glides over my clit. "You don't come until I'm fucking your ass, Bea."

"Oh my God, you're horrible," I gripe, biting my lip.

"You love it."

I do. So fucking much.

He folds back and uses one forearm to keep my knees pressed to my chest while he fists his cock with the other. And then the real teasing begins. He circles my clit with the head, presses the tip inside me, gives me a couple of inches, but pulls out again. Over and over. He keeps barely fucking me. Filling me for one stroke before pulling out again. Amidst the maddening torment, he leans in to kiss me. "Soon, baby. You're almost ready."

I'm mindless with want. Desperation and acute need consume me. I'm so wet, so close to coming it's a physical ache.

This time, when he fills me again, I wrap my legs around his waist, desperate not just for the orgasm just out of reach, but for him, for this closeness, for this feeling to never end. Just as I'm about to tip over the edge, he pulls out. He sits back on his heels and taps the plug with his erection.

"Please, Tristan. Oh, God. Just please."

"Knees to your chest," he orders.

And I comply. Because all I want is to come, and I trust that he'll make this good for me. He always does. He works the plug free, thumb circling my clit to keep me on the edge. He tosses it to the floor and grabs the lube from the nightstand, coating his cock and my ass before he rubs the head over the opening.

"Nice and slow, Bea." He presses the blunt tip against me and carefully eases the head inside. He's thick, a lot thicker than the plug or his fingers. I tense and whimper at the sharp sting and the sudden burn.

His thumb circles my clit. "Just relax, baby, deep breaths. You got this."

I take a deep breath, and another, and another.

"Focus on what feels good." He eases a finger inside my pussy, then resumes circling my clit as he pushes in another inch, past the first barrier. I exhale a shuddering breath as the sting subsides and pleasure follows.

"That's it. Good girl," he praises.

He doesn't push in farther, not yet, just rocks his hips a little and keeps circling his thumb. The orgasm hits me like a slow rolling wave, washing over me, dragging me down with the intensity, radiating through my entire body. I quake and shudder and moan. And then he's pushing in deeper, past the next barrier, and I keep coming, wave after wave of bliss.

"Mine. All fucking mine," Tristan grinds out. He adjusts me so I'm on my side, my knees hooked into the crook of his left arm. His nose brushes mine. "So good, little Bea. You're doing so good. How does it feel?"

"I c-can't st-stop c-coming," I stammer.

His fingers are gentle on my cheek, his smile all satisfaction and primal desire. "And I haven't even started fucking you yet."

He takes it slow, hip rolls and gentle thrusts and endless praise, until I ask for more. Until I'm begging him to fuck me. Until I'm screaming his name and digging my nails into his arms as I shudder and clench my way through another intense orgasm.

Afterward, he runs us a bath and fills it with bubbles. He helps me into the tub and gets in behind me, settling me between his legs. He kisses my neck and squirts body wash on a pouf, gently wiping the sweat from my body. We stay in the tub until I start to doze off. Then he towels me dry, changes the sheets, and brings me cake in bed. When I'm full and sleepy, he wraps himself around me and tells me how perfect I am.

As I'm drifting off, I swear I hear him murmur, "You're the only one I want, Bea. Only you."

But in the morning, I wake up alone.

"**T**his needs more of something, but I don't know what." Hemi frowns at the guac.

I dip a tortilla chip into the concoction and take a test bite. "A little lime juice and a dash of salt and we're all set."

"Thanks for hanging out with me tonight," Tally says.

Hammer gives her a side hug. "We've got you."

Tally went on a date that ended badly. They went to a movie with a group of friends, and at the end of the night, he dropped her off and kissed her. It was a sad, overly tongue-filled experience. He's already suggested they go out again, just the two of them, via text. So now she has to tell him she thinks they should just be friends. Poor little thing is stressed out.

"Maybe it wasn't as bad as I'm remembering it." She spins her phone on the table. "Or maybe he was nervous. That could explain it, right?"

"So you're saying you imagined that he was basically making out with your chin?" Hammer asks.

Tally crosses her arms on the counter and drops her head. "It was so weird. Why did it have to be so weird? It was literally the worst kiss ever." She lifts her head. "He's so cute. Maybe he's teachable, though? Maybe it's a fixable problem?"

"Do you want to be the one to fix it?" I ask.

She wrinkles her nose. "No. I really don't."

"Then you let him down easy. But not today." Hammer pushes the bowl of black licorice candies toward her. They're

Tally's favorite. "Today we eat guac and candy and feel bad about shitty kissers."

"Amen to that." We clink our glasses and all take a drink.

My phone rings, the tone telling me who it is. I assigned a song to everyone at the top of my contact list. "Hey, 'sup?"

"My cock. Wanna come ride it?"

I snort a laugh. It's been a week since the anal devirginizing. It took a couple of days before sitting down didn't induce a wince, but man, it was worth the slightly uncomfortable aftermath. I'd been irked that Tristan was gone when I woke up, and even more irritated that he hadn't left so much as a note. But Brody had asked to shoot the puck with him, and he hadn't wanted to wake me before he left. He sent peonies to my work with a slightly inappropriate card that I had to hide from my colleagues. "Such a tempting offer, but I'm with the girls," I tell him.

"I hoped to see you tonight." The disappointment is clear in his tone.

"We have a girl emergency. But we can do dinner and a sleepover tomorrow night," I suggest.

"Are you okay?" Concern laces his tone.

"Yeah. I'm fine. It's not a me emergency."

"Right. Okay. How late will you be with the girls?"

"I'm not sure. I wouldn't wait around for me." I don't want to leave early just so Tristan can get a vagina fix.

"I think I'll go out with Flip tonight," he grumbles.

My stomach tightens. "Don't sound so excited."

"I want to spend time with you, but you have plans." He sighs. "Tomorrow you're mine, though?"

"Tomorrow I'm yours," I agree.

"Have fun with the girls." He ends the call without saying goodbye. Irritation flashes through me, but he does that with everyone.

"Everything okay?" Hammer asks.

"Yeah, Tristan wanted to hang out, but I have plans, so now

he's going out with Flip." I set my phone on the counter face-down and take a hefty gulp of my drink.

"Does that worry you?" Hemi asks.

I shrug. "We're spending all this time together, and my heart is pretty invested. I think it's the same for him, but I don't know if he's ever going to be at a point where he's willing to label it."

"He's totally in love with you," Hammer says.

"He is," Hemi agrees.

"He looks at you like you're the sun," Tally adds.

"But can he commit? That's the thing." I blow out a breath. "I find myself trying to build my life around his. He travels half the year, so I'm going to need some assurance. As nice as it is to hear from everyone else that he's in love with me, I'm not sure when or if he'll ever be able to tell me himself."

CHAPTER 26

TRISTAN

"Nate, man, I'm sorry." I keep shaking my head. My brother messaged a few minutes ago to ask if I was home and if he could video-call me. I'd just gotten home from practice, and I'm always up to talk to my brother. But I wasn't prepared for the reason why.

"It's such a gut punch. I thought we were going through a rough patch because of our workload this semester. Now I find out she's interested in some other guy." His voice cracks, and he clears his throat.

I scramble for words, but I'm at a loss, so I end up repeating myself. "I'm sorry. I know how much you liked her."

He looks like he's on the verge of tears. "I didn't like her, Tris. I was in fucking love with her. I still am." He rubs his chest. "Fuck. I thought we would move in together this summer. We were looking at graduate programs together. We applied to all the same places. And now I find out she's been talking to this other guy in one of her classes. Like, how long have I been missing the signs?" He runs a frustrated hand through his hair. "Love fucking sucks."

I hate that I can't fix this for him. He looks wrecked. "You need to come for a visit? I can get you a train ticket. You can stay with me. I'm not traveling until next week," I offer. "Or I can fly you to an away game."

"I would if I didn't have exams in a couple of weeks. The timing of this is just shit." He presses the heels of his hands against his eyes. "She told me I wasn't emotionally available enough. That I didn't show her I care enough. I told her I loved her. I don't know what else she wanted from me. What else did she need?"

I blow out a breath. I always felt like Nate had it together better than I did when it came to relationships. He had a girl-friend in high school for two years. And he dated another girl his freshman year of university. Both of those breakups sucked, but they have nothing on this one. Watching my brother fall apart over a woman scares the shit out of me. "I don't know, man. I'm probably not the best person to go to for relationship advice."

"You and Rix have been together for a while, though, right? And you've dated a lot," Nate says.

"Well, I don't know if I'd use the term *dated* to describe what I've been doing, and Bea and I have only been seeing each other for a few months. It's not the same," I argue. We spend a lot of time together, and we have a lot of sex, but we don't have a label. The closest I've gotten is calling her my girl. Labels feel like unnecessary pressure. Like there's more at stake. Like I have more to lose.

Nate's brow furrows. "But you're in love with her."

I immediately reject that possibility. "No, I'm not."

Nate's expression turns incredulous. "Bro."

I swallow past the sudden lump in my throat. "What?"

"Dude, there are media shots of the two of you together. It's pretty obvious you're into each other."

"Yeah. We have a good time together, and I like her, but it's not serious."

Even I realize that sounds like a lie coming out of my mouth. I've been fighting my feelings for Bea for a while. Not putting a label on it isn't going to make the way I feel about her go away.

Neither is trying to stuff them into a box and keep them there. As I sit here, arguing with my heartbroken brother, I realize he might be right, and fuck if I want to end up in the same position as him. He's gutted, and they were together for a year. He's way nicer than I am, better at relationships. Nate was planning their future, and she just bailed.

"All right. Whatever you say." He glances away, maybe so I can't see his watery eyes. "I gotta go. I've got class in half an hour, and I need to get my shit together."

"I'll text you later. Check in to see how you're doing, okay?" I say.

"Yeah, that sounds good. But can you not tell Dad, please? He was excited to see Lisa over the holidays, and I can't deal with the disappointment right now."

Our dad is a big fan of Lisa, so I understand his concerns. And he's asked if I'm bringing Bea. I said I wasn't sure, assuming she'd go north to visit her parents for at least part of the holidays. "It'll stay between us," I assure him.

I end the call and stare at the ceiling for a few minutes. Seeing Nate wrecked like this freaks me out, especially because the more I think about it, the more I realize he's right. I'm in love with Bea. But I'm not good at long term. I haven't attempted a real relationship since the one in high school blew up.

Being in love with Bea isn't something I know how to deal with. Nate and Lisa went to the same university. I travel too much, my life is hockey, and my contract is up at the end of the season. The odds that it could work aren't fantastic. And Bea's last relationship ended because he moved across the country. Getting invested feels like I'm setting myself up for failure. I'll let her down eventually, and she'll leave. And then I'll be alone, again. Except I'll have a giant hole in my chest where Bea used to be.

Even if Toronto renews, I don't know how long I'll be here. And I could still end up anywhere in North America come June. Bea needs stability. Hell, she deserves it, considering how unstable so much of her life has been. It's not like she'll move across the country with me if I get traded. Unless it was Vancouver. Then she'd at least have Essie. But I don't want her to do that, anyway. What if I fuck shit up again and she's stuck in some province or state with just me? She'd be miserable.

I'm off my game during practice, the conversation with my brother weighing on me. When I get to Bea's, she's on a video call with Essie. She's got her earbuds in. It's a common occurrence these days. But it reinforces all the shit rolling around in my head. That I won't be enough for her. That I'll fuck this up, and she'll get tired of dealing with me and my bullshit. That she'll walk away again.

"Just give me two minutes." She ushers me inside. "Tristan just got here. Yeah. Next week, same time works for me. I know. I'm so excited that you'll be home for the holidays. I need my Essie fix like nobody's business. We can go to all the Christmas markets. And you can help me look for new recipes to try out. Oh! And I want to show you the plan I've been working on. Yeah. I'm stoked." Her eyes are all lit up. "Yeah. I know. I was looking at some really cool night courses. I might even be able to take one this winter, which would be amazing. We can talk about that when you're here. And we'll go to a game. You can meet all the guys. We'll check the winter schedule and see if there's a Vancouver game I could come your way for, especially since I can start taking vacation days." There's a pause, presumably while Essie speaks. Then Bea laughs. "I know. I can't wait either. We'll have sleepovers, and I'll get the girls together for a night in, so we can include Tally. We'll have a blast." Another pause. "Miss you! Love you too!" Kissy noises. "Talk soon."

She ends the call and sets her phone on the counter, pulling out the earbuds. "Hey. Sorry about that."

"What kind of courses are you looking at?" It's the first I've heard of this, apart from when I mentioned it on that secret date we went on.

"Just a nutrition class. It's no big deal."

"It kind of seems like a big deal, though, since it's kind of your passion."

She shrugs. "I haven't even applied, and they only have so many spots, so it might not even happen." She wraps her arms around my neck and smiles up at me. "How was practice?"

I want to push this more, but I don't have the bandwidth for it. Not tonight. Instead, I settle a hand on her hip and let her pull my mouth down to hers. But I don't make a move to deepen the kiss. Everything feels off. Wrong. Like I'm standing outside myself, watching this happen instead of experiencing it. Like I'm encased in concrete—my emotions too. "Not great."

She pulls back, lips tugging down at the corners. "Did something happen?"

"Nate's going through some stuff." A year plus down the drain. And he's heading into exams. It could affect his grades, along with everything else. If Bea leaves me, how will I handle that? The thought of her walking away makes me feel ill, and it's only been a few months. How bad will it be a year from now? Two? Longer? It was bad enough when she moved out. That kind of hurt will destroy me. We haven't been together long, and already she's woven herself into my everyday. If that disappears, if she disappears, I'll have this massive hole. In my life. In my chest. It won't be like my mom leaving, either. At least I can't run into her. But Bea is my best friend's sister. I'll know what's going on in her life. She'll find someone else, *love* someone else, and it won't be me.

Her hands settle on my chest. "Do you want to talk about it?"

"Not really." Because then I risk telling her how I feel. I'm in love with her. I don't see how she could feel the same, be in so deep she can't see straight.

Her smile is soft, uncertain. "Do you need a distraction?"

"Maybe, yeah." I'm drowning in fucking feelings. Falling on them like swords. It's pain and fear, and it's eviscerating me from the inside. My heart is in a vise, and the ache just keeps expanding.

"Okay. I can do that for you." Her hands skate down my chest, and she finds my belt buckle. She undoes my pants, pulls her shirt over her head, and unclasps her bra, letting it fall to the floor as she drops to her knees in front of me.

I skim her cheek with my fingers. "You're so fucking beautiful."

"So are you." Her lips brush the tip of my erection. "Let me make you feel better."

I give myself over to the sensations and stop trying to find a way out of the pit I'm in. It's better this way. I'm saving her from a lifetime of misery. She'll realize eventually what I already know: I can't be what she needs. But I can do sex. I'm good at it. I love giving her orgasms, making her feel good. But I'm hopeless at feelings, and I'm sure as hell not good at love.

She takes me in her mouth, but I can't handle her gorgeous, guileless eyes. So I pull her up and bend her over the counter. I can't look at her perfect face. Can't have her eyes on mine. Can't let her see the truth. The entire time, I try to convince myself that she'll be better off without me. That I don't want to wake up beside her every day. That I won't miss the sound of her voice, or the feel of her body against mine when I hold her. That I'm fine without her smiles and her laughter and the smell of her citrus and vanilla shampoo.

But based on the nearly debilitating pain in my chest, I won't be fine without her, and that scares the living shit out of me. She has all the power, and I already know how much it hurts when someone I love leaves. This will be so much worse. Especially if I don't end things now, before she's in as deep as me.

Afterward, we make dinner. I'm on autopilot, not really hearing anything she's saying. I don't taste the food as I chew and swallow. My head is all over the place. My chest is tight, and I keep thinking about the look on Nate's face when he told me Lisa broke up with him. He's devastated. Broken. I'll be the same when it happens to me and Bea—worse probably, based on the way I already feel.

I help Bea clean up, and when the last dish is put away, there's nothing left to do. I fold the dish towel and set it on the counter. "I don't think I can do this with you anymore."

Bea closes the cupboard door and turns to face me. "Do what?"

"This." I motion between the two of us. "I don't think it's going to work."

"I don't understand," she says softly.

I can't be what she needs long term. Not when I don't even know where I'll be next year. What if I get traded? What if she wants to stay in Toronto? Flip is here, and she has friends. Her parents are a few hours away by car. Most of the people she cares about are here, apart from Essie. My job might be financially stable, but I'm gone half the time. What if what happened to Nate happens to us? I'm an asshole, the probability is high.

"My contract with Toronto is up at the end of the season. It's anyone's guess where I'll end up." Hollis is having a kickass season. Anything could happen. What if I get signed by Arizona or California? We'd hardly see each other. It's hard enough to deal with away games now; being hours away by plane would be unbearable. My mind spins faster and faster.

She props her hips against the counter, expression reflecting her confusion. "But they might renew your contract. You're having a great season. Hollis being back doesn't change that."

Being in love with her won't stop her from leaving me eventually. Because Nate is right: this hollow ache in my chest, this rising panic, it's all the feelings I've been trying to avoid. Roman saw it, fucking Hollis saw, Ashish saw it, and here I am, the last fucking one to figure it out. Walking away now will wreck me, but if I stick around it'll be worse when the inevitable happens and she decides she's done. She'll meet someone better for her. Someone stable, easygoing, someone who can be there to take care of her like she deserves. She deserves flowers and date nights and someone who will tell her every fucking day how special she is.

My stomach continues to roil. The nausea is almost unbearable. "Hollis is having a great season. He's got one more year on his contract, and I don't. I have no idea what next year will look like. I'm probably going to move, and you just got settled in a new job."

She crosses her arms. "We have months before that's an issue."

"But it's going to be an issue eventually, Bea. It's just a matter of when. We're not a good fit." I run a hand through my hair. There are so many things I wish I could say, but all those words are frozen in my mouth. So I tell her the one truth I can. "I can't open up the way you'll need me to in a relationship. I'm going to let you down, Bea. I can't be what you need. We were having a good time, but we should just call it now. Before either one of us gets hurt."

The ache in my chest turns into a crushing pain. I remember the last time I felt like this—the day I found my mom throwing her suitcase in the car. There's no fucking way I can go through that again.

"Where is this coming from? I don't understand."

"Now or in a few months, the outcome will be the same. It's not like we're serious about each other." I can't be here anymore. Can't deal with more questions. Can't face the truth. I'm terrified of how I feel about her, and that fear will only grow, become more unmanageable, the longer I stick around. I thumb over my shoulder. "Okay, well, Beat, I'm going to go."

She doesn't stop me. Just stands in the kitchen, looking lost, and lets me walk out the door.

CHAPTER 27

RIX

I'm still standing in the middle of the kitchen, trying to figure out what the hell happened, when Hammer walks through the door.

Her nose scrunches up, and she thumbs over her shoulder. "I saw Tristan in the hall, and he looked like he was about to commit a heinous crime. Possibly murder."

I nod and try to swallow past the lump in my throat.

"Are you okay?" She drops her purse. "Rix, what's going on?"

"I don't know what just happened." My chin wobbles. "I think Tristan broke up with me."

"What? Why? Did you get into a fight?" Hammer looks as confused as I feel.

I shake my head. "We don't fight. I mean, we haven't gotten into an actual fight." Not since the cake incident. Anything other than that has just been mild bickering, which quickly turns into sex. "He doesn't like arguing because there was so much of it in his house when he was growing up."

"You've never had a disagreement?"

"He shuts down."

"Is that what happened? Did he shut down and leave?"

"No." I shake my head. "Maybe? I don't know. I'm so confused." My eyes prick with tears.

"Okay, don't panic. Sit down and tell me what happened. Maybe it's nothing. Maybe he's having a day." Hammer grabs a box of tissues and guides me to the couch. "Start from the beginning."

I explain what happened—that he was upset when he got here and said his brother had stuff going on, that I distracted him with sex, and we made dinner, but he was quiet and off in his own world. "Even the sex was...not typical. Like, it happened, and I came more than once, but he seemed... detached."

"Detached how?"

I roll my eyes to the ceiling. "Like usually there's dirty talk, and he'll do...things."

"Like fuck you with a cucumber, spit in your mouth, and try to fit his entire hand in your vagina?" she asks.

"Yes. No. He likes to feel my pulse. Fuck." I close my eyes and shake my head. I'm about to start bawling because this might have been the last time. "He kept kissing my neck and burying his face in my hair. It wasn't the way it usually is with us. We're typically like an explosion. Oh..." I press my fingers to my lips. "Oh, God. It was like he was saying goodbye." Stupid tears leak out of my eyes. "Maybe he came over here knowing he was going to break up with me."

"But *how* did he break up with you?"

"He said he couldn't do this anymore." I rub my temple. "That he might get traded because his contract is up at the end of the season, and that we weren't a good fit. That he couldn't give me what I needed. That it didn't matter if we ended things now or in a few months because we weren't serious about each other."

"I don't understand why he's worried about that now when the season has just started." Hammer looks like she's trying to decipher hieroglyphics.

I dash the tears away. "I guess he doesn't feel the same way about me as I do about him." I wrap my arms around my middle. "I feel sick. I can't believe he broke up with me."

"Tristan is stupid in love with you, Rix." Hammer hands me a fresh tissue. "Maybe you should call him."

"And do what? Ask him point blank if he's breaking up with me?"

"Yeah." Hammer gives my hand a sympathetic squeeze. "If he's breaking up with you, he at least needs to own that shit and not do it in some weird way that makes you question what happened. Which is completely on brand for Tristan, by the way."

"Okay. You're right. I'll call him." I grab my phone and pull up his contact. I feel like I'm going to hurl as I hit Call. It rings four times before he answers.

"What's up?" It's clear he's in his car. Horns blare in the background.

"Did you break up with me? Is that what happened?"

He sighs, and I'm pretty sure my heart falls out of my chest and hits the floor with a splat. "Yeah. Like I said, we weren't serious. I can't be what you need. I'm not the best choice for you long term." He's silent for a moment before he asks, "Do you need clarification on anything else?"

I'm going to vomit. "No, I think you've made it pretty clear."

"Okay. You probably shouldn't call me anymore."

And now it feels like my heart has been punted into traffic and run over by a transport truck. "Fuck you, Tristan." I end the call before he can say anything else to pulverize my heart.

Hammer's expression tells me she heard everything he said. "Why is he being such a horrible prick?"

"I don't know." A low sob bubbles up.

She opens her arms, and I fall into them, letting her hold me while I cry my heart out.

The next morning at work, everyone who sees me asks what's wrong, and my boss pulls me aside and tells me it's okay to take a few days off if I'm sick. It's flu season, and two other employees have called in this week. I don't need to be a hero.

I don't tell her I don't have the flu. Although this feels just as bad, if not worse. I am heartsick, though. I can't stomach food. Sleep is evasive. My chest aches. I was in a relationship with Rob for more than a year, and I was sad that it ended, but it didn't hurt a fraction as much as this does. Which tells me a lot about my feelings for Tristan. There were a few times recently when I considered telling him, but I didn't know how he'd react, so I didn't. That seems to have been the right choice.

I leave before lunch and do something stupid on the subway ride home: I check all the unread messages from Rob.

ROB

Hey, checking in, I shouldn't have left that in a text message. It was a shitty thing to do.

It's been two weeks, Rix, please message just so I know you're okay

You're dating a pro hockey player? I guess maybe that explains the silence. I'm still sorry about the text I sent, and I hope you're doing well.

My fingers hover over the keys, I start and stop a few times, but I finally type the message and send it:

RIX

Was I easy to leave?

The humping dots appear and disappear three times before a message appears.

ROB

I'm calling you, please pick up.

My phone vibrates just as I exit the train. I clear my throat before I speak, "Hi."

"Hey. Hi. I'm glad you picked up. Are you okay?" Concern laces his tone.

"Right now I'm not the best, but I'll be okay. Was I easy to leave?" I ask again. Because this is the second time in a year someone has broken up with me. I feel like the common denominator.

"No, Rix, you weren't easy to leave," he says softly.

"One day you were texting that you missed me and then a couple of weeks later you were dating someone new."

He sighs. "That wasn't fair of me. But loving you from the other side of the country wouldn't have been fair to either of us. Breaking up with you was hard, Rix. Really fucking hard. It's why I didn't message for a couple of months. I just...couldn't hear your voice and not hurt. Why are you asking me this?"

"The hockey player broke it off with me."

"He's a fucking idiot, and I would know since I was one too when it came to you. Did he say why?"

"He said he couldn't be what I needed."

"That sounds like a him problem, not a you problem. Look, Rix, you're an incredible woman. Driven, smart, fun, funny. Maybe he realized the same thing I did, that it would only be a matter of time before someone better for you came along. But breaking up with you was one of the hardest things I've ever done."

"It was the right thing to do, though. Thank you for taking the time to call."

"Thanks for answering."

We say a slightly awkward goodbye and I feel like at least where Rob is concerned, I have some closure. I manage to keep it together until I get home. But the second I walk through the door, I break down again. That's the state I'm in when I call Essie.

"That fucking asshole. He's damn lucky I don't live in Toronto, or I'd hunt his stupid ass down and kick him in the nuts," she says after I explain.

I start bawling again. I'm not afraid of crying, although I prefer to do it in private. But the number of tears I've shed since last night is ridiculous. I should probably drink something with electrolytes to replenish all the salt I've lost.

"Can you take a few days off work?" Essie asks.

"My boss thinks I have the flu." When I saw my face in the subway mirror, it made a lot of sense. My eyes are red rimmed, with dark circles under them, my nose is red, and I have a pocket full of tissues. So yeah, it was a logical leap.

"Come see me. Get out of Toronto for a few days. Let me take care of you," Essie says softly. Her fingers click away on a keyboard. "I found a flight that leaves at three this afternoon and returns to Toronto on Sunday for three hundred bucks. I'm booking it. Start packing."

"Wait, what? Don't buy my ticket."

"It's an early Christmas gift. I can't watch you fall apart from across the country. I need to see you, and I'm working an event on Friday. Otherwise I'd get on a plane."

"I love you so much." More tears fall.

"I love you, too. I'm sending you the information. You can cry for five more minutes. Then turn off the faucet and pack a bag."

"Okay. I can do that." I get my eyes to stop leaking after three minutes and prop my phone on my nightstand, talking to Essie while I pack a suitcase. Afterward, I lie on the couch for ten minutes with tea bags on my eyes to help the swelling go down. Essie has to meet with her team for this weekend's event, and I need to get my ass to the airport, so I end the call.

On the way to the airport, I call Hammer to explain, then leave a message in our group chat to tell the girls I'm going to

Vancouver, but I'm just a text away. I'm about to email my boss about working from home for the rest of the week, but she's already sent me one saying she'll see me on Monday and to get some much-needed rest. And then I'm off.

"I 'm so glad I'm here." I melt into Essie when she picks me up from the airport that evening.

"Me too. Tristan is an idiot." She wraps her arm around my shoulder. "Come on, let's go back to my place and drink wine and you can tell me what happened."

Essie lives in a small one-bedroom apartment in downtown Vancouver. It's fun and artsy and full of her effervescent personality. Soon we're sitting on her hot pink couch, me hugging a zebra print pillow and nursing a glass of wine while I recount the events that brought me by plane to my best friend's living room.

"I just don't understand why he felt like he needed to end things now when you have the whole season in front of you," Essie says.

"He said he couldn't be what I needed."

"What does that mean, though? What does he think he can't give you?"

"His heart, I guess. He said he couldn't be open with me the way he thought I needed him to." I sigh. "Maybe he realized I have stronger feelings for him than he does for me. That might explain it?"

"I don't know, Rix." Essie taps her lips. "Maybe he didn't tell you how he felt in words, but he sort of showed you, in his own weird way—like that cake, and the basket of veggies shaped like penises, and taking you to the maple farm. He cares about you, Rix. So whatever happened to cause the breakup, it wasn't because he doesn't have feelings for you." She gives me a sad smile. "I think you're used to being second best. Not because you are, but it's a mindset you've adopted. When you were young, you never wanted to be in the way. Your brother stole the limelight, and you always stepped back into the shadows. But you were never less important. Ultimately, it's up to you to reject that or accept it. Especially with someone like Tristan."

My chin wobbles, and my eyes prick. I pluck a tissue from the box beside me. "He was so awful at the end. It was like a switch had been flipped, like he'd turned off all his emotions."

Essie's eyebrows pop. "Maybe he did. You said he was off and something had happened with his brother that he didn't want to talk about. He's super tight with both brothers, right?"

"Yeah. He talks to them all the time. He goes to Brody's games, and he and Nate text every day and talk on the phone as much as you and I do."

"Okay." She crosses her legs. "He said something happened with Nate, the one who's our age, right?"

"Yeah."

"Maybe whatever happened with Nate triggered Tristan and that's why he shut down. But we can't know for sure because we're not in his head."

"I just hate that I don't know because he wouldn't tell me." I let my head fall back. "Why did I fall in love with my brother's best friend? Why couldn't I stick to casual sex and that's it?"

"Because he gave you plenty of reasons to like him. And from what I've seen, he cares about you the same way you care about him. I just think you've had a lot more experience at relationships with substance than he has. Maybe his feelings for you scare him."

"I'll never know since he told me I shouldn't call him anymore." I hug a pillow to my chest. "I'm running in circles, going nowhere. How can I face him after this? All my friends in Toronto are connected to the freaking team now. I built this whole network of support, and now it'll be super awkward." I lift my head. "What time is it? They have a game tonight." I left my phone in her bedroom because I didn't want to obsessively check my messages or be disappointed by the lack of contact from Tristan.

"It's eight."

"Shit. The game's already over." I set my wine down and hop off the couch. Hammer and I were talking about this game. They played Colorado, and they've been on a winning streak. Toronto was hoping to be the ones who broke it.

I pull up the team social media feed. "Yes! They won!" My smile drops when I realize I can't message Tristan to congratulate him. I message Flip instead.

> **FLIP**
>
> Thx. Hammer said you're in Vancouver. And Tristan said you're not dating anymore? WTF?

> **RIX**
>
> I'm with Essie.

> **FLIP**
>
> For how long???

> **RIX**
>
> ¯_(ツ)_/¯   Have fun celebrating.

Before I toss my phone aside, I do something stupid. I check my brother's social media. And my poor battered and bruised heart takes another hit. Because the first image to pop up is one of Flip and Tristan, amidst a group of bunnies.

"Uh-oh. What happened now?" Essie asks.

I toss the phone on the cushion so she can see. "Looks like he's already over us."

Maybe it's time to consider moving to Vancouver.

CHAPTER 28

TRISTAN

We won again tonight. No thanks to me. I've been playing like shit since I ended things with Bea. But going home to my empty condo didn't seem appealing, so I'm out with Flip and the rest of the guys, celebrating even though I don't feel like it. At least we're in the VIP section with a table of our own and a bottle of scotch that Flip surprisingly paid for.

Two days ago, I found out Bea went to Vancouver. It's my fault she's there. I broke up with her like an idiot, and the first thing she did was hop on a plane. I sip my scotch. I hate my life.

"So why is my sister in Vancouver?" Flip asks. He's been texting her the past couple of days, but I guess she hasn't given him much information. And Hammer and Hemi are pissed at me. All I've gotten from them are side-eyes and middle fingers. Shilpa won't even acknowledge my existence.

"Because Essie is there." I've said this half a dozen times already. I don't know what else he needs me to say.

"Yeah, but what happened between the two of you that she went there with no warning?"

I've been pretty vague about things. Mostly because I don't want him to punch me in the face again, even though I deserve it. "Bea misses her. They say it every time they talk on the phone.

They're always planning visits and talking about portals or whatever. And her boss already said there's a position out there."

Flip frowns. "She seemed perfectly happy in Toronto. She and Hammer and Hemi and Tally are like the four freaking Musketeers."

I drum on my knee. "Yeah, but who knows where I'll be next year. It's not like she needs her life upended. Especially not because of me."

"Well, didn't you just do exactly that by breaking up with her?" Roman asks.

Flip uncrosses his arms and reaches for his glass. "Dude. This isn't about you and where you'll be next year."

"Then what's it about?"

He drains his drink and refills it. "Your mom."

"I haven't spoken to my mom in years."

"Exactly."

"Oh, fuck this." I start to stand, but Flip puts his hand on my shoulder.

"Listen, man, that shit fucked you up. She was a coward and a garbage mother. Her leaving the way she did, how it all went down, it wasn't cool, man." I don't know how to deal with the empathy in his tone or on his face. "You're in love with my sister, and you're projecting your issues onto her because you're fucking terrified of losing someone else you care about."

"That's not—"

"It is. That's exactly what this is about. It's why your relationships don't last more than a couple of months. And why you rolled with all the fun times before Rix moved in with us. The same night Nate tells you he and his girlfriend broke up, you end things with Rix." He makes a circle motion with his finger. "It's all connected. You think because Nate couldn't make his relationship work, you won't be able to either."

"That's not... It's more than that," I say.

"Of course it's more than that," Flip says with a sigh. "Nate's breakup is just a piece of the puzzle. You broke up with Rix because you went into a panic spiral. You possibly being traded at the end of the season—which, based on stats and logic, isn't probable—is a convenient excuse."

"It could happen, though. And it's not like Bea is going to come with me if I have to move."

"Dude, it's months away. Have you talked about it with her? Asked her what she wants? I mean, come on. Stop burying your head in the sand and just admit you're in love with her." We stare at each other for a few long, painful seconds before he shakes his head. "I always knew your mom leaving fucked you up, but I didn't realize how badly until now. You broke up with Rix because you're afraid she'll bail if things get hard. So you did it first."

"She would leave eventually. I'll fuck it up."

"Congratulations, you've already managed to do that by breaking her fucking heart, you idiot!" Roman snaps. "She sobbed for hours after you left. Peggy said she was beside herself. She couldn't figure out what she did wrong."

"I can't give her what she needs. I can't be what she needs," I say.

Flip raises a hand before Roman can rip my head off again. "Look, I get that you've got some real hang-ups about relationships because of your mom, and they're totally understandable. But Rix isn't the type of person to up and bail. It's not who she is. So don't blow it because you're too afraid to face what you already know. She's it for you." He sighs.

"I know what it's like to have your heart ripped out of your chest, and that's what you did to Rix. Maybe you should try telling her how you feel instead of circling the issue and wallowing in a pit of despair," Flip adds. "I know what you're like, man. You avoid conflict. It's the reason it took you falling for my fucking sister to finally tell me you didn't want in on all the bedroom parties. And I'm sorry for that, man. I should have realized you were going with the flow." He seems genuinely apologetic.

I don't have a chance to respond, because a woman in a sequined dress rushes over.

"Flip! Oh my God! I thought it was you!"

He gives her a chin tip. "Hey, how you doing? You're looking hot tonight." He slides out of the booth and offers her his arm. "I gotta hit the bathroom. You wanna keep me company?"

She giggles and slips her arm through his. "Of course I do."

Hollis watches them leave with a disbelieving look on his face. "He's going to fuck her in the bathroom, isn't he?"

"Probably. Yeah." I gulp my scotch.

If Bea was here, we'd probably be on the dance floor together. It was always extended foreplay, and then I'd get her home and naked. Afterward, I'd feed her snacks in bed, and she'd fall asleep tucked against my side. And my arm would always fall asleep, but I'd deal with the pins and needles because I didn't want her to move. Because all I want is to be near her— however she'll take me. Or I would have, before I broke up with her.

I let Flip's words sink in. Did I really push her away? Did I sabotage myself because I'm too fucking afraid of my own feelings? Did I put words in her mouth because I'm the one who believes I'm not worth staying for?

"You're a fucking pussy," Roman says.

"Tell me how you really feel," I grumble into my glass.

"Oh, here we go," Hollis says.

"I called you out on this months ago. *Fucking months*," Roman says. "I was sure you were going to fuck things up by not being honest with Flip, and I was right. Because Rix ended up moving in with Peggy. And who helped you get your head out of your ass back then?"

"You did," I admit grudgingly.

"Well, here's another one: relationships are hard and messy and sometimes they're scary as fuck, but don't end one because

372

you're too fucking scared to admit how you feel to her and yourself."

It's like he's inside my goddamn head. "What if she doesn't feel the same?"

"What if she does?" Hollis counters. "What if you're everything she's been looking for? What if you're it for her? Are you really going to let her walk away without a fight?"

"She's in Vancouver." What if she decides to stay? What if her visit becomes permanent?

"And?" I've never seen Hollis look this annoyed. "What the fuck is wrong with you? You have the chance to be with the one person you really want, and you're still sitting here like a dejected asshole. Not all of us are that lucky. Go get her back, dipshit."

Flip returns with messed-up hair and lipstick prints on his shirt. "What'd I miss?"

"I gotta go." I knock back the rest of my scotch, which probably isn't my best move, and slide out of the booth.

"Go where?"

"The airport."

"Halle-fucking-lujah," Hollis mutters.

"Go get her." Roman claps me on the shoulder and tucks something in my pocket. "That's the name of a therapist. When you get back, do yourself a favor and make an appointment. You getting your head out of your ass is only step one."

I don't argue, just thank him—even though the idea of talking about my fucking feelings with a stranger is about as appealing as swimming with piranhas.

I drink three bottles of water on the way to the airport and buy a pack of gum before I approach the ticket counter. I get a seat on the first flight out to Vancouver, leaving at six-oh-five a.m. I sober up in the lounge by eating breakfast and drinking more water, then stop at the airport store and buy a ridiculous number of overpriced bags of candy—all Bea's favorites. I also buy a backpack because I have nothing else with me. Then I board the plane, loosen my tie, pop the top button on my shirt, and sleep the entire way to Vancouver.

But when we land, I immediately second-guess my decision. What if I tell her how I feel, but it's too late? What if she wants to move to Vancouver after visiting Essie? What if she comes back to Toronto and I do something else to fuck it all up? I stand in the middle of the airport, wishing for a set of fucking balls. But I'm frozen. Unable to move. Unable to do the one thing I desperately want to, which is find my way back to Bea. I'm choking on my fear. Drowning in the panic that I'm here and so close to what I want, but certain I can't have it.

People brush by me as I war with myself to do something—anything but stand here, paralyzed by my own fucking fear. I hate how weak it all makes me feel. How powerless I am, and how much power Bea has over my feelings without even knowing it. But as the minutes tick by, I can't make myself text her or find another way to get Essie's address.

I pull the card Roman gave me out of my pocket. I don't know what I expect—for some magical fairy godmother psychologist to pick up and immediately give me the backbone to get the fuck over myself?—but it goes to voicemail.

"Hi. My name is Tristan Stiles. My teammate, Roman Hammerstein, gave me your number. I'm in love with my best friend's sister, but I don't think I deserve her. She also hates me right now because I'm an asshole, and I'm fucking up my life because I don't know how to handle my feelings. I could use some help. Please. When you have a chance, can you call me back so I don't lose her forever? Thanks." I leave my number and end the call.

I still can't make myself call Bea, so instead I go to the counter and buy a ticket home. It leaves in less than an hour. Since I have no bags and a Nexus pass, I make it through security and onto the plane without causing a delay, even though I'm the last passenger to board. I'm grateful there was an open seat in first class, because I don't fit well in regular seats.

As soon as we take off, I regret my choice. It's possible I'm losing my mind. But we're already in the air, and there's nothing I can do about it. It's only ten in the morning Vancouver time, but it's already afternoon in Toronto so I order a scotch.

An hour into the flight, I'm scrolling through pictures of Bea on my phone, and I swear I catch a hint of citrus and vanilla as someone passes me on the way to the bathroom. When I look up all I see is the bathroom door closing as the flight attendant tells someone they should use the washrooms at rows twenty-eight or fifty-four.

The smell makes me wish, again, that I hadn't changed my stupid fucking mind and gotten back on the plane. I drain the rest of my scotch and grab the backpack from under my seat to rummage around for candies. I opened a few of the bags when we were landing earlier to get the taste of sleep out of my mouth.

The bathroom door opens.

"Miss, please return to your seat, and please use the designated bathrooms."

"Sorry. Sorry. There was a taco incident. It won't happen again."

I'm in the middle of ripping into a bag, and the voice shocks me. The bag explodes, Fuzzy Peaches landing everywhere. One hits the man next to me in the cheek.

"Shit. Sorry."

Bea's head whips around. "The fuck?"

For reasons I don't understand, I shove a bunch of Fuzzy Peaches in my mouth, even though they make my mouth itchy and I hate them. Bea loves them.

She stalks down the aisle. Her brow is furrowed in confusion, which is reasonable since I'm supposed to be in Toronto. "Why are you on a plane home from Vancouver when you played a game in *Toronto* last night?"

"I'm not. I mean yes, we played in Toronto last night. And yes, I'm flying back from Vancouver." I say this through a mouthful of candy I can't stand. My tongue is already itching. I want to spit it out, but the flight attendant already took my glass. Bea is standing in the aisle, looking beautiful, and tired, and really perplexed. Now's my chance to tell her how I feel, but she looks the opposite of happy to see me. I remind myself that this makes sense because I was such a dick to her when I broke things off. What if she's only coming home to get her stuff and move to Vancouver permanently?

"Why are you eating Fuzzy Peaches? You hate them," she asks.

"No, I don't." I shove more in my mouth. I don't know why I'm lying. Other than I'm panicking and didn't expect to see her for at least another twenty-four hours.

"What are you doing here?" Bea's eyes narrow. "Why would you fly to Vancouver?"

"Because." I chew furiously, but my mouth is dry, and swallowing is the worst. "I wanted to talk to you." If I had something I could spit them into, I might be able to think a little more clearly. I should tell her the truth. All the lying is what got us into this mess in the first place. "But I changed my mind when I landed. I couldn't even make myself leave the airport or text you. So I got back on a flight home."

"You changed your mind?" Bea's confusion shifts to disbelief.

"Yeah." I swallow the mouthful of horrible candy. "And now we're on the same flight." I need to stop stating facts and start saying something that actually matters. But she looks so damn angry. And I don't want to do this in front of a plane full of people. Especially if she confirms what I already believe to be true: she doesn't want me anymore.

"You are an asshole of the highest order," Bea snaps.

"I think we came to that conclusion a long time ago," I concur. Bea has known I'm an asshole for a long time.

"Miss? Please, I need you to return to your seat." The flight attendant is standing behind her with her arms crossed.

"I know. I'm going." She pins me with a hateful glare. "Fuck you, Tristan. Fuck you for being a thoughtless, overwhelming dick." She looks around, maybe realizing we have the attention of all of first class. "I'm so sorry. Drinks are on him. And snacks." She points to me.

"Drinks and snacks are free in first class," says the guy I hit with the Fuzzy Peach.

"Right. Thank you." She flips me the bird and disappears back into economy.

Well, that went the opposite of how I'd hoped.

"You're Tristan Stiles, number forty-four, right wing for Toronto Terror," Fuzzy Peach Guy says.

"Yeah." My mouth is so itchy, and I think I totally blew any chance I had of getting Bea back.

"Think I could get your autograph for my son? He idolizes you."

"Sure. Yeah." I sign his baseball cap and his laptop. "You wouldn't have an antihistamine, would you?"

"I don't. Sorry."

"No worries."

My mouth is already starting to peel. The next three and a half hours are going to be long.

CHAPTER 29

RIX

I am fuming. Absolutely fuming. I cannot believe Tristan flew to freaking Vancouver to talk to me, changed his mind, and ended up on the same damn flight home. Having my heart tossed into a meat grinder once is bad enough, but to have him do it all over again less than a week later is more than I can handle. For a second I was excited to see him. Until he went and opened his word hole.

I fucking *hate* him. HATE him. Selfish, arrogant fuckboy.

As soon as we land, I disappear into the first available bathroom and unleash a nightmare made of refried beans and heartbreak. I spend a good forty-five minutes in there. Ten of them actually using the bathroom, another ten waiting out whoever is in the bathroom with me out of sheer embarrassment, and then another twenty-five after Tristan texts me to tell me he's at baggage claim. Maybe as a warning? Who the fuck knows?

I send him an excessive number of middle fingers in reply:

RIX

ᶜᵐ (-_-) ᶜᵐ ᶜᵐ (-_-) ᶜᵐ

ᶜᵐ (-_-) ᶜᵐ ᶜᵐ (-_-) ᶜᵐ

ᶜᴖᴖ (-_-) ᶜᴖᴖ   ᶜᴖᴖ (-_-) ᶜᴖᴖ
ᶜᴖᴖ (-_-) ᶜᴖᴖ   ᶜᴖᴖ (-_-) ᶜᴖᴖ
ᶜᴖᴖ (-_-) ᶜᴖᴖ   ᶜᴖᴖ (-_-) ᶜᴖᴖ
ᶜᴖᴖ (-_-) ᶜᴖᴖ   ᶜᴖᴖ (-_-) ᶜᴖᴖ
ᶜᴖᴖ (-_-) ᶜᴖᴖ   ᶜᴖᴖ (-_-) ᶜᴖᴖ
ᶜᴖᴖ (-_-) ᶜᴖᴖ   ᶜᴖᴖ (-_-) ᶜᴖᴖ

Eventually, he messages back with a thumbs-up.

The tears start again. It takes twenty minutes to calm down enough to leave the bathroom.

Normally I would take the train home. It's infinitely cheaper than an Uber or a cab, but my emotional state is unstable, so I opt to spend the extra money. Crying in front of one person is preferable to crying in front of potential hundreds.

I have messages from Essie asking if I made it home okay. And my brother has called twice but hasn't left a voicemail. I wonder if Tristan is home already. Probably. His place is a short trip from the airport.

I call Essie once I'm in the back of a cab—they can't give me a bad rating for being emotional. "You won't believe who was on the plane."

"Ryan Reynolds?"

"I wish. I bet he's just as funny in real life as he is in movies," I say.

"Do you really want me to guess, or should this be a rhetorical question?"

"We can go with rhetorical. Tristan was on the plane."

"What? Why? Didn't he have a game in Toronto yesterday?"

"Yeah. Apparently, he flew out to Vancouver to talk to me, but changed his mind when he got there and ended up on the same flight home as me."

"What? But why?"

"I don't know. It was so humiliating. I had a bathroom emergency on the plane and snuck up to use the one in first class since there usually isn't a line and no one pees on the seat. Also, that dinner we had last night was so stupid. Why do I always eat the refried freaking beans?"

"Because they're delicious and impossible to resist."

"It's so annoyingly true." I glance at the cab driver, who is dutifully ignoring me. "Anyway, I came out of the bathroom and guess who was sitting in first class wearing the same suit from the game last night."

"Oh my God."

"Right? He was shoving candy into his face. And when I confronted him, he said he flew out to talk to me, but changed his mind. Like breaking my heart once wasn't bad enough. He had to go and do it again in front of a bunch of people. I made a scene on a freaking plane. Today is the worst." Tears leak out. I don't stop them. It's pointless. They'll fall regardless.

"Oh, muffin. I'm so sorry. What happened when you got off the plane?"

"I had to use the bathroom for obvious stress-induced and refried bean reasons. He messaged to say he was at the baggage carousel. I don't know if it was a warning or what. I sent an excessive number of middle finger emojis, and he sent a thumbs-up, and then I cried for twenty minutes, and now I'm in a cab on the way to my apartment."

"I feel like there are pieces missing to this story," Essie muses.

My phone beeps with an incoming call. I check to see who it is. "Crap, that's my brother. It's the third time he's called in the past ten minutes, and he hasn't left a message."

"Okay. Call me when you can with an update. I love you."

"I love you back. Wish I was still in Vancouver. I'll call you later." I end the call with Essie and take the one from Flip. "Hey."

"Hey. How was Vancouver?"

"Great until the flight home."

"What happened on the flight home?"

"Tristan."

He's quiet for a second. "Can you explain that?"

"Evidently he came to Vancouver to talk to me, then decided he didn't want to talk to me anymore, and we ended up on the same flight home."

He blows out a breath. "That pussy-ass fucker."

"It was humiliating." Especially the part where I said he would pay for everyone's drinks and the guy beside him reminded me they're free in first class. And then I tried not to cry for the rest of the flight home. I was unsuccessful.

"What were his exact words? Did he say he didn't want to talk anymore?" Flip asks.

"He said he changed his mind. Can we not do this right now? I'd prefer not to relive this experience more times than necessary," I snap.

"For fuck's sake. You two are hopeless."

"Thanks for being a supportive brother." I hang up and turn my phone to silent.

It's nearly dinnertime when I roll in the door to my apartment. I leave my bag in my room and hop in the shower to rinse off the smell of plane. When I come out of my bedroom, Hammer, Hemi, and Tally are in the living room.

"Yay! You're back! How was Vancouver?" Hammer bounces across the room and hugs me.

I hug her back. "Vancouver was great."

She steps back. "It sounds like there's a but in there?"

"There is, and his name is Tristan. However, I do not feel like crying anymore over that asshole, so can we not talk about him and go get something to eat? All I've had today is a mini container of plain Pringles and a Kit Kat. Also, please, for the love of all that is holy, do not allow me to order anything that includes refried beans."

Hammer and Hemi exchange a look. "Okay. Let's grab dinner."

"But no refried beans," Tally adds.

Hemi invites Shilpa to join us since she knows Ashish is with Hollis and Roman. She meets us in the lobby, and we file out of the apartment and over to the restaurant across the street.

"So Essie was good?" Hammer asks once we're seated in a booth.

"She was great. I needed the break from life. How was everything here this weekend? Tell me what I missed."

"I made Dallas go to a horse farm to witness the birth of a foal for a promo op," Hemi says. "The family has a son with a serious medical condition who idolizes him. It was a great opportunity."

"The legal hoops were absolutely worth it," Shilpa adds.

"Oh my God, that's terrible and awesome at the same time."

"I know. He passed out. It was glorious."

"The paperwork would have been a nightmare if you hadn't caught him going down," Shilpa says.

"I'm so glad they caught that part on camera." Hemi smiles evilly for a second before her smile softens. "But there's a brand-new foal in the world named Dallas Bright, and a very happy boy, so I feel like the embarrassment of fainting on live video is worth it. Dallas doesn't totally agree with me, but I'm okay with that."

"You really can't stand him, can you?" I muse.

"Nope. Not at all. It's my life's mission to make his as miserable as possible, one embarrassing promo op at a time."

We order a pile of appetizers—no tacos or refried beans—and dig in. While I was gone, Tally let the bad kisser down without having to tell him he's a bad kisser, and Hammer has decided to go into sports-team PR because she loves her internship. Shilpa is considering letting Ashish knock her up. It's been a weekend.

Flip shows up while we're paying the bill. I'm not in the mood for any kind of I-told-you-so conversation. "If you're here to rub this in my face and tell me I'm an idiot for dating Tristan, you can save your breath."

He purses his lips and stuffs his hands in his pockets. "That's not why I'm here. Can we talk? Just us?"

"Not if you're going to make me feel shittier than I already do."

"That's not my plan."

I sigh. "Fine." I shrug into my jacket, hug the girls, and follow Flip into the cold Canadian evening.

We make it half a block before we duck into a coffee shop. I get the most expensive decaf latte on the menu, and he gets a black coffee. "I need to apologize," he begins.

"For?" I take a seat across from him and wrap my cold hands around my hot coffee cup.

"A lot of things. I was an asshole about you and Tristan."

"You were, but it's over now." I focus on my coffee because saying that makes my heart hurt. "And you were right anyway. He's a fuckboy, and I should have known better than to fall for him."

Flip sighs. "He's not great at relationships, but he's not really a fuckboy. Or he wasn't until I moved in with him. I should've curbed my extracurriculars while you were living with us. Especially after finding out you could hear every detail. And I shouldn't have brought home Tiff and Trinity after I found out about you and Tristan. It wasn't the right way to handle things."

"It was a particularly shitty thing to do, but so was sleeping with Tristan behind your back," I admit. "I honestly didn't think it would go on for as long as it did, or that I would develop real feelings for him. The longer we were in it, the harder it was to be honest about it, especially knowing what I know about how things went down with you two and your fuck friends."

A pair of teenagers glance our way. Flip is wearing a baseball cap and a hoodie, nothing team related, so he mostly blends in. "I was hurt more than anything," he says. "And maybe pissed at myself for not seeing what was right in front of me. But I could have dealt with it a lot better than I did. Tristan is a good guy, but he's got a lot of baggage, Rix. A lot. What happened with his mom really screwed him up. When he said he changed his mind about talking to you, I don't think it's because he didn't want to. I think it's because he's scared that you're going to tell him to go fuck himself. So maybe give him a chance to explain. He's bad at feelings, and he has a lot of them when it comes to you."

"I don't get why he would fly all that way just to turn around and fly right back home."

"Neither do I, to be honest. But he's miserable without you and scared to admit it. Before you write him off, at least let him explain his actions."

"Who says he's even going to try?"

"He's waiting for you at your apartment."

"What? How do you know that?"

"Because I dropped him off before I came to see you. Hollis let him in the building." He stands and looks at me expectantly. When I don't make a move to follow his lead, he sighs. "I need both of you to stop being miserable, and the only way to do that is by talking. So please go home and deal with him."

I exhale an anxiety filled breath. "Okay. I really hope you're right about this, because I honestly can't handle any more heartbreak."

"I'm right. I've known him for a long-ass time. He doesn't show his feelings much, but the ones he has for you are excessive and plentiful."

I follow Flip out into the cool evening, and he walks me back to my building. "Give him shit and make him own his," he says when we arrive.

"Okay."

"I love you, Rix."

"I love you, too, Flip."

I push through the doors and hit the button for the elevator. My palms start sweating on the ride up to my floor.

Sure enough, Tristan is sitting in the hall outside my apartment.

He picks up an enormous bouquet of peonies and a cake

from Just Desserts and scrambles to his feet. "Bea, can we talk, please?"

I approach him slowly. I will not be swayed by cake and flowers. Not this time. He looks rough, but also delicious. He's changed into a T-shirt that hugs his thick biceps, a pair of jeans, and some flashy running shoes. Guy loves his freaking running shoes. His coat is lying in a heap on the floor. He's sporting two days of stubble and dark circles under his eyes that match mine. These are things I didn't notice on the plane.

He steps aside while I use the keycard to unlock the door. Thank goodness this place doesn't have old-school locks. My hands are way too shaky to deal with getting the key in the hole. I usher him inside and put the island between us.

Hammer comes out of her bedroom with a bag slung over her shoulder. "I'm going to visit my dad. For the night."

"I'm not kicking you out of the apartment," I say, my eyes bouncing between her and Tristan.

"I know. I'm offering. He's been bugging me to have a movie night anyway." She gives me a brief hug. "Just hear him out."

"Hey, Hammer." Tristan sets his armload of grovel gifts on the counter and waves.

"Hi, Tristan. The cake and flowers are a nice touch, but please communicate your feelings to each other so you can both stop being sad." She slides her feet into a pair of fluffy slippers and leaves us.

I cross my arms. "I'm listening."

He runs a hand through his hair. "I miss you, Bea. I can't eat, I can't sleep. All I think about is you. I can't even look at a cucumber anymore without feeling like my chest is caving in. I fucking hate this."

My heart squeezes. These are all things I want to hear, but it's not an explanation. "I hate it, too, but it doesn't clarify why you were on a flight back to Toronto. Why come to Vancouver to talk to me and then change your mind?"

He starts pacing. "I chickened out. I'm a fucking pussy. I

admit that. Last night, the guys sat me down and told me as much. And then I flew to Vancouver to tell you I want to be with you, but when I got there I just…couldn't do it. Because I'm a chickenshit. So I got back on the plane, and then you were on it, and I didn't expect to see you, and I started eating those horrible Fuzzy Peaches that make my mouth peel, and you were so beautiful, and real, and right fucking there, and I wanted to touch you and talk to you, but we were trapped in first class, and I just…choked. There were all those people watching. I know I fucked it up. But even if I hadn't lost my nerve, I would have been too late because you were already on a plane back here, so my plan would have been shot to shit anyway."

"Why did you lose your nerve?"

His eyes are wild, and he swallows compulsively.

"Because…because the way I feel about you terrifies the fuck out of me." He runs a rough hand through his hair. "And I'm afraid that you'll realize I don't deserve you, or that I'll get traded at the end of the year, and you'll decide you don't want to do this with me anymore."

"So you broke up with me because you're afraid of your feelings and what the future might look like?" I ask.

He looks so forlorn and lost. "It was a stupid thing to do, Bea. I know that. I know I screwed things up. But I couldn't get out of my own fucking way. I could barely handle it when you moved out. I was miserable then, and all these feelings I have about you, for you, they just keep getting bigger. And what if you leave me again? Or I have to move, and you don't want to come with me? Or you decide Vancouver is a better place for you? I thought if I ended things now it wouldn't hurt as much, but I was wrong, Bea. So fucking wrong. Everything sucks without you."

I cross my arms. "You don't get to keep doing this to me. You can't lash out every time things get hard, or you get scared. Shutting down when there's a tough conversation isn't something I'll accept from you."

His nostrils flare, and his knee bounces with his anxiety. "I know, and I'm sorry. I was overwhelmed and I didn't know how to deal with it."

"Sorry isn't going to cut it, Tristan. You ripped my heart out last week and tossed it in a meat grinder. You treated me like one of your bunny hookups and made me feel like a giant piece of shit. I was fucking devastated. *Devastated*. You *discarded* me like trash. Like I meant *nothing* to you. Is that what you intended? Is that how you wanted me to feel?"

His eyes are haunted, and I swear for a moment he looks like a lost little boy.

"If you want to fix what you broke, you need to decide what you want and do something about it. I can't be the only vulnerable one here. You can't take and not give."

"You're right. I know you're right. I'm sorry." He rubs his bottom lip. "I think I'm pretty fucked up."

"What do you mean?"

"Remember how I told you I came home when my mom was leaving?" he says softly.

I nod. "You had to tell your brothers and your dad when they got home." That alone would do enough damage to warrant years of therapy, which I'm not sure he's ever had.

He nods. Swallows a few times. "I, uh...I asked her not to go." He drops his head. "Begged her not to leave, even though a lot of the time all she did was get angry at us." He exhales an unsteady breath. "But I didn't want her to go. I told her I'd do better, that I'd do anything if she would just stay." He kneads the back of his neck.

His gaze lifts, and my heart breaks for the boy who was crushed that day, because he's still very much inside the man before me. He opens his mouth once, twice. Grinds his teeth together and releases a huge exhale before he continues.

"She said it didn't matter what I said or did. It would never be enough. She didn't want us anymore. And then she left." His eyes drop to the floor. "I never told anyone that part. Not Flip, definitely not my dad, or my brothers."

My heart feels like it's shattering. What a horrible, hateful, selfish thing to do to another person. Especially her own child. Everything falls into place. Because when she said that to him, she created a core wound, leaving him to believe he's not enough. He still believes it. One of the most important, influential people in his life, one who was supposed to show him unconditional love, took that away from him and did so much damage in the process. She scarred his heart and made him believe he was intrinsically unlovable. Of course he's afraid of his feelings. His love wasn't enough to keep his mother from leaving, so how could it keep me from doing the same? He equates love with loss. Big loss. The life-changing, heart-eviscerating kind.

"I'm so sorry for the way she made you feel, and that she was too selfish and too much of a coward to admit she was the one who didn't feel like she deserved to be part of your family. I'm sorry she put that on you." I pause until he meets my eyes. "It isn't your fault that she left, Tristan. You didn't cause it. You're not the reason for it. *She* wasn't enough, not you. But you can't keep hurting the people you care about because of it."

"I know."

"Do you, though? Because I hear the words, but your actions say something else," I tell him gently.

"I fucked this up so bad, Bea. I know that. How I acted last week, the way I shut you out, it wasn't fair." He draws a long, shuddering breath. "Lisa broke up with Nate—and he's got it together when it comes to relationships. He was just...ruined over it. And then you were talking to Essie about stuff you never even told me." He stares at his hands. "I didn't think I could ever be what you needed. I couldn't be the person you came to with things that matter. I know this doesn't make what I did better, and I understand if you're done with me. With us. I would get it if you decide you can't deal with me anymore. But if you give me another chance, I'll do everything I can to be better. I want to be the one who gives you what you need, if you'll let me."

He takes another deep breath and his gaze lifts. "I love you. I'm so in love with you, Beatrix." He swallows thickly. "I've fucked up so hard. Maybe too much. But I want a future with you. It doesn't matter if we're living in the same city, or you're here and I'm somewhere else. All I want is you, Bea. I'll do anything and everything I can to make it work if you'll take me back. I'm scared out of my fucking mind, but I would rather be terrified and have you in my life than not have you at all. And I'm probably going to get things wrong, but I promise I'll try to be the guy you deserve."

His hopeful, scared expression breaks my heart and makes it swell. "Perfection isn't something I expect from you, or anyone in my life. You're allowed to be imperfect. I expect you to be the best version of yourself every day that you can be. Some days will be great, some won't. Sometimes we'll make mistakes. But when that happens, we talk things through and figure out how we can do it better next time. We just don't shut down, or bail, or turn into a grade-A asshole."

"I've done that a lot to you. Shut down and turned into an asshole," he says quietly.

"You have, but I've also allowed it. I've accepted being second best for a long time, and I won't do that anymore because it's not good for me, or us. And moving forward, I won't let you get away with that shit. But I also won't walk away when it gets tough, and I won't let you do that either. Sometimes it'll be uncomfortable and scary. But I want to try to make this work if you do."

"Does that mean you'll give me another chance?" His expression is so uncertain, I almost want to hug him.

I smile and nod. "Sweet, dirty boy, I love you."

His eyes flare with surprise. "Really?"

"Really."

"You love me?" He tries out the words, like they're new to him. "Even when I'm an asshole?"

"Even when you're an asshole. But we'll work on that, and on you being less of a dick when you're feeling vulnerable."

"That's going to take some practice, but I will do whatever it takes to keep you." He blows out a breath. "Roman gave me a name of a therapist, and as much as I hate talking about fucking feelings, I won't risk losing you again. I'm working on getting an appointment." He tips his head. "You really love me?"

"I really love you."

He shifts on the couch, and suddenly he's kneeling on the floor between my thighs. He cups my cheek in his palm. "Is this okay?"

"It's okay."

"I love you so fucking much, Bea." He leans in and rubs his nose against mine. I almost melt into the couch. It's so sweet. His thumb strokes along the edge of my jaw. "I love how thoughtful you always are. I love your kindness, and your intelligence, and your drive." He kisses me softly. "And I love how patient you've been with me while I try to figure out how to deal with all these fucking feelings."

I laugh, and he grins.

"And I love the sound of your laugh. I want more of that. I want to be the reason you smile. And I never want to be the reason you cry again. It breaks my fucking heart." He nuzzles into my hair and breathes me in. "I want to take care of you, give you all the things you deserve. I want to make you happy." He bites the edge of my jaw, and I whimper. "I want to make you feel good in all the ways that count."

He covers his mouth with mine, and I wrap my arms and legs around him, hooking my feet behind his back. His tongue sweeps my mouth, and he groans. He grips my ass, rising in one smooth motion.

At the same time, our apartment door flies open. "Peggy honey, I brought you donuts from your favorite pl—" Roman comes to an abrupt halt. "Oh shit."

"Hammer's already at your place and she's staying the

night," I tell him. This isn't the first time he's let himself in without knocking.

"Right. Good call. I'll knock next time." He leaves the way he came, his face an exceptional shade of red.

Tristan crosses to the door, puts on the safety, then carries me across the apartment. He kicks the door to my bedroom shut behind us and climbs onto the bed with me wrapped around him like a koala.

He tears his mouth from mine long enough to ask, "No one else is going to barge into the apartment uninvited tonight?"

"No. Hammer will text and wait for a reply before she comes back."

"Good, because I want to show you exactly how much I love you tonight."

He comes in for another kiss, but I put a hand on his chest. "Can I make a request?"

"Absolutely."

"I know we just did the whole love-declaration thing, and maybe there's an inclination to, you know, make love, and I definitely think there's a time and place for that. But I'd rather you turn me into a sex pretzel and do dirty things to me tonight."

One side of his mouth curls up in a salacious smile. "Careful what you wish for, little Bea."

"Fuck me like you mean it," I taunt.

He folds back on his knees. "Strip."

Everything below the waist clenches, and my nipples peak. I yank my shirt over my head and toss it on the floor. I struggle with the button on my jeans, especially when Tristan lazily discards his own shirt and unzips his pants. I shimmy out of mine as he slides his hand into his boxer briefs. I kick my jeans off and work on unfastening my bra. It takes two tries because my hands are shaking. Tristan frees his erection from his boxers and gives it a slow stroke as I push my panties over my hips.

His eyes travel over me, and I feel it in my vagina. "I love your body. I love your curves and your softness."

"How do you want me?"

"Every way I can have you, but first I want you to sit on my face." He shucks off his jeans and stretches out on the bed. He makes a circle motion. "Bring that ass over here. You're gonna be a good girl and suck my cock while I tongue-fuck your pussy."

I scramble into position, straddling his chest and shimmying back until I'm hovering over his face.

"So fucking eager." He smacks my ass. "Look at you, dripping already." He licks up the inside of my thigh on a low groan. "Come here." He grabs my hips and pulls me down, then spreads me and licks all the way from my clit to my ass. "So goddamn good."

He buries his face in my pussy, and I grab his knees, which are bent, so I don't fall face-first into his erection. I roll my hips along with his strokes of tongue and nipping teeth.

I keep one hand on his knee for balance and grip his shaft, stroking from base to tip before I drag my tongue through the slit, tasting precum. I cover the head with my lips and run my tongue around the crown. I'm rewarded with Tristan's tongue pushing inside me.

I pop off and lick a path up his shaft. He mimics the movement by lapping at my clit. When I bob on his cock, he sucks and nibbles my clit.

"You're a fucking gift, Bea." He latches onto my clit, sucking hard as I take as much of him as I can. I'm pretty sure his nose is inside me when the head of his cock hits the back of my throat, and I'm not sure how he's breathing. I dig my nails into his thighs as his thumb takes the place of his tongue, which plunges inside me. The orgasm hits me with a force I don't anticipate. I pop off, sucking in a gasping breath that leaves me as a moan, and topple forward, my face mashing into his thigh. His spit-covered shaft slides over my cheek.

One second, his erection is pressed against the side of my face and the next, I'm on my back, Tristan stretched out between my legs.

His eyes search my face as one hand cups my cheek. "You okay?"

I nod.

"Fuck, I love you." He kisses me. It's sloppy and wet, but neither of us seems to care. When he pulls back, his expression is almost tender. "My sweet, filthy girl. I missed you so much."

"I missed you, too." I moan as his shaft glides over my clit. "Please fuck me now."

The blunt tip pushes against my entrance, and he hooks the backs of my knees into the crook of his arms, pushing my knees to my chest. He fills me with one hard thrust. The orgasm I was in the middle of a moment ago fires back up, and I grip his biceps.

His hips pull back and he slams back in.

"Oh my sweet lord," I moan. And then I moan some more as he starts a punishing rhythm. And I keep coming, the wave of bliss seemingly endless. He's definitely fucking me like he means it.

Eventually, he releases one thigh so he can curl his hand around my throat. He props himself up on his other forearm and finds the perfect angle, his strokes measured and even. He drops his head to kiss me, matching the roll of his hips to the stroke of his tongue. And when I'm close to coming again, he breaks the kiss so he can watch me unravel beneath him.

"I love you, Bea," he whispers as his rhythm falters.

"I love you, too." I run my fingers through his hair and press my palm to his throat. "Eyes on mine, baby. I want to see you when you're coming inside me."

His smile turns into a snarl as he thrusts, once, twice, a third time. He shudders, and his eyes soften as his erection kicks. I see it, all the love he's been hiding. I see that boy I used to have a crush on as a teenager, who's become the man I've fallen for.

"There you are." I smile up at him. "That's the Tristan I've been in love with all along."

CHAPTER 30

TRISTAN

I wake up in the morning wrapped around Bea. It's only six, and her alarm doesn't go off for another ten minutes. She's still asleep. I can tell by her slow, even breathing.

She loves me.

She loves *me*.

It's hard to get my head around that. That she's not leaving. That she'll stay in Toronto and be with me instead of moving to Vancouver where Essie is. That I'm worth the headache. I'm not easy to be with. I'm not good at feelings.

But I want to get better at them. I have to. There's no way she'll stick around for more of me shutting down on her.

As I lie here, her body tucked against mine, I think about the way I treated her at the beginning. All those negative feelings I thought I had about her weren't hate at all. I didn't want another person to take care of. To worry about. But I was just afraid. I'll gladly take care of Bea for the rest of my life. She's worth every effort. Loving her isn't a chore, it's an honor.

She was a reminder of the family I didn't have but wanted. She was the kindness I never believed I deserved. Why would I, when one of the most important people in my world walked away without a backwards glance? I didn't want another person to be responsible for. And I sure as hell hadn't wanted to like her, to find her endearing, or sexy, or sweet, or smart, or intriguing. I'd wanted to put her in a neat box labeled "Flip's Little Sister." She'd been untouchable, forbidden fruit. But I'd taken a bite anyway, sure she'd be bitter and I wouldn't want her again.

But I had. I *do* want her. She hums and rubs her ass against my erection. I nose her hair out of the way and kiss her warm neck. It's a distraction from all the things in my head that I don't know what to do with. Besides, morning orgasms are a good start to the day. And a way for me to keep her happy. I let my fingers trail down her stomach and between her thighs. She sighs and wriggles against me.

Her alarm goes off.

She makes a discontented noise and grumbles, "I forgot it's Monday."

I silence her alarm. "I can make it a good one." I roll her onto her back and reach across the nightstand to hand her the pocket pack of breath strips before I start kissing my way down her body.

"You don't have to eat my pussy to make my Monday better," she mumbles.

"I want to, though." I settle in, getting comfortable, and bring her to orgasm with my mouth before I get inside her. Last night was a lot of pretzeling, so this morning I take it nice and easy, focused on making it good for her. She comes again while I'm inside her.

Afterward, we hop in the shower, then make breakfast together. "Do you have to go to work today? Can you call in sick?" If she goes to work, she could change her mind about how she feels.

"I was off for four days, and you have practice this afternoon." She tips her head, expression pensive.

"You could come to practice." I run my hand through my hair and knead the back of my neck. I don't know how to deal with this new version of us. Or what to do about the tightness in my chest and the rising panic. Maybe giving her another orgasm will make it go away. I grip her by the hips and lift her onto the counter. She's wearing one of my team shirts. She might have panties on under it. Or not. I'm about to find out.

I try to kiss her, but she covers my mouth with her palm. "What's going on?"

She drops her palm so I can answer. "I want to make you feel good again."

"Why?"

"Why?" I echo.

"I've already come twice this morning, and like four million times last night. As much as I appreciate your dedication to providing me with an exceptional number of orgasms, my vagina could use a break." She drags her finger along my temple and settles a warm palm against my cheek. "What's going on up there?"

"I don't want you to go to work today." It's the truth, which I think she's looking for.

"Why not?"

"Because."

She smiles softly. "What are you afraid will happen if I go to work?"

I bite the inside of my cheek while she stares at me expectantly. "What if you change your mind?"

"About?"

"How you feel about me."

"Why do you think after all of this I would just not love you anymore?"

When she says it like that, it doesn't make a lot of sense. "What if you change your mind? What if you have time to think and you realize I'm not worth the hassle?"

She's silent for a few long seconds before her palm curves around the back of my neck. She pulls me down for a kiss. But she doesn't let me deepen it. Instead, she gives me one of her patient smiles. "Your ability to keep me in a perpetual state of bliss isn't the reason I fell in love with you, Tristan." She squeezes my hand. "Why do you love me?"

"Why?"

"Yeah. Aside from my ability to deep throat your ridiculously large penis and my excitement over being turned into a fuck pretzel, why else do you love me?"

"You're strong and independent, and kind and thoughtful. You're patient and driven and you have a great sense of humor, and you're fun to be around, both in and out of bed. And you take care of the people you love, and you're loyal."

"So in the same vein, just because I'm not next to you, I won't stop loving how you're a caretaker for your brothers, and you're always there when they need you. You always make time for them. You're thoughtful and observant. You're generous and giving, both in and out of bed. You're also driven, a team player, and when you're not feeling emotionally vulnerable, you can be incredibly sweet and affectionate." She runs her fingers through my hair. "I appreciate how much you want to please me, and that we're on the same page in the bedroom, but that isn't the reason I want to stay, or try to make this work."

I nod once. "I think sex is my default when I don't know what to do with my feelings. Like I can erase my fear with orgasms."

"You can put it on hold that way, but it'll still be waiting for you when they're over. Just remember, you don't need to be perfect, and we'll both make mistakes along the way. Sometimes you'll want to shut down because all the feelings that come with love can be overwhelming. Everyone has coping strategies. You can go for what's safe and hide yourself or hide behind sex. Or you can do what's hard and know that I'm going to be here to accept you on the good days and the bad days. You have to show up for yourself if we're going to make this work. I won't accept your shitty behavior, Tristan, but I will accept you. All of you."

After a moment I nod, so she continues, "The most important

thing to remember is that I love you. Not an idea of you. I didn't just fall for the sweet side that comes out when you let your guard down. I fell for *all* of you. Everything that makes you uniquely you. The sweet and spicy parts. The hard and the soft edges. I love every part of you, Tristan."

"I'm going to do everything I can to deserve that love." I push her hair over her shoulders. "You were right here, all this time. If I'd gotten out of my own damn way, we could have been together sooner."

Bea shakes her head. "We found each other at exactly the right time, Tristan. And we're here now. That's what matters." She opens her arms. "Give me one of those melty hugs where you bury your face in my hair and huff me, hoping for some kind of contact high."

I curve myself around her, and she does the same. I burrow through her hair and shove my nose against her neck. "I really love the way you smell."

"I really love that you love the way I smell."

When I pull back, I circle her throat with my hand and brush my nose against hers.

She sighs and hooks her leg over my hip. "Now you're playing dirty."

"How's that?"

She bites her lip. "Doing what you're doing."

"You mean this?" I sweep my thumb across the edge of her jaw and give it a gentle squeeze, then rub my nose against hers again.

"Mmmm..." Her hands slide down my chest. "Two of my favorite sides of you at the same time. It's hardly fair." She frees me from my boxers and drags the head over her clit, lining us up.

"I promise I'll make it worth it."

I drive Bea to work—she makes it with minutes to spare and a promise from me that I won't pull that move before she goes to work again or she'll one hundred percent find an unpleasant way to get me back for it—and head to team practice. On the way, I get a callback and my first appointment with Roman's therapist—another step toward being the best version of me that I can.

Flip takes one look at me when I reach the locker room and nods slowly. "You fixed things?"

"I fixed things."

"It's a real mindfuck, knowing what your afterglow face looks like. I can't decide if I want to punch you or slap you on the back, or both."

"I can understand that." Living together for the past year has shown us sides of each other that we can't erase. "But I love her. I'll do anything to keep her happy."

"Yeah. I know that, too. It's the reason I haven't knocked out your front teeth yet." He puts on his shoulder pads, which hide a bunch of nail marks. "You finally tell her how you feel about her?"

"Yeah. I did." I pull my shirt over my head, revealing a few crescent-shaped marks and a set of teeth marks about an inch away from my nipple, so I turn and give him my back, which isn't in much better shape with all the scratches down it.

"Good, good."

Ashish gives me props as he passes on the way to the shower. "Happy you got your head out of your ass, Stiles."

"Same, man. Same."

Roman slaps me on the back. "Good work finding your balls, Tristan."

"I'm not sure if that's a compliment or a dig," I reply as I pull my pads on.

"A bit of both," Hollis says with a smirk. "But we'll all appreciate having your head back in the game now that you're no longer wallowing in a pit of self-loathing and despair."

Turns out he's on to something there. Getting Bea back and finally coming clean about my feelings is a weight lifted, and I play better than I have since I stupidly broke it off with her. Practice is smooth, my mind is clear, and even though I didn't get a whole hell of a lot of sleep last night, I'm still on my game.

I pick Bea up from work and we head to Ajax so we can watch my brother's hockey game together. It's a stupidly long drive in Toronto rush-hour traffic, but I don't want to miss it. This is the team they've had the most trouble with this season, and I want to be there to support him.

"Your dad will be at the game?" Bea asks.

"Yeah, he goes to pretty much all of Brody's games."

She squeezes my hand. "I love that *you* show up for Brody, too."

"I try to as often as I can since my mom can't be bothered with any of us. I want him to know he's supported."

"I think you do a good job of that as his brother," she says.

"I know I don't do the feelings stuff well, but I try to be as present as I can with my schedule." Although I've been pretty caught up in my own shit recently. "I checked in with Nate today. He seems better than he was last week." Between rounds of I'm-sorry-for-being-an-emotionally-repressed-idiot-thanks-for-taking-me-back-and-I-love-the-fuck-out-of-you sex, I told Bea about what happened with Nate and his long-term girlfriend and how it seemed to be the thing that pushed me over the I-can't-deal-with-my-feelings-so-I'll-just-implode-my-relationship ledge.

Bea nods. "That's good. I imagine it'll take a while for him to get over it. They were together a long time," she says softly.

"Yeah, he didn't expect it, so he's pretty crushed. But right now he's focused on exams and putting all his energy into that. When he's finished, he'll probably visit for a couple of days."

"That'll be good. Just be careful with Flip around. He's not the best influence," Bea warns.

"Yeah. I know. But Nate is different from me. He's never really been the kind of guy to engage in meaningless hookups, and he doesn't try to fit other people's expectations of him. I did that a lot." It's not Flip's fault that I didn't say no to the endless women he brought home. I always had a choice. I just never exercised my options the way I should have.

Bea adjusts her position, so she's facing me. "We all do things to make other people happy, even if they don't make us happy."

"Yeah. I did that a lot. I wasn't the best role model for Brody."

"In one area of your life, for like what? A year? Don't beat yourself up about being a hot, famous hockey player everyone wanted a piece of."

I pull into the arena lot and find a parking spot. "You're a kickass girlfriend."

"Girlfriend?" Bea gives me a small, hopeful smile.

I hit the release on my seat belt and do the same with hers. "Is that okay? Maybe you don't want to put a label on it."

"Do you want to put a label on it?" she asks, putting the ball back in my court.

I've purposefully avoided labels for a long-ass time. In part because they scare the shit out of me. But it doesn't matter if I call her my girlfriend or not; I'm still hopelessly in love with her. Not giving it a title doesn't make those feelings any less present or real. "Yeah. I do, but it's okay if you're not ready for that."

"I'm ready for that," she whispers.

"Yeah?"

"Yeah."

I drag my fingertips along the edge of her jaw, and she pushes her hair over her shoulders, exposing her throat for me. I take the not-so-subtle hint and circle her throat. "You want to be my girlfriend?"

"I want to be your girlfriend," she replies.

401

"I'm your boyfriend?" I ask, leaning in close.

"You're my boyfriend," she agrees.

I rub my nose against hers, and she whimpers.

"You better make up for keeping me hanging like this for hours by fucking the living hell out of me tonight."

"Consider it extended foreplay." I tip my head and claim her lips.

When her hands start to wander, I end the kiss and promise I'll take good care of her later.

We join my dad in the arena and watch Brody play his ass off. And afterward, when we're waiting for Brody in the arena restaurant, a few of the girls who watched his game come over and ask for autographs, and a couple of his teammates stop to say hi. I've just finished introducing Bea when Brody appears. Bea excuses herself to the bathroom, and as soon as she's out of earshot, both my dad and Brody give me knowing looks.

"Girlfriend, eh?"

"Yeah. We made it official and stuff."

"You always had a soft spot for her," Dad says.

"How's Flip feel about that?" Brody asks.

"He's good with it now."

"So he wasn't good with it at first?" he presses.

"He knows how I feel about her."

"You mean he knows you're in love with her?" Brody says with a smirk.

I give him a look.

"Dude, you were looking at her like she was the freaking sunrise at Thanksgiving. I'm surprised it took this long."

I roll my eyes. He has a point. "Yeah, Flip knows I'm in love with her."

"She's good for you," Dad says.

"She is." And I plan to do everything I can to be good for her, because that's what she deserves.

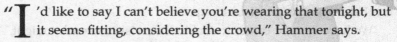

CHAPTER 31

RIX

"I'd like to say I can't believe you're wearing that tonight, but it seems fitting, considering the crowd," Hammer says.

We're in Vancouver for an away game. Tristan wanted to fly me out, and I convinced the girls to make a trip of it since the game falls on a Saturday. And it means I get in an unexpected visit with Essie right before the holidays—like a pre-holiday gift.

"You know what they say… If it looks like a bunny, and it dresses like a bunny, and it acts like a bunny…"

"It is a bunny?" Tally says.

Essie's eyes light up. "He has to fuck you like a bunny."

"Oh, shit," Hemi laughs.

"That's actually genius," Hammer says.

"I must try this." Shilpa's eyes are alight with excitement. "You are opening my eyes to the possibilities."

"Get ready for some fun times in the bedroom." I pat her arm.

"Why would you want to be a bunny when you're Tristan's girlfriend, and he's totally in love with you?" Tally asks. Bless her sweet, untainted heart.

"Because sometimes it's fun to shake things up, and he'll have to behave himself while we're out. It'll be a win-win all the way around. No matter what, we'll have victory or consolation sexy times."

"Relationships mystify me." Tally sips her giant soda.

While it's typical for me to wear a jersey with STILES and number 44 on the back, it's unusual for me to have turned that jersey into a dress with a low-cut V neck. I also don't usually wear thigh-high boots with ridiculous heels. Outfits like these are reserved for the bunnies who attend games and compulsively troll the players' social media accounts, hoping to figure out what bar they're going to after. I've seen plenty of altered jerseys. I've also never forgotten Tristan's and Flip's comments before we started hate-fucking each other about how Vancouver has the best bunnies.

Am I secure in my relationship? Absolutely. Tristan worships me. I also know what riles him up.

We have seats at center ice behind the visitors bench tonight, and we get settled as the teams take the ice to warm up. A few minutes in, Tristan comes over to take a drink from his water bottle. When his gaze lands on me, he tips his chin up, like he's asking me to stand. Which I don't do because the cameras have caught us interacting and suddenly, we have their attention, as well as what feels like that of the entire arena. But not for long since I'm wearing a Toronto jersey and we're in Vancouver.

It isn't until later, when the team files onto the bench, that he's able to get a load of my outfit, or lack thereof. He gives me a devilish smirk.

"Oh, you are in for it tonight," Hammer snickers. "It's a good thing he booked his own room or Flip would be sleeping on my dad's couch."

As soon as I agreed to come for the weekend, Tristan booked us a suite in the hotel. It's ridiculously lavish and has its own separate bathroom and living room. Essie stayed with me last night, and Hemi, Hammer, and Tally have two other rooms on the same floor. Ashish obviously got a room for him and Shilpa. Hopefully they have a fun night, too. Essie's original plan was to go home tonight, but we convinced her to bring an overnight bag.

It's an incredible game, and much to Vancouver's dismay and Toronto's delight, Tristan scores a goal in the first five minutes of play. After that, Toronto keeps the lead all the way through. At the beginning of the third period, Hollis is on the ice, and Tristan is on the bench. Thirty seconds into his shift, he gets checked into the boards and they pull him from the game, sending Tristan back in. Vancouver gets a two-minute penalty, giving Toronto a power-play advantage.

"I don't think Hollis will be back on the ice tonight," Hammer says.

"Yeah, that was a dirty hit," I agree.

We've been waiting for another team to use last season's injury against him. Hopefully, the trainers are being extra cautious and he's fine. The power play works to Toronto's advantage, and Tristan manages an assist while Flip scores a goal in the first minute. They almost score again, but Vancouver's defense finally wakes up and starts playing. Still, we win five-three, which is amazing.

As expected, we end up at the hotel lobby bar—the location is intentional, even if it means the place is packed with people. Tally can't join us at a regular bar or nightclub, and we don't want her to be left out of the festivities. Here she has the entire team and us to watch out for her.

"Nineteen feels really far away." She sips her mocktail.

"Eighteen is around the corner." Hemi gives her shoulder an affectionate squeeze.

"A kid in my school can get fake IDs," she says wistfully.

"The headline on that one wouldn't be the best," Hemi replies.

"Or the paperwork for me," Shilpa adds.

"Yeah. I know. A girl can dream, though." She sighs.

The team shows up soon after, and with them, a ridiculous number of thirsty bunnies.

Tristan makes a beeline for our table, his gaze electric in a way I feel between my legs. He's wearing a charcoal gray suit with a team tie. He looks entirely too fuckable for his own good. This is the third in a stretch of four away games. While regular video calls and mutual self-gratification sessions help ease the sting of separation, flying out here has helped quell the ache of his absence.

I don't have a chance to exit the booth before he reaches me. He cups my cheek for a moment, thumb skimming my chin as he adjusts his palm and it comes to rest against my throat. He leans in and brushes his nose against mine. "I'm going to do filthy things to you later."

"I missed you, too."

"This outfit is drawing way too much attention," he grinds out.

I grin. "That was the plan."

"Figured as much. I'm guessing you won't let me take you up to the room now."

My smile widens. "It's like you know me."

"Game fucking on, Bea." He slants his mouth over mine and gives me a panty-melting kiss.

"Geez, get a room," Hemi mutters.

"That's borderline obscene," Hammer observes.

"No one's ever kissed me like that," Tally whispers.

"I am learning all the things," Shilpa declares.

"Who wants to place bets that their next-door neighbors will be calling in a noise complaint tonight?" Essie says.

"Better yet, they call the police because they think someone is being murdered," Hemi adds.

"Oh, yeah, that's totally possible. I've heard them from the hallway before," Hammer says.

Tristan tears his mouth from mine and smirks. "Bea can be vocal."

"This is true," Hammer agrees.

"You sure you don't want to come upstairs now? I'll go easier on you later if you let me take the edge off now," Tristan whispers.

"I'll take my chances," I murmur.

"You get the flowers I left for you?" he asks.

I nod. "And the veggie basket and cake."

"Good. I'll be back for you later." He releases me and nods at the girls. "Ladies."

They all say hello, and then he heads to the bar.

"Every interaction is like extended foreplay for you two, isn't it?" Hammer observes.

I sip my drink and ogle him from across the room. "We haven't seen each other in almost a week."

"You're kind of couple goals. I want to find someone who wants me with the same intensity as he wants you," Essie says.

"He's definitely good for my ego," I reply.

Flip stops by our table. "What's up with the outfit?"

The girls snicker.

"Just trying to blend in."

He gives me a confused look. "Pretty sure it's having the opposite effect." He scans the table. "Anyone need anything?" His gaze lands on Tally's empty glass. "Tals, you want another Coke?"

Her eyes flare, and she ducks her head as her cheeks flush. "I'm okay. Thanks, though."

"All right. You girls stay out of trouble." He heads for a table full of players, including a couple of rookies.

"Seems like he's mostly over what happened the other week, eh?" Hammer muses.

"What happened the other week?" Hemi asks.

Hammer's eyes go wide. "Shit, sorry."

I wave off her apology. "It's fine. I stayed over at Tristan's, and we thought Flip wasn't coming home. He walked in when things were happening. On the kitchen counter."

"Cucumber-salad things?" Tally asks on a whisper.

"Seriously. Hell is going to have a special place for us in it." Hemi sighs.

"I enjoy cucumber salad," Shilpa says.

Essie laughs.

Tally's cheeks flush, but she's grinning.

I shrug. "Sort of serves him right for all the times I had to listen to him boning randoms while I was living there."

"Truth." Essie clinks her glass against mine.

"It worked out the way you needed it to, anyway," Hammer adds.

"Exactly."

The day after that happened, Tristan started looking at condos in my neighborhood. There was a penthouse for sale in the building across the street. He set up a walk-through and put an offer in. He moves in the new year, and Flip will take over the mortgage for the current condo. The increased revenue from his investments will more than cover what Tristan used to pay each month.

It means we'll have much-needed privacy, and he can fuck me with cucumbers any damn time he wants.

An hour later, I have to use the bathroom. On my way back to the table, I run into Tristan.

He wraps his arms around me and drops his head, nose pressed into my hair, lips ghosting the column of my throat until they brush my ear. "You do realize the longer you make me wait to get you up to the room, the longer I'll make you wait for an orgasm, right?"

"I love it when you threaten me with a good time."

"Tell the girls you need to call it a night, and I won't keep you on the edge the way you've done me for the past two hours."

"Just let me say good night."

He narrows his eyes.

I pat his chest. "I'll be back in five."

I hug all the girls good night. Hammer's gone to grab a

round of drinks. I spot her at the bar, getting chatted up by some random guy. She flips her hair over her shoulder.

"Check it out," I say to Hemi.

She follows my gaze. "Roman went up to his room ten minutes ago."

"What about Hollis? Is he still here to play bodyguard?" I ask. We scan the bar together.

"There he is, nine o'clock." Hemi tips her chin in his direction.

He's standing with Dallas, Ashish, and Shilpa.

I head back to Tristan, who's leaning casually against the bar. But his gaze is all fiery promises.

He tips his chin at Dallas, Ashish, and Shilpa as we pass.

Hollis isn't with them anymore. I assume he's gone to manage the situation with Hammer and the flirty guy. But she's still talking to him—she's only half paying attention to what he's saying, though. I follow her gaze to the elevators, where Hollis is. The doors open, but before he steps over the threshold he glances back. I swear, for a second, a hint of longing crosses his face. Then he disappears inside the elevator, and the doors close behind him.

"Did you see that?"

"See what?" Tristan asks.

"Nothing. Never mind. Let's go up to the room so you can make me regret wearing this."

Two guys join us in the elevator, and Tristan slings his arm over my shoulder and pulls me in close. He kisses my temple. They get off on the twelfth floor. We're on the fifty-third. As soon as we're alone, he presses me against the mirrored wall. One hand circles my throat, the other finds its way between my legs.

His eyes flare when he skims bare flesh. "Where are your panties?"

"My purse."

He withdraws his hand and holds it out. "Give them to me."

I retrieve them and drop them into his open palm.

He rubs the crotch between his fingers. "They're soaked. Did you take care of yourself in the bathroom? I'll know if you're lying," he warns.

I shake my head.

He glances above the doors. We have twenty floors to go. He lifts the hem of my jersey dress and edges a foot between mine, widening my stance. Tristan drags a single finger up the inside of my right thigh, then brings it to his lips and licks the pad. "I haven't even touched you yet and you're dripping wet. Does the idea of getting fucked like a naughty little bunny excite you?"

I bite my lip and nod.

We're at the fortieth floor now.

"We should stop the leak before you make a mess all over the elevator floor."

For a second, I'm confused, until he drags my damp panties up the inside of my thigh, then pushes them inside me.

"Oh my fucking God," I whisper-moan.

His lip curls in a salacious smile as he fills me with my panties. The elevator dings our arrival at the fifty-third floor as he tucks away the last of the fabric and pulls my dress back into place. He laces our fingers, and we stroll leisurely down the hall.

I'm vibrating with anticipation.

The second we're inside the room, Tristan pins me against the door. His mouth covers mine in a searing kiss, and I try to hook one of my legs around his.

"You think I'm going to let you rub that greedy pussy of yours all over my thigh?" His nose brushes mine as he traps my legs between his. He pushes his hips into me, his erection pressed against my stomach.

I groan as I grip his hair and try to pull his mouth back to mine. He tips his chin up and looks down at me through hooded lids. "Get my cock out."

I abandon his hair and find his belt. With shaking hands, I free the clasp, pop the button, and drag the zipper down. Tristan makes a deep, needy sound when I slide my hand into his boxer briefs and wrap my fingers around his erection. I free it from the black fabric and stroke from base to tip.

He steps back and arches a brow. "It's not going to suck itself, is it?"

I drop to my knees on the plush carpet and lick up the length, then cover the head with my lips, running my tongue around the crown, sliding over the weeping slit at the tip.

"Fucking hell," he grunts.

I pop off long enough to ask, "Am I the best bunny?" Then wrap my lips around him and roll my tongue around the head.

He pulls me off long enough to ask, "Is that what you want? For me to treat you like a bunny?"

"Your only bunny," I clarify.

"I fucking love you, Bea. More than anything," he declares.

"I love you, too. But tonight, I want you to fuck me like a toy."

He blinks a couple of times. Blows out a long breath. "You'll tell me if it's too much?"

"You know my limits," I assure him.

And he does. Every time, he pushes me right to the edge, and I love every freaking minute of it. I want to drop a hand between my thighs and rub my clit, but I know if I do, I'll be delaying my release. Instead, I grip his base and cup his balls in my other hand as I bob up and down on his cock. I hum and moan and make loud slurping sounds. When I pop off, I spit on the head and rub it over my lips before I take him into my mouth again, deeper with every pass.

He gathers my hair in his hands and wraps it around his fist. His other palm settles against the soft space under my chin and tips it up. "You gonna take it all like a good little bunny?"

I make an affirmative sound, and he holds my head still, hips pulling back and snapping forward. The head hits the back of my throat, and I gag. I grip my thighs, determined not to grab his in a wordless request to temper his pace. He pulls back and gives me a moment to find my composure and my breath. And then he thrusts again. This time I'm ready.

"That's it. So fucking good." His thumb sweeps along the contour of my bottom lip.

He finds a rhythm, holding my head in place while he fucks my mouth, and I moan around his cock, make all the noises I know he loves, drooling all over him. When he comes, I swallow it down. Spit runs down my chin and my neck. My eyes are watering, and I'm on edge and desperate for release, but aware I'll get it when he's ready to give it.

He bends to kiss me. It's sloppy and wet, but he doesn't seem to care. "You okay with hard and dirty?" he asks.

"Yes, please," I whisper.

"Such a sweet little bunny, aren't you?"

A moment later, I'm on my back on the plush carpet in the middle of the living room. From where I'm lying, I can see the roses he had sent to the room for my arrival. My knees end up at my chest, and he licks up the length of me and latches onto my clit. I almost lose my mind at the sensation of it all. Every time I think I'm about to tip over the edge, he stops. And then starts the same torment over again. My panties are still tucked inside me.

He latches back onto my clit, teeth grazing the sensitive skin, and at the same time, he eases a finger inside. He hooks the lacy fabric and tugs as he sucks, and I go careening over the edge into bliss. As I'm coming down from the high, he shoves his fingers into my mouth and pulls my panties free with his teeth. He drops them on the carpet and replaces them with his fingers, making the orgasm feel endless.

He flips me over on my stomach and brackets my legs with his. My cheek is pressed against the plush carpet.

He kisses my temple and orders, "Open."

I part my lips, and my panties end up in my mouth. And then he slides into me.

I'm so fucking wet. And already coming again. He slips his

palm under my cheek so I don't end up with rug burn on my face and fucks me into the floor. My nipples scrape the carpet, and I taste my own desire as I moan around my panties. As far as dirty fucks go, this absolutely takes the cake.

"I love you." His lips brush my cheek. "So fucking much."

I make a noise around my panties.

He pulls them free so I can speak.

"I love you, too."

On the next thrust, he pulls back, flips me over, and fills me again.

When I come this time, it's with his eyes on mine, his hands framing my face, and his love for me a mantra on his lips.

EPILOGUE

TRISTAN

ONE MONTH LATER

"All your kitchen stuff is put away," Bea announces. "Do you want me to put lunch out for everyone yet, or hold off and tackle the bedroom now that the furniture is where you want it?"

Her hair is pulled up in a ponytail. Sweat makes flyaways stick to her skin. She's wearing one of my loose tanks that doesn't hide anything with a blue sports bra underneath. Her yoga pants hug her ass in a way that makes me want to tell the guys to come back later.

I wrap an arm around her waist and nuzzle her neck. "I'd rather get started with you in the bedroom."

She tips her head to give me access to more skin. "I'm a gross mess."

I lick her salty skin. "You taste like you want to be naked."

She laughs and pushes on my chest. "Put a pin in it, Tristan. We'll be alone in a few hours. You can lick every inch of me then."

"Waiting sucks."

"Says the king of withholding orgasms."

"I'll give you one right now to tide you over," I bargain.

"Alluring, but my brother and your teammates are on the way back up with living room furniture, and Hammer, Hemi, Shilpa, Dred, and Tally are setting up the spare bedroom." The chatter of female voices filters down the hall. "We both know you'll do something dirty, and I'll probably be louder than I mean to, and it'll be embarrassing, mostly for me."

I open my mouth to argue, but she's not wrong.

As if on cue, Dallas, Flip, Hollis, Ashish, and Roman grunt their way through the propped-open door, each carrying huge boxes containing new furniture. I probably should have hired movers, but Flip argued that it was an unnecessary expense when we have an entire team who can unload a truck within an hour.

"Stop looking at your girlfriend like that, Tristan. We'll be out of here in a couple hours," Hollis grumbles as he passes.

Bea laughs and untangles herself from my arms.

A few seconds later, more of my teammates appear with boxes.

I give up on getting into Bea's pants for now. She's right. We'll have all night together. The more we get done now, the less I'll have to manage on my own.

"Just a couple more trips and the truck will be empty," Flip says.

"I'll check on the girls, and we can get started on lunch." Bea's fingers skim my back as she passes.

I latch onto her wrist before she can get very far.

She spins to face me, her expression expectant.

"Thanks for being here today, and for going to all the trouble to make sure the fridge is stocked." She brought over two coolers of food this morning and a case of vitamin water, plus beer and wine for after we've finished unloading the truck.

She smiles up at me. "I'm happy to help."

I lean in and brush my nose against hers. "I love you."

"I love you, too." She squeezes my hand and winks. "Go help the guys and I'll get lunch ready, so we can kick everyone out sooner."

I pull her in for a brief hug. I'm getting better at affection. It's not something I'm inherently good at because I didn't get a whole lot of it growing up. My dad was good with praise and back pats and being present, but hugs were rare, and my mom's version of affection usually involved telling me she was surprised I hadn't screwed something up. Or sometimes throwing shit around me instead of at me when she was particularly frustrated. I equated hugs with weakness. But Bea is slowly changing that, and I try to show her through more than just gifts and words how important she is.

The therapist Roman suggested has been helpful, too. Talking about my feelings isn't my favorite, but I want this to work with Bea, so I go every week. The more I do it, the easier it gets.

"You're poking me in the wrong hole," Bea mutters when my erection nudges her navel.

"He loves you, too."

"When everyone leaves, we can start christening rooms. The bathroom should probably be first."

"I vote kitchen. I saw all the cucumbers in the crisper."

She laughs and pushes on my chest.

I release her and head for the living room, where the guys are unboxing my new furniture. Bea came with me to pick most of it out.

An hour later, the living room is set up, along with my bedroom, the spare room, both bathrooms, and the kitchen. The dining room table is covered in a lunch buffet of wraps, homemade pizzas, salads, and a dessert platter. My teammates all go back for seconds and ask who catered. I tell them Bea put it together on her own, and Hollis and Roman talk up how awesome it's been to have her prepping meals for them when they have home games. She doesn't have time to take on more right now, but she loves it, so I'm hopeful that could change in the future.

We've been discussing what it would take for Bea to go back to school for sports nutrition. I have a plan that includes getting her to move in with me. I'm not pushing her, though. I know she wants to forge her own path, but when she's ready to take that step, I'll be here to help her achieve that dream.

An hour or so later, as soon as everyone leaves, we christen the kitchen island and the shower. Then I grab us drinks so we can hydrate in the living room. Which we'll christen next.

"You're staying over tonight." I move Bea to straddle my lap.

"Don't think I haven't noticed the absence of the word *sleep* in that statement."

I run my hands up her thighs. "You should bring some clothes over and leave them here."

"I literally live across the street," she points out with a smile.

I finger the hem of her shirt. "Yeah, but I left a couple of empty drawers in my dresser for you, and the closet is freaking massive, so you should help me fill it."

Her grin widens. "Okay. I can do that."

I squeeze her thighs, working up my nerve. "You're welcome to move in any time you want."

Bea runs her fingers through my hair. "You've been here for a handful of hours. How about you take a little time to get settled, and we can enjoy being a couple while that happens?"

I swallow past the thickness in my throat. "You don't want to move in with me?"

"It has nothing to do with wanting to." Her eyes grow soft, and she leans in to rub her nose against mine. "Because I absolutely do. But we've only been officially official for a couple of months. And your place is still full of unpacked boxes. Toronto is having a great season, and you'll be traveling on and off until June."

"If we make it to the playoffs," I add.

She nods but doesn't say anything else about that. We're

having a kickass season, and as long as we keep playing like we are, we have a good chance of making the playoffs this year. "When you're in town, I'll be spending most of my nights in your bed."

"You can stay here even when I'm not in town."

"I know. But it's nice having a roommate and girlfriends to hang out with. I need the support system, especially with Essie in Vancouver for the foreseeable future, and because your job has you on the road so much. It makes sense for you to settle in, and we can date, and I can sleep over when you're in Toronto for the next few months. Then I can fill your place with my crap and put my throw pillows everywhere."

"They should be called throw-me-away pillows," I grumble.

She laughs. "Besides, it'll be good for you to have your own space too. No cleaning up after Flip. And then you can appropriately appreciate how awesome it is to have me around to take care of all the things like meal prep when I finally do move in."

"I already appreciate those things about you." I finger the end of her ponytail. "But it makes sense that we wait until the end of the season. You'd be alone half the time, otherwise." Bea and Hammer get along well, and while she's not a replacement for Essie, they've become close friends over the past few months. All those girls have.

"Once I move in, you're stuck with me." She runs her fingers through my hair.

"More like you're stuck with me. I'm the clear winner in this arrangement."

Her smile softens. "I don't know about that. You're proving to be a pretty awesome boyfriend." Her fingers drift down my cheek. "You're thoughtful, sweet, and giving."

"Especially in bed," I add.

"And out of it." She brushes her lips over mine. "You're a catch, Tristan, and you're all mine."

"And you're mine."

"All yours," she agrees.

I can see my future unfolding with Bea. For the first time in my life, I understand what home feels like. It's not a place for me; it's her. She's where I want to be.

She has my heart.

Bea is the person it beats for.

BONUS EPILOGUE
BIRTHDAY CELEBRATIONS IN BAD PLACES

RIX

Consciousness is slow to tap me on the eyelids this morning. Something feels off. Wrongish. And then I realize there is no dick poking me in the back or the butt. There is also no six-five man wrapped around me like Saran, huffing my hair and breathing against my neck. I could do a visual check, but I'm not committed to opening my eyes yet, so I roll onto my back and stretch my arms in both directions. The bed is empty apart from me. And based on the coolness of the sheets, it has been for some time.

I reluctantly pry my lids open and turn my head toward Tristan's pillow, which is empty. The clock on the nightstand reads 10:42. That explains why I'm alone. Tristan never sleeps past nine-forty-five, even after marathon sex. His internal alarm clock only allows him to stay in bed for so long. I have the enviable ability to access my teenage-sleep capabilities on weekends and sleep until noon. This only happens on weekends when Tristan has away games. Apart from today.

I smile as I take in the bouquet of bright yellow flowers sitting on the nightstand beside the clock, and the giant, ridiculous balloon arrangement beside it. Several of the balloons are bumblebees, which has become Tristan's favorite cute thing to buy me, along with stuffed cucumbers or pickles, for obvious reasons. The biggest balloon reads Happy Birthday! in cursive.

I throw the covers off and roll out of bed, stopping at the bathroom to brush my hair and my teeth before I go in search of my boyfriend for birthday orgasms. I find him in the kitchen, sitting at the island, flipping through a hockey magazine.

A huge bowl of fruit salad and the makings for egg sandwiches take up most of the counter.

His face lights up when he sees me, and my heart gets all melty.

He spins on his stool and opens his arms as I approach. "Morning, birthday girl."

I step between his legs, and he wraps his arms around me, burying his face in my hair.

"The flowers and the balloons are beautiful," I say against the side of his neck, then lean back.

"Just like you." He pushes my hair over my shoulders and wraps his hand gently around my throat, then leans in and brushes the end of his nose against mine.

My vagina gets all gushy, along with the rest of me. "Should we go back to bed so you can turn me into a sex pretzel and give me a birthday-gasm or two?" Or more. I try to pull him off the stool, but he doesn't budge.

"I've got a full day planned for you." He glances at the clock on the stove. "And we have to be somewhere in an hour, so the birthday sex pretzel and orgasms will have to wait."

I push my bottom lip out. "No birthday-gasms?"

He sighs. "Fine, I'll give you one to tide you over, but the rest will have to wait."

He pulls my sleep shorts off and I quickly do the same with my tank. I'm about to climb into his lap, but he wraps his hands around my waist and lifts me onto the counter, then pushes the stool out of the way and drops to his knees. I spread my legs wide and rest my heels on his shoulders. There's zero lead up, no teasing, no gentle test licks. Nope. Tristan hoovers my clit like he's sucking my life force out of it. I shriek and grab his hair, and attempt to slam my legs closed, but his forearms are already pressed against my knees, holding me open.

His gaze lifts and he eases up on the suction, swirling his tongue around my clit instead. I relax and stop trying to rip his hair out. For a few seconds, anyway. I know better than to believe he'll be this nice for long. He laps at me, fucks me with his tongue and rubs his nose on my clit and then, just as I'm about to lean back on my elbows so I can watch the show in comfort, he latches back onto my clit, sucking like a damn demon. Annoyingly, it does the trick and I come like a fucking freight train.

Tristan grips the edge of the counter and pulls himself back up. He uses the bottom of his shirt to wipe my girl-gasm off his face. "I think that was a new record. What did that take, less than two and a half minutes?"

"Freaking pro hockey players." I roll my eyes. "Always making it a competition."

He shrugs, unapologetic. "Can't help that I'm exceptionally gifted at making you come." He gives me a peck on the lips and settles his hands on my hips. "You think you can stand up, or you need me to carry you back to the bedroom and help you get dressed?"

"You could carry me back to the bedroom and fuck me before I get dressed," I suggest.

"No can do, little Bea, time's a ticking." He taps his bare wrist.

"This day better end with you fucking me into next week." I slide off the counter, but hold on to the edge, in case my legs aren't willing to do their job yet.

"Babe, have I ever let you down in the fucking you into next week department?"

"No." I sigh. "But it's my birthday and my birthday wish is to be turned into a sex pretzel." I'm whining now.

"And you will be. Later." He taps my bare ass. "Now get dressed. I'll make us egg sandwiches and then we gotta be somewhere."

"Are you going to tell me where? And how should I dress?"

"It's a surprise, and just casual is good." He's already turned on the stove, so clearly I'm not getting my way right now.

Whatever. It's easy to make him regret not giving me what I want on my birthday. A strappy sundress that's bordering on inappropriately short is a good start. I consider not wearing panties just to be a brat, but decide against it in case there's a breeze today, which is likely since we're right by the lake. I opt for lacy cheekies and do a bend test to make sure I won't accidentally flash people.

Tristan is plating our egg sandwiches when I return to the kitchen. He sets a mug of coffee and my breakfast in front of me and joins me at the island with his own. "So is the whole day a surprise, or just whatever you have planned next?"

"The whole day. But I promise you'll love every minute." He kisses my shoulder.

"Any hints you want to drop? Can I guess what we're doing and where we're going?"

"Guess all you want, but nothing you can do will convince me to ruin the surprises."

"Not even if I offered anal?"

He side-eyes me while chewing.

"How about the *Chasing Amy*? You love that. I'll even let you tie me to the bed again." I'm pulling out the big guns.

He sets his sandwich down, wipes his hands on his napkin, and slowly turns to face me. He reaches across me and curves his hand around the outside of my left knee, using it to spin me toward him. His knees bracket my legs. He closes them so I can't spread mine and show him my panties. I swallow thickly, thinking I've won for a hot second as he wraps his hand around my throat. The smile that spreads across his face makes my pussy clench. He leans in and sucks my bottom lip between his. "It's cute that you think those things aren't already on the table later tonight."

He releases my throat and parts his legs, spinning my stool back to face the counter and my half-eaten sandwich. "Be a good girl and finish your breakfast so we can get to the fun part of the day."

TRISTAN

Thank fuck I whacked off twice already this morning, otherwise Bea would have successfully shot my entire birthday plan to shit already. She's currently pouting in the passenger seat of my car. Her sundress is riding so high that I can see the yellow lace panties that match her yellow dress. Clearly, this is purposeful.

I remind myself that we'll circle back home after this first outing, and that I'll be able to fit in a round of sex pretzeling before part two of the birthday celebrations begin.

"Are we going to Just Desserts? That's where we're headed, isn't it?" She perks up.

"Nope." I went there yesterday to pick up her cake. It's currently across the street in Hammer's fridge.

"Oh." She's back to pouting.

I make a right and pull into the grocery store parking lot.

"Oh! I love this place!" She bounces in her seat, excitement setting in.

All The Best Things is a specialty grocery store that carries retro treats and snack foods from around the world. I've taken her here a couple of times. Bea has some hang ups about splurging on treats, so usually I come on my own and pick up a few of her favorite things. But today is different since it's her birthday, and the whole point is to spoil the living shit out of her.

I circle the lot twice, but it's full, so I end up parking on a side street instead. Rix hops out of the car before I even have it in park. I fire off a message to Flip, letting him know we're here so we can implement birthday surprise part two. Rix knocks on the window, impatient.

I exit the car and meet her on the sidewalk.

"I hope they have Thrills gum, and the Haribo Berries, and those sherbet powder things. I love those so much." "Fingers crossed they have all your favorites." I know they do because I called ahead a couple of weeks ago requesting specific items.

She hugs my arm and bounces as we walk, her boobs rubbing on my biceps. I think about gross things, like clumps of hair in the drain, or dog crap stuck in my shoes to distract me. A public hard-on is not ideal.

I grab a cart once we're inside the store and follow Bea to the specialty candy aisle. "They have everything I love! How am I going to choose?" She tugs at the end of her ponytail, brushing it over her lips as she surveys her options. She's so fucking cute when she's giddy.

"It's your birthday, Bea. You don't have to choose. You pick whatever you want, and I buy it for you. That's how birthdays go." It doesn't matter if I give her free rein. She's always conservative with food and indulgences. I check my phone again to make sure part two of the surprise is in place.

"Should I get a Whatchamacallit or a Payday?" She holds both, weighing them in her hands, like the decision will save the world.

I pluck both from her hands and toss them into the cart. "You should get both." I reach above her for the sherbet tubes and toss three in, since they're her personal favorites. Forty-five minutes later, we stop in the ice cream aisle for a pint of her favorite and head for the checkout counter.

"This is a lot of candy. Like too much, we should put some back," Bea says as I drop an armload on the conveyor belt.

"It's candy. It won't go bad. And it's your birthday, which means I get to spoil you. End of discussion." I kiss her forehead and drop another armload of candy onto the belt. Two-hundred and fifty dollars later, we're stocked with treats and surprise part one is a success.

Bea tries to take the bags from me, but I refuse to let her carry them.

"We're taking these home, right? There's ice cream, so we have to go home first. And the chocolate will melt otherwise. We'll have time for more orgasms, right?" Bea asks as we cross the parking lot to the side street where I parked.

"Yeah. We'll have time for more orgasms," I assure her.

"Yay!" she claps excitedly. "I already know what position I want to start with today."

I smirk. "I'm sure you do."

Bea stops short when we reach the spot where my car was parked. She glances around. "Did we go down the wrong street? Where's your car?" She frowns and points to the house on our right. "You parked right in front of the one with the red door, didn't you?" She grabs my arm. "Oh my God, Tristan. Did someone steal your car?"

"Nobody stole my car, baby."

"But it's gone! It's not there! Look!" She motions with both hands to the brand new custom painted SUV sitting in its place.

I transfer the bags to one hand and dig around in my pocket for the fob. The taillights flash as I hit the unlock button. Bea's brows pull together, and she looks around, as if she expects someone else to magically appear.

I dangle the keys in front of her, biting back a grin. "Surprise."

She looks at them in confusion, then at the SUV, then at me.

"Happy birthday," I say, waiting for it to sink in.

Her mouth drops. "Oh my God. Are you serious?"

I arch a brow and jangle the fob.

"You're serious." She holds her hand under mine, expression still reflecting disbelief as I drop the fob into them. "You bought me a Mercedes for my birthday."

"I know you're nervous about driving mine, so I figured it would be good for you to have your own wheels," I explain. And I just wanted a reason to spoil her, but also appeal to her practical side.

"This is a very extravagant birthday present," she murmurs.

"I'm a lot to deal with, so I feel like you deserve it." I kiss her temple. "It's got great safety ratings, it's hybrid, so better for the environment, and it gets excellent mileage." All features that will make her happy.

"This is ridiculously over the top, but I love it, and you." She takes my face in her hands and lays a kiss on me.

"I love you, too. Why don't you check it out?" I nod toward the car, pleased by her excitement. If anyone deserves nice things, it's my girlfriend.

"Right! Yes!" She skips over to the driver's side and opens the door.

"Want to open the trunk for me?" I hold up the bags in my hand.

"Yes! Of course!"

I put the groceries in the trunk, then I join her in the car. "So, what do you think?"

"I think it's amazing. Is this custom interior?"

"Yeah." It's yellow and black. Like a bumble bee since I call her my little Bea.

"This is the most incredible birthday gift. The sound system is already synced to my phone! And the backseat looks so spacious. We should check it out!" She clambers over the center console, flashing me her lace covered ass on the way. "There's so much room back here! Even you could fit comfortably!" I exit the SUV and climb into the back with her.

"Nice and roomy, right?" I observe.

"I love it." She grabs the front of my shirt and pulls my mouth to hers. "You are so getting a thank you blow job when we get home. I'll make all the gagging noises and drool all over your balls."

"It's your birthday, Bea. Today is all about you," I mumble around her tongue.

"I love choking on your cock." She shifts to straddle my lap. "My head doesn't even hit the roof."

I laugh and then groan as she adjusts her position and her panty covered pussy presses against my erection. "We should christen my birthday present."

"Right here?" I'm not opposed to car sex, or even public sex, but it's the middle of the day and we're parked outside of someone's house.

She glances around. The side street is empty of people. "The windows are tinted. We should be safe, right?"

"We should. Yeah." Like I'm going to fight her on car sex when she's already popping the button on my jeans.

Bea drags the zipper down and I shimmy them over my hips so she has access to my cock. She curves her warm, soft hand around my shaft and gives it a squeeze, followed by a slow stroke. "I'm going to deep throat you when we get home," she whispers. "And get you all dirty when Tristan fucks my ass with you later."

"You realize it doesn't have ears, right? And that it's part of me."

"Shh." She presses a finger to my lips. "Don't be jealous that we're having a moment."

. I'll have plenty of opportunities later to remind her just how in control of her favorite appendage I really am.

She pushes her yellow lace panties to the side and rubs the head over her clit, sighing as she drags it lower. And then she sinks down, wet heat surrounding me as she takes me inside her. She always feels so fucking good. I settle my hands on her hips, fighting not to take control, not to move her over me. She rolls her hips and moans.

"Shh, little Bea, you don't want to get caught fucking in your brand new car, do you?" I ask.

She buries her face against my neck, muffling her needy sounds as she shifts in my lap. Her fingers drift down my arm and I already know what she wants without her asking for it. I urge her head up and wrap one hand around her throat. She bites her lip to stifle a whimper as our eyes lock.

"This is a great backseat," she pants, and her eyes roll up. "So close."

I grip her hip to help move her up and down my length. "You gonna come all over my cock like a good girl?"

"Yes. Shit. Fuck. Oh my—" I slide three fingers into her mouth to stifle her moan.

Her pussy clamps around my cock and I fight with my body not to let go. It's fine for her to come all over me, but a tissue would be a smarter location choice for me to let go, so she's not leaking all over the seat on the ride home.

She tugs on my hand, and I remove my fingers from her mouth. She sags against me, face pressed against my neck again. "I love you, and this car, and car sex."

"Same on all three." I squeeze her hip.

"You need to finish." She starts to shift her hips again.

"But not inside you."

"Oh, right. That would be messy." She lifts off me and her nose wrinkles as she takes in my coated cock. "Or messier."

I reach around her and pluck a packet of tissue free from the center console.

"Oh, fuck that." She bats them away. "I got this." She shimmies off my lap onto the floor between my legs, wraps her hand around my shaft, and covers the head with her perfect, soft lips.

A couple with a dog walk by as her head bobs and she makes gratuitous slurping noises. Thankfully, no one else walks by and it doesn't take me long to come.

She pops off, all smiles and satisfaction. "Anal when we get home?"

"Whatever the birthday girl wants, the birthday girl gets," I tell her.

She clambers back into my lap and her eyes go wide. "Oh crap! We have ice cream in the trunk. It's probably all melted."

"It's okay, Bea, the grocery store is right there." I thumb over my shoulder and kiss her cheek. "We can get more."

Want even more bonus content?

Sign up for my newsletter to receive the "Chasing Amy NSFW Scene"

ABOUT THE AUTHOR HELENA HUNTING

NYT and USA Today bestselling author, Helena Hunting lives on the outskirts of Toronto with her amazing family and her adorable kitty, who think the best place to sleep is her keyboard. Helena writes everything from emotional contemporary romance to romantic comedies that will have you laughing until you cry. If you're looking for a tearjerker, you can find her angsty side under H. Hunting.

OTHER TITLES BY HELENA HUNTING

OTHER TITLES BY HELENA HUNTING

STANDALONE NOVELS
The Librarian Principle
Felony Ever After
Before You Ghost (with Debra Anastasia)

FOREVER ROMANCE STANDALONES
The Good Luck Charm
Meet Cute
Kiss my Cupcake
A Love Catastrophe